should be returned to any branch of the
County Library on or before the date shown

Debra Webb AUG 2018
bestselling auth
including those
the Colby Agency
than four million b
countries, Debra's
childhood on a farm
www.debrawebb.com.

D0726925

Cindi Myers is the author of more than fifty novels.
When she's not crafting new romance plots, she enjoys
skiing, gardening, cooking, crafting and daydreaming.

A lover of small-town life, she lives with her husband
and two spoiled dogs in the Colorado mountains.

Also by Debra Webb

Finding the Edge
Sin and Bone
Dark Whispers
Still Waters
Bridal Armor
Ready, Aim...I Do!
Colby Law
High Noon
Colby Roundup

Also by Cindi Myers

Murder in Black Canyon
Undercover Husband
Manhunt on Mystic Mesa
Soldier's Promise
Missing in Blue Mesa
Stranded with the Suspect
Colorado Crime Scene
Lawman on the Hunt
Christmas Kidnapping

Discover more at millsandboon.co.uk

BODY OF EVIDENCE

DEBRA WEBB

SAVED BY THE SHERIFF

CINDI MYERS

MIX
Paper from
responsible sources
FSC
FSC® C007454

This book is produced from independently certified FSC™
paper to ensure responsible forest management.

For more information visit: www.harpercollins.co.uk/green

Printed and bound in Spain
by CPI, Barcelona

MILLS & BOON

First Published in Great Britain 2018
by Mills & Boon, an imprint of HarperCollins*Publishers*
1 London Bridge Street, London, SE1 9GF

Body Of Evidence © 2018 Debra Webb
Saved by the Sheriff © 2018 Cynthia Myers

ISBN: 978-0-263-26582-8

39-0718

BODY OF EVIDENCE

DEBRA WEBB

This book is dedicated to the amazing nurses and doctors we often take for granted. Thank you so much for all you do.

Chapter One

Dr. Marissa Frasier ruffled the hair of her six-year-old patient, Jeremiah Owens. "You were very brave, Jeremiah."

The little boy had arrived at the ER two hours ago with a greenstick fracture to the radius about three inches above his left wrist. After an examination and then X-rays to confirm, he had stoically watched as Dr. Pete Myers, the ortho on call, applied the cast for keeping the arm stable. Jeremiah had chosen royal blue for his cast. Though there had been no serious shift in the bones as a result of the fracture, they wanted it to stay that way, and children couldn't always be counted on to follow instructions or to keep on a splint. A cast was typically the better route to go with younger patients.

The child's lips had quivered and his eyes had grown bright during the procedure, but Mom was the only one who cried. The poor woman had apologized profusely. Her sweet son had repeatedly told her that he was okay and that it didn't really hurt. Being a parent was difficult at times, and this had been one of those times.

Dr. Myers had quickly moved on to an elderly patient who'd arrived with a fracture to the upper quarter of the femur. Never a good thing, but particularly problematic in older patients. Apparently tonight's theme was broken bones. They'd had three others this evening. Marissa was reasonably confident that was a record for a Thursday night.

"Thank you, Doctor," Mrs. Owens said, her tears all but dry now. "He was a very brave boy." She kissed the top of her child's head.

Marissa smiled. "Perhaps when Nurse Bowman has gone over the dismissal instructions, a reward is in order for your outstanding bravery, Jeremiah."

"I think that's a very good idea." His mother patted him gently on the back. "A reward would be very nice, don't you think, Jeremiah?"

He nodded eagerly, the hint of a smile tugging at the corners of his mouth.

"Nurse Bowman will let you pick something from our special treasure chest." Marissa gave Eva a nod as she walked to the door. "Have a safe drive home."

This time Jeremiah actually flashed her a real smile. She couldn't decide whether he was happier about the treasure chest or going home.

The ER had been buzzing for the past several hours. A couple had misjudged the time it would take to reach their preferred hospital and ended up having to stop at the Edge for their little girl's entrance into the world. A two-car accident with five victims; a bicycle crash involving two teenagers who suffered broken bones, nasty lacerations and no shortage of bruises; and two concertgoers who'd taken tumbles while crowd surfing had shown up with fractures similar to Jeremiah's. There was also a knife fight between two thugs in a drug deal gone wrong. Both victims had arrived in the backs of police cruisers.

And yet another little boy, Timmy, who arrived with a scary-looking laceration to the upper arm, caused by a bad idea. The boy had decided he wanted to practice knife throwing the way a character in some movie he'd watched recently had done. Amazingly he had actually hit the tree with the knife he'd sneaked from his mother's kitchen. The trouble had occurred when he braced his left arm against the tree and attempted to dislodge the knife with his right, slicing across his left arm only a couple of inches above the elbow. He was a very lucky little boy. A little deeper, and he might not have arrived at the ER in time. The brachial artery was closest to the surface near the elbow. Marissa was very thankful the injury was not so deep and had missed the artery.

At the double doors that led back into the lobby, Jeremiah slipped free from his mother's hand and raced back to where Marissa stood near the nurses' station and gave her a hug. She crouched down and hugged him back. Her heart reacted. She had so wanted children of her own.

Not meant to be. At least not so far, and with no prospects of a boyfriend, much less a husband, the outlook was rather dim.

When the child skipped back to where his mother

waited at the open door, Marissa waved goodbye. As the doors closed, she turned back to the chart she was reviewing.

"Dr. Frasier."

Marissa paused and looked up at the registration specialist, Patsy Tanner, who'd called her name. "Yes, Patsy?"

"There's a man in the lobby who says he needs to see you." She shrugged. "I told him you were with a patient but he just keeps pacing the room. He asks for you every five or so minutes." Her expression turned uncertain. "He looks very upset."

A frown furrowing its way across her weary forehead, Marissa dredged up a smile. "Thank you, Patsy. I'll take care of it."

Sometimes a father or husband or even boyfriend of a patient would grow agitated and demand to speak with the doctor who had cared for his loved one. Since Marissa hadn't lost any patients or even attended to any patients with a dire prognosis this evening, she couldn't imagine the trouble would be too serious. Perhaps one of the two who'd been carried off to jail after their knife battle had a disgruntled friend. She sent a quick text to Security and asked that they keep an eye on the situation as she spoke with the man pacing the lobby.

The moment Marissa stepped beyond the double doors that stood between those waiting for care and the emergency department, she knew it wasn't going to be so easy.

Even before the man turned around, she recognized him. The rigid set of his broad shoulders. The silky dark brown hair that brushed his collar. He wore jeans and a shirt, not the khakis and a polo he'd preferred before their lives had fallen apart. William Bauer turned around as if he sensed her presence, despite the fact that eight or nine other people were scattered around the room, speaking softly or searching their social media feeds on their phones.

It had been that way between them in the beginning. Even a few hours apart had felt like an eternity. They had sensed each other across a crowded room, their hearts seeming to beat harder and harder until they touched.

Marissa's ex-husband strode toward her, his gaze narrowing, homing in on her. The anger twisting his lips—the lips she had kissed so many times—warned this would not be a pleasant visit by any definition of the word. Unfortunately, this was not his first unannounced appearance, and she feared it would not be his last.

When he stalled toe-to-toe with her, his six-foot-two form looming over her five-foot-six one, she asked, "Why are you here, William?"

"You changed your cell number. I had no choice."

Thankfully he kept his voice down, but there was no mistaking the fury in his tone.

Marissa glanced around the room. "Why don't we step outside where we'll have some privacy?"

The subtle shift in his posture told her he liked the idea of privacy. Uneasiness pricked her, but security was nearby. Her ex-husband stepped back, allowing her to go ahead of him. She moved toward the exit, keeping her step steady and her smile pleasant. No need to let anyone see the worry and the dread pulsing beneath her skin.

She and William had been married for five years. The first year had felt happy, or at least as happy as any two people with newly minted medical degrees diving into their residencies could feel. More often than not they were either flying high with adrenaline or utterly drained from exhaustion. They had married at the courthouse the day after they finished medical school. Miracle of miracles, the NRMP, National Resident Matching Program, had matched them both to hospitals in the Chicago area. A whirlwind trip to the city had ended with them leasing the cheapest apartment they could find, and they'd been completely thrilled that it had a reasonably large shower, a bedroom and was near both their hospitals.

Then, slowly but surely, everything had changed.

Marissa had done exceedingly well. She'd garnered praise and numerous opportunities for her hard work. William, on the other hand, had floundered. He couldn't seem to keep up. His work was subpar. He didn't get along with anyone. He'd barely survived his residency. By the end of the second year, they had argued every minute they were together, which wasn't nearly enough to sustain a relationship.

A little less than two years ago, he had been asked to leave the practice he'd joined after residency. It was either he leave voluntarily, or legal steps would be taken to remove him. The senior doctor in the practice was a mutual friend. Though Marissa and William had already been divorced for a couple of months by then, he'd called to explain that he had grave concerns about William's mental health.

Sadly, he hadn't been telling Marissa anything new. The breakdown in their marriage had mirrored the disintegration of his mental health. Twenty-three months and two weeks ago, he'd finally snapped and he'd turned physical. Marissa had ended up with a concussion and a fractured arm much like little Jeremiah's. At her ex-husband's trial, the judge had been particularly peeved by the fact that William was a doctor, and subsequently sentenced him to a year for felony domestic violence. He'd been released six months ago.

The first thing he'd done was come to Marissa and apologize for his behavior. Since that time he'd been volunteering in the community and appeared to be working hard to redeem himself. Marissa had no idea how he was earning any sort of income. He'd exhausted the meager savings they had managed prior to the divorce with his need to prove his status with a new car every year. Unfortunately, his salary as a general practitioner was not that of a cardiothoracic surgeon, as he appeared to want the world to believe.

However much he wanted to act as if he had learned his lesson, Marissa knew better. He was still drinking. Before and, foolishly, even after the divorce, she had tried to help him, but she'd soon recognized that she could not help a man unwilling to help himself. No matter that they had been officially divorced for eighteen months and twenty-two days, he never left her alone for long.

In part, she blamed herself. If she'd made a clean

break after he attacked her physically rather than attempting to help him, things might have been different. Now, no matter how many times she told him to back off, he always found a way to insert himself into her life. He discovered something among his things that belonged to her. A letter addressed to her had come to his apartment. A relative was ill and he thought she might want to know. When he'd run out of legitimate excuses, he'd started showing up simply to argue about how she had ruined his life.

She suspected this evening's visit was the latter, though he had never showed up at her ER before. Too many potential witnesses.

Once they were a few yards from the ER entrance but still within sight of the security guard who monitored that entrance, William lit into her.

"Why would you change your phone number? You've had the same number since we moved to Chicago."

He stood very close to her, his face so near she could feel his breath on her cheek, could smell the liquor when he spoke. William was a handsome man still. Classic square jaw, straight nose, nice lips, assessing brown eyes. But once things started to fall apart, his eyes were always bloodshot from the sheer volume of alcohol he consumed daily. The final year of their marriage, he would come home from work and drink until he passed out in his chair or on the sofa or wherever he happened to be when the saturation point of alcohol in his blood took control. It was as if he couldn't bear his life, so he attempted to wash away each day's memories with booze. Every month or so he would promise to join Alcoholics Anonymous. He even went *once*.

So ironic. He'd been the best all through high school. Best GPA. Best player on the football team. Best all-around student. Class president. College had been much the same. Even in medical school, he had been the golden boy among the professors and his peers. Never had to work very hard to achieve his class ranking.

Whether it all merely caught up with him in the end or he just couldn't keep up the pace any longer, he plummeted. From all reports, once he went into practice he was a satisfactory doctor. There had never been any complaints from patients. Certainly no malpractice suits. It was his colleagues who couldn't tolerate his bullying and bad behavior.

And his wife. For a while, Marissa had taken his mental abuse and, ultimately, his first and only departure into physical abuse. But that mistake would never be repeated. She refused to be a victim like that ever again. Granted, he had been drunk out of his mind at the time, but she would not allow him to use his drinking as an excuse. He had hurt her and that was that.

"I changed my number because I would like you to stop calling me." She kept her gaze steady on his. It was important that he understand her decision was not up for discussion. She knew this man intimately. At the moment he appeared reasonably sober, and she wanted him to see and to hear that she meant business. The life they had once shared was over. They were not friends, and they never would be.

"You've finally found someone else, haven't you?" Rage blazed in his dark eyes.

An alarm she knew better than to ignore triggered. There was something about his eyes, his tone that seemed different tonight—colder, harder. "This is not about anyone else, William. This is about you." She kept her voice steady, her tone firm. A year of counseling had helped her to overcome feelings of guilt about the breakdown of their marriage and to stand up for herself, even against the man she had once loved and with whom she had expected to spend the rest of her life. "Now, if you'll excuse me, I have to get back to my patients."

"Is that another kick in the teeth?" he growled. "I don't have a career anymore. No patients. No nothing."

She braced herself and summoned her waning courage. "You don't have a career anymore because you drink too much. You need help, William. I can't help you. Until you commit to changing your life, this is how it will be." She backed away a step. "You should go back to AA and seek private counseling."

He grabbed her arm, his fingers clutching like a vise. A wave of panic flooded her.

"Don't tell me what to do," he warned. "If you had been a better wife, maybe I wouldn't have needed to drink. You could have helped me, but you chose to throw me—our life—away."

It was the same exchange every time. When he grew angry, he always blamed someone else for his mistakes. "Goodbye, William." She yanked her arm from his grasp and turned away.

One day he would surely come to terms with the

reality that *he* made his own choices, and *he* executed those choices.

"Issy."

She hesitated. Shouldn't have. Damn it.

"Look at me. Please."

How was it that she could still feel sympathy for this man? He had made her life miserable for four years before the divorce. He'd done his damnedest to do the same thing the past six months since his release from prison, but she had managed to handle it better. It was always easier to deal with issues from a distance. And though he insinuated himself into her present every chance he got, they did not share a home...they did not share a bed. He was no longer her responsibility, legally or morally.

She took a deep breath. Turned to face him. "First," she said, "if you ever touch me again, I will take out a restraining order, and then you'll have yet another black mark on your record. Now, what is it you want to say?"

He stared at her for a long moment. Even from several feet away, she could feel the sheer hatred emanating from him. The bright exterior lighting allowed her to see the desperation in his eyes. She shook her head and started to turn away but his lips parted and, once more, she hesitated.

"I'm going to kill myself."

Shock slammed into her gut. She sucked in a sharp breath. "You don't mean that."

He nodded. "I do."

"Please, William, you need help. See someone before you destroy any chance of ever rebuilding your life and career. Everyone deserves a second chance. Give yourself one before it's too late."

He shook his head. "I'm going to kill myself. But first—" he stared at her so hard she could feel the cold, ruthless pressure of his fury "—I'm going to kill *you*."

He walked away.

Marissa's knees buckled, forcing her to grab for the sleek limestone wall to steady herself. She watched him settle behind the steering wheel of his car and drive away. As much as she wanted to believe that he was only attempting to frighten her, she knew better than to be that naive. As a physician, she was well aware that people could snap and do unspeakable things.

William had been teetering on the precipice of total self-destruction for years now. Her first obligation as a physician was to report the threat. Since he was no longer practicing medicine, that was one less concern. She would call the office of his former practice and let their mutual friend know about the threat he'd made. If William was so angry with her, it was highly probable that he felt a similar rage for his former colleagues.

Making her way back inside, she prepared a mental list of everyone she should call. Her brain raced with the idea that this wasn't supposed to happen to her. She had been a good student all through school. She'd never gotten involved with drugs or alcohol. Even in college and then medical school, she was the consummate Goody Two-shoes. Focused, reliable—that was Marissa Frasier. As her marriage fell apart, she'd endeavored patiently and persistently to try to repair their relationship. But nothing worked. When she had done all within her power, she had extracted herself from the ever-increasing volatility of the situation. He'd already destroyed her ability to love him. She'd felt sympathy—as she did now—but that was no basis for a marriage.

The waiting room was nearly clear now. Maybe things would slow down, giving her a chance to pull herself together once more. A few more deep breaths to slow her racing heart, and she was getting there. Once she was through the double doors and headed toward the nurses' station, she relaxed.

Eva caught her in the corridor before she reached the doctors' lounge. "Are you okay, Dr. Frasier?"

Marissa produced a smile. Eva was one of those people whom everyone liked. With her white-blond hair and creamy porcelain skin, many of the older patients called her an angel. But it was her green eyes that Marissa first noticed. Their eyes were a very similar emerald green. Marissa, too, had the extrapale skin, but her fiery red curls set the two of them apart. Patients were always saying that if not for the difference in hair color, they could pass for sisters.

Marissa took her friend's hand and pulled her into the lounge. With a quick glance around she said, "It's William. He showed up again. *Here*." She moistened her lips and wished her heart would not start that confounded pounding again. "It was different this time."

"Are you serious?" Eva took both Marissa's hands in hers. "Listen to me—this situation is not getting better. He's escalating. If you continue to interact with him—"

Marissa shook her head. "I won't. I can't." She inhaled a deep breath. "He said he's going to kill himself, but first he's going to kill me."

"That's it." Eva released her and reached into the pocket of her scrubs for her cell phone. "I'm calling Todd. You need protection."

Eva's fiancé was an investigator at the Colby Agency. Eva had urged her repeatedly to go to the agency for help about William. Somehow Marissa had been certain she could do this herself, but now she wasn't so sure.

His desperation and fury had been palpable. He was not playing.

He wanted her dead.

The bottom dropped out of Marissa's stomach and she wrapped her arms around her middle. How on earth had they gotten to this place? How could a man who had once loved her—and she knew in her heart that he had—now want to kill her?

She had no answer. William was broken. He had allowed envy and whatever other hidden mental health issues that plagued him to take over. Add the alcohol on top of that, and he was a mess. A desperate mess who didn't care anymore. He wanted the pain and misery to end, and he wanted the person he saw as responsible for that pain and misery to pay for ruining his life.

Eva was right. She couldn't handle this situation any longer. Now she was the one who needed help.

Eva ended her call. She took Marissa's hands once more and gave them a squeeze. "Victoria, the head of the agency I've been telling you about, will see you first thing in the morning—if that works for you."

Marissa nodded, her entire being numb. "I'll go. I can't ignore this situation any longer."

"You have to believe me when I say that Victoria will know what to do. Her agency helped me, and they helped Dr. Pierce. They can help you."

The first spring of tears burned her eyes, and Marissa cursed herself for being so weak. "Thank you."

"Listen," Eva said gently, "Todd and I don't want you to be alone tonight, so I'm taking you home with me."

"No." Marissa shook her head. "I can't do that. The two of you are just finding your way in your relationship. I don't want to intrude. I truly appreciate the offer, but really, I have a security system and I'd feel much better at home. I need to be able to think all this through and prepare for tomorrow's meeting."

"Okay, but if you need anything, all you have to do is call." Eva hugged her hard. Marissa closed her eyes and fought the damned tears.

This was not the time for her to fall apart. Staying alive and safe required her to keep it together. It was well past time she focused on taking care of herself.

Tomorrow she would take the necessary steps to purge William from her life once and for all.

Chapter Two

Hampden Court, Friday, June 29, 6:00 a.m.

The sound of traffic on the street outside her East Lincoln Park graystone woke Marissa. The room-darkening Roman shades she'd ordered when she first bought the house nearly two years ago did their job very well, ensuring that the room was pitch-black. Working nights more often than not at the ER required sleeping in the daytime. Not so easy to do without the darkness.

There were times when total darkness was a good thing.

This was her rare long weekend, so she could sleep in this morning. Her next scheduled shift was Tuesday. She intended to treat herself the next couple of days. Some long-overdue shopping, maybe a mani-pedi. She pulled the silky sheet close around her and toyed with the idea of actually sleeping in. How long had it been since she'd stayed in bed until noon unless she'd worked until seven or eight in the morning? Besides, the shops wouldn't open for hours.

Then she remembered William's cruel words—the angry promise that he was going to kill himself and her.

She had an appointment at the Colby Agency at nine. A weary sigh whispered across her lips. She should get up, shower and figure out something to wear. Well before her divorce, her social life had died a slow, suffocating death. It had been so long since she'd needed something professional to wear that wasn't scrubs, much less anything vaguely dressy, that she had no idea what had survived the move from the Lake Shore condo she and William had shared.

It was now or never. With the intention of getting up, she threw back the thin, silky sheet. Her hand bumped a strange lump in the bed.

What in the world?

Had she left all the throw pillows on the bed? She generally piled them on the chaise lounge when she drew back the covers before bed. But she'd been tired last night. Maybe she'd just tossed them aside. Her hand moved over the mound.

Firm.

Not pillows.

Her fingers traced what felt like a leg that became a hip.

Human.

Marissa shot up from the bed and stumbled as she groped at the lamp. Her heart pounded against her sternum. Light pooled across the king-size bed.

She saw the hand first.

She tilted her head and studied the familiar fingers. Long, round-tipped.

Even before her gaze swung up to the pillow and the head resting there, she knew it was William.

Lying on his side, facing her, he stared, unblinking eyes cloudy with death. *Impossible*. She squeezed her eyes shut and tried to dispel the image. Yet, when she opened her eyes once more, he was still there. The room spun around her. She shook herself. Swayed precariously before she snapped from the shock of seeing her former husband lying in her bed, obviously *dead*.

Marissa scrambled across the bed to him. Blood had puddled on the pillow behind his head and oozed down onto the sheet behind his shoulder. His dark hair was matted at the back of his neck. This could not be happening. She leaned closer to determine the source of the blood—a small hole at the base of his skull. The flesh around it was puckered and purplish. The life-giving fluid no longer seeped. Heart and pulse racing, her mind screaming at her to do something, she touched her fingers to his carotid artery.

Nothing.

Dear God, he was *dead*.

His skin was cool. Gray.

No. No. No.

He couldn't be dead. Not here. Not like this. Not possible.

She pushed him onto his back and ripped open his shirt. Buttons flew across the bed and the floor.

Pressing her cheek to his chest, she listened for a heartbeat, tried to feel his chest rise and fall.

Nothing. No heartbeat. No rush of blood.

Would CPR do anything?

She stared at his ashen skin. Cold. No pulse. Somewhere on the periphery of her consciousness, she noted the darkened area along the right side of his body where he'd been lying...*livor mortis*. The blood had pooled at the lowest point when his heart stopped beating. His eyes remained open, his unseeing gaze now fixed on the ceiling.

Feeling completely numb, she fought to summon some sort of emotional distance as she picked up his hand, felt the stiffness in his fingers and in the entire length of his arm.

He had been dead for several hours.

Trembling, she placed his hand on the sheet and scooted back to her side of the bed and off. She stood and grabbed for her cell on the table next to the bed. A quick tug pulled it loose from the power cord. She hit the three digits that would bring help.

When the dispatcher finished her spiel, Marissa spoke with remarkable calmness. "My name is Marissa Frasier." She provided her address. "My husband— ex-husband," she amended, "is dead. Please send the police."

The brief blip of calm deserted her, and Marissa collapsed onto the floor as she answered the rest of the woman's questions. Was she injured? No. What was her ex-husband's name? William Bauer. Had there been a violent encounter? No. What was the nature of the victim's injuries?

"He's been shot." The words were whispered. How could this be? She'd been sleeping in the bed right next to him.

For that matter, how had her husband been shot and

ended up in her bed? Did he even have a key to this house? She had never given him one…

More questions from the dispatcher. Was she armed? No. Was there anyone else in the house? No. Wait. Her heart slammed into a frantic rhythm once more. She didn't think so. Marissa scrambled to her feet and moved slowly through the second floor of her home. She thought of the only weapon she owned. It was in the lockbox in the drawer of her bedside table. Should she go back for it?

The front doorbell sounded from downstairs and the dispatcher informed her that it was the police and emergency services; she should answer the door now. Marissa descended the stairs, disbelief swaddling her like a thick fog. Every creak of the century-old staircase echoed in her brain, seeming to ask how anyone—even William—climbed these very stairs to her room without her hearing. How had he climbed in bed next to her without her rousing?

She'd been tired, for sure. She'd slept hard. Even had a bit of a sleep hangover. Still, when they were married and working different shifts, she never failed to wake up when he came home. In college, she'd always awakened when her roommates came in—no matter how quiet they had tried to be.

As she approached the front door with its three-quarter glass panel, she realized she should have changed or grabbed a robe. Her lounge pants and tank covered her, but the fabric was thin. She suddenly felt exposed and so very cold.

Two uniformed officers stood on her stoop. The

flashing lights of an ambulance sat at the curb. Another couple of uniforms hustled up the steps to join the group. This was real. William was dead…in her home.

Steadying herself, Marissa twisted the dead bolt to the unlock position and opened the door.

"Ma'am." The first man in uniform gave her a nod. "I'm Officer Jacob Tolliver. One of my fellow officers is going to stay out here on the stoop while another has a look around outside. My partner and I are coming inside to have a look around. Do you understand?"

His question warned her that she apparently appeared as much in shock as she felt. She nodded. "Yes. He— he's in the bedroom. Second door on the left upstairs."

"You're certain there is no one else in the house?"

"Just me and…my…him, and he's dead." She tried to remember her precise steps. "I didn't check the third floor."

Officer Tolliver nodded, then he and his partner walked past her and headed for the stairs. Marissa blinked slowly as the paramedics from the ambulance came inside next. She leaned against the wall and slid down until her bottom hit the floor.

William was dead.

He'd said he was going to kill himself.

The location of the bullet hole—and she was certain that was what it was—wasn't consistent with a self-inflicted gunshot wound. She had seen her share. But, even if he had somehow managed to shoot himself in the back of the head, how did he get into her room? Into her bed?

She had no idea how much time passed before one of the officers helped her up and escorted her to the sofa.

"Dr. Frasier," he said gently, "first, is there anyone we can call for you?"

Marissa's lips parted, the reply on the tip of her tongue, but then she closed her mouth. There was no one to call. Her brother, her only living relative, was in South America with a group of doctors who were donating the next two weeks to areas with little or no available medical care.

William was dead…not that she had been able to call upon him for any sort of help in ages.

Eva…*the Colby Agency.*

"I should send a text to one of my colleagues and let her know what's happened." Dear God, she needed to call William's family.

"Why don't you let us take care of that?"

Marissa provided Eva's number to another of the officers who appeared, and he assured her he would make the call. She wasn't entirely certain why the officer preferred to make the call himself rather than have her do it. She supposed it had something to do with ensuring she didn't share the details of William's death, since there would be an investigation.

Investigation. Murder. Someone had murdered William.

Her lips trembled. This was a homicide investigation, and she was a person of interest. Her hand went to her mouth, and the urge to vomit was nearly overwhelming. Dear God.

"Dr. Frasier, can you start from the beginning and tell me what happened?"

Her mind still steeped in disbelief, she recounted all that had happened since she woke up. Twice he stopped her and urged her to take her time. The clearer the details, the better. She tried her very best to speak slowly and not leave anything out.

More people came into her home. The latest two were fully clad in disposable garb—gloves, white coveralls, matching hair covers, masks and booties. Forensic techs, she realized. They were here to collect evidence of the crime that had taken place in her home.

The shooting. The *murder*.

How in the world had William been shot right next to her without her hearing it? Wouldn't there have been a struggle?

No sooner had she finished her story to the officer than another pair of official-looking men walked in. These two wore business suits.

"Dr. Frasier," Tolliver said as he stood, "this is Detective Nader and his partner, Detective Watts. They'll be taking over from here."

The man named Nader took the chair that Tolliver vacated. Watts followed the officer up the stairs.

Marissa's throat felt dry. She wished for water or coffee. Anything.

"Let's start at the top, Dr. Frasier. I want to know everything you remember from the time you got home last night."

Marissa started at the beginning once more and told the detective the same story she'd told the officer.

Nader asked her about her relationship with William. She flinched. Of course he would want to know those details. Most likely the officer simply hadn't gotten that far in his interrogation.

Because this *was* an interrogation. Not merely an interview. A man was dead.

As briefly as possible, Marissa explained her relationship with William, culminating with the recent volatile history—his words to her last night outside the ER.

Nader did a lot of scribbling.

Marissa wrung her hands together, wished again that she had a jacket or sweater and a bottle of water or a cup of coffee.

A female officer approached Nader and whispered something in his ear. The two of them glanced at Marissa.

"Give me a minute," Nader said.

The officer stepped back to the front door and waited there.

"You know a fellow named Lacon Traynor? Says he's part of your legal and security team from the Colby Agency."

Relief rushed through Marissa. "Yes." Though she didn't know the name Lacon Traynor, she absolutely knew the Colby Agency. Eva likely knew the man.

"Does the Colby Agency represent you?"

Marissa wasn't sure how to answer that question. They did, in a manner of speaking, she supposed. Though she hadn't technically met with Victoria yet and hadn't signed any documents.

But William was dead—in her bed.

She needed help.

"Yes." She hated that her voice quivered. "Yes, the Colby Agency and I are working together. Because..." She moistened her lips. "Because William's behavior was becoming increasingly erratic and threatening."

Nader sent a nod toward the waiting officer, who disappeared out the door.

"Nader!"

The shout came from the landing at the top of the stairs. Marissa's gaze moved to the man who had called out. It was the other detective, Watts.

"Yeah?" Nader glanced over his shoulder.

"Bring the doc up here for a minute, will you?"

Nader stood. "Let's have a look at your bedroom."

Marissa followed the detective to the staircase. They waited at the bottom until the two paramedics had descended.

"Coroner's on his way," one of the paramedics said to Nader.

The detective nodded and the paramedics left. Marissa watched as they, too, disappeared out her front door. Suddenly she wanted to do exactly that. She didn't want to be here any longer. She didn't want to go back upstairs. There was blood in her bed.

Bile churned in her belly.

William was dead.

Nader gestured for her to go ahead of him. Her entire body had started to shake by the time they reached her bedroom door. She hugged herself tight. It wasn't until she walked into the room this time that she smelled the stench of death. That unmistakable odor of rapidly decomposing cells, mixed with the metallic fetor of blood. The shades had been raised, filling the room with morning light. William remained on the bed. He would be there, she reminded herself, until the coroner arrived to take possession of the body.

The body. Dear God, why? Why would he do this? Yet the gunshot had been to the back of his head. He had not done this. She had to keep her thoughts straight. Her mind whirled madly. He had been murdered. She had to remember that. Someone had come into her home…

Her stomach clenched, and she suffered through another round of nausea. She had assumed that William had somehow gotten her key. But William couldn't have done this…not alone anyway.

His killer had stood over her bed…had done these awful things while she slept.

"At any time after you awakened and found your husband—"

"Ex-husband," she corrected Nader, her voice weak, practically a whisper.

He nodded. "After you discovered your dead ex-husband lying next to you, did you at any time walk to that side of the bed?"

Marissa had to think about the question for a moment, then she shook her head. "No. I scooted across the bed and pushed him onto his back." She shrugged. "All I could think was that he needed CPR, but then I realized it was too late. I suppose I was in shock." Her hand went to her throat. "I don't see how this could have happened." She looked around the room. "Here. With me asleep right next to him."

Watts held up a clear bag with a handgun inside it. "Is this .22 caliber automatic yours, Dr. Frasier?"

Marissa peered at the bag. "It looks like mine." She gestured to her night table. "May I?"

Watts and Nader nodded. One of them muttered, "Sure."

She moved to the table and pulled open the top drawer. A fingernail file, a brush, the book she'd started reading months ago and never gotten back to. The nail polish she never seemed to have time to use, and the lockbox. She removed it from the drawer and opened it. No weapon.

Where was her gun?

"It's not here." She turned back to the detective holding the weapon. "Is there a way to determine if that one is actually mine?"

She instinctively understood that the weapon in the bag, the one that was probably hers, had been used to kill William.

"Our forensic experts will make that determination," Watts assured her.

"We'd like to swab your hands," Nader said.

She nodded. "Of course." She had nothing to hide. Apparently she had slept through William's murder. How was that possible? Wouldn't she have heard the weapon fire? It might be small, but it was loud nonetheless. She'd fired it numerous times when she took that gun safety course. The sound would certainly have awakened her. The entire scene was sheer madness. None of this made sense.

Horror churned inside her.

Watts motioned for one of the techs to come do the honors. Marissa held her hands in front of her—they shook. The forensic tech carefully collected the samples from the skin on her hands then stepped away from her without ever making eye contact.

This was a nightmare. She squeezed her eyes shut, wondered again how this could be happening.

"We'd also like the clothes you're wearing, Dr. Frasier."

Marissa opened her eyes and met Nader's steady gaze. The female officer was there now, as well.

"Officer Holcombe will accompany you to your closet. You might want to pack a few things. I'm afraid you won't be able to come back into the house for a few days. We need time to properly process the scene."

The scene.

"Of course."

With Holcombe right behind her, Marissa went through the en suite to the large walk-in closet that had been a key selling point for the home. Moving mechanically, she packed jeans and T-shirts and her favorite sneakers into her overnight bag. She wasn't due back to work until Tuesday. Surely they would be finished here by then. Just in case, she grabbed a set of scrubs as well as a pair of black dress slacks and a matching blouse, along with her favorite flats for meeting with Victoria Colby-Camp. She went back into the bathroom and gathered her toiletries.

Once she'd zipped the bag, Holcombe said, "I'll just need you to remove your pajamas, ma'am."

It wasn't until then that Marissa remembered she was

still wearing her pj's. Rather than answer Holcombe, she returned to the closet and found another pair of jeans and a University of Illinois T-shirt. While the officer stood by, she stripped off her pj's and dropped them into the waiting bag.

"I'll need your underwear too, ma'am."

Naked save for her underwear, Marissa went back to the closet, Holcombe on her heels, and snatched another pair of panties from the drawer. She slipped off the pair she was wearing and quickly shimmied into the clean ones. While Holcombe readied the bags for turning over to one of the forensic techs, Marissa quickly dragged on the jeans and a T-shirt. She'd already packed her sneakers, so she pulled on a pair of thong sandals. With the officer waiting for her, evidence bags in hand, she abruptly remembered she would need pj's, too. She grabbed a pair and stuffed them into her bag with the rest.

With her bag hanging over her shoulder, she exited the bathroom and walked straight up to Nader. The coroner had arrived and was examining the body.

The body. It sounded so clinical. This was the man with whom she had thought she would spend the rest of her life...

"May I leave now?" She kept her gaze carefully averted from the activities across the room.

"You can." He reached into his jacket pocket and removed a business card. "Call me if you think of anything else." When she'd taken the card, he added, "I will have more questions, and there's the official statement you'll need to come downtown and make, so keep me informed of your location."

Marissa nodded and hurried from the room. She felt sick and disgusted and aggrieved. How the hell had this happened? When she went to sleep last night, her biggest concern had been how to extract William from her life. Now she had to worry about whether she was a murder suspect.

Her heart hurt for William. She would never have wished him dead.

Downstairs, yet another new arrival stood near the stone fireplace perusing the framed photographs there. This one was male and tall, with sandy blond hair. He wasn't like the others. He wore well-loved jeans, a sky blue shirt and a tan summer-weight suit jacket, but it was the cowboy boots that really set him apart from the others. He turned as she descended the last step and thrust out his hand, looking for all the world like a character from a modern-day Western movie who'd just stepped off the screen and into her living room.

"Lacon Traynor," he said, "from the Colby Agency."

Marissa took the final steps between them and accepted his hand for a quick shake. She wasn't sure what she had expected when Eva mentioned calling the Colby Agency, but this towering, cowboy-boot-wearing guy was not it. He looked vaguely familiar, but for the life of her she couldn't place him.

She finally found her voice. "Have we met?"

He gestured for her to follow him toward the kitchen. Her graystone was three stories and quite deep, but very narrow. When you walked in the front door you could see all the way out the back, with nothing but the staircase with the powder room tucked beneath it to hamper the flow. Beyond her kitchen was a set of French doors that led onto a rear deck. Beyond the deck was the small driveway. No garage, just a driveway. She was immensely grateful for something beyond street parking. A garage was on her wish list.

"We may have run into each other at the Edge when I was working with Bella and Dr. Pierce."

Now she remembered. She'd seen him once with Dr. Pierce during that awful business about his deceased wife. She remembered thinking then that this guy looked like a sheriff from a modern-day Western. Ruggedly handsome and utterly capable. She hoped he could help her the way Bella Lytle had helped Dr. Pierce, and Todd Christian had rescued Eva.

"Let's get out of here," he suggested.

She was more than ready to do that. In the kitchen, she grabbed a bottle of water from the fridge. Traynor took her bag and led the way out onto the deck and down to where her car was parked. He walked right past her vehicle and to the alley.

She followed, too overwhelmed to put up a fuss. "Where do we go from here?"

"My car. They'll want to go over yours at the lab."

Marissa hissed a disgusted sigh. They were taking over her entire life. Not that she actually minded, as long as it would help find William's killer.

A killer who had been in her home. Fear tightened around her throat.

She waited until they were seated in Traynor's car and he'd driven away before she said as much.

"Until they've collected all the evidence they believe they can find and have ruled you out as the shooter, they're going to be all over you and your property. You might as well get used to that now." He sent her a side-long glance. "The good news is that while ruling you out, they'll also be looking for the actual perpetrator. It's no fun, but it's the way it works."

Marissa closed her eyes and leaned back against the headrest. She was so tired.

"Why don't you tell me why someone would want to make it look as if you killed your ex-husband?"

Marissa's eyes snapped open. Good God, he was right. The entire setup was about making her look responsible for William's death. But who would do that? Other than her friends at work, she had none. Her social life had fizzled out during her final years of marriage to William. He'd chased away every friend they'd ever had.

"I have no idea." Why did this have to happen now? Her life was finally headed in the direction she wanted, and this insanity had to descend upon her? What had William gotten himself into that someone would want to murder him?

"Eva filled me in on your past with Bauer. Officer Tolliver brought me up to speed on your statement, so I'm not going to make you repeat any of that for now."

Thank goodness. She'd already repeated it twice.

"Since his release from prison, have you kept up with Bauer's activities?"

"No. I tried to evict him from my life, but he still showed up every so often to antagonize me."

"So you don't know how he made money or who his associates were?"

"No." God, she'd thought she was doing the right thing distancing herself, and suddenly it felt as if all the things she didn't know were coming back to haunt her. "He sold the condo when he went to prison. Honestly, I don't even know where he lives."

Saying the words out loud made her feel all the guiltier. How could she have been married to the man for five years and not know where he was living the day he was murdered?

What kind of person did that make her?

"No worries," Traynor assured her. "We can track down all that information. But first, I'm taking you to breakfast. You need to eat."

"I'm really not hungry."

He flashed her a smile. "Maybe not, but I'm starving."

At that moment, the reality of her predicament settled fully upon her.

How in the world would she ever prove that she hadn't killed her ex-husband?

He had been murdered in her bed. The murder weapon was her gun. The security guard from the Edge could confirm that she and William had had a heated exchanged less than twenty-four hours ago.

She swung her gaze back to the man behind the wheel.

Her only hope was this cowboy who wanted to eat before they got down to business.

She was in serious trouble.

Chapter Three

Lincoln Avenue, 10:00 a.m.

Lacon had practically shoveled in the stack of pancakes he'd ordered while Dr. Frasier picked at her eggwhite omelet. When she'd descended the stairs in those tight-fitting jeans and the navy university T-shirt, she'd looked like a college freshman, not the thirty-four-year-old doctor he'd been sent to protect. He'd learned a lot about her last night from Eva Bowman, fellow Colby investigator Todd Christian's soon-to-be wife. Eva and Frasier were close friends. Frasier spent an hour in the gym most every day running on the treadmill—which was different from the way she used to run through the neighborhood she loved. Her ex-husband had followed her by car several times so she'd changed her routine.

She worked hard and lived frugally to cover the mortgage for the restored graystone she'd bought when she left Bauer. She'd allowed him to keep the equity in their condo as well as the furnishings to facilitate a speedy divorce.

Between Eva and his online research, he'd learned

a great deal about Dr. William Bauer, as well. Like his ex-wife, he'd graduated medical school with lower than average student loan debt because of scholarships and hard work, but the practice he'd been invited to join had not offered much in the way of fringe benefits to cover any of those loans. Frasier, on the other hand, had landed a great offer with complete coverage of any loans still outstanding. Dr. Devon Pierce, the administrator at the Edge, had given her a hefty bonus to join him when he opened the prototype advance emergency medicine facility. That bonus had served as a down payment on her new home.

While Frasier's career blossomed, Bauer's had flopped. After ferreting out all he could online about the guy, Lacon had called a friend of his who had made a career writing about life in Chicago and who kept his finger on the pulse of Chicago's streets. Since Bauer's prison stint, he sold his services as a physician to anyone who had the money to pay the exorbitant prices, and he asked no questions. He lived in a hotel and used his cell phone like an answering service.

Based on the few questions Lacon had asked her since placing their breakfast order, Frasier was completely unaware of her ex's dangerous and likely illegal activities. He'd kept the conversation fairly light in hopes she would eat. After the shock she'd suffered, she needed protein.

When she'd finally gotten down a few bites of her food and started on her second cup of coffee, Lacon decided to give her the bad news. "I did some research on Bauer."

She looked at him, her face reflecting her confusion. She had the greenest eyes. Friendly green eyes, like Eva's. And then there was that fiery red hair. He wondered if the lady had the temper to go with those wild red locks.

"You did?" She shook her head. "I'm so out of it, I didn't realize you were already looking into my situation."

"I started last night, right after I spoke to Eva."

"Oh." She looked slightly less confused now, and even a bit hopeful. "I forgot Eva called you last night." She placed her fork on the table. "I wasn't actually sure who she called. Only that it was someone from the Colby Agency."

"We would have had this discussion this morning in my boss's office except..."

She nodded. "Yeah. Except..."

"Anyway," he went on, "I discovered a number of things you probably aren't aware of. You might want to brace yourself."

The flicker of hope that had flashed in her eyes faded. "Was William in trouble?"

"Considering what happened in your bedroom, I'd say most definitely."

"What was he involved in?" She moved her hands to her lap, but not before he saw them tremble.

Now for the bad news. "He was practicing medicine as a sort of concierge doctor."

Marissa sat, obviously stunned, for a moment. "But he was only released from jail about six months ago." She shook her head. "He had patients? The state board suspended his license for unprofessional conduct. I don't understand. Had the board reviewed his case recently?"

"I don't have all the details, but I can tell you his patient list is better suited for the wanted posters on a post office wall than the files in a doctor's office."

She sat back. "I'm not sure I understand. Are you saying he was treating criminals?"

Lacon nodded. "As in, he gets a call when a drug lord or mob boss needs a bullet removed from one of his favorite henchmen."

"Oh my God." She closed her eyes in a futile effort to block the reality of what his words meant.

"My source was able to name a couple of top-of-the-food-chain thugs he's done work for. They were paying him big bucks for the work and for his silence."

She allowed this news to sink in before asking, "So whoever came into my home last night and killed William may have been hired by an actual drug lord or mob boss?"

"That would be my guess."

All those soft curls swished as she shook her head. "Then why not kill me, too? What if I had suddenly awakened in the middle of what they were doing? Or if my neighbor heard the gunshot?"

"From what you described and what Officer Tolliver told me, this was a professional hit. Bauer stepped on someone's toes, and they showed him who was boss. Why they chose your place to carry this out, no clue just yet. If the shooter used your gun, my guess is the police will find a pillow or something along those lines that was used to muffle the sound."

Her face clouded with worry. "I hadn't thought of that. Still, I'm not a heavy sleeper. I can't believe I slept through someone coming into my home and killing my husband right next to me."

Lacon was having trouble with that one, as well. "While I waited for you to come back downstairs, I noticed there was a half-empty bottle of wine on the counter in your kitchen. Did you have wine last night?"

"Yes. I had one glass. I told the detective as much."

"Anything unusual about how you felt after you drank the wine or when you woke up? Groggy? Headache?"

"I remember I felt really tired last night, but that's not unusual. I work long, hectic hours at the ER. So I went straight to bed after the wine. This morning, I did feel a little sluggish, had a mild headache, but I assumed it was about finding William dead next to me. I told this to the detective, too."

"They're probably drawing the same picture I am, Dr. Frasier. Most likely they'll have the wine tested for drugs. It might be best if you had a blood test to see if there's anything we need to know about."

"We can stop by the Edge."

"From there we'll go to the safe house and get you settled. We can start going over what we know and what we don't from there. We've already got people gathering more accurate and detailed information about your ex-husband's activities since his release. It won't take us long to figure this out."

"Safe house?"

"The police won't release your home for a day or two, and it's best that we keep you out of reach of whatever trouble Bauer found himself in until we determine the source and any potential threat to you. You don't need to worry. We've got you covered."

The first hint of a smile tilted her lips. "Thank you."

Colby Safe House, 1:30 p.m.

WHEN MARISSA HEARD the words *safe house*, she hadn't expected a fortress. The house sat in the woods on the edge of Lake Michigan, a good forty-five minutes from downtown Chicago. A towering brick wall surrounded the property on all sides save the one facing the lake. Enormous iron gates had opened for their entrance onto the property and immediately closed behind them. If not for the large windows, the house would have looked more like a stone prison than a mere house. Lush flowers and shrubs bordered the stone facade, softening it a bit.

Traynor parked his car in front of the house. He gazed up at it. "State-of-the-art security system operated by keypad or voice control. Steel shutters can be closed over all the windows and doors. No one can touch you here."

For some reason, she didn't feel the slightest bit better about this nightmare. Part of her held on to the fleeting possibility that any moment she would wake up and discover that the whole morning had been a dream. Things like this didn't happen to regular, everyday people. She felt as if she'd been shoved onto the set of a thriller movie. Any minute now the director would give the order to run.

Traynor climbed out of the car and rounded the hood to her side. She emerged to join him. She shook off the troubling thoughts and focused on the reality staring her in the face right this second. She was standing in front of a safe house. A place where she would stay until William's murder was all sorted out.

"It's beautiful, in a sort of austere way," she said, mostly to make conversation.

"You'll feel more comfortable inside."

At the door, he pressed his palm onto a keypad and the door locks released. He pushed the door open and waited for her to step inside before him. The walls were a warm beige with lovely gloss white trim. Rich furnishings and draperies added a very elegant touch. All those large windows allowed sun to pour in between the slats of the shutters. Unlike the exterior, inside it actually felt warm and inviting.

"You're right. It's a very lovely house."

"Take whatever room you'd like upstairs, and then join me for coffee in the kitchen."

She took her bag from him and headed for the grand staircase. Upstairs, she wandered into the first room with a view of the rear gardens and the lake. The rock paths and dense greenery made the stone patio and gorgeous pool with its rushing waterfall look as if they had always been there—as if they were part of the natural landscape. She sighed. Too bad this wasn't some exotic resort where she'd spend the next few days soaking up the sun. She hadn't taken a vacation in years.

But this was no vacation.

Feeling more exhausted than she had since medical

school, she tossed her bag onto a chair and opened it. One by one she hung her jeans and T-shirts in the largest closet she'd ever seen. Maybe hanging them would help with the wrinkles from being stuffed into her bag. She carried her toiletries to the massive en suite. A luxurious marble tub, a shower for at least four and two sinks designed in colorful glass that crowned the endless vanity. The window over the tub looked out over the lake, as well. The view put the bathroom over the top.

"A grand hideaway," she mumbled.

She leaned against the counter and stared at her reflection. Her pale skin looked even paler. The dark circles under her eyes spoke loudly of the morning's horrors. The stop they'd made at the Edge had taken longer than she'd anticipated. Eva insisted on knowing exactly what happened. She drew the necessary blood samples and ensured them the analysis would be handled stat.

Eva had promised to explain everything to Dr. Pierce. As much as she adored Eva, Marissa really hadn't wanted to talk about it anymore to anyone except those involved directly in the investigation. Her body and soul felt tender, and she needed time to think and process all that had happened. But sweet Eva had coaxed the story out of her. In the end, Marissa supposed it was better if her dearest friend, as well as Dr. Pierce, understood the precarious situation.

She supposed *precarious* was the best way to describe her current dilemma. Part of her wanted to call her brother, but he would only insist on coming home, and that wouldn't be fair. He was doing important work.

She doubted this was going away anytime soon. There was always time to call her brother later if the situation deteriorated.

Pushing away from the vanity, she trudged back into the bedroom. She made it as far as the bed before she collapsed. Traynor was waiting for her downstairs, but she couldn't seem to make her body obey the command to get up and move.

Tears rushed over her lashes and down her cheeks. She didn't want to cry. It was too late for tears, but she couldn't stop them. Giving up the fight, she dropped her face into her hands and let them come. Her shoulders shook with the sobs that tore at her heart. No matter that she and William had been over for years—she had loved him so deeply before everything fell apart. She had expected to spend the rest of her life with him…to have children with him. Eventually. Though she couldn't say that she still loved him, she cared about him and wanted the best for him.

Now he was dead.

He'd threatened to kill himself and her mere hours before his death, and somehow that made the tragedy all the sadder. Had he really wished her dead? She'd tried so hard to help him before his abuse turned physical. She had already stayed in the marriage too long. Why was it women so often stayed, somehow believing they could salvage what remained of their marriage?

Foolish. Simply foolish.

A soft knock on the door drew her attention there. Traynor stood in the doorway, his tall frame and broad shoulders filling the space. She swiped at her eyes and attempted to pull herself together. "You'll have to excuse me. I don't know what's wrong with me. I can't stop crying."

Most men usually found an immediate excuse to disappear when a woman cried. To her surprise, Lacon Traynor crossed the room, grabbed the box of tissues on the bedside table and sat down on the bed next to her.

"You needed to cry," he said gently as he offered her a couple of tissues. "It doesn't help to keep all the emotions bottled up inside. This has been a seriously bad day for you. If anyone I've ever met needed a good cry, it's you."

She dabbed at her eyes and nose. "I keep asking myself how it happened without me waking up. No matter how I examine it, it doesn't make sense."

"We'll have a better handle on things when the lab results are in. For now, just know that none of it was your fault. You're a victim in this."

Marissa stared at the soggy tissue in her hand and asked the question that had been pounding in her brain since Traynor told her what he'd discovered about William. "Why do you think they didn't kill me?" She shrugged. "I mean, I can see how, if William was lurking around my house and they followed him there, it was a coincidence of sorts. But it feels like more than just a coincidence."

"The body was staged," Traynor said. "Since there was no sign of a struggle in your home, I believe they drugged Bauer and put him in position, then shot him."

Marissa shuddered. She'd seen enough gunshot wounds involving .22s to know that when dealing with a caliber that small, all kinds of things could go awry. The bullet could have glanced off his skull, traveled around beneath the skin and come out someplace else. The damned thing could have ended up hitting her. After all, William had been lying on the bed facing her.

But that wasn't what happened. The coroner's report would tell the detailed story, but shoving the muzzle against the back of his neck just below the base of the skull in that particular spot pretty much guaranteed the brain stem would be damaged. The likelihood of death was extremely high. Since there had been no exit wound, the bullet no doubt penetrated the skull and bounced around in the brain, doing all manner of additional damage. Even if by some twist of fate William had lived, he would in all probability have suffered significant physical and cognitive damage.

She pushed away the thoughts. If he'd been drugged, perhaps he hadn't suffered. She hoped he hadn't suffered. As horribly as he'd treated her in recent years, he hadn't deserved to be murdered.

"Were they trying to send me a message for some reason?" Marissa couldn't see the thought process behind such a move. She had nothing to do with William's work or any debts he might owe to angry loan sharks. Frankly, she hardly knew the man who had once been her husband anymore.

Traynor didn't answer for a second that turned into five. "That's it, isn't it?" She stared directly at his face, silently demanding that he meet her gaze. "You believe the person or persons who did this wanted me to know they could come into my home and commit murder right in my most intimate space. They left me alive for some reason, didn't they?"

"That's one of the theories, yes. Are you certain you're not aware of any activities Bauer was involved in? Could he have given you something to keep for him? Something they might want?"

"No. After I landed in the hospital from the beating he gave me, I cut all ties with him. The only times I've seen him since his trial are when he has shown up unexpectedly on the street outside my house or in the parking lot at the market where I shop. He's called and left messages, but I never answer them. Eventually I changed my number. I never allowed him into my new house. When he came to the ER yesterday, that was the first time he'd come to my work."

"If they believe you have something that belongs to them or something they want," Traynor offered, "we'll know soon enough."

She drew in a deep breath and squared her shoulders. "I think I need a walk."

"Come on." He stood. "I'll show you around the property."

Downstairs, he took her on a tour of the kitchen, which was huge and filled with gleaming cabinetry and sleek countertops. The appliances were commercial, restaurant-style pieces of art with enough bells and whistles to make any chef happy. A dream kitchen by anyone's standards. Traynor's next stop was the gym. The array of equipment would satisfy the most hard-core workout enthusiast. Marissa would spend some time here for sure. Next to the gym was the garage that housed six luxury vehicles; some were even bulletproof. She had to admit, she was impressed.

Back through the kitchen and the dining room was a den at the back of the house. A floor-to-ceiling fireplace sat against one wall; big comfy furniture filled the center of the room, and a sizable television was tucked into a discreet nook. But the part that stole Marissa's attention was the wall of French doors and windows that zoomed all the way to the vaulted ceiling to allow as much of the lake view into the room as possible. She could live in this one room.

Outside, the breeze coming off the water chased away the afternoon heat. They followed the stone path, and Traynor pointed out the boat dock and the helipad. The safe house was prepared with a number of escape routes, as well as a safe room that could withstand just about any sort of attack.

"When did you join the Colby Agency?" She leaned against the steel railing that topped the seawall at the back of the property. The air was crisp and fresh, and she felt herself starting to relax.

"Six years ago." He propped his arms on the railing and stared out at the water. "Before that I was a bounty hunter."

Marissa smiled. No surprise there. She'd had him pegged as a rugged law enforcement type. "Where did you grow up?"

"Floresville, Texas," he announced proudly. "Half an hour south of San Antonio. The family ranch is there. I have two brothers and a sister who run the family business, one of the biggest cattle operations in the state. My dad's retired now, but he still gives his input."

She gazed out over the water for a moment before searching his face. "You didn't want to stay with the family business?"

He smiled, and the expression startled her. Lacon Traynor was an attractive man, but when he smiled it was a genuinely beautiful sight. She liked his smile. His eyes, too. He had those light brown, almost golden eyes. The blond hair and gold eyes were a vivid contrast to his tanned skin.

Her detailed analysis of his physical assets puzzled her. It didn't seem appropriate to admire the man's attributes after what had happened. Honestly, she couldn't even remember the last time she'd paid attention to whether a man was attractive or not, much less noticed his smile or his eyes. Something inside her had shut off all those feelings after William threw her up against the wall a few times and then tossed her down the stairs. It really was a miracle she'd survived without truly devastating injuries.

But no matter that he had done that awful thing to her, she still never wished him dead.

Yet he was dead, and somehow even in death he'd found a way to punish her for being a better doctor than he could be…for working harder than he ever considered working. And for trying to do the right thing when he no longer cared.

She had a right to be happy, and William—alive or dead—had no right to try to take that happiness from her. Anger sparked deep inside her.

"I was far too cocky and too full of myself to be happy on the ranch. I needed adventure. For a long time—" his gaze drifted back to the water "—rounding up the bad guys and bringing them in was enough. But then a really bad one got out of jail after a two-year stint, and went back home and killed his ex-wife. I saw things differently after that. Doing the job no longer held the same appeal. I needed distance and a fresh start."

"The ex-wife was someone you knew?" She had a terrible feeling the story didn't end with a job going wrong. His words carried the weight of far more than mere facts or statistics. This was personal.

"She was my fiancée. We were getting married the next month. He killed her just to get back at me for hauling his sorry ass to San Antonio to stand trial the first time."

"I'm so sorry."

He nodded, stared down at his hands. "I was out of town when he was released, a week earlier than expected. I had a bail jumper to pick up in El Paso. The local cops took care of the bastard though. He made the mistake of trying to fight back when they cornered him, and they took him out."

"So you moved away." She didn't blame him.

"I needed a change of scenery."

"The winters are very different here," she commented, easing the topic of conversation away from his painful past.

"You're not kidding. But I wanted to work for the best. It was important to me to find work that allowed me to help people before the worst happened. The

Colby Agency gave me that opportunity." He sent her another smile, this one considerably dimmer than the first. "Most of the time anyway."

"Sometimes there's just no way to see what's coming." Not in a million years would she have suspected William of this behavior. She'd had no idea his fall from grace had taken him so far down.

Lacon placed one of his broad palms over her hand on the railing and gave it a reassuring squeeze. "We'll figure this out."

His promise warmed her. Her cell vibrated against her hip, shattering the moment of encouragement. She pulled it from her pocket and checked the screen, expecting it to be Eva or one of the detectives. Blocked Call flashed on the screen. "Marissa Frasier."

"Hello, Dr. Frasier."

The deep voice was male, but not one she recognized. She hesitated, waiting for the man to go on.

"You have a very lovely home. I sincerely apologize that my business with your husband caused you any inconvenience."

Fear rushed over her, and she instinctively grabbed Traynor's arm. "Who is this?"

"You'll know soon enough," the man promised. "For now, I need your help. You see, your husband left me in a very difficult situation. Now you're going to have to pick up his slack."

"I have no idea what you're talking about," she argued. Traynor's head was next to hers now so he could hear, as well. "William and I divorced a long time ago.

Whatever business he had with you has nothing to do with me."

"You are a doctor, are you not?"

She didn't answer. She didn't need to, because he already knew.

"Yes, I know you are. Your late husband bragged about you quite often. He still kept photos of you in his phone. You're still listed as *wife* in his cell phone. How does that make you feel, Dr. Frasier?"

The bastard had William's phone. The police had asked her about his phone. The news about the photos and the way she was listed in William's phone sent a strangely unnerving sensation chasing along her spine. She wasn't sure how she was supposed to feel about that announcement. Maybe William simply hadn't taken the time to clear the past from his phone. Now she would never know. *Didn't matter.*

"What do you want?" she demanded.

"Drive into the city, Dr. Frasier. When you reach Division Street, I will send you the address you need to find. Involve the police, and you will regret it. Refuse to come, and you will regret it."

"Why would I do this when you won't tell me who you are?"

Her phone vibrated, making her heart skip another beat.

"Have a look at the photo you just received," he said as if he, too, had felt the vibration.

She drew her phone from her ear and touched the screen to open the text message. A photo of Jeremiah Owens wearing his blue cast appeared on the screen.

It was obvious the photo had been taken as he and his mother exited the ER earlier last evening.

"Did you receive the photo?" the man asked.

Marissa didn't have to question why he sent it. The realization sat like a boulder on her chest. "Yes."

"Your late husband told me how much you love your patients. I'm certain you will want to ensure little Jeremiah remains safe, no matter the cost or the inconvenience."

Fury overrode all logic. "I don't know what sort of game—"

"This is not a game, Dr. Frasier. You will do exactly as I say. Any supplies you require will be provided by my associates. Do not notify the police. Trust me, I have eyes and ears everywhere in this city. Do not make a mistake, or little Jeremiah's mother will be burying her son while you stand by and wonder why you didn't listen more carefully to my instructions. I'm certain you do not want that to happen."

The fury drained instantly, leaving only the fear. Her heart hammered so hard she could scarcely manage a breath. "It'll take me nearly an hour to get back to the city."

"I'm counting on you, Dr. Frasier. Respond to the text I sent to let me know when you have arrived at Division. Instructions will follow."

The call ended.

She lifted her gaze to Traynor's. "I have to go. I don't know who this man is or what he expects from me, but I have to go."

"No." He took her hand. "*We* have to go."

Chapter Four

"You need to drive faster."

Lacon couldn't remember the last time anyone had asked him to drive faster. "I'm running ten miles an hour over the speed limit now, Dr. Frasier. We don't want to risk a traffic stop."

Frasier twisted around in her seat and stared out the back window, then did the same on the passenger side. She stretched across the console and checked behind him and then in front of him to see his side of the highway. "I don't see any cops. Please, you need to hurry."

"Try to calm down," he urged. Hell, she was making him nervous. He got it. She was a doctor, and this wasn't part of her daily routine. He'd probably pass out if he had to cut open a patient and poke around their organs. "Bella will be patching through the conference call any second now. We need to keep our heads on straight until we get a better handle on the situation."

"Bella Lytle?"

"The one and only." Bella was soon to be Bella Pierce. Dr. Devon Pierce, the Edge administrator, had already popped the question. "She's coordinating a call between us, Victoria and Chicago PD."

"What?" Frasier glared at him. "He said no police! He claimed to have eyes and ears in the department."

Had she not been listening when he called Victoria? "Victoria and Lucas know the police department inside out. They won't be calling Nader or Watts. Whoever they work with will be someone completely trustworthy. Their connections go well above any possible leaks."

"Oh, my God." Frasier hugged herself. "If something happens to that child…"

Lacon made the next turn. "He wants you scared, Marissa." He used her first name in hopes of getting her full attention. "Men like him—whoever the hell he is—use fear as a means to gain power. Don't give him the power."

She stared at the cell phone clutched in her hand, the picture of the little boy on the screen. "Mrs. Owens doesn't have any other children, and she can't have any more. Her husband was killed in a construction accident two years ago." She held up the phone, aiming the screen at Lacon. "This child is all she has. I can't risk taking him away from her, do you understand?"

"I do understand." He pressed a little harder on the accelerator, adding another five miles per hour to his speed. "I will do everything I can to make sure nothing happens to the child or to you."

His cell rang, the call coming over the speaker system in the car. He'd set it that way so they could both hear the conversation and respond as needed.

He touched the screen. "Traynor here. I have you on speaker so Dr. Frasier can hear you, as well."

"Dr. Frasier, this is Victoria Colby-Camp. On the line with me are Lucas Camp, Ian Michaels, Bella Lytle—all from the Colby Agency. From Chicago PD's Bureau of Detectives we have Chief Connie Staten. We also have Chief Anthony Waller, who commands the Bureau of Organized Crime since, based on what we've learned about the late Dr. Bauer, we feel we're dealing with an element of organized crime."

"Have you learned something new about William?"

Frasier's voice sounded small and weary. Lacon hated not being able to take the weight of this fear off her shoulders. Before Victoria or the others could respond, he interjected, "I've brought her up to speed on what we had as of this morning."

"Dr. Frasier, this is Chief Waller. We had been watching Dr. Bauer for about two months. We have reason to believe he was deeply involved with Vito Anastasia. To give you a quick overview of our position, in recent decades we've made great strides in eliminating the mob element in Chicago. It still exists, but nothing like it did thirty years ago. Anastasia is doing all within his power to give rise to a new group called the Network. In the last year we've seen a startling increase in homicides and all manner of organized crime. We believe Anastasia is behind that deadly increase. Our goal is to take him down as quickly as possible but, as you are aware, I'm sure, we need evidence against him for that. We could use your help toward that end."

"We will not allow you to use our client in any way that will endanger her life," Victoria stated, her tone professional but firm.

Lacon was grateful his boss had spoken up. He'd been struggling to hold back that same warning. He had been with the Colby Agency long enough to know Victoria's feelings on the subject.

"Ms. Colby-Camp—" a female voice joined the conversation "—this is Chief Staten. You have my word that we would never allow an operation that would endanger Dr. Frasier's life. We're only asking that she share information with us. The fact of the matter is she's already in Anastasia's crosshairs. Whatever his goal, he will not stop until he accomplishes that goal. If anything, we can help protect her."

"How was William—Dr. Bauer involved?" Frasier demanded.

Lacon glanced at her, wished he could give her arm a squeeze of reassurance, but at this speed he needed both hands on the wheel. He had a bad feeling about this. With people this high up the department food chain involved, Bauer had been more than just involved with Vito Anastasia. Lacon would bet everything he owned that he had been caught by the department and forced to feed them info—acting as a confidential informant. Why else would Anastasia assassinate his doctor? He hadn't said as much to Frasier, but the murder was a blatant assassination. The mob executed their people when they stole from them and when they ratted them out. Bauer had done one or the other, no question.

"As a doctor, you're aware that all gunshot victims are reported. Anytime a known criminal shows up in an ER, if he's recognized, he's reported. To avoid those types of situations and to keep his family and crew healthy, a man like Anastasia hires a doctor to take care of things discreetly. Dr. Bauer had been working for Anastasia in that capacity for five months."

Lacon noticed the way Frasier's hand trembled as she covered her mouth. This was not the man she'd known, the man she'd loved. By the time he was murdered, Bauer had been a stranger. A stranger who had dragged her into a world so vile and so dangerous that she couldn't possibly comprehend the risk involved with merely being on the bastard's radar.

"What level of cooperation are you looking for?" Victoria asked the question blazing in Lacon's brain.

"For now, see what Anastasia wants," Waller said. "If it turns out he wants Dr. Frasier to assume the position left open by Dr. Bauer, then we would want her to take it for a period of time and feed intelligence to us."

Lacon couldn't help it—he laughed. "Why don't you just ask her to put a gun to her head and pull the trigger? The result would be basically the same."

That Victoria didn't caution him to back off spoke volumes. She agreed. The proposal was unreasonable.

The two cops on the call started talking at once, arguing why it made complete sense. Victoria countered their denials, backing Lacon's concerns.

"I can't make any promises right now," Frasier spoke up, her voice loud and firm this time. "All I care about at the moment is making sure Jeremiah Owens is safe. Unless you can do that, we have nothing else to talk about at this time."

Lacon smiled to himself. *Way to go, doc.*

"We have undercover surveillance on the Owens home. Mother and son are both inside," Staten assured her.

Frasier shared a look with Lacon. He knew what she was thinking. "Whatever you do," he warned the representatives of the department on the line, "under no circumstances can Anastasia discover that we've contacted you, so those boots you have on the ground better be damned careful."

"I am confident Chiefs Staten and Waller will not allow that to happen," Victoria said, echoing his warning a tad more diplomatically.

The two chiefs gave their assurances that the operation was locked down tight, and the call ended with one final urge from Victoria for Frasier to be careful.

Lacon's phone immediately rang again. This time it was only Victoria. She reminded him that his sole obligation was to Dr. Frasier and keeping her safe. Frasier thanked her.

When they reached Division Street, Lacon parked at a gas station on the corner of West Division Street and North Winchester Avenue. "Send the text."

Frasier held his gaze for several seconds before typing, I'm at Division.

Half a minute, maybe more, elapsed and a soft ping announced a response. Corner of 1735 West Hubbard St. at intersection of Hermitage Ave.

Frasier showed him the screen. Lacon nodded. "I know the area."

Five turns and hardly more than five minutes later, they pulled up in front of a warehouse for lease. Tension rippled through his muscles. Lacon shifted into Park and turned to face her. "Stay close to me. No matter what else happens, stick to me like glue. I do not want you out of my sight for any reason. Got it?"

"Got it." She swallowed hard, the muscles of her throat working. "How will your people know where we are?"

"Every Colby investigator has a tracking device installed in their personal vehicle. The same goes for my phone. Just remember, no matter what else happens, we cannot be separated."

She nodded. "Wait. What's my excuse for having you with me?"

Her voice trembled, and he wished he knew the words to say that would ease her fears, but there were none. "Your ex had been threatening you. You hired personal security through a private firm. I'm your bodyguard."

She nodded. "Good. Okay."

"I'll get out first and open your door."

She moistened her lips. "Make it look real. Right."

"Make it look real," he agreed.

Lacon cleared her fear from his head and reached for the door handle. He emerged from the car and scanned the street in both directions. No traffic. Only a parked car here and there. He walked around to the passenger side and opened the door, again surveying the area. As soon as she was out of the car, he ushered her to the front entrance of the building marked 1735.

"Stay behind me," he said before opening the door.

She nodded. He grasped the knob, gave it a twist and pushed the door inward. She stuck close behind him just like he'd instructed.

Lights were on, but the place looked deserted other

than a few stacks of shipping crates. As soon as the door closed behind them, four armed men materialized from behind the crates and fanned out in a circle around them. All four were dressed in black suits, black shirts and full-face masks, also black. One skirted around them until he was behind Lacon and started the expected pat-down. His weapon was removed from his side holster.

Taking a step forward, putting her side by side with him, Frasier said, "I'm Dr. Marissa Frasier. Your boss is expecting me."

The tallest of the four walked toward them until he stood toe-to-toe with Lacon. "You were instructed to come alone." He stabbed the muzzle of his .44 caliber automatic against Lacon's forehead. "Now I have to take care of this excess baggage."

"If you kill him," Frasier said, her voice strangely calm, "I won't do whatever it is your boss called me here to do."

As much as Lacon appreciated her support, he did not want her to be a hero.

The man in front of Lacon, who appeared to be in charge, turned his head toward her. "Then I'll have to kill you, too, and the boss will be most unhappy."

Frasier took a step toward the man. Lacon gritted his teeth. He had to hold himself back from grabbing her. Three weapons shifted their aims toward her head. She ignored them and stared directly at the man in front of Lacon. "Then you might as well do what you have to. This is my personal bodyguard, and wherever I go, he goes. Are we clear?"

Lacon held his breath, prayed she hadn't just signed her death warrant.

The thug in front of him pressed the fingers of his free hand to his ear, touching the earpiece he wore. The boss was listening, and he had made a decision.

Let it be the one we need.

"Let's go," the man in charge announced. He stepped aside and gestured for Lacon and Frasier to precede him.

Lacon was able to breathe again. He leaned toward her. "Do not do that again."

She ignored him the same way she had the other guy. Maybe the doctor was a lot tougher than she looked.

Thug number two walked beside Lacon, and the others walked behind them. The procession continued into a corridor behind the large space they had entered. Three doors down on the left another man, dressed all in black like his friends, opened a door and stepped aside for them to enter.

Frasier was ushered into the room first. Lacon stayed right behind her. In the center of the room, beneath the fluorescent light that flickered incessantly, a man lay on a white sheet that looked much like a drop cloth used for painting. His hands were tied in front of him and his feet were secured at the ankles. Blood soaked his shirt. The gag in his mouth prevented him from speaking, but he made frantic sounds as they approached.

Next to the man on the floor was an open box loaded with what looked like medical supplies. Lacon didn't need a map or a block of instruction to see where this was going. Along with the medical supplies, spread out on the floor were a number of torture devices. A battery and jumper cables for delivering shocks. Dental forceps for extracting teeth. And an array of other nasty tools for generating pain.

The thug in charge answered a call on his cell. He made a couple of agreeable sounds and then set the phone to speaker.

"Dr. Frasier, I need this man alive," the voice of their caller—the one they suspected was Vito Anastasia—announced. "Your survival depends completely on his. Do not let me down, or this is where the police will find your body."

Frasier charged forward and dropped onto her knees next to the man. She surveyed his injuries. Lacon moved closer to her, but the Top Thug pulled him back. Lacon stared him dead in the eyes. Hoped like hell he got the chance to kick his ass.

"I may need his assistance," Frasier said.

Top Thug pushed Lacon toward her. "He's all yours."

Lacon crouched next to Frasier. "What can I do?"

She poked around in the box, surveying the supplies. "First, I need to sedate him." She picked up a bottle and a syringe.

"No!" Top Thug snarled. "We need him conscious."

"I cannot remove the bullet while he is conscious," Frasier snapped. She gestured to another drug bottle. "We'll wake him up when I'm done."

Top Thug stepped back.

Damn, Lacon was impressed. The doc was holding her own with these dirtbags.

Frasier cleaned her hands and forearms with an antibacterial solution before donning a pair of gloves. Lacon removed his jacket and did the same. When she had everything she needed spread on a white towel that the instruments had been wrapped in, she moved closer to the injured man and began her work. She checked his vitals and then ripped open his shirt to get a closer look at the injury.

Tears ran from the guy's eyes. He'd wet himself. Frasier spoke quietly to him as she worked. "I'm going to give you morphine. You won't feel any of this."

While she attended to the man, Lacon committed his face and physical features to memory. Whoever he was, he'd pissed off Anastasia or had information he wanted. Lacon considered how they might be able to help him, but not a single idea came to mind that wouldn't get one or both of them killed.

When the man had lost consciousness, she removed the rag stuffed in his mouth. To Lacon she said, "I want you to keep an eye on his blood pressure."

He grabbed the blood pressure cuff she had removed from his left arm and moved to the other side so he wouldn't be in her way. He strapped the cuff into place and pressed the button to start the process. Luckily for him, this particular monitor did all the work.

"About the same, one-ten over seventy."

Frasier nodded and continued cleaning the area around the injury. Her moves were so precise and so rhythmic, Lacon found himself mesmerized by the steady, quick steps. She opened the entrance wound a little wider, had the bullet out in a few precise moves and began closing the wound in a matter of minutes. Lacon checked the guy's blood pressure periodically. Thankfully it stayed fairly consistent.

When she had dressed the wound and peeled off her gloves, the top thug said, "Wake him up."

Frasier pushed to her feet and turned to him. "First, I didn't see any additional bleeding, but I can't be certain there isn't damage I couldn't see. He needs an ultrasound and other tests to determine if there are additional internal injuries. This is not a sterile environment. He'll need an antibiotic, and I still can't say that he'll get through this without a serious infection."

Top Thug shook his head. "Doesn't matter. Just wake him up and then you can go."

Lacon removed the cuff and slowly stood, careful not to make any sudden moves. These guys wanted the man awake and patched up so they could continue torturing him for information. The last thing they wanted was for him to die without divulging his secrets. Damn.

"He should be in a hospital," Frasier argued.

"Wake him up," the thug ordered, the muzzle of his weapon nudging her in the chest.

When she didn't make a move to do so, his cohort stuck his weapon in Lacon's face. He didn't flinch, but his gut sure as hell clenched.

"Wake him up or your bodyguard dies," Top Thug warned.

Frasier trembled visibly. She glared at the piece of shit a moment longer before crouching next to the box of supplies and preparing a shot of Narcan. Seconds after she administered the injection, the man's eyes opened.

Top Thug yanked her to her feet. "Now go, or watch your friend die."

She started to argue, but Lacon took her by the arm

and ushered her out of the room. Two of the thugs followed them out of the building; one returned Traynor's weapon. She kept looking back, and he kept pushing her forward. They had to get out of here or they could end up dead, too.

Damn. Damn. Damn.

He ushered her into the car, fastened her seat belt and then closed her door. When he dropped behind the wheel, he started the car and drove away immediately, his pulse throbbing. Son of a bitch!

They were leaving that guy to die.

And if they warned the police, Anastasia would know.

There had to be something he could do to stop this travesty.

Then the answer hit him square between the eyes. He called 911.

Frasier stared at him, her eyes wide with fear. "What're you doing?"

When the dispatcher had finished his spiel, Lacon said, "Man, you gotta get the fire department to 1735 West Hubbard. Smoke is boiling outta that old warehouse. I think some homeless people are living in there. Hurry!" He ended the call.

He glanced at Frasier. Her green eyes filled with tears, and a barely perceptible smile tugged at her lips. "Thank you."

And then she broke down and cried.

Lacon reached across the console and took her hand in his.

Chapter Five

Marissa pulled on her pj's. The lavender bottoms and white tank top with its matching lavender phrase, Doctors Are People Too, were badly wrinkled from being stuffed carelessly into the bag. Didn't matter. She stared at her reflection, images of the gunshot victim she'd patched up—the man whose name she didn't know—flashing over and over in her head.

She hoped the fire department had arrived before the bastards in the masks could finish him off. No matter that she understood doing anything further to help him was impossible given the situation, she still ached at the idea that she and Traynor had walked out of that damned warehouse and left the wounded man there. She had taken an oath to heal…not to walk away and leave someone injured on the floor.

Despite thinking she was all cried out, more tears flowed down her cheeks as she thought of the call she'd had to make to William's parents. Though they had stopped speaking to her after the trial, she still felt their anguish. William's death was such an immense waste. He was still so young. Eventually he might very well have been able to pull his life back together. William had obviously been desperate; otherwise he would never have resorted to such unexpected criminal behavior.

But the decision had been his alone. Some part of her felt the weight of guilt, but it was not her fault. Intellectually, she understood that irrefutable fact. On an emotional level, it was a different story. She had loved him. They had lived as husband and wife for five years. She had wanted to see the good in him even when he'd stood outside the ER and told her he intended to kill her. She hadn't wanted to believe he'd meant it.

Had that been his warped way of warning her something bad was about to happen? Had he thought such a threat would prompt her to go to the police? She would likely never know.

Men like Vito Anastasia cared nothing for human life—only about what they could take. She wasn't naive. She watched the news, but she had never been forced to bear witness to that cold, harsh reality until today. The sick and injured came to her, inside the safety of the ER. She wasn't out there witnessing the atrocities that occurred far too often on the streets of most cities. She'd certainly never walked away knowing somebody she'd provided care for would surely be murdered in the hours to follow.

Was what she'd done any different from treating a gunshot victim in the ER who ended up right back on the street hours or days later to dive into the same life of crime that had put a bullet in him in the first place?

Where did her obligation end and that of the police begin? Or the patient, for that matter?

Her arms went around her body and attempted to stop the trembling. Had Traynor not hauled her out of that warehouse and she'd stayed, what could she have done to stop four armed thugs? Nothing.

There was no going back. At this point, she just needed to know the fire department had arrived in time.

Her damp curls tucked into a hair clip, she emerged from her room and went in search of Traynor. Some errant brain cell reminded her that she needed to eat. It had been many hours since she'd forced herself to swallow a few bites of the omelet. But her stomach didn't feel capable of accepting food. Her throat felt so dry and constricted, she wasn't sure she could swallow even a tiny bite.

You need the energy to keep going. That much was true.

Downstairs she found Traynor making sandwiches. "I was just about to come find you." He set a plate on the counter in front of her. "Ham and cheese. I didn't know if you wanted mayo or mustard."

Her stomach rumbled and knotted at the same time. She pushed into place what she hoped passed for a smile. "Thank you."

"Whatever you want to drink, you'll probably find in the fridge." He placed the second piece of bread atop his own sandwich. "They keep this place stocked like a five-star resort. Make yourself at home."

She put a hand to her mouth, then allowed it to slide down her throat. "I'm not sure I can eat."

He lifted his sandwich. "Try it. You'll probably be

surprised how hungry you are after you get down the first couple of bites."

Maybe he was right. Before she dared try, she wandered to the fridge and grabbed a bottle of cold water. She downed a long swallow, her throat immediately feeling better. He picked up her plate as well as his own and moved to the table. She followed, too tired and too overwhelmed to do much else.

Hoping she could actually swallow something more than water, she took a bite of the sandwich.

"This is hard for you," he said. "You're accustomed to a clinical environment where the variables, though at times outside your control, are a different kind of battle. Everyone in the room is generally attempting to help the patient, not cause harm. It doesn't work that way in the environment set up by a guy like Anastasia."

She closed her eyes for a moment and tried her best not to sound as angry and bitter as she felt. "I watch the news, Mr. Traynor. I'm well aware how the world works."

"But you don't usually find yourself caught in the middle of the lead story. This is a whole different world. The people who end up in front of you want help, and there's rarely anyone trying to prevent you from providing the necessary help."

"True," she said wearily, "unless you count insurance companies."

He laughed and she couldn't help smiling, even if it hurt her face to do so.

"Have you heard if the man in the warehouse made it?" She held her breath as she waited for his answer.

Whatever the man was guilty of, she wanted him to be alive. Deep down, she understood that she was likely kidding herself. Men like Anastasia wouldn't leave those sorts of loose ends.

Why in the world would William have risked working for a man like Anastasia?

Guilt heaped onto her shoulders. Because she pressed charges against him for what he did to her. Because he went to prison and lost his license to practice medicine. Because he was desperate, and she could no longer deal with the mood swings and the drama…she had only wanted out of the marriage.

What kind of person did that make her?

The single bite of bread, ham and cheese she had swallowed sat like a rock in her stomach.

"Unfortunately he was dead when the firemen arrived on the scene."

The words pummeled her like stones. She really had left the poor man to die.

"You did not put him in the situation he found himself in, Doc. The man you pulled that bullet out of was Brent Underwood. According to what Bella could find on him, he was one of Anastasia's long-time accountants. Rumor on the street is that he was skimming the books. That doesn't make what happened to him right, but it damned sure tells you he chose his own path."

She forced down another bite. Told herself he was right. This was not her fault any more than William's death was. "So what do we do now?"

"We wait and we rest while we can."

"What if he calls again?" This time when the bite

lodged in her throat, she forced it down with a long swig of water.

"We'll deal with that issue when the time comes."

She stared at her plate. Pushed it away. "You make it sound so easy."

"This ain't my first rodeo, Doc." He stacked her plate on top of his. "Most of the cases I investigate involve people who do very bad things. The best I can hope for is to protect the innocent and to help make sure the bad guys don't get away with it."

She couldn't think about this anymore. It was time for a change of subject. "Do you get back to see your family often?"

He glanced at her as he cleaned up the remains of their dinner. If he was surprised by the abrupt change of topics, he showed no indication. "Every Christmas and every Father's Day."

Father's Day was barely two weeks ago, so he must have just seen him. "So you said your father's still involved with running the ranch despite being retired?" she asked.

He nodded, tucked the plates into the dishwasher. "More than my older brother would prefer, I think."

"What about your mother?" She leaned against the counter, forced her mind away from that warehouse and the man who had died there.

Her bodyguard dried his hands and tossed the towel aside. "She was injured in a horseback riding accident when I was twelve. She died a few hours later. She was a damned good rider, but, as I've gotten older, I've realized that even the best swimmer can drown. Just one of those freak accidents you hope will never happen. But it happened to her."

"That must have been very difficult." She couldn't imagine being twelve and losing her mother. It was bad enough at thirty.

"What about you?"

She looked up at him. "My brother and I grew up in southern Illinois. My mother was a substitute teacher. Dad managed a supermarket. It was a small town so everyone knew everyone else. My parents were determined that both their children would be doctors. I suppose like most, they wanted better for us than they had."

"Your brother's a doctor, too."

"He is. Steven's three years younger than me and still finding himself." She laughed, picturing her brother, the free spirit who felt completely comfortable grabbing his passport and taking off at the drop of a hat. "He spends all his free time traveling, but his travels usually involve volunteering in support of those in areas where there isn't adequate medical care available."

"You lost both your parents." He walked to the coffee maker and started a fresh pot.

"A few years ago. Mother died of cancer, and Dad had a heart attack a couple of years later. It was a tough time." She'd longed for the comfort of simply talking with them when her marriage disintegrated. She hadn't shared the dirty details with her brother until after William was in prison. Her little brother might be younger than her, but he was very protective. She only wished she could see him more often. The once-a-year thing was not nearly enough.

"Sit," he suggested. "I'll serve the coffee. Cream, no sugar, right?"

"Right." She weaved her way around the island and climbed onto one of the stools. "Is this what you do most of the time? I mean, are your cases typically like this one?"

"Sometimes providing protection is involved, sometimes not. Depends on the situation."

The bold smell of fresh-brewed dark roast coffee filled the air.

"Are your clients usually female?" She clasped her hands atop the granite counter and studied her bodyguard. She wondered how many of his clients wanted more than just his protection.

What in the world? She shook herself. Her brain was obviously muddled.

"Two out of three, maybe." He poured the coffee, added cream to hers and then walked toward her with a mug in each hand. "Victoria assigns the best man or woman for the case. Gender has little to do with her decisions."

"Thank you." Marissa wrapped her hands around the warm mug. "I imagine you have plenty of damsels in distress hoping for more than your protection."

The silence that followed exploded in her ears. Had she really asked that question out loud? To think it was bad enough. Oh…dear… God. She really, really needed to go into that room upstairs and close herself inside. What he must think of her!

He finally laughed, a sort of choked sound. "I have to say I haven't encountered that situation yet."

What did the mere thought say about her? The answer echoed in more of that embarrassing silence.

"I think maybe television and the movies glamorize the kind of work I do a little too much. I can see how you might think these situations could easily drift off into a romantic interlude."

Now she was really embarrassed. She tried to laugh, but it came out more like a squeak. "I guess I read too many romance novels growing up. My mother was a big romantic. She had a library of hundreds of books. They all had a couple themes in common—boy rescues girl, girl falls in love with boy."

This time his chuckle was the real thing, the sound pleasant. She liked it. "My mom had one of those, too," he offered. "She and my sister always had a book on their bedside tables."

"How old is your sister?"

"A couple of years older than me. She's a veterinarian. Takes care of the horses and the cattle. You two would get along well. The only difference is her patients generally have four legs."

Marissa was the one laughing this time. It felt good, made her relax marginally.

Traynor told her which of his siblings were married and who wasn't, who had children and who wanted more. He loved his nieces and nephews. Loved his family. The pride in his eyes and in his voice made her smile. She liked listening to his voice. His laughter made her feel normal again. How long had it been since she'd had a conversation like this with anyone besides her colleagues at work? She couldn't even remember.

"I have to say, Mr. Traynor, listening to you talk about your family, you almost sound homesick."

He held her gaze for a long moment. "Sometimes. But my work here makes me happy. I don't see myself going back." He reached for his coffee. "By the way, you have to stop calling me that. Mr. Traynor is my father. Call me Lacon."

"All right, Lacon. Then you should call me Marissa or Issy. That's what my friends call me." She made a face. "Except Eva. She insists on calling me Dr. Frasier whenever we're wearing scrubs and at work. Any other time she calls me Issy, too."

"Issy it is, then."

Her cell vibrated against the granite and she jumped. Blocked Call. Her blood ran cold. "It's him."

"Stay calm," Lacon warned. "Don't let him hear your fear. When you answer, put it on speaker."

She accepted the call and tapped the speaker icon. "Marissa Frasier."

"I wanted to thank you, Doctor."

It was him.

"No need to thank me. I didn't do it for you," she replied, barely keeping a snarl out of her tone. "I did it for the man who'd been shot."

"Be that as it may, I appreciate your work. I was able to extract the information I needed, and I couldn't have done it without your help."

And then his thugs had killed him.

"You son of a bitch!"

Lacon held up his hands and gave her the signal to bring it down.

She tried, she really did, but she was so angry. "I hope you die screaming."

Laughter echoed from the damned phone. It took every ounce of control Marissa possessed not to fling it across the room.

"I would have been disappointed if you hadn't been angry, Dr. Frasier. In fact, I have to give you credit. Having your friend call in the fire department was ingenious. I'm genuinely grateful my men were able to get what I needed before the men in the turnout gear arrived. You see, if my people had failed and been forced to abandon this traitor, I would have been most unhappy. No one likes it when I'm unhappy, Marissa. May I call you Marissa?"

Lacon silently cautioned her again.

"If this arrangement is going to be so informal, then I'll need to know your name, as well."

A soft laugh whispered in the air. "Vito. You can call me Vito, which is far better than 'son of a bitch.'"

She would not apologize.

Lacon made a hand signal for money. At first she was confused, then she understood.

"If you think I'm going to continue this arrangement out of the goodness of my heart, you're mistaken, Vito. I expect far more than whatever you were paying William."

Another laugh, this one not so soft. "You have one more test before we talk about money. There is one matter, however, we should discuss. Your bodyguard. He cramps my style. Get rid of him."

Fear bloomed in her chest. Lacon shook his head.

She swallowed back the fear. "Except," she countered, sounding almost casual, "now I have you threatening my safety, so no deal."

The silence dragged on long enough to make her sweat.

"I like you, Dr. Marissa Frasier, so I will grant you this one demand. But make no mistake, if you or your bodyguard screw with me, you will both die—screaming, as you say."

The call ended.

Marissa grabbed the countertop to brace herself.

Lacon gave her arm a squeeze. "Really good job, Issy."

She turned to him. "I don't know if I can do what he wants…" She shook her head. "God only knows what the next scene he sends me to will look like." Her body shook with the fear she wanted to keep at bay.

Lacon pulled her to him, gave her a big hug. "You're strong, Issy. You can do this. If you help the police take him down, think how many lives you'll be saving."

She pressed her face against his chest and closed her eyes. "I keep telling myself that's the upside of this situation."

"But any time you want out, say the word and I'll make it happen." He drew her away from him to look into her eyes. "My job is to keep you safe. That's all that matters to me."

She hugged him this time.

Maybe, just maybe, with the help of this man, she could get through this.

Vito Anastasia was going down, by God.

Chapter Six

Saturday, June 30, 7:45 a.m.

Marissa slowed the speed of the treadmill for her final mile. Her heart pounded and sweat clung to her skin. It felt good. She'd missed the stress release that went with a long, hard workout. The entire week had been so busy, she'd fallen behind on her usual workout routine.

The first thing that entered her mind when she woke this morning was the jarring and painful memory that William was dead. In a few days, his family would be claiming his body, there would be a funeral and then he would be laid to rest.

Would she be able to attend his funeral? Should she? They had been in love once. Five years as husband and wife was significant. In truth, she had worked hard to evict any good memories along with the bad ones over the past two years. After what he'd done to her toward the end, who could blame her?

Slowing to a fast walk, she pushed the questions aside. The second thought to pop into her head before she threw back the sheets and climbed out of bed was about Vito Anastasia. He had to be stopped. But the police were right; that wouldn't happen until they had a significant body of evidence to make it happen. They needed a way in, a way to get close to him. All she had to do was play along until *she* could make that happen. For whatever reason, fate had dropped that terrifying potential into her lap.

How could she ignore the possibility of taking one more ruthless murderer off the streets?

The treadmill stopped and she swabbed her face with the towel hanging around her neck. The thought of dealing with another injured person Anastasia might murder made her shudder. But he would never stop unless someone stopped him.

She could be that someone. All she needed was the right kind of backup.

Traynor—Lacon—was her protector. He'd made it clear that his top priority was to protect her. She was very grateful to have the Colby Agency backing her up. But would he be willing to cross certain lines and boundaries for her? She wasn't a cop. She wasn't tied to the same rules. There were things she could say and steps she could take where Anastasia was concerned that the police could not.

She had heard the interest in Anastasia's voice. For some reason, he was intrigued by her. Or maybe that part had been her imagination, though she didn't think so. He'd also acquiesced to her demand to keep Lacon around. Perhaps she was reading too much into the conversation, but she had nothing to lose by exploring the potential.

Except the same thing William had lost—her life.

You have to be smarter, Issy. William was desperate. Desperation breeds mistakes. If she could keep her wits about her, she could do this. For William and all the other victims Anastasia had taken and would take in the future.

She could help stop him. *Maybe.*

After she'd showered and dressed in a pair of the jeans and a T-shirt she'd packed, she went in search of Lacon. She found him in the kitchen pouring orange juice. Bacon, eggs and toast waited on the stove.

"Good morning." He set the bottle of juice aside. "You feel like breakfast?"

Today she was starving. "I do. Thanks."

He passed her a plate and they met in front of the stove. He wore jeans and a button-down cotton shirt— this one in white—much like yesterday. And, of course, the cowboy boots. Another of those casual suit jackets hung on the back of one of the stools facing the large island. Today's jacket was navy. Somehow the outfit was perfect for the man. She couldn't imagine him in a dress suit.

"I wasn't sure how you liked your eggs, so I figured scrambled was the way to go."

"This is exactly how I like my eggs."

His smile was contagious. "Good."

Marissa settled onto a stool and dug in. The eggs were soft, the bacon crispy and the toast lightly buttered. Certainly not her usual fare of yogurt and granola, but so scrumptious. Maybe it all tasted so good because she'd hardly eaten in the past forty-eight hours.

The ER had been so busy Thursday night, she'd barely had time to grab a bag of veggie chips.

Or maybe it was just because she was alive and not dead.

When she'd slowed down, she asked, "Any news on the drug tests?"

"Ian Michaels called first thing this morning. You tested positive for Rohypnol. We haven't heard from PD's lab yet, but I'm sure they'll find it in the bottle of wine you drank from that night, and something similar in Bauer's tox screen, as well."

"Wow." She placed her fork next to her plate as the news traveled through her.

The confirmation that one of Anastasia's men came into her home and laced her bottle of wine with a date rape drug made her furious. As a teenager and a college student, she had been extra careful about having so much as a soda in public places where her drink might be left unattended even for a second. The fact that this drink—this drug—had been administered in her own home, in a bottle of her wine, made her feel ill.

The queasy feeling abruptly morphed into outrage. "I will not allow him to get away with this. If there is any way I can help stop him, I'm up for it."

"We're doing all we can toward that end, as well," Lacon promised.

She wanted to tell him, to blurt out the decision she'd made this morning, but that wouldn't be the smart move. He would see the emotion behind the announcement. When the time was right, her words had to be calm and logical.

"I know you are." She picked up her plate and fork. "Thanks for the breakfast. I didn't know chef was a part of your repertoire of skills."

He chuckled as he followed her to the sink. "Chef, personal shopper, chauffeur—it all goes with the territory."

Putting her cleaned plate into the dishwasher, she asked, "Do you ever make operational decisions without consulting the boss?"

"There are times when—" he placed his plate behind hers "—split-second decisions have to be made. At the Colby Agency, we receive extensive training and daily briefings. Victoria trusts her investigators to make the right decisions."

Marissa doubted very seriously if the operational decision she wanted him to make fell within the agency's approved guidelines. "Victoria is right to trust you." She peered up at her bodyguard and again acknowledged the warmth in his eyes. "You were spot-on with every move last night. If I had any doubts about any aspect of moving forward, they disappeared when you made that call to summon the fire department to help that man."

"Unfortunately it didn't help."

"True." She nodded. "But you tried, and that effort helped me tremendously."

He held her gaze, searching her eyes. Was he looking for the motive behind her words? Did he sense that she was up to something? He was, after all, a top-notch investigator trained to spot potential issues.

Her cell vibrated and she jumped. She snatched it

from her hip pocket, her pulse racing as she considered the possibility that it could be Anastasia again.

Please don't let it be him.

The number was the staff line at the Edge.

"Marissa Frasier."

Lacon watched her expectantly. She mouthed the word *work*. He nodded.

"Dr. Frasier, this is Patsy. I realize this is your weekend off, but Jeremiah Owens's mother is here and she says it's imperative that she speak with you in person." The rustle of sounds on the other end indicated Patsy had moved to a different location. "She seems pretty upset. What would you like me to do?"

Fear thumped in Marissa's veins. "Tell her it'll take me about forty-five minutes to get there, but I'll leave right now and head that way."

"I'll tell her. Thanks, Dr. Frasier."

Marissa slid her phone back into her pocket. "It's the Owens boy's mother. She wants to speak with me in person."

Lacon reached for the keys on the counter. "We should see what she has to say."

If Anastasia had harmed that child in any way…

Well, Marissa would make him pay. Somehow.

The Edge, 10:00 a.m.

MARISSA HAD WORKED herself up by the time they reached the Edge. She fluctuated between utter outrage and sheer terror. She should have called Jeremiah's mother to check on him. She could have done so without giving away why she was calling. If something had happened to the boy, it would be her fault.

She hurried to the desk and waited for Patsy to finish registering a new arrival. As soon as the elderly man had shuffled away, the registration specialist said, "I put her in the small conference room."

Marissa thanked Patsy and headed for the double doors that separated the large lobby that served as a waiting room and the emergency department. Lacon was right behind her. She waved to Nurse Kim Levy and hurried past the nurses' station to the small conference room.

Mrs. Owens sat alone, her hands wringing together atop the small round conference table. Her worried face lit up as Marissa walked in. "I'm so sorry to bother you on your day off."

Marissa slid into a chair next to her. She patted the woman's clasped hands. "No problem. Is Jeremiah okay?"

She nodded. "He's doing fine. But I wanted to ask you about those men."

The bottom dropped out of Marissa's stomach. "What men?"

"Two men have been watching my house. They were there all day yesterday, and they're back today. I finally worked up my nerve this morning and walked out to the car. I asked the driver if there was a problem, and he said no. He said they were just keeping an eye on things and that they're friends of yours. I'm not trying to be mean, but they make me very nervous."

Fury roared through Marissa's blood. "I will take

care of this, Mrs. Owens. There's been a miscommunication. Those men aren't supposed to be there. You go home and don't worry about this anymore."

She nodded, relief washing over her face. "I figured there was a mix-up of some sort." Her face pinched with worry once more. "I hope whoever those men are supposed to be looking after is okay."

"They're fine. Just fine."

Marissa, with Lacon right next to her, walked her back to the lobby. "Thank you for coming by. I really am sorry for the confusion."

When Owens was halfway across the lobby, Marissa yanked her phone from her pocket once more. She sent a text to the contact who had sent her Anastasia's instructions last night. The message was brief and straight to the point.

Tell Anastasia to call me. Now.

Surprise sent Lacon's eyebrows shooting up. "That should get his attention."

Marissa stormed back to the conference room to wait on a response. She did not want to be closed up in a car if she was able to speak with him. Lacon closed the door behind her and took a seat. She couldn't sit. She paced the small room, anger building with every step she took.

"You might want to take a breath," he suggested.

She stalled and flashed him a fake smile. "I am breathing."

He held up his hands. "Okay."

As angry as she was, she stalled and did as he said. She inhaled long and deep, let it out slowly. A couple more times, and her heart rate had calmed somewhat. Her phone vibrated and she snatched it from her pocket.

Blocked Call.

"I think it's him." She accepted the call. "Marissa Frasier."

"Dr. Frasier." He sighed. "You are determined to test my patience."

"Call your dogs off the Owens home. I did what you asked—now I want you to leave them alone."

Lacon sat back in his chair, his arms crossed over his chest. She couldn't decide if that amused smile he wore was about pity or pride.

Silence, thick and suffocating, reverberated across the line.

"Your friend the bodyguard should explain the hierarchy in this relationship, Dr. Frasier." Anastasia's voice was cold, hard. "He's employed by the Colby Agency. I'm certain he's well aware of how things work."

"If you don't live up to your side of the bargain," Marissa warned as if he hadn't said a word, "then there is no relationship. Leave the Owens family alone."

More of that tense silence filled the air. Her heart thumped harder and harder with each second that elapsed.

"Done."

The call ended. Marissa stared at the screen. Could it really have been so easy?

Lacon stood. "You okay?"

She shrugged. "I honestly don't know."

He chuckled. "I have to tell you, Issy, I'm torn between being damned impressed and freaking terrified."

A laugh burst from her, but before she could say she felt basically the same way, the door opened and Kim poked her head into the room. "A balcony collapsed while a bridal party was taking photos on it. We've got fourteen injured five minutes out. Dr. Reagan wondered if you might be able to help out for a couple of hours."

"Glad to." She glanced at Lacon.

"Don't worry about me. Do what you've got to do. I have calls to make."

Marissa wasn't exactly dressed for work, but that hardly mattered. She washed up, donned a white coat and was ready by the time the lead ambulance rolled in.

The first gurney to come through the doors was the bride. Marissa moved toward trauma room one with the paramedics.

"Caroline Boehner, twenty-seven, BP one fifty over ninety, pulse a hundred ten. Complaining of pain in the right leg."

"Thank you." Marissa put a hand on the young woman's arm. "Don't worry, Caroline, we're going to get you taken care of. You'll be ready for that walk down the aisle in no time."

The younger woman's mascara had made black streaks down her cheeks. The updo her blond hair had been arranged into had come undone. Beyond the tangled mass of hair, her veil appeared to be intact. The beaded bodice of her gown had managed to avoid damage, but the lower portion of the mermaid-style lace-

and-tulle train had not fared so well. Whatever shoes she'd been wearing were long gone.

"Are my parents okay?" A sob tore from her throat. "I'm so worried about them. We were doing the photos—you know, the ones you do before the wedding." More tears flowed down her face. "My whole family was on that balcony."

Marissa gave her arm a squeeze and turned to the paramedic. "We'll get you an update on everyone as soon as we can. For now, let's get you taken care of."

After a quick examination, Marissa sent the bride off to Imaging. The six bridesmaids and the flower girl were all treated and released with nothing more than scrapes and bruises. The bride's two brothers and one sister, who was the maid of honor, were shaken and bruised but had no serious injuries. The mother suffered a fracture of the left scapular body.

By far the worst injury was the father's, a hip fracture that would require surgery. The sixty-year-old man was in excellent physical condition, so there was every reason to be optimistic about a speedy recovery. The bride suffered a stable fracture in the tibial shaft. Surprisingly, there wasn't one concussion among the whole lot.

They were a very lucky group.

The groom and the rest of the wedding party arrived and filled the lobby. Anyone else coming in would think a wedding was imminent right there in front of the registration desk. Thankfully, the news Marissa had to pass along was all reasonably good, considering the fall the bride's party had taken.

When the last patient was out the door and the ER

was quiet again, Kim watched as Marissa peeled off her gloves and left the white coat in the laundry hamper.

Marissa shot her a look. "What?"

"So, tall, blond and handsome is your bodyguard?"

Marissa laughed. She couldn't help herself. "He is."

"Wow. I mean, I know you're still reeling from what happened to Dr. Bauer, but the two of you were divorced for a really long time before…he died. And you've hardly dated since. Seriously, you should enjoy some of that."

"Some of that?" Marissa dried her hands, thankful they were in the locker room. "What on earth are you suggesting?"

Kim pushed away from the door frame. "I'm suggesting, Doctor, that you relax and let go. You're always so busy giving that you never take anything for yourself. Take something!" She threw her hands in the air for emphasis. "Something gorgeous and hot and better than six feet tall."

Rather than scold her friend as she normally would have, Marissa nodded slowly. "I'll take it under advisement."

Kim rolled her eyes. "You are so predictable."

Ah, if she only knew. "The one thing I am not these days, Kim, is predictable."

"Where your love life is concerned you are." Kim sent her a look daring her to counter that statement.

Love life. Marissa didn't have a love life. The most recent three men in her life were her deceased ex-husband, a mob boss and a bodyguard. Even if she were in the market, it was hard to make anything romantic out of the combination.

"I saw him watching you," Kim argued. "He thinks you're hot."

Marissa laughed out loud. "Okay, I think that's my cue to get out of here."

"Just sayin'."

"As you said from the outset, this is not exactly the right time for romance," Marissa pointed out.

Kim gave her a skeptical look. "Who said anything about romance? I'm talking about sex. Hot, down-and-dirty, mind-blowing sex."

Before Marissa could summon a proper response, her friend hustled off to check on her patients. Marissa sighed and went in search of Lacon. He was waiting for her at the nurses' station. Every female on duty smiled at him and called goodbye.

The man was undeniably handsome, cowboy boots and all.

Marissa shook her head at the foolish notion. She had a mob boss to take down. This was no time for sex, not even the hot, down-and-dirty, mind-blowing kind.

Colby Safe House, 9:30 p.m.

MARISSA STARED AT the glass of wine in her hand. If she had been impressed with Lacon Traynor's breakfast-making skills, she was truly fascinated by his prowess at the grill. Steaks and potatoes and a nice, leafy green salad. When she'd asked him how he'd acquired such a command of the culinary arts, he'd simply replied that being single and closer to forty than thirty, it was either learn to cook or starve.

When he'd first offered the wine, she'd passed, but the more he'd made her laugh during dinner, the more she'd relaxed, and a couple of glasses of wine began to sound far more appealing. He'd stopped at one, and she'd felt a little guilty when she moved on to number two. But not that guilty. She sipped her wine. Rich, red and bold flavored. She needed the relief—that was a certainty.

"According to Anastasia," she said, abruptly recalling the conversation, "you should be able to tell me all about him and how the hierarchy of my new relationship with him works."

Her bodyguard considered the statement from his relaxed position on the sofa. She'd curled up in one of the massive upholstered chairs for the best view of the water. Rather than answer her right away, he pulled off his right boot, then he moved on to the left. He set them side by side on the floor.

Marissa frowned. "Do you always wear boots?"

"Most of the time." He leaned back and propped his sock-clad feet on the large leather ottoman. "I have running shoes for working out. And the boots." His shoulders went up and then down in an easy shrug. "That's about it."

To avoid staring at his long lean body like a smitten schoolgirl, she said, "Tell me what makes Anastasia so special." She wanted to make the bastard feel the pain he inflicted upon his victims. Despite the wine, anger simmered inside her.

"He's young to be sitting at the top. Forty-two. He's doing all in his power to resurrect the 'family,' as he calls it. He's smarter than the average criminal. Ruthless. Single. No children. So he has basically nothing to lose. It's hard to best a man who doesn't have an Achilles' heel."

"Except he wants to win," Marissa decided. "Power is his weakness."

"You're saying that he's so fixated on getting what he wants that he might not see what's right in front of him?"

"Exactly. Psych 101." She downed the last of the wine and set her glass aside. "Is he unmarried and childless because he's so focused that he ignores his own needs? If so, that makes him a ticking time bomb. Eventually, that kind of focus comes back to haunt you. You can't ignore what the mind and body require forever."

Lacon assessed her for an endless moment. "Sounds like words spoken from experience."

She assessed him right back. "Experience we have in common."

A grin hitched up one side of his mouth. "Touché."

They lapsed into silence for long enough to make her feel restless. She pushed out of her chair and went to the wall of windows. The sun had set, leaving the moon to reflect its golden glow on the water. Way out here, away from the city, the world felt so peaceful, so quiet. So innocent.

"Why did you become a doctor?" He moved up beside her, his gaze settling on the dark water.

"Because I wanted to help people." She crossed her arms and leaned against the window frame. "And it was all my mom and dad ever talked about."

"Have you ever regretted your decision to go into medicine?"

"Never." A smile tugged at her lips. "I spend a lot of time working with kids. I donate every other weekend to the Chicago Children's Center. I love seeing them smile when they're happy. It makes my heart glad to see the relief on their parents' faces when I tell them everything will be fine."

"What about when you can't tell them everything will be fine?"

He was watching her closely now, as if the answer was somehow incredibly important to him.

"It's the most painful thing I've ever felt. In that moment, I would give anything to have a different answer."

"Is that why you didn't have children of your own?"

She met his analyzing gaze. "No. William didn't want children right away. Then it was always later, later. When everything fell apart, it no longer mattered. I guess I assumed I'd one day meet someone new and things would be different, but that window is closing all too quickly."

"You deserve things to be different," he said softly. "And that window is far from closed."

"What about you?" She lifted her chin and made the same deduction about him. "Don't you deserve for things to be different in your personal life? A wife, kids, maybe?"

"What makes you think I want anything different from what I have right now?"

Maybe he didn't. Maybe she had misjudged him. "I

don't know. You just seem a little lonely when it's quiet like this and no one needs rescuing."

He reached out, tugged at a wisp of her curly hair. "How could I be lonely with you standing right there?"

His fingertips traced her cheek, trailed down her throat, moved around her neck and pulled her close. Her breath caught, but she didn't resist. Deep down she'd wanted to know what he tasted like from the moment they met.

His lips closed over hers, and the taste of wine and man had her melting against him.

He drew away all too soon. "As much as I would like to, it's probably best that we don't cross that line tonight, Issy."

She curled her fingers in his shirtfront and held him close when he would have moved away. "We're both adults. We can do whatever we like." Her voice was thick with the desire sizzling in her veins.

"You think about that, and if you don't change your mind, we'll revisit the subject tomorrow or the next day."

She released him and he walked away. She watched him go before turning her attention back to the moon and those glittering stars that she never saw in the city.

The truth was, she'd already made up her mind. Going after Vito Anastasia was incredibly dangerous. She could end up dead just like William.

Maybe it was the wine, but at the moment, she could not imagine dying without knowing Lacon Traynor intimately first.

Chapter Seven

Sunday, July 1, 5:30 a.m.

Marissa lay in the darkness. She didn't want to get up. What she wanted was to lie right here and keep replaying that brief but incredibly sexy kiss over and over. Almost two years, that was how long it had been since she'd been kissed—really kissed—even just briefly. Sure, she'd had the peck on the cheek from friends after an evening out or in thanks for the perfect birthday present. But a real kiss, cloaked in desire that burned all the way through her, had not landed on her lips or anywhere else on her body in so very long.

Of all the times for her libido to suddenly turn itself back on. She closed her eyes and replayed one more time the tender way his lips—lips that had looked so firm and yet felt so soft—had molded to hers. The sweet, hot taste of his mouth and, mercy, the feel of his fingers tracing her skin. She shivered, feeling warm and needy.

In medical school and then in her residency, she'd done psych rotations and she'd completed the necessary coursework, but it didn't take a psychiatrist to comprehend the problem here. The murder of her ex-husband and the fear and chaos of being drawn into the dangerous world he'd crashed into since his release from jail had her survival instinct in overdrive.

Her reaction was completely natural. Faced with the possibility of death, the instinctive response was a relentless urge to procreate—to celebrate the mating of the human body. No great mystery. The problem was her instincts didn't quite understand that she was like a starving person suddenly faced with a mouthwatering buffet. She wanted desperately to assuage the emptiness and insecurity smothering her with what he had to offer well beyond his ability to keep her safe.

Not a smart move, Issy.

She climbed out of bed and dragged on a pair of jeans and another T-shirt. The outfit was the last of the casual wear she'd brought with her. She'd have to try out the laundry room at some point today or get permission to stop by her house for fresh clothes. Considering her name and face had already shown up in the news related to William's murder, she had no desire to go shopping. Stuffing her feet into her sneakers without bothering to untie them, she reached for her phone, tucked it into her back pocket and then thumbed the backs of the shoes over her heels.

Lacon was probably already downstairs prowling around in the kitchen. If not, she didn't mind taking her turn to prepare breakfast. She was far from a great cook, but she made a mean egg sandwich. She'd hit the bottom step of the grand staircase when she smelled the pancakes. Her stomach rumbled. She could get used to this.

Lacon stood at the stove, a dishtowel slung over his shoulder. She paused at the door and watched as he flipped pancakes onto a plate. Like her, he wore jeans again today, paired with a khaki-colored shirt this time and the boots, of course. The usual jacket, this one black, hung on a chair at the table.

She enjoyed watching the sure movements of his hands—broad, long-fingered hands. She'd felt his arms, his chest. There was plenty of hard muscle beneath all that soft cotton. Long muscular legs and a great back-side that filled out the jeans he wore. Kim, damn her, had sparked her imagination, and now it was running away with her. She sighed.

The object of her naughty musings glanced over his shoulder as if he'd sensed her presence or heard that sigh of defeat. "Morning."

"Morning." She pushed away from the door and went to the fridge. "Orange juice?"

"Yes, ma'am. Nothing goes with pancakes like orange juice."

"Except—" she reached for two glasses "—sausage and syrup."

"That part goes without saying. Pancakes aren't pancakes without syrup and sausage. It's a rule."

She laughed as she poured the juice. A tiny part of her wanted to feel ashamed that she could laugh and feel desire so soon after William's death, but that wasn't fair. Their relationship had been over for two years. Though she certainly still had feelings for him, those feelings were more about basic human compassion, the loss of an old friend...of the man who had once been the center of her universe. In reality, she had grieved the loss of their love and the intimate part of their relationship years ago. She refused to continue blaming herself for William's problems or for what she might have done differently.

It was well past time she moved on. As soon as she helped put Vito Anastasia where he belonged.

One some level she recognized that she should be afraid, terrified even. But the man flipping those pancakes made her stronger, braver, not to mention desperate for another of his kisses.

"Anything new this morning?"

It was likely too early, but it never hurt to ask. One of his colleagues from the Colby Agency may have called him already or sent him an update by email or text. She doubted their investigations operated on a nine-to-five schedule.

"Nothing new yet." He carried the two plates loaded with pancakes and sausage links to the table. "Grab the syrup."

She set the glasses on the table and returned to the counter for the syrup. Old-fashioned maple, her favorite. "Will the police keep me updated on their investigation into William's murder?" She had no idea how this worked. She'd never personally known anyone who was murdered.

"The two detectives will contact you as necessary. They don't like to give up too much information during the course of an investigation, so don't expect a lot of interaction—unless they need information they believe you have."

Since she'd told them everything she knew, she didn't expect to hear from them anytime soon unless it was to do the formal statement. They ate for a while without saying more. There really wasn't a lot more to say. It felt as if they were in a time warp, and everything relevant to the out-of-control situation had suddenly stopped.

Her cell vibrated. She stilled. Lowered her fork to her plate and reached into her hip pocket. *Please don't let it be him.*

Blocked Call.

Dread swelled in her belly, pushing away her appetite and making her heart thump harder. "It's him."

Lacon gave her a nod. "Answer it."

God, she did not want to. What if he demanded that she go to another scene like the one she'd gone to yesterday?

She accepted the call and immediately set the phone to speaker. "Marissa Frasier."

"I need you, Dr. Frasier."

His voice, cold, calculating, twisted her insides. Without giving her time to question his demand, he stated the address and severed the connection.

She stared at the phone for a moment, her stomach churning, threatening to rebel against the few bites of breakfast she'd taken.

"We'll need forty minutes to get there," Lacon said.

Nodding slowly, she tucked her phone away. "Do we tell anyone?"

He stood. "Never make a move in an op like this

without keeping your backup informed. That mistake is the fastest way I know to get yourself dead."

Nothing like another dash of reality to undermine her bravado.

FIVE MINUTES LATER they were en route. Lacon gave Ian Michaels a heads-up. Michaels would coordinate with their contact at Chicago PD. Issy spent the better portion of the drive lost in thought, or maybe she was mentally preparing herself for what she might have to do.

Don't let it be like last time. He didn't want her to have to go through that again.

Lacon liked this plan less and less. He didn't see an end to Anastasia's use of her as a pawn. The bastard was far too careful to get himself caught in a trap so easily foreseeable. Bottom line, something had to give soon. Every event like the one they were about to walk into endangered her life.

While every night they spent together tested his ability to maintain control.

That kiss. That damned foolish idea that he could scare her off by making a move. Damn it. All he'd accomplished was to fan the flames already blazing inside him. He wanted to know her...every inch of her.

Backing away from that perilous cliff, he focused on the here and now. Their destination was a small older convenience store located at the corner of Hirsch and Kildare. He parked near the front entrance. There were no other cars near the store. They were probably parked in the back.

From the outside, the store looked closed. He emerged

from the car, scanned the area and moved around to the passenger side. Issy was already climbing out. As they approached the front entrance, the single glass door with its steel bars opened. Like the thugs from yesterday, the man wore a mask. Fury had Lacon gritting his teeth. He hoped like hell these bastards got what they deserved.

Soon.

The goon took Lacon's weapon, locked the door behind them and then led the way to the storage area at the back of the building where stock was kept. Two men lay on the vinyl-tiled floor. Both were dressed in black, sans the masks. Their battered faces appeared to be the least of their worries. Blood had soaked their shirts and leaked onto the floor. The most telling aspect of the situation was that neither of the two masked thugs was aiming their weapons at them. The injured were part of their team. One of them, the one farthest from where they stood, kept trying to raise himself up onto his elbows.

"It's about damned time," the injured guy doing the moving growled. "What the hell took you so long?"

"What happened?" Issy moved toward the first of the two victims and lowered to her knees. She didn't bother responding to the other guy.

"A disagreement over a debt," the second of the masked men said.

Lacon recognized the voice. Same top thug as before. *Bastard.*

He surveyed the space. This time a bag of medical supplies sat on the floor next to where the men lay. Issy tugged on a pair of gloves then passed a second pair to Lacon. "I may need your help."

"You got it." He pulled on the gloves and crouched down beside her.

"Have they been given anything for pain?"

Since the two weren't howling in agony, Lacon was reasonably sure they'd been given something to take the edge off.

Top Thug confirmed it. Issy shot him a disgusted look and then prepared to open the shirt of the first victim. From the slit in the fabric, it was evident he'd done a little dance with a knife. When the shirtfront was pulled apart, a nasty laceration about eight inches wide made a bloody smile across his abdomen. There was a lot of blood, and the guy grumbled about needing something more for the pain.

"I need to explore this wound to ensure the penetration didn't reach into the abdominal cavity and nick an organ." She nodded to the other guy. "Have a look at his injuries for me. If there's a BP cuff in the bag, check that for me, as well."

The guy who wanted to sit up spewed a few more curses.

Lacon moved into position next to the grumpy patient. "Be still," he ordered. When the guy had relaxed onto the floor, Lacon ripped open his bloody shirt. Two bullet holes to the torso. There was a lot of blood still oozing from the wounds. "Two entrance wounds just above the naval." He rolled the guy forward just enough to check for any exit wounds, prompting some angry curses. "Got one exit wound to the lower back." He pushed the damaged shirt a little higher up his back. "Don't see a second one. Looks like a .38."

When he allowed the man to settle back against the floor, the thug kept his mouth shut. His face had paled, and he seemed to have lost interest in complaining. "You want me to check his BP?"

"Try to stop the bleeding," Issy ordered. "I'll cover this wound and change patients with you." She nodded toward the grumpy guy who'd decided to keep quiet for now. "I need to have a closer look at him before I finish here."

Lacon applied pressure to the two wounds that were no more than two inches apart. The bleeding eased somewhat, but the glazed look in the guy's eyes told him things were going south. "That's probably a good idea. I don't think he's doing too well."

Dividing his attention between Issy and the two thugs hovering over them, he noticed one of the bastards appeared to be videotaping the whole thing like an episode of some reality show. Probably an order from Anastasia. His increasing interest in Issy was more than a little troubling.

Issy quickly peeled off the bloody gloves and stretched on a new pair. She hurried around to get into position next to Lacon. "Keep an eye on the other guy. I'll want that bag closer so I can grab what I need from here."

Lacon scooted the bag next to her. When he'd changed his gloves and covertly taken what he needed from his pocket, he knelt down next to the guy with the laceration to the gut. He made a show of checking his injury, ensuring that the fingers of his right hand dipped into the man's trouser pocket.

"She gonna finish patching me up?" he asked.

Lacon gave him a nod. "As soon as she takes care of your friend."

Issy tore a scalpel from its packaging and used it to make an incision between the wounds to facilitate getting a closer look inside his gut. She shook her head. "I need more light."

"There's one of those headlights in the bag," Top Thug told her.

Lacon reached across the two injured men and dug around until she located the headlight. He turned on the spotlight and held it in place. Judging by Issy's face and her voice when she'd asked for the light, the situation was deteriorating quickly.

She mumbled a *thanks* as she carefully examined the area she'd opened. Lacon monitored the guys with the guns. Blood abruptly oozed far faster from the wound she was probing. She swore and worked to find the source. The seconds ticked off, and her attempts were futile. The blood just kept coming. The patient was obviously going into shock from the blood loss. He'd gone still as stone and barely blinked.

"We need to get this man to the ER!" she shouted at the two thugs. "I can't do what needs to be done for him here."

"No hospital," Top Thug tossed back. "It's your job to fix him. Now. Here."

Tension rifled through Lacon. She was losing this battle. Blood continued to pour out of the man now.

She looked up at Lacon. "Call 911 or we're going to lose him."

He reached for his phone just as a muzzle bored into the back of his skull. "Move and I will blow your head off."

Issy swore again as she fought to get the bleeding under control. "He's dying," she snapped. "I cannot make the necessary repairs using what you've given me to work with!"

"Can I help?" Lacon said, the phone in his hand seeming to burn his palm. He should call the guy's bluff. Make the phone call.

"Check his pulse," she ordered. "You may need to start CPR while I…"

Her words trailed off but Lacon didn't hesitate. He pulled the headlight around his head so he could still direct some light toward the injury, tuned out all else and focused on finding that rhythmic beat at the base of the man's throat.

Nothing. "No pulse."

"Begin CPR." Her entire focus was on the wound and stopping the bleeding.

Lacon tossed his phone aside and began the chest compressions. His instincts said it was too late, but he would do whatever Issy told him to do until she made that call.

Two or three minutes later, she sat back and shook her head. "It's over."

The look of defeat, of desolation on her face tore Lacon apart.

"What about me?" the other guy shouted.

"Move away from the body," Top Thug ordered. "And take care of him." He waved his gun toward the other man.

The thug who had been recording the ordeal tucked his phone away and waited for Lacon and Issy to move away from the dead man.

The defeat gone now, replaced by absolute fury burning from her eyes and hatred etched in her face, Issy stood and peeled off her gloves. Her T-shirt and jeans were a bloody mess. "And what about infections? I can make the necessary repairs to your friend here, but he'll need an antibiotic, and even that might not be enough. Don't you understand this is not a sterile environment?"

"Just do it," Top Thug commanded.

Lacon stared at the man, hoping he saw the intense need to tear him apart in his eyes as he peeled off his gloves. He itched to kick this guy's ass. For Issy's sake, he restrained the urge. This guy wasn't worth risking her life.

With clean gloves, she made quick work of cleaning and closing the laceration to the man's abdomen.

As soon as a dressing was applied, Top Thug ordered, "Get out."

When she'd removed her gloves, Lacon pulled Issy tight to his side as he ushered her toward the front of the store. Just outside the door, Top Thug returned his weapon and slammed the door shut, locking them out. Lacon guided her to the car and settled her into the passenger seat. He fastened her seat belt and hustled around to the driver's side. Rage roared inside him.

There had to be a way to stop this insanity.

For her.

He glanced at Issy repeatedly as he drove. She didn't speak, just stared out the front window, barely so much as blinking.

She couldn't take much more of this.

They'd barely gone a dozen blocks when she spoke. "Stop the car."

He glanced at her. "What's wrong?"

Dumb question. Right now the whole world was wrong. She'd had to watch a man die because she didn't have the necessary tools to save him. Her pleas to call 911 had gone unheeded. The dead man's blood was all over her, the smell thickening inside the car.

"Stop the car," she repeated, her voice so low he could scarcely hear her.

He pulled over at a gas station that had closed down. Windows and doors were boarded up. Gas pumps were missing.

She flung the door open and hurried to the edge of the parking lot where old broken concrete hit grass, and dropped to her knees.

Lacon got out more slowly, surveying the area for any trouble. When he felt confident they were safe, he lowered to his knees next to her. He held her hair back as she vomited. When the heaving had stopped, she sat for a long moment. He squeezed her shoulder. "You okay?"

She nodded.

He helped her up and they walked back to the car. She said nothing else, and he wished like hell there was more he could say or do.

Her ex-husband had screwed her over, had thrown away his own life and left her to clean up the mess.

Lacon slid back behind the wheel and drove. To his way of thinking, there was only one way to end this—a bullet right between Vito Anastasia's eyes. The sooner the better.

He hoped like hell he was the man who got to pull the trigger for that one.

Maybe that tracking device he'd tucked into the trouser pocket of the guy with the knife wound would provide the first step toward that end.

Chapter Eight

Marissa stood in the middle of the bathroom. She couldn't seem to make herself move. She stared at her hands. Blood still stained the lines and creases, no matter that she'd washed them twice already. That man—in spite of the fact that he had been a criminal and had likely done terrible things—hadn't deserved to die on the floor from injuries that could very likely have been taken care of in the proper medical setting.

How many times had William done this for that son of a bitch Anastasia?

For years she had recognized his lies, knew he kept secrets. Why had she stayed so long after realizing the sort of man he had become?

Her body started to shake. She really had no idea how long she had been standing here in this same spot. Lacon had driven her back to the safe house and ushered her through her room and into this bathroom so she could shower. He'd said he would be back to check on her after his shower.

How long ago had that been?

She told her body to move, to do what needed to be done, but she couldn't seem to make it happen. What she really wanted to do was collapse onto the floor in a pathetic heap and cry until there was no more regret, no more pain and no more fear of what might be coming next. But how would that help anything? If she fell apart, she would be no good to anyone else, let alone herself.

She needed to shower. She stared at the blood soaked into the clothes she wore. It was mostly dry now, though the smell was sickening. But she didn't care how it smelled. Not really. She was too tired to care. What hurt was the reality that all the blood represented a lost life. Part of her just wanted to go to the bed and crawl under the covers.

She stared down at her feet. Somehow she'd managed to toe off her shoes and peel off her socks. She'd left them by the sink downstairs in the laundry room when she'd tried to scrub the blood from her hands— an effort that hadn't worked too well.

Forcing one foot in front of the other, she walked toward the shower. She reached inside and turned on the water. Her fingers found their way to the hem of her T-shirt. All she had to do was pull it up and over her head but somehow she could not. Images of the man who had died this morning flickered in her head. The face of the other man—the one Anastasia's people had murdered after she took care of him—joined the stream of images. She should have done more for both of those men. They were dead, in part, because of her.

She opened the glass door and stepped into the

shower. Didn't matter that she still had on her clothes. She no longer cared. She leaned her head against the cool tile wall and allowed the hot water to pound against her back. Her eyes closed and she struggled to hold in the sobs, but they would not be contained.

Wilting helplessly against the wall, she slid down onto her knees. The steam rose, swirling around the sobs echoing from her throat that were tearing at her heart.

The door opened, drawing the heated air out and allowing the cooler air to rush in. She opened her eyes but she didn't move. Didn't care if Anastasia himself was coming for her. She just wanted this nightmare to be over.

Lacon crouched next to her, the water raining down on his blond head, slipping down his muscular shoulders and chest, soaking into the waistband of his jeans. She blinked just to make sure she hadn't imagined him.

"Come here." He helped her up when all she wanted to do was let the hot water melt her and wash her away. "I'll take care of you," he whispered.

His hands found the hem of her T-shirt and pulled it upward. She instinctively raised her arms so he could pull the sticky T-shirt up and over her head. He tossed it onto the built-in bench on the other side of the shower. She closed her eyes and let the hot water patter against her chest. His hands unfastened her jeans. Her eyelids fluttered open, and she watched his long fingers and broad hands work the wet jeans over her hips, down her thighs. She raised one foot and then the other for him to pull the denim free. The stained jeans landed next to the T-shirt.

Then he stood, water rushing over his gorgeous body,

soaking into his clean jeans. She realized suddenly that he'd already had his shower. She scrubbed her arm across her face, the hot water mixing with her salty tears. A shudder of defeat quaked through her and she wanted to collapse on the floor once more, but he pulled her into his arms and held her against his strong, warm body.

She cried some more, wishing she could stop, but she couldn't. He held her, caressed her wet hair and her back. Eventually he drew her away from the comfort of his body and leaned her against the tile wall. It was slick and hot now, no longer cold. He reached for the body wash and filled his palm. Slowly, so very slowly, he smoothed the cherry-blossom-scented soap over her skin. He started with her throat, then traced his hands over her shoulders, down her chest, over the silk encasing her breasts…down her arms.

Her body trembled at his touch. Fire rushed over her skin wherever his hands landed. He clasped his fingers with hers, washing her hands, then traced a trail up her sides. With a gentle prompt, he turned her around and washed her back. Every inch of skin was caressed and massaged thoroughly.

He leaned close, whispered against her temple, "Close your eyes."

Her breath catching at the nearness of his lips, she did as he asked. His every touch, every move was so very gentle. He ushered her under the spray of water and began washing her hair, massaging her scalp until goose bumps spilled over her skin. When he'd rinsed it thoroughly, he started all over again with the conditioner, slowly, methodically working a kind of magic she had never felt before. Her body was on fire, so hot and languid she could barely stand.

Then he dropped to his knees and washed her feet, her ankles, calves and thighs, his touch patient, intent. When she thought he might stop, he added more body wash to his hands and washed her intimately through the strappy bikini panties she wore. She whimpered in spite of her determined efforts to curb the reaction.

He stood. Pressed a kiss to her cheek and turned for the door.

"No."

The single word was rough, desperate, demanding.

She couldn't let him go.

She needed him.

She wanted him.

He looked into her eyes, his as full of desire as she knew hers were. She wasn't the only one who wanted more.

"This is not what you need," he murmured.

"Last night you said we'd revisit the subject tomorrow." She reached behind her back and unhooked her bra, let it fall down her arms and onto the tile where the water swirled and rushed down the drain. "It's tomorrow."

"You're just looking for a distraction," he warned. "I don't want to be something else you'll regret."

She leaned against the wall, allowing her breasts to jut forward. "I think you missed a spot."

He grabbed the body wash and squeezed a little more onto his palm. He held her gaze as he reached for her breasts. She gasped when both hands closed over her and squeezed. He teased her nipples, leaned down and kissed her, his mouth devouring hers.

Her arms went around him, slid down his back until she encountered the waistband of his jeans. She trailed her fingers around to his fly and unfastened it. She stuck her hands inside that soft denim and ushered them slowly down his lean hips, then pushed his back against the wall this time. She kissed her way down his chest as she pushed his jeans lower and lower. When her tongue dipped into his navel, she dropped to her knees and tugged off the soaking wet jeans.

She kissed her way back up his muscled thighs, past his fully aroused penis and onto the center of his wide chest. He lifted her up, and her legs instinctively went around his waist. He shut off the water, shouldered his way out the door and headed for the bed. He lowered her onto the comforter and reached for the one thing left between them, those damned panties. He dragged the damp, strappy things down her legs, following that same path with his lips. He tossed the panties away and settled between her welcoming thighs.

As she arched her hips, his erection pressed against her, and she shuddered with need. He pulled away, apparently satisfied to taste and tease her mouth with his own.

"I can't wait any longer," she murmured between kisses. She lifted her hips into him once more.

He grinned and reached down to guide himself into her, filling her quickly and completely. She cried out with the pleasure of it. Shivers rushed through her, rippling along every muscle, pushing her toward that place of pure sensation. He held her tight, his muscled chest rubbing her breasts, grinding against her nipples until she thought she would lose her mind.

Her fingers found their way into his hair, and she relished the silky feel of it. She traced his square jaw, nipped his lips with her teeth. The rasp of his hips along her inner thighs, the stretching sensation of each thrust, the brush of his chest against her breasts...all of it had her plunging toward sensory overload.

The distant ache of climax teased her, coming nearer and nearer until the pleasure exploded inside her. One, two, three more thrusts and he came, too.

He growled as he rolled onto his side, pulling her with him, their bodies still intimately joined.

Tears burned her eyes, but she refused to cry again. She didn't know why she felt that particular urge. He was...amazing. What they'd just shared was amazing. There was no other word for it.

As if understanding, he pulled her close and whispered into her damp hair. "Please don't regret this."

"I couldn't even if I wanted to," she whispered back.

2:00 p.m.

"WHERE ARE WE GOING?"

She'd asked him that same question four times already. "It's a surprise." Lacon grinned at her.

"Okay. I like surprises. Sometimes."

"You'll like this surprise, I promise."

He'd had to select a car from the garage. All the blood in his would just remind her of the nightmare at Hirsch and Kildare. For now, he intended to do all in his power to keep that smile on her face and that sweet laughter coming from her luscious mouth.

He'd taken her to his favorite burger joint for lunch. They'd eaten all the bad stuff: burgers, fries, shakes. He'd had her pegged for a vanilla girl, but she'd gone straight for the chocolate. He couldn't remember the last time he'd laughed so much as she'd told him stories of her and her brother's antics as kids.

She'd asked a million questions about his family and childhood, as if all he'd previously told her hadn't been nearly enough. So he'd decided to give her the grand tour—at least the one he could give without driving all the way to Texas.

He parked in front of his town house on Rockwell. She peered out the window at the two-story redbrick duplex. It wasn't as fancy as her place, but it was his home away from home, and he was comfortable here.

She whirled in the seat to face him. "Is this where you live?"

He nodded. "You want to come in?"

"Yes." She reached for the door.

He emerged, checked the street in both directions and met her on the sidewalk. He resisted the urge to take her hand as they strolled up the walk. Six steps up to the stoop and through the common door. A small hall that had once been a glamorous foyer went left to his town house and right to his neighbor's.

As soon as he'd unlocked the door, Issy rushed in ahead of him. His gut tightened. What she thought of his place suddenly mattered way too much.

She wandered all around the reasonably spacious living room. He should probably get a rug for the hardwood, but the bare wood floors had never bothered him.

His sofa and chair were big, overstuffed and comfortable. A couple of handy tables, a big-ass television and he was good to go. About the only other thing he needed was someone to curl up on that big old sofa with him.

That his gaze rested on her warned him that he was moving way too fast into personal territory. He'd been trained to avoid that dangerous deviation. He knew better. But he couldn't slow the momentum.

"I love the fireplace."

"It comes in handy on those cold Windy City nights." He joined her at the mantel where she was examining the family photos that lined it.

"Your sister is beautiful."

"Thanks. My dad insists she looks just like our mother did at that age."

Issy smiled at him and moved on to the group photo they'd taken on Father's Day. "Wow. All you Traynor men are handsome."

A spark of jealousy burned in him. "Really?" He took the framed photo from her. "Those two?" He shook his head. "No way. I got all the looks in the family."

Another of those relaxed smiles spread across her face. He could barely breathe just watching the happiness bloom on her countenance.

"Let's see the kitchen. Do you cook as much here as you do when you're on duty at the safe house?"

"Absolutely."

He led the way through the small dining room to the kitchen. "There's a patio out back."

She walked around the kitchen, touched the cabinet doors, trailed her fingers over the counter. His mind conjured up the memory of his fingers trailing over her skin, feeling her body shiver against him…feeling her coming around him. He swallowed hard, tried to think of something witty to say.

"It's cozy." She surveyed his spice rack and the stack of cookbooks in the corner, then she touched the hand towel that hung on the oven door handle. It said Cooking Good. His sister had given it to him at Christmas. "I can tell you spend a lot of time in here."

He shrugged. "When I'm home I cook."

"Can I see upstairs?" She bit her lower lip as if she was worried he would say no. "You've seen where I sleep."

"Sure." He gestured toward the stairs. "Make yourself at home."

She strolled past him and hurried up the stairs. He climbed a little slower, mostly because that way he got to watch the sweet sway of her hips. It wasn't like there was a lot to see up there—beyond the gorgeous woman in front of him. There were two bedrooms and one bathroom, besides the tiny half bath downstairs. She wandered from room to room, lingering in his bedroom. Soft music whispered from the clock radio.

"Nothing to see." He gestured to the bed. "Bed. Dresser and closet." He shrugged. "And one small bedside table. I leave the radio on like that all the time." The volume was turned down so low you could barely hear the music. He liked the gentle sound, like the soft roar of the ocean.

She grabbed him by the hand and pulled him toward the bed. "I want to lie here with you and listen."

"Really?"

"Yes. It's kind of silly, but I want to *feel* your space."

"Okeydokey."

He climbed onto the bed and lay down beside her. They stared at the ceiling fan going round and round, listened to the soft notes of the music filtering through the air.

"Your bed is comfy."

"Yeah."

Her hand found his, and their fingers instinctively intertwined.

The tight feeling in his chest worried him. He was liking this way too much.

The vibration in his jacket pocket alerted him to a call. He exhaled a big breath and dug the damned thing out. At least it wasn't hers. Anastasia wouldn't call him.

He stared at the number. Didn't recognize it.

"Traynor."

"Mr. Traynor, this is Chief Anthony Waller."

Lacon stilled. "How can I help you, Chief?"

"We need to have a meeting."

Surprised, Lacon asked, "What time and where?"

"Now, if possible. I've contacted Victoria. She's already en route. We're meeting near the old station house on Halsted Street in Lincoln Park. I realize it's short notice, so how quickly can you be there?"

Lacon sat up. "Half an hour."

"Bring Dr. Frasier with you. This can't wait."

"We'll be there."

Issy was sitting up now, her gaze searching his face. "What's going on?"

"Chief Waller wants a meeting. He said Victoria is already en route."

Issy finger combed her hair. "Then I guess we have to go."

Lacon didn't have a good feeling about this. As they moved back downstairs, he decided it would be best to contact Michaels en route to confirm this impromptu meeting. They had no control over Anastasia's actions, but this felt wrong somehow. His instincts were sounding off.

At the front door, he hesitated. "Stay inside while I have a look around outside."

She hugged her arms around herself. "Okay."

He hated the fear that took the place of the happiness he'd watched light up her face until that damned phone call interrupted. She'd been through too much already. He didn't like any of this, not one little bit.

Outside, he surveyed the street. Checked the car. All seemed as it should be. He put in a call to Ian Michaels. Got his voice mail. He left a message for Michaels to let him know what was going on with the Waller meeting. He left the location just in case.

Once Lacon felt confident there was no danger lurking nearby, he locked his place and ushered Issy out to the car. He took a few shortcuts to reach the neighborhood where the old defunct police station still stood. He'd added a little time on to what was necessary when Waller questioned him. His instincts still nagged relentlessly at him.

Something wasn't right.

He parked behind another vehicle on the side street next to the bank across from the old police station and cut the engine. He surveyed the street in front of the old station house. So far he saw nothing unusual, but that didn't mean something unusual wouldn't come out of the woodwork like roaches after dark.

"What do we do now?" She looked at him, her eyes clearly conveying that she was worried because he was worried.

"Let's just stay in the background and see how this plays out until we hear from Michaels."

Five minutes later, an SUV arrived. Chief Waller got out and walked halfway down the block. Maybe ten seconds later a dark car, big with heavily tinted windows, eased to the curb. Waller leaned down at the rear passenger side and appeared to be talking to someone.

The vehicle was not an agency vehicle. There was no sign of Victoria or Michaels. This was definitely not right, by any stretch of the imagination.

"This is all wrong." Traynor started the car and slowly backed down the side street. When he was far enough from the intersection to avoid detection, he executed a u-turn and sped away.

"Do you think Chief Waller was trying to set us up?"

Lacon checked his rearview mirror. "I don't know, but I didn't recognize that car as one of the agency's. I didn't see Victoria or Michaels either."

His cell vibrated and he checked the screen. This time it was Michaels. "Traynor."

Michaels confirmed his gut instinct. Victoria had not received a call from Waller. The chief had lied.

The meet was a setup.

Chapter Nine

Colby Safe House, 6:30 p.m.

Victoria had already met with Chief Connie Staten regarding Chief Waller's potential criminal activities. Marissa hated the idea of one of the top cops in the city being on Anastasia's side, but she wasn't foolish enough to believe it didn't happen. For some, money was more important than anything else, even executing their sworn duties.

"Does this mean that Anastasia knows where we are?" The idea had only just occurred to her. Her heart thumped hard against her ribs.

Lacon raised his hands in a hold-up gesture. "Right now we have no reason to believe he knows where you are. Waller was never given this address. He only knows that you're at one of the agency's safe houses. The addresses are a closely guarded secret."

"So there are others?" She relaxed the tiniest bit. This feeling of not being in control of her own destiny, of being totally at someone else's mercy, had her completely on edge. She had agreed to do this, but she hadn't expected to not be able to trust the good guys. The reality of the situation felt far graver now. Caused her to doubt herself.

"Several." He glanced around the kitchen, set his hands on his lean hips. "You up for chicken? I've mastered several mean chicken-and-rice recipes."

As unsettled as she was about this latest turn of events, she had to smile. He really was such a nice man. Whatever happened, when this was over, she hoped they could remain friends. Her body heated just standing here looking at him. She wasn't sure friends would ever be enough. But she also realized that right now she was his job—his work—and this wasn't necessarily the beginning of anything deeper.

It just felt that way.

So not smart, Issy.

"That sounds great." She pushed all the troubling thoughts away. "What can I do?"

He grinned. She loved that grin. Her heart stumbled. *Don't even go there, silly.*

"Find something green that goes well with chicken and rice."

"I think I can handle that." She went to the fridge. "Someone stocks this place whenever there's a guest?"

Or maybe he'd done the shopping, too. But no, she didn't think so. She couldn't see how he would have had the time between when she reached out to her friend Eva Bowman and when Lacon showed up at her house after William's murder.

"There's a staff that takes care of the cleaning and the shopping."

She had been surprised when they returned to find the en suite in her room spotless, the bloody clothes gone. She hoped they had thrown those clothes away because she certainly never wanted to see them again.

Her exploration of the fridge turned up kale and spinach, two of her favorites. All they needed was the right dressing for a healthy salad.

The cell in the hip pocket of her jeans vibrated, reminding her that she had nothing clean left to wear after today. This pair of jeans and the "Doctors would be lost without nurses" T-shirt were the last of the casual wear she'd packed. Obviously her idea of how long this business would take had been far too optimistic. Cutting herself some slack, she had just discovered her ex dead in the bed next to her. Her ability to think clearly had been seriously compromised. She pulled the phone from her pocket and checked the screen.

Blocked Call.

Fear swam through her veins.

"It's him."

Lacon nodded for her to answer.

The fridge started that annoying sound that warned the door had been open too long. She pushed it closed with her hip and touched the screen, accepting the call and putting it on speaker. "Frasier."

"It's time we met, Dr. Frasier."

She held on to the counter, his declaration making her knees weak. "If you've managed to get two more of your men gravely injured, save us both some time and trouble and just shoot them."

"Now, now, Doctor, you wound me. Sometimes it's impossible to keep my people safe. I suppose I have far too many enemies to hope for peaceful negotiations in business."

Marissa dropped the kale and spinach onto the counter. "If no one is in need of medical care, why are you calling?"

"As I said, I think it's time we met in person."

A new fear surged into her chest. She stared at Lacon. He moved his head side to side. But how was she supposed to stop Anastasia if she didn't do as he asked? She couldn't bring this guy down from afar. She had no choice.

"What time did you have in mind?"

Lacon looked away, but the set of his jaw told her he wasn't happy with her decision.

"Tonight. Eight o'clock. We'll have dinner in my home. I rarely invite anyone into my home. Consider yourself honored, Dr. Frasier. My chef is one of the finest in the city. I'm certain you will fall in love with his culinary skills."

His comment gave her pause. Did he somehow know that she had raved about Lacon's abilities in the kitchen? That was impossible. The security here was far too state-of-the-art.

Reaching for her most cavalier tone, she said, "I'll need your address."

He provided the Lincoln Park address without hesitation. "I'll see you at eight. Bring your bodyguard if you like."

The call ended. One look at her *bodyguard* and she held her breath. To say he appeared upset would be a monumental understatement.

"You know we have to do this," she ventured.

"No way in hell are we going to his house."

"Yes." She took a deep breath to bolster her waning courage. "We are. It's the only way I'll be able to get close to him. I can't stop him from a distance. I need to be closer. Close enough to connect him to a murder or some other criminal activity."

"So you've decided this is your mission in life? You're just going to take whatever risk necessary." He passed a hand over his jaw. "Not happening. I'm calling Victoria."

"Suit yourself. I'm going to get ready."

He was already making the call when she walked out. Maybe it wasn't a smart move. Anastasia could be planning to kill her. The trouble was, she couldn't keep living this way. She had a career. Was she supposed to go back to work not knowing when he would call and demand she appear and make a house call for him? How long would she have to play that game before she got close enough to find some sort of leverage to help bring him down?

She didn't want to live that way. Didn't want to follow in William's footsteps.

Peeling off the jeans and T-shirt, she went into the closet. The dress clothes she had brought for meeting Victoria would have to do. The black slacks were some of her favorites. The blouse, too. The flats were comfortable and dressy enough. She didn't actually care what this piece of shit thought of how she looked. She just wanted to get closer—close enough to learn at least one of his secrets.

She hadn't brought any makeup, which was fine by her. She rarely wore it anyway. She brushed her hair, let it fall in those wild curls that were the bane of her existence. Perfume was the last thing she'd been thinking about when she'd packed. The cherry blossom scent of the body wash still lingered on her skin. Good enough.

She'd just shut off the light and exited the en suite bath when Lacon walked into her room, the tension in the set of his shoulders like a flashing neon sign that screamed frustration.

"You're determined to do this, aren't you?"

"It's the only way I'll ever be free of him." She clasped and unclasped her hands. "I can't stay hidden like this forever."

He dropped his head. "You're right. He's not going to stop using you until someone stops him." He lifted his gaze back to hers. "I don't know if we can count on the police to make that happen. He's a powerful guy, and the kind of money he throws around can sometimes sway even the most honorable man."

"Which means it's up to us."

"I just don't like it."

She walked over to where he stood and wrapped her arm around one of his. "I don't like it either. But I can't think of a better plan."

"I don't want you alone with him."

"I want you right beside me every minute."

"All right. Let's do this. Give me five to change clothes."

"I'll have a glass of wine while I wait."

They parted in the hallway. He went to his room and she descended the stairs. In the kitchen, she picked through the chilled white wines until she found one of her favorites. In the past couple of years, she'd become quite the expert at removing wine corks. Before it had always been William's job. Funny how so many little things changed when a marriage ended. Luckily, the cork gave her no trouble. She poured a glass and savored a long drink. Though she needed a clear head for tonight, a little fortification was in order, as well.

She had finished off the healthy serving by the time Lacon appeared at the door. Her breath caught in her throat. "Wow."

It wasn't until he grinned that she realized she had said the word out loud. Her face warmed with embarrassment.

She shook her head and confessed, "You look… *wow.*" The black trousers and the black shirt fit him like a glove. But the perfect crowning touches were the boots and the jacket. "Really nice."

"You set a high bar, Doc. You look amazing yourself."

Her blush deepened, and she felt the blood rush even harder to her cheeks. "I think maybe you have a little cabin fever, Mr. Traynor. You're delirious."

"I don't think so." He put the wine away while she rinsed her glass. His gaze settled on hers, and the doubt there was unmistakable. "Shall we go?"

She put her arm in his. "It's too late to back out now."

Maybe tonight she would learn something important to the mission without anyone having to die. That would be the best-case scenario, at any rate.

North Burling Street, 8:00 p.m.

MARISSA HAD BEEN to her share of mansions. The Edge administrator, Devon Pierce, lived in a gorgeous mansion out in Highland Park. It was genuinely beautiful. But this house with its manicured grounds, discreet landscape lighting, an iron fence and gate that sprawled along a full city block on Lincoln Park's most prestigious street. The term *mansion* seemed wholly inadequate.

An armed guard opened the intricate iron gate and greeted them at the sidewalk. The landscape and fountains alone probably cost more than Marissa's entire house. The home's towering front double doors opened as they climbed the limestone steps.

"Good evening, Dr. Frasier," the man dressed all in white said. He ignored Lacon. "Mr. Anastasia is waiting for you in the parlor. Directly ahead and to your left."

"Thank you." She smiled for the man, whom she decided was a butler. Did butlers even exist anymore?

"Sir, I will need your weapon," the butler said to Lacon.

He relinquished the weapon in his side holster without fanfare but kept the one in his boot. He'd told her about it on the drive here.

The entry hall was enormous, with a ceiling that soared up three floors. The winding staircase railing was black and gold, with marble steps twisting around the grand hall all the way up to the second floor and beyond. The gleaming marble floors flowed forward, changing to rich hardwood as they entered the parlor. Unlike the crisp white walls of the entry hall, the parlor walls were clad in rich mahogany paneling. A stone fireplace was surrounded by comfortable chairs in an elegant conversation grouping. In the center of the room, two sofas faced each other. An impressive chandelier hung from the soaring ceiling.

Anastasia stood at the wall of windows that looked out over the back of his urban estate. He turned to greet her, and she was surprised to find that he was not as old as she'd expected. The photos of him that Lacon had showed her were always taken from a distance, and his face was rarely clear enough to see the details. He was undeniably young and attractive. But his gray eyes were predatory, cunning. She didn't like his eyes, particularly as they roved over her as if she were his prey.

He smiled, surprising her again. "Dr. Frasier, it is a pleasure to meet you."

Before she could answer, he crossed the room, took her hand and brushed his lips across it. She barely restrained a shiver of revulsion and hoped she had managed to conceal the reaction.

"I'm sorry I can't say the same, Mr. Anastasia." She withdrew her hand from his. His touch made her feel ill.

"What would you like to drink?" He gestured to the elegant bar across the room. "Wine? A martini?"

She had to be careful to keep a clear head, but chances were if she drank, he would, as well. Then again, maybe she'd read far too many mysteries. "White wine. Thank you."

"And you, Mr. Traynor?" He looked beyond her. "Scotch? Bourbon?"

"Nothing for me."

Marissa glanced at him. Hearing his voice, though weighted with irritation, made her feel safe. He stood a few feet away, arms hanging loosely, hands clasped in front of him. He and the man pouring the drinks could not be more different. Lacon's silky blond hair and light golden brown eyes were a stark contrast to Anastasia's raven-black hair that brushed his shoulders and eyes so dark they were nearly black.

Both men were tall, but Lacon had the lean, muscular build of an athlete. Anastasia was thinner. He wore black trousers as well, but rather than a button-down shirt, he had donned a silk V-neck pullover that clung to his body like a second skin. He appeared fit, but she doubted he possessed the physical strength of the man who had made love to her last night. She shivered at the memories. This time she could not restrain the pleasant sensation.

Anastasia brought the stemmed glass of wine to her, his own tumbler of bourbon in his other hand.

She lifted the glass to her mouth, but then hesitated as she remembered that this man had ordered someone to drug her wine so she wouldn't wake up while her house was broken into and her ex-husband was murdered and left in her bed.

"It's the best." He sent a pointed look at her wine.

When she still hesitated, he nodded. "I see. You think there might be something in the wine."

Before she could answer, he took her glass and downed the contents. "Now," he licked his lips, "would you like a glass of wine?"

"I would." Only then did her heart begin to slow from its frantic race.

When he'd poured her another glass of wine, the butler who'd taken Lacon's weapon appeared and announced that dinner was served. They migrated to the equally luxurious dining room that would easily accommodate forty. The table was set for three at the end nearest yet another wall of windows.

Anastasia held her chair and then sat down at the head of the table. Lacon was seated directly across from her. Marissa felt as if she were in one of those old gangster movies.

More staff dressed in white, a woman and a man, rushed around the dining room delivering their salads and leaving cutting boards loaded with fresh bread. Water goblets were filled. Linen napkins were placed across their laps.

Anastasia wanted to know everything about her, from her childhood to her work at the Edge. He acted as if he knew nothing of her background. She knew this was a lie, but his performance as the uninformed was nothing short of award winning. He said nothing to Lacon. It was as if he wasn't in the room.

By the time dessert arrived, the tension between the two men was palpable.

Marissa stole glances at Lacon, but his full attention

was on the man at the end of the table. The dessert was delicious. The raspberries and blackberries provided the perfect tart contrast to the creamy ricotta mousse with its distinct hint of orange liqueur. She nibbled at the dessert while coffee was served.

Her mind wouldn't stop with the questions. Why had Anastasia invited her here? What did he want? What did he need to prove? That he had the grandest mansion in all of Chicago? That he had a hell of a chef and a loyal staff?

Or was it that he wanted to show her he could be just another billionaire businessman?

Whatever his intent, he wasn't fooling Marissa. She knew what he was. A heartless, greedy criminal who would do anything to achieve his goal. This man had murdered William. He had killed at least two other people in the short time since she learned of his existence.

He was a monster.

ANASTASIA STOOD.

Lacon had never been so grateful for anything in his life. If he survived this night without punching the guy's face in, it would be a flat-out miracle.

This meeting, however important they had hoped it would be, had proven utterly pointless. The only thing Lacon had learned was that the bastard was seriously obsessed with Issy.

Anastasia couldn't keep his eyes off her. He took advantage of every damned opportunity to touch her. Her hand, her arm. Lacon was about ready to explode.

You have really screwed this one up, buddy.

Lacon had allowed the relationship with Issy to become personal. Images of last night flickered through him, reminding him that he'd made a serious mistake. But he couldn't call what he'd felt a mistake. It wasn't just sex…it was more. Still, protecting her had to be his top priority. Nothing else could get in the way.

"I'd like to show you something," Anastasia said to Issy.

Fury eating at him, Lacon trailed behind the two as they exited the house through the French doors that lined the dining room. A terrace flanked the back of the house. Overhead, a balcony ran that same length. Down the steps was a reflecting pool and fountain, as well as a large gazebo that covered an outdoor living room. The property was bordered with thick shrubs and trees, giving more privacy than he would have expected to find in such an urban setting.

Anastasia appeared to be headed for the garage. Like the one at the Colby safe house, the garage was a six-bay structure that faced the street running behind the house. Considering the property covered an entire city block, there could potentially be street access on all four sides. Lacon had only spotted this one access.

Between the gardens and the garage was a carriage house. Anastasia placed his hand at the small of Issy's back and ushered her in the direction of the carriage house. Fury exploded deep in Lacon's gut.

Damn it. Where was his objectivity when he needed it?

Anastasia entered the code that unlocked the door and pushed it inward. Lacon stepped ahead of Issy. "I need to have a look first."

Anastasia gestured to the door. "I have premiere security, but by all means, be my guest."

Rather than a guesthouse as he'd expected, the carriage house was like a small medical clinic. He checked the other doors. One led to living quarters and the other to a small private courtyard.

Lacon gestured for Issy to come on in, then he stepped aside to observe. He had a feeling he wasn't going to like what came next.

"This is the clinic I had prepared in anticipation of taking on a private physician as part of my staff."

Issy wandered around the room. Lacon was no doctor, but he'd never seen a better-equipped clinic. Not surprising, really, since Anastasia was megarich. *Bastard.*

The other thing Lacon had recognized tonight was the sheer jealousy he felt every single time Anastasia looked at her, much less touched her. He shook his head, frustrated with himself.

"This is pretty incredible," Issy admitted.

Lacon reminded himself she was playing along, but he still didn't like her positive reaction.

"This is where you will work." Anastasia shook his head. "No more rushing to locations where what you need might not be available. I've put you through a great deal this week, but I needed to know I could count on you—that you could handle the demands of my business. I have no doubts now. You possess the necessary skills, and you are beautiful. You're exactly what I've been looking for."

"This is all very nice," she said, drawing Lacon from

his fixation with beating the guy to a bloody pulp. "But I already have a position that means a great deal to me. The people, the facility—I can't walk away from either."

Lacon didn't miss the flash of anger in the other man's cold eyes.

"You work for me now," he reminded her. "Going back to the way your life once was isn't possible, so don't waste your time fighting the inevitable. This is where you will work."

Issy cocked her head and studied him a moment. "What's in it for me? Contrary to what you obviously believe, I don't live my life for you or to serve your every whim."

"I thought you understood the nature of our relationship, Issy."

Who the hell gave him permission to call her Issy? Lacon clenched his teeth, kept his mouth shut. His fingers curled into fists.

"What is our relationship?" She took a step toward Anastasia. Lacon tensed. "You drugged me, murdered my ex-husband and left him in my bed, and you think that constitutes a relationship? Please, you must know that I can't just forget those two ugly facts. You've put me in an untenable position."

Anastasia's jaw worked a second before he spoke. "Bauer left me no choice. He should have known better than to double-cross a man like me. He made a very bad decision and he paid the price."

"A lapse in judgment, for sure," she agreed. "I've done my research, Mr. Anastasia. I'm aware of the kind of man you are."

"Vito," he reminded her. At some point over dinner, he'd urged her to call him Vito. "What has your research told you?"

"The most lucrative part of your business is done behind the scenes. But then there's the legitimate business you operate. You have many powerful friends and allies. How would it look to them if they learned you had hired a murder suspect? Until this business with William is cleared up, I have to face the very real possibility that I could be charged with murder."

"You needn't worry. I will clear up any questions related to your involvement in that unsavory business immediately. You'll receive the call tomorrow."

Issy seemed uncertain how to respond. Then she went for the jugular. "You murdered the man I once loved. How can you expect me to pretend that didn't happen?"

He stepped nearer to her, and Lacon prepared to step between them.

"William Bauer killed himself. He understood when he took matters into his own hands what he was doing." Anastasia studied her for one seemingly endless moment. "Would you be so quick to jump to your ex-husband's defense if you knew that he spoke often of how he hated you? Of how he wished you dead?"

She blinked. Lacon flinched.

"I don't believe you." She shook her head. "We didn't get along and he was angry that I pressed charges—"

"He hated you. He asked me to have you killed, but I refused."

The color drained from her face. "What are you talking about?"

"He wanted you dead because he knew you hadn't changed your will or your insurance policies. All that was yours would be his and, in time, he would regain his license to practice medicine. He couldn't risk killing you himself." Anastasia frowned. "I did worry toward the end that he might snap and attempt to harm you."

"*You* worried about me?" Disbelief underscored her tone.

Lacon was proud of her. He'd just thought the same thing.

"I did. When I learned of William's latest bad decision, I decided it would be in both our best interests to put an end to his plotting."

"So you drugged me and had him killed—and put in my bed—in an effort to protect me." She laughed. "That's rich, Vito, but I'm not buying it."

Lacon resisted the urge to smile.

"Well, there was the matter of getting your attention and, of course, your cooperation."

"Thank you for dinner and the tour of your home." She turned away from him and strode toward the door.

Lacon hesitated going after her just so he could see the man's reaction when he realized she was actually leaving.

Outrage streaked across the bastard's face. "No one walks away from me."

Lacon moved toward her. She stood at the door now, staring back at the man who had spoken.

"If you want me to work for you," she said, "then

you need to make it worth my while. The police have been all over me, as a murder suspect and as a potential way to get to you."

Renewed tension slid through Lacon.

"The police have asked you to be their eyes and ears against me?"

"They have."

Lacon decided she would make a damned good detective. She was aware that if Waller was the leak in the department, then Anastasia already knew this. His respect for her increased exponentially.

"And what did you do in response to this request?"

She shrugged. "I heard them out. I figured maybe if I helped them, they might stop trying to prove I had anything to do with my ex's death."

Anastasia waited for her to go on, his gaze narrowed.

"But then I realized they were just using me." She shook her head. "I was used by my ex—I'm not going to be used by anyone else. The next time they asked for a meeting, I blew them off."

A smile cut across the bastard's face. "I will pay you three times your current salary if you come to work for me. The benefits," he said the word so salaciously Lacon wanted to puke, "will be immeasurable."

"I'll think about it." She turned back to the door, but then hesitated again. "Just one thing." She gestured to Lacon. "He goes where I go."

Anastasia sized him up again, this time more slowly. "I have no issue with that request. I'm certain he would be an asset to me, as well."

Lacon was relatively certain from his tone that he didn't mean as a member of his security team.

Issy shook her head. "Sorry. He's all mine. You can look, but no touching."

Another of those sick smiles lit the other man's face. "As you wish."

She held the other man's gaze as if she might say more. Lacon wanted to urge her out the door, but she'd done a damned good job of handling the situation so far. He wasn't about to mess with her momentum.

"How am I supposed to trust you, Vito?" She folded her arms over her chest. "First you regale me with stories of how often William spoke of me. You mentioned that he said I loved my patients. Now you want me to believe that he hated me. Wanted me dead."

Anastasia moved closer to her. Renewed tension coiled in Lacon.

"He spoke of you often, but none of it was good. It was his obsession with hating you that led me to see for myself all that you were. William Bauer was a fool. A liar and a fool."

Issy ignored his thinly veiled compliment. "Just one more question."

Anastasia lifted his eyebrows in inquiry.

"Why me? There are lots of talented doctors in this city. Why does it have to be me?"

"All these months I found myself watching you, learning about you. You intrigue me, Dr. Marissa Frasier. It must be you. It cannot be anyone else. You have forty-eight hours to make your decision."

The stare-off lasted another ten seconds before she walked out the door.

Lacon followed her without a backward glance. He was more than ready to get out of this snake den.

At the front door, the gray-haired man in the white suit returned his weapon and bid them a good evening. The same guard opened the gate at the street for them to pass, then closed and locked it. Lacon checked the street and his car before allowing Issy to get inside.

He didn't breathe easy until they were a mile or so away from Anastasia's compound.

"You okay?" He glanced at her, wished he could see her face better, but it was too dark.

"I'm good. I just need to get back to the house so I can take another shower. I feel dirty having breathed the same air as that scumbag."

Lacon laughed. That was the best line he'd heard all night.

Chapter Ten

"We have a tail."

Marissa clutched the armrest and glanced at Lacon. "You think it's Anastasia's men?" Like she had to ask. Her stomach was still churning from the time spent with the man. The things she had read about him in the research Lacon had shown her sickened her. What kind of man could do those things?

She wasn't naive. The world could be a dangerous place. She knew men like Vito Anastasia existed. She saw the harm one human could wreak upon another in the ER more often than she would like.

But somehow it felt more oppressive and far more terrifying when the horrors came from a person who looked so normal…so polished and who presented himself so graciously.

"That would be my guess," he said in answer to her question. "He wants us to know there's no escaping his reach."

Marissa felt suddenly cold. She hugged her arms around her body. "I wanted to do this. I hoped I could get us one step closer to accomplishing the goal, but all

I did was open up another door in this maze of insanity. I don't see how we can ever hope to stop him. He's... I..." She sighed. "I failed."

"You did great, Issy. It was the right decision. I was the one who wasn't thinking clearly."

She didn't question what he meant by the statement. She had to admit that having him say as much made her feel better about the outcome of tonight. Not only had she not learned anything usable, now she was in deeper trouble than before. She had forty-eight hours to give the bastard a response to his demand.

"What do we do about whoever is following us?"

He reached into his pocket and withdrew his cell. "Traynor."

Marissa chewed her lips as she waited for him to finish the call. When he'd tucked the phone back into his pocket, he said, "Michaels says our tail is an unmarked cop car."

"Mr. Michaels is following us, too?"

"I never go into a risky situation without backup."

She'd wondered why he caved so easily in the end about the dinner invitation. "So what do we do about the cop following us?"

"Maybe I'll just have a talk with him and see what it is they want. Brace yourself."

She pushed back into the seat, braced one hand on the armrest, the other on the dash. He hit the brakes, bringing the car to a rubber-burning, tire-squealing abrupt halt.

Behind them more tires squealed. The car charged up so close their headlights disappeared from the rearview mirror. Marissa held her breath. When there was no crash, she relaxed. The car hadn't slammed into theirs. Thank God.

A car door slammed hard. Whoever was in the car—presumably a cop—was getting out. Lacon drew his weapon, held it on his lap.

There was a knock at his window, followed by a detective's shield being pressed against the glass, and Marissa sagged with relief.

Lacon powered down his window. "What can I do for you, Detective?"

The man leaned down and peered into the car. *Detective Nader.* He glared at them. "We need to have a conference, Mr. Traynor."

We? Only then did Marissa realize a man was standing outside her door, too.

"There's a coffee shop over on Clark that's still open," Lacon suggested. "We'll meet you there." He hit the accelerator and took off, leaving the two detectives standing on the street in the dark.

"Do you think they're involved, like Waller?" She put her hand to her chest and ordered her heart to stop its pounding. She needed to calm down.

"I don't know, but we'll play along and see what we find out."

The short drive to the coffee shop allowed Marissa to collect herself. Whatever Nader and Watts wanted, she needed to at least appear calm. No doubt they had followed them from Anastasia's place. Should she tell them what she'd seen so far? She couldn't be sure.

When Lacon parked, she asked, "Will Michaels be watching?"

"He will, and then he'll follow us back to the safe house."

Marissa was impressed with the Colby Agency all over again. She was immensely grateful Eva had referred her to them.

She considered Lacon's profile. She was grateful for the recommendation and a whole lot more. Whatever happened when this was over, this man had shown her that she could feel again...that she should trust herself completely. She hadn't done that in a long time.

Lacon Traynor was one of those guys that girls dreamed about meeting. When it came to knights in shining armor, he was the real deal. The thought made her smile.

The coffee shop was quiet. Only a handful of patrons were scattered around the small dining area. Lacon ordered two black coffees and found them a table as far away from the few customers as possible. Nader and Watts were given coffee on the house for being members of Chicago PD. They wove through the tables and joined them. Both looked as weary as Marissa felt. Their long day showed in their rumpled suits and bleary eyes. She really hoped these two could be trusted and weren't on Anastasia's payroll.

"You two have a hot date tonight?" Nader asked as he settled into a chair.

"I'm sure you know where we were," Lacon said. "Whatever you have to say, say it. No games. We're tired of games. Especially games initiated by the police."

"We just wanted to give you an update." Nader sipped his coffee.

"Yeah," Watts echoed, "we thought you might want to know."

Lacon glanced at the clock on the wall. "It's after eleven at night—whatever you need to tell us couldn't have waited until morning?"

Watts shrugged. "It isn't like we got you out of bed." He sent a knowing glance at Marissa. "You don't mind hearing news about your late husband, do you, Doctor?"

Marissa fisted her hands together in her lap so no one would see them shaking. "What news?"

"He was drugged with the same one used on you," Nader announced.

An ache pierced her chest. "So he was unconscious when he was shot?"

Watts nodded. "Most likely."

Marissa was glad he hadn't suffered. "So, are you ruling me out as a suspect?" Anastasia's promise reverberated inside her, but she doubted he could possibly work that fast. This new development had to be coincidence. Or maybe Anastasia had already heard what the police had learned, and that was why he'd offered to get her name cleared. She had never met such a cunning monster.

"Well, it's not quite that simple," Nader said. "We have a few more things to work out, but you definitely dropped considerably down our short list."

That was something. She nodded but didn't go so far as to say thank you.

"I do have one question." Nader leaned back in his

chair. "Why would you be visiting Anastasia at his home? The only people we see going in and out of his private residence are those closely associated with him. This has been nagging at me all evening, Dr. Frasier. You see," he leaned forward once more, propped his arms on the table, "I really want to believe you're one of the good ones, but this looks awfully suspicious."

She met Lacon's gaze. How did she answer that question? She hoped he had picked up on how lost she was here.

"Gentlemen—" Lacon leaned into the table as Nader had "—our mutual enemy invited Dr. Frasier for dinner. Is there a law against having dinner?"

Watts snickered. "Depends upon who you're dining with."

Lacon looked from one to the other. "You see, we're receiving mixed signals from the folks in your department. Maybe you expect us to tell you all our secrets and what we were doing tonight, but I'm afraid we just can't trust you on that level. Dr. Frasier's protection is my top priority."

"What mixed signals?" Nader demanded in a furious whisper.

"Well—" Lacon leaned even closer to him "—you might want to ask Chief Waller about that."

Nader and Watts exchanged a look. "All right." Nader glanced around the shop. "Lookie here. Me and Watts, we know there's trouble in the department where Anastasia is concerned, but we're not part of that trouble. In fact, we don't know anyone who is."

"But what we do know—" Watts joined the huddle

"—is that someone way higher up the food chain is, as they say, thick as thieves with him."

Marissa wanted to just blurt out all that she knew. It would be so easy to trust them and tell them everything she and Lacon suspected so far, but Chief Staten had instructed Victoria to pass along the advice that Lacon and Marissa should not trust anyone but her. At least until she figured this out. Marissa felt certain the woman was still grappling with the idea that a man at Waller's level could be bought.

"Well," Lacon said, "we appreciate that you fellows are good cops, but you've got to understand our position. We're just trying to stay alive."

Nader gave a nod. "I can understand that. I'm just saying that if you happen to learn something we need to know, you can feel comfortable calling us." He looked to Marissa then. "You have our number."

"I do." There was a card somewhere in her purse.

"The bottom line is," Watts said, "someone—and we all know who that someone likely is—broke into your home, drugged you and your ex, then put him in your bed and killed him. I'm just a little confused as to why you'd want to break bread with the man and not give us a heads-up."

Marissa held the man's gaze, anger rushing into her throat. How dare these two accuse her of such a thing when she was only doing what she believed she had to do?

"Sometimes…" She hesitated to steady her voice.

"Sometimes," Lacon agreed, "you do what you have to do because no one else can do it for you."

Nader nodded somberly. "I would just hate to see you follow the same path your ex followed. It'd be a shame for that to happen."

"I can guarantee you both," Lacon assured, "that I'm not going to allow Dr. Frasier to get hurt."

Marissa shook her head. "You shouldn't worry about me, Detective. I have no plans to emulate any of the mistakes my ex-husband made in the final years of his life."

Nader withdrew his cell phone. "We found a couple of guys in a Dumpster over off Kildare. We thought one or both might be connected to your dinner date. Have you seen either one of these men before?"

Lacon stared at the screen before Nader turned it toward Marissa and showed her first one and then another photo. Fear tightened her throat. The first had been the man with the two gunshot wounds that she hadn't been able to save. The other was the man who'd suffered the laceration across his abdomen—the one who'd been alive when Anastasia's men had taken him from that storeroom.

Lacon pushed back his chair and stood. "Good night, gentlemen."

Marissa couldn't take her eyes from the screen even as Lacon rounded the table and stood behind her chair, waiting for her to follow his lead. A dozen things she could have said whirled in her head as she rose from her chair, her legs shaky, but none of those things felt right. Instead, she turned and walked out of the coffee shop with Lacon.

He was the only person she trusted in all this.

Colby Safe House, Monday, July 2, 12:50 a.m.

LACON PLACED HIS weapon on the bedside table. He couldn't remember the last time he'd been this pissed off. He shouldered out of his jacket and pitched it on a chair.

He'd given Michaels an update on the drive back. Like Lacon, the senior investigator couldn't get right with the timing of the visit from the detectives. How the hell could they have known about the invitation from Anastasia? It wasn't like they could have followed them from the safe house.

There was always the chance that Nader and Watts had made it a personal mission to watch Anastasia as often as their work schedule would allow. They obviously understood that Bauer's death was on Anastasia, not to mention a truckload of other murders.

Both men from the scene at the old store were dead. At least now Lacon understood why the tracking device he'd tucked in the one guy's pocket had never left the neighborhood. Nader had shown them the photos of the bodies. Anastasia's men had apparently executed the man with the superficial knife wound.

Marissa had been devastated all over again by the photos. He'd watched the tears fill her eyes before she closed herself in her room. For that and so many other things, he wanted to rip Anastasia's arms from his body and beat him to death with them. Even a slow, torturous death wouldn't come close to covering what Anastasia deserved.

"Son of a bitch." He yanked his shirt free of his jeans

and started unbuttoning it. He wanted to hurt Vito Anastasia like he'd never wanted to hurt anyone before. Lacon understood that he had crossed the line so far he couldn't even see it anymore, much less get back to the other side. If he messed up and Issy got hurt...

"Idiot." Hopping on one foot, he dragged off a boot, tossed it aside. He pulled his backup piece from the other boot, left it on the bedside table and tugged off the other boot the same way. One by one, he peeled off his socks and flung them at the chair.

He exhaled a big breath wrought with frustration and reached for his fly. A knock at the door stopped him in the middle of the task.

One, two, three—he counted to five, reminded himself of his duty in all this, and ordered his body to relax before crossing the room. At the door he stood there, mentally repeating the words—*This is a case. She is a client. The agency's client.* His job was to protect her. Not take her to bed. Not get all tangled up emotionally with her.

Don't screw this up any further.

He opened the door, and she stood there in a T-shirt and nothing else—at least nothing else he could see—staring up at him. "I can't sleep."

"Would you like a glass of wine? Maybe a vodka on the rocks?" He would be more than happy with either one or both. Despite his best efforts, his gaze slid down her body, along those long legs and back up to the nipples jutting against the thin fabric of the T-shirt. He was pretty sure a whole bottle of vodka couldn't quench his thirst right now, or keep him from going any stupider than he'd already gone.

You have so screwed this up.

She shook her head and a tear slid down one cheek.

Oh hell. He pulled her into his arms and held her tight against him. The feel of her soft cheek against his chest made him weak as a kitten.

Damn. Damn. Damn.

"Hey now. We'll get you through this. It might take a little more time, but I'll keep you safe until we do."

She turned her face up to his. "I trust you completely. You're the only person I can trust." Another tear trekked down her cheek.

Holy hell, he was in trouble here. He swallowed back the warning he probably should have given her—*Don't trust me at the moment*. He couldn't even trust himself right now.

"Let's go downstairs and get you a nightcap. That'll help you sleep better."

She shook her head. "I don't want anything to drink."

He held his breath, his heart pounding so hard he was certain she felt the effect she was having on him.

"I want *you*."

"Issy."

She went up on her tiptoes and kissed his mouth. He froze. Told himself to resist. Warned himself not to take advantage of her vulnerability.

One soft hand slid inside his jeans. He growled. "Whoa, now."

She ignored him, her fingers reaching and finding

his dick that was hard as a rock. He was doomed. She squeezed him. He shuddered. "Issy."

Her mouth latched on to his right nipple. She sucked hard. He blinked repeatedly. Struggled to get air into his lungs. With every ounce of willpower he possessed, he pulled her away, those warm fingers slipping away from his dick.

"You're killing me here."

Her green eyes sparkled with desire. "You're an adult. I'm an adult. I don't see the problem." She rested her palms against his chest, and his entire body reacted.

"My objectivity is already compromised," he confessed. "I can't risk making a mistake with your safety."

She shook her head. "I don't understand. Are you saying because you got upset every time Anastasia touched me or stood too close to me that your reaction was a bad thing?"

Irritation—at himself—spiked inside him. "Yeah. That's what I'm saying."

"I see." Her hands fell away from him, but her gaze locked on his. "I'll need the number for that Ian Michaels guy who serves as your backup."

A frown tugged at his brow. "Why do you need his number?" He'd be happy to give it to her and all but... why?

"Because you're fired." She braced her hands on her hips. "If you feel compromised by this—" she gestured from her to him "—then you're fired."

He had to admit he hadn't expected that reaction. "I'll call him right now, if that's what you want."

He felt for his phone, remembered that it was in the

pocket of his jacket. His hands fell to his sides, mostly because he suddenly felt sick to his stomach. "You really want to fire me?"

"No, Lacon. I want to make love with you, but you feel that would compromise you even more and—"

He hushed her with his mouth. Her arms went around his neck and he lifted her into his arms. He kicked the door shut and carried her to the bed. His mind was on fire, his body aching for her. She'd bested him and there was nothing he could do to stop this rush toward crash and burn.

He wanted her.

All of her. Now. This minute. He pulled off her T-shirt, lost his breath at the sight of her naked body. "Man alive." She was so beautiful.

She came up on her knees, matching his stance. "First, I just want to touch you."

Taking her time, she touched his face, traced the line of his jaw, the hollows of his eyes, the shape of his lips. When he could move, he did the same, touching her face, memorizing every beautiful detail. His fingers toyed with the shell of her ears, tugged at those lush red curls. They traced each other's throats. Shoulders. Arms. Fingers. They held their hands up, palm to palm, her creamy-white skin against his rougher tanned skin. Just touching her overwhelmed him.

"My turn," he whispered.

He backed off the bed, shucked his jeans and then returned to her. He ushered her down onto the comforter and learned the rest of her body all over again. His mouth traced a path over her breasts. He sucked each nipple until she begged him to finish. Her body writhed beneath his touch as he kissed his way down her flat belly and to that sweet spot between her soft thighs.

He made her come with his tongue, then he did it again with his fingers. Every part of him was hard with need, and she was everything he needed.

"No more," she murmured. "I want you inside me."

He moved into position, nudged into her hot, wet opening just an inch or two then he held still and watched her come a third time.

When she was done, he got started, pushing all the way inside, making her scream his name.

He brought her to the edge once more, then he sat back on his heels, pulling her with him, forcing himself deeper inside her. She gasped, those pink lips damp from their kisses, her green eyes glazed with pleasure. He rocked her back and forth until she found that instinctive rhythm in this new position. When those sweet muscles deep inside her tightened on him again, he bent forward and lost himself to the final thrusts that would take him over that edge with her.

When they had caught their breath, he held her tight. Never wanted to let go.

Chapter Eleven

9:30 a.m.

Using Lacon's sculpted chest as her pillow, Marissa propped her chin on her hands and smiled at him. "I want to hear more."

He laughed. She felt it rumble through his chest. She loved the sound of his laugh.

"My sister is going to be completely embarrassed about all the stories I've told." He stroked her hair. "She has kids of her own now. She'll swear to you that she never participated in any of those sneaky pranks."

His words tugged at something deep in Marissa's chest. It sounded as if he expected that she would meet his family. No matter how very often she reminded herself that this time was not real, not a foreshadowing of a future together, some part of her simply refused to accept it. Yet the rest of her fully understood that this was only a shared moment trapped between tragedy and uncertainty. Survival was encoded in human DNA, the mind programmed to sort through and to find the most optimistic possibilities and to take them.

She propped a smile into place. "You have my word. I will never tell."

He cupped her face, his thumb sliding across her cheek, his gaze serious now. "You are so beautiful."

They'd gotten up at three this morning and eaten, then they'd come back to bed and made love again. And again after that. They'd fallen asleep in each other's arms. He'd made breakfast around seven, and then they'd ended up back in his bed again. Maybe they would spend the day here hiding from the world.

Tomorrow was soon enough to face reality.

"You make me feel beautiful."

He pulled her upward, drawing her mouth to his. He tasted like rich coffee and the sweet jam he'd spread on his toast. Her hands rested on his hot skin, and her body relaxed along the length of his.

His cell phone rattled on the table next to his side of the bed. He groaned.

She wanted to tell him not to answer it because she wasn't ready to let go of this moment, but she rolled onto her back instead and closed her eyes against the intrusion.

"Traynor." He listened for a bit. "You're sure about that?" More listening. "Glad to hear it." A few seconds more of his silence, and then the indistinct murmur of the caller's voice. "All right. Thank you."

She held her breath as he tossed the phone back onto the table.

"That was Detective Nader."

Marissa sat up. Feeling naked at the mention of the

detective's name, she pulled her knees to her chest to cover her bare breasts. "Did he have news?"

Lacon trailed a finger down her leg, drew a circle around her ankle. "He did." His gaze met hers. "The prints of the two guys they found in the Dumpster came up a match to the ones in your bedroom. So you're no longer a suspect in Bauer's murder. They're now looking to some element of organized crime—considering the two dead thugs are known players."

"We can connect those two to Anastasia." Hope bloomed in her chest. "We can take him down."

Lacon sighed. "I wish it were that easy. We can tell the police what we saw, what we did. We can tell them it was Anastasia who told you to do it. But we can't prove it. If the goal is to take him down, we need evidence."

He was right. Damn it. At least one part of the nightmare was over. Yet the relief she had expected would not come. The worry on Lacon's face told her he wasn't relieved either. The fact that she had tried to help those two made her angry. They had drugged her and killed her husband, and she'd felt bad she couldn't save them. She wanted to be glad they were dead but she couldn't bring herself to have so little regard for human life. What she understood with complete certainty was that those two men had been sacrificed.

She hated Vito Anastasia.

"Anastasia handed the police those two men to keep his promise to me."

Lacon nodded. "He sacrificed them to prove a point to you."

She pressed her forehead to her knees and fought

back the damned tears. She was sick of crying. Sick of feeling the guilt for things out of her control. "I want to be grateful they're dead. I want to feel good about it. What kind of person does that make me?"

"This isn't your fault, Issy. What you're experiencing is your response to the perfectly orchestrated machinations of an egomaniac. You are the victim, not those two thugs who chose their own destiny."

She lifted her head and met his gaze once more. "How will I ever be free of him?"

He didn't respond, because they both knew the answer.

The only way to stop a man like Anastasia was to kill him.

Hampden Court, Noon

THE ONE UPSIDE to the news from the detectives was that her home had been released from evidence. The exterior signs that it had been a crime scene were now gone. No more yellow tape, no red warning bulletin taped to the door. But inside was a whole different story.

Dust from the search for fingerprints was everywhere. Drawers and shelves were disorganized from the rummaging of the police. Upstairs, the sheets from her bed and the pillows had been taken to the lab, so the bare mattress with its glaring round bloodstain was all that remained of where she had slept her last night in her home.

"We can call someone to remove the mattress and

have a new one delivered," Lacon offered. "Pillows, too. Just tell me whether you want soft or firm."

She nodded. "That would be good. Soft. Definitely soft."

He checked the brand of her mattress, did a quick search on Google and made the calls. She wandered around the room, surveying her things as if they were foreign objects. It didn't feel like home anymore. How would she live here again?

"There's a service we use frequently that can clean everything up for you," he offered once his other calls were complete.

"No." She shook her head. "I'll do it."

She didn't want anyone else here, touching her things. If there was any possibility of her ever feeling at home again in this place, the effort had to start somewhere.

"Sounds like we have our work cut out for us." He gave her a wink. "I can handle myself surprisingly well with a mop."

"I think maybe I'll have to see that one to believe it," she teased.

Downstairs, they raided the laundry room for supplies. When Lacon pulled on a pair of plastic gloves that went halfway up his forearms, she had to laugh.

"You know," he said, ignoring her, "after my mother died, my sister and I usually got stuck with the housekeeping chores." He shrugged. "We were the youngest. My older brothers were needed in the barn or the pastures. Doing all the fun stuff."

"You looking for sympathy, tough guy?"

"No, ma'am." He gave her another of those winks that made her want to smile despite this awful mess.

"Where do you want to start?" She hefted her bucket of supplies. "While you tell me about your terrible childhood, I mean."

He pointed up. "Did you ever have to wash dishes for a whole crew of ranch hands?" He shook his head. "Not a walk in the park."

"My mother," Marissa explained as they trudged up the stairs, "was a throwback housewife from the fifties. She wore the apron and made cookies every day. Whatever shopping needed to be done, she took care of it while I was at school. Whenever I was home, she was home. The only exception was if the school needed her."

"Mine was the same way until she got sick."

At the top of the stairs, Marissa waited until he stood in front of her. "That must have been really hard. Kids need their mothers, even tough little boys."

One corner of his sexy mouth hitched up. "You have got to stop tempting me, Dr. Marissa Frasier."

Despite the fact that he smiled, she heard the sadness in his voice. He was right. This was a case. She was his job. If they were lucky, it would be over soon. She shouldn't keep prying into his personal life. In a few days he would be long gone.

And then the real hurt would come.

A glutton for punishment, Marissa nudged him into telling her more stories of his childhood while they cleaned. His stories kept her mind off the one currently unfolding in her life. She could not recall ever having seen a man more handsome in yellow plastic gloves and brandishing a bottle of furniture polish.

"Now, you're prodding all these stories out of me," he said as they settled in the kitchen for a late lunch. "When am I going to hear more about your childhood? You and your brother must have had plenty of adventures."

She smiled as she nibbled a cracker. The bread had expired so they had to make do with crackers and cheese. "I was the good girl. Never got into trouble at home or at school."

His gaze narrowed. "I find that difficult to believe."

"It's true. I spent all my time keeping my little brother out of trouble."

"No slipping out of the house with your friends after your parents were in bed, or sneaking a beer when no one was looking?"

"Nope. My brother did all those things, but not me. I was too busy studying and watching out for him."

"Is that why you stayed with Bauer as long as you did?"

He asked the question so casually, in between bites of cheese. "He was nice. Always in need of a study partner. I never thought about it that way, but I suppose the relationship felt comfortable because I was taking care of him the way I had my brother."

"He never took care of you?" Lacon searched her eyes, as if the answer were immensely important to him.

"Maybe." She shrugged. "In his own way. Not with romance, per se, no flowers or chocolates or spontaneous dates. But at one time we enjoyed talking about work."

Lacon's expression was pained. "He didn't take care of you, Issy. You deserved a lot better then, and you do now."

"My brother told me that from the moment I announced William and I were getting married." She shrugged. "I didn't listen because it felt good *enough*, and there just wasn't time to do better. I was so busy, it was easier to take what was right in front of me than to try to find time to look for something different."

He tucked a wisp of hair behind her ear. "Life gets in the way sometimes."

"I would never have imagined he would do the things he's done the past two years. I thought I knew him." She shook her head. "I guess I really didn't." That was the saddest truth of all.

"Some people are good at hiding the blackness that lurks in their soul."

He was right. She had beaten herself up plenty of times for the bad decisions she'd made with William. It was time to get past those mistakes and look to the future. And she sincerely hoped this man would be a part of her future.

His turn to talk about the more painful part of his past. "What was your fiancée like?"

He ate the last cracker on his plate, seemed to mull over her question. When he'd washed it down with the grape juice that was all she had in the house, he said, "She was kind and sweet. Pretty." He smiled. "My boss at the bonding agency where I worked warned me not to get too attached. He knew how much I loved people projects."

His words disrupted the rhythm of her heart. "People projects?"

He shrugged. "I was always helping someone. A beggar who lived on the street. A kid who just needed a father figure. A woman whose husband abused her. It was like my hobby. Helping folks is a good thing but I didn't stop at helping. I had to get emotionally involved. Attached, my sister called it. Sherry—that was her name, my fiancée—we got so tangled up with each other, I couldn't see my hand in front of my face. I should have realized what that bastard would do the first chance he got. I knew his kind. But I was blinded by love—the idea of it anyway. She died, and I will carry that burden to my grave. I should have paid better attention."

Marissa felt as if she'd been slapped in the face. He could be describing their relationship to this point—or whatever it was. She felt ill. She reached for her water and tried to dampen her parched throat.

"I was young," he went on, seemingly oblivious to her shock. "I didn't recognize the difference between infatuation and love, and the need to protect someone versus the need to be with someone."

She tried to think of something to say, but no words would come.

"I have never allowed myself to get personally involved with work again." He set down his glass and looked directly at her. "Until now."

Somehow she forced the words out around the lump

in her throat. "We're both experienced adults. This isn't the same."

"No." He stared so intently at her that she ached with the weight of it. "It's not the same."

The doorbell echoed through the house. She blinked away the damned tears that crowded into her eyes. How foolish had she been? She'd allowed her feelings to go unchecked. William's death had made her vulnerable. Lacon had tried to warn her but she hadn't listened.

He stood, drew the weapon from his waistband at the small of his back. "Stay put. I'll see who it is."

When he'd headed for the door, Marissa closed her eyes and put her shaking hands over her mouth to hold back a sob. She was a mess. Her life was a mess. A great deal of the fallout bombarding her just now was William's fault, but *this*—this emotional entanglement—was hers alone. She had no one to blame but herself.

She drew in a deep breath. She was no little girl, no young woman so involved in her career she couldn't think straight. She was a grown woman, a physician. Acting like a foolish jilted girl would be ridiculous. What she and Lacon shared was sex, mutual need. Nothing more. It was perfectly healthy to enjoy sex between consenting adults. This did not have to be complicated for either of them. His attention and tenderness had helped her get through this unspeakably difficult time. It wasn't a big deal.

Keep telling yourself that, Issy.

Lacon was suddenly standing in front of her. The abrupt pounding at her door made her jump. "It's Anastasia."

Her heart swelled into her throat. "Your car is out front. He knows we're here."

He nodded. "Stay out of sight. I'll talk to him."

She nodded and went through the kitchen to the laundry room. She kept the door open a crack so she could hear.

A few seconds later she heard Lacon say, "What can I do for you?"

The strength in his voice warmed her. All else aside, she was so grateful to have him standing between her and Anastasia. He was a good man. A loyal man. Tears burned her eyes again and she blinked them back. Whatever happened in the future, she was immensely thankful for this time with him. For his strength, his honesty and every single moment of the rest.

"I'd like to speak with Marissa."

The other man's voice made her shudder with revulsion.

"She's not available at this time," Lacon said.

Marissa held her breath, hoped he would leave.

"I'll wait."

There were footsteps and then the unmistakable squeak of leather. He was staying. Damn him.

"I think maybe you didn't hear me," Lacon said. "She's not available, now or later. You should go before I get frustrated."

Marissa pressed her hand more firmly over her mouth. The silence terrified her.

"I'm certain you've misunderstood me," Anastasia countered. "I will wait to see her. If you take issue with that, then you may sort it out with my associates."

How many did he have with him?

"Would you like to step outside, Mr. Traynor?"

Another voice. Male. Hard.

Enough.

Marissa opened the door and walked back through the kitchen and into the living room. Two men hovered around Lacon. Anastasia sat on the sofa.

"I'm a little busy," she said to the man in the sleek black suit now staring at her. "The police left my house in a mess. I won't feel at home until everything's back in order. Perhaps we can visit another time, Mr. Anastasia."

"Vito," he reminded her as he stood. "The reason I stopped by won't take long."

Lacon pushed between the two thugs and came to her side.

Anastasia glanced at him as he moved ever closer to Marissa. "I thought you might want to thank me for clearing your name. It was quite a sacrifice, as I'm sure you've learned. Two of my men died for the honor."

Fury blasted through her. "What a waste." She held his stare. "I'm certain I would have been exonerated in any event. I'm touched that you felt compelled to intervene on my behalf, but I can assure you it was a waste of your resources."

Rage flickered in his eyes before he schooled the reaction. "You are a fighter, Marissa Frasier. I've decided that forty-eight hours is far too much time. I will have your answer to my proposition today. Will you accept my proposal?"

If she told him no, he might kill them where they stood. If she said yes...

"As you can imagine, I haven't really had time to consider your proposal. Once I'm resettled in my home, I'm sure I'll be able to think more clearly and focus on where I go from here."

He moved closer still. Next to her Lacon tensed.

"Is there something or someone keeping you from making the right choice, Issy?"

His use of her nickname made her stomach churn. "I make my own decisions, Vito. I thought you would know that by now. Didn't William tell you how stubborn I can be?"

"I will have your answer," he pressed.

Lacon put a hand to the man's chest. "I'm beginning to think you suffer from selective hearing, *Vito*. She said she doesn't have an answer for you."

The other men in the room instantly drew their weapons and aimed them at Lacon. Marissa touched his arm. "It's all right. I think Vito understands."

The glare-off between Lacon and Anastasia lasted another ten disturbing seconds.

Anastasia stepped back from Lacon's firm hand. "You, Mr. Traynor, are pushing your luck."

Lacon dropped his arm to his side and laughed. "I've been pushing my luck my whole life, Anastasia. I don't think you're going to have anything at all to do with changing that. You see, Dr. Frasier is my responsibility. I listen only to her. Until she tells me to back off, I will be in your face. Got it?"

Five pulse-pounding seconds passed before the other

man spoke. He turned his attention to Marissa. "I'll expect your answer before midnight. Do not disappoint me, Issy. You won't like my reaction."

Anastasia turned and walked out. The two men backed out behind him, weapons still trained on Lacon.

When the door closed, he moved lightning fast across the room and locked it. He stepped to the window and checked beyond the shade.

Marissa struggled to remain standing when her knees threatened to give out.

"They're gone."

Lacon turned and started walking toward her. Somehow she couldn't bring herself to move from this spot.

"He isn't going to let me go."

LACON WISHED HE could promise her that Anastasia would eventually move on, turn his attention elsewhere, but he knew that was not true. He'd done more research. The man was like a dog with a bone. Once he set his sights on something, he wouldn't let go until it belonged to him.

"Let's take a break while I update Michaels. Maybe he'll have some news for us."

"You go ahead. I need to stay busy." She rubbed her hands up and down her arms as if she were cold.

He touched her cheek and offered the most reassuring smile he could. "I'll only be a minute."

She nodded and returned to the cleanup work. They'd finished upstairs. She pulled on her gloves and started scrubbing the bookshelves in her living room. Lacon put through the call and brought Michaels up to speed.

He and Victoria had spoken, and her concern was that Anastasia would simply take what he wanted and kill anyone who got in his way. This was his MO, Michaels reminded him. Lacon had come to the same conclusion.

With a warning to get back to the safe house as soon as possible and to be careful, the call ended.

The sooner he helped Issy get through the work down here, the sooner he could coax her into going back to the safe house. She had mentioned staying here, but that was a no-go. She wouldn't like it, but he was confident he could convince her to listen to reason.

By the time the last of the fingerprint dust was cleaned up downstairs, the delivery truck had arrived with her new mattress and taken the old one away. Issy had lit her favorite scented candles to chase away the lingering odor of death. She'd opened a bottle of wine but Lacon had passed on the offer. His instincts were humming. Whatever Anastasia had planned when he didn't hear from her or didn't get the answer he wanted, Lacon wanted to be well prepared.

He tucked in his side of the clean sheet. "I don't think I've ever seen so many books outside a library," he teased.

She smiled, the first since that idiot's visit. "I've always loved reading. Growing up, we spent more time with books than with the television. I've never been able to give one away, so I keep them."

He reached for one of the new pillows and tucked it into place on his side of the bed. "I think you might need to consider a bigger house, maybe with a room to serve as a library."

"I thought about turning the third floor into one but I kind of like having a guest room when my brother visits. How about you, are you a book guy?"

They finished making the bed. "To tell you the truth, I haven't read a book since college. Never enough time."

"What now?" She glanced around the room as if searching for one more chore to do.

"We should head back to the safe house. I can protect you better there."

"What do I do about Anastasia? If I ignore his demand, he'll just come after us."

"We'll figure it out as we go." Lacon smiled, lifted her chin with his knuckle. "I do not want you overanalyzing this. We will figure it out."

She drew away from his touch. "You're probably right. I should pack a few things before we go."

He watched her walk toward the closet, worry nagging at him. He'd said or done something to upset her. When he felt more comfortable about her safety, he would make right whatever he'd done wrong.

Chapter Twelve

"You've got everything?" Lacon picked up the bag she had packed.

Issy stood in the center of her living room looking lost. She had been more quiet than usual the past couple of hours. They'd finished the cleanup and set her home to rights. Every hour that passed seemed to make her draw more into herself. He wanted to ask if he'd said or done something, but the situation was getting far too intense for him to go there now. Keeping his head on straight was crucial.

She finally nodded. "I guess so."

He, on the other hand, was already worried about how he would protect her when she returned to work tomorrow. By morning, Anastasia would be searching the city for her. He would be pissed as hell. No doubt he would come here and also go to the ER where she worked. The bastard would not stop until he found her.

Déjà vu was messing with Lacon's head. Flashes of memory from his attempts to protect Sherry had his gut in knots. *You're older and wiser now.* He hoped like hell the wisdom he had gained over the years would keep him smart and prepared for what he could feel coming.

"You're ready then?"

"I suppose." Issy glanced around one more time before walking toward him. "I'm ready if you are."

"I'll have a look around outside and check the car, then we're off."

"And I'll stay right here until you give me the all clear," she said, repeating his usual order.

They'd been over the way things would go from here. With Anastasia's edict, every move they made out in the open was riskier. He was growing more impatient. And that impatience made him all the more dangerous.

"You got it." Lacon reached for the door.

"You'll let your backup know?"

He gave her a nod. "Always do." He reached for the door once more.

"Wait."

He turned back to her as she pulled her cell phone from her pocket. She stared at the screen. "It's Anastasia."

His heart bumping into a faster rhythm, Lacon nodded. "Answer it."

She took a breath, touched the screen. "Marissa Frasier."

"I need you to make a house call, *Issy.*"

Her gaze collided with Lacon's. He gave her a nod to continue.

"What kind of house call?"

"Based on your previous house calls, you can well imagine. My people work in the most dangerous parts of the city. The reception is not always a positive one.

However, this particular one, I'm sure you can handle quickly."

"What's the address?"

He provided a South Calumet address, thirty-five minutes away on the other side of the river. Lacon instinctively calculated the most direct route.

"I'll go now," she said, her tone weary.

"When you're finished, Issy," Anastasia said, "I need your answer."

The call ended.

Her gaze moved up to Lacon's, worry clouding her green eyes. "We have to go, I know." She shook her head, tears welling in her eyes. "But I don't want to. I don't want to be his puppet again."

For the first time in his career, he second-guessed the decisions he'd made about the case so far. "We could just leave. Get in the car and keep driving."

She smiled sadly. "We could."

For a couple of seconds the possibility crackled between them with such promise. But they both knew running wasn't the answer.

He laughed. "But then we'd just have to be back by tomorrow so you could make your shift at the Edge."

Her smile lightened the tiniest bit. "True." She sighed. "I guess we should just do this thing."

He nodded. "Guess so." He reached for the door once more. "I'll have that look around first—just in case— and then we'll go."

"I'll be waiting for your signal."

His right hand on the grip of his weapon, he moved out the door and down the steps. Sidewalk was clear.

No passengers in any of the parked vehicles as far as he could see. He walked to the car, popped the trunk and dropped her bag inside. He sent Michaels a text with the address of where they were headed, then surveyed the street again as he closed the lid.

He sensed the man behind him before the bastard made a sound.

"Get your hands out where I can see them."

Son of a bitch.

When he didn't obey the command quickly enough, a muzzle bored into the back of his skull.

"Take it easy." Lacon held his hands out on either side of him.

A hand patted his jacket then reached beneath for his weapon. "Let's go back in the house now."

For an instant he considered trying to tackle the guy. There was always the chance the first shot would miss. The trouble was, there were likely two of them, and if he did anything stupid and got himself killed, Issy would be completely at their mercy.

So he did as he was told.

They climbed the steps and walked through the door.

Lacon had cleared the door when Issy screamed.

He pivoted.

The thug's weapon discharged.

Lacon's brain assimilated a number of things simultaneously. Issy had hit the man's arm with something that looked like a fireplace poker. The man with the gun howled in agony. The weapon he'd dropped spun across the floor.

Lacon made a dive for the weapon. He hoped like hell a neighbor would call the cops about the gunfire.

"Leave the weapon or I will shoot her."

Lacon didn't immediately remove his hand from the gun on the floor. He shifted his attention to the new man in the room, the one holding the muzzle of his weapon against Issy's temple. The first guy had snatched the poker from her and stood glaring at her as if he wanted to deliver a little payback.

Damn it all to hell. Lacon pushed to his feet, hands in the air. "You probably should call your boss. He wants Dr. Frasier to take care of a situation over on South Calumet."

The two men exchanged a look, and then the one with the gun on Issy laughed. "That was for your backup. He'll be rushing over to South Calumet, but not the two of you. Now, let's go."

The guy with the poker strode toward Lacon, nudged him with it. "Back off."

When Lacon had taken a couple of steps back, the bastard reclaimed his weapon and tossed the poker aside. "Anybody else does something stupid, and I'm putting a bullet in *your* head." He pointed to Lacon. "You got that?" he growled at Issy.

She glowered at him. "Got it."

The younger thug took Issy out the back door first. The older guy trailed Lacon, nudging him regularly with the muzzle of his weapon. They walked down the narrow driveway Lacon had opted not to use for parking when they arrived today to avoid the possibility of his car being trapped in the event of a takeover exactly like this one.

So much for trying to cover all the bases.

Once they reached the street that ran behind Issy's home, they made a right and walked half a block to a black sedan.

"You." The man behind him jabbed Lacon in the ribs with his weapon. "Get in the front passenger seat."

The other guy forced Issy into the back and slid in beside her.

When they were all in the car, the guy in the back warned, "Keep in mind, Traynor, you make one wrong move, she gets it."

"Give me your cell phones," the driver demanded.

Lacon handed over his phone. The guy tossed it out the window.

"Let's have it," the guy in the back snapped at Issy.

A couple seconds later his window went down, and Issy's phone hit the ground.

Lacon should never have allowed her to leave the safe house. He shouldn't have allowed her to go along with the police in hopes of trapping Anastasia.

The problem was, none of those choices had been his. Issy had wanted to take Anastasia down. She had known that he would never stop coming after her as long as he was out there and still drawing breath.

Lacon had every intention of changing one or both of those things.

North Burling Street

IT WAS DARK by the time they pulled through the gate onto Anastasia's compound. Marissa imagined they had waited for the cover of dark to approach his home. They'd driven around far longer than necessary to come straight here from her place by any reasonable route.

The thug who'd dragged her out of the car and was now gripping her arm ushered her across the expansive yard. He was still favoring his right arm, which she supposed was why he held on to her with his left hand. She wished she had hit him harder and on the head. If she'd moved faster, maybe Lacon would have been able to grab his weapon before the other man could stop him.

She glanced around, wishing there was a full moon tonight. The landscape lighting she had noticed on her and Lacon's previous visit was missing tonight. The sound of the water in the reflecting pond dribbled in the darkness, adding another layer of eeriness to the fear expanding inside her. Her heart beat faster and faster as they neared the rear of the house. She glanced over her shoulder twice, making sure Lacon and the other thug were still behind them.

She was going to get him killed. William's stupidity and her plummet into that same stupidity were going to cost this man his life. She had to do something. He was doing his job, yes. He was aware of the danger, yes. But the potential end result wasn't right any way she looked at it. She could not allow this to happen.

Once through the French doors, the thugs ushered the two of them away from the main living area and down a long hall. Finally, they crowded into what appeared to be a storage room. Shelves loaded with dry goods and household supplies lined the walls. The bastard clutching her arm reached for a box of detergent, but when he moved it a portion of the shelving slid away, revealing a staircase.

Just like in a bad movie. How would Lacon's backup, Ian Michaels, or the police find them here?

At the bottom of the stairs was a fair-sized room that looked somewhat like a small den. The typical U-shaped sectional sofa was arranged atop thick beige carpet. Rich paneled walls gave the basement room a more classic look. A large television and a fireplace sat on opposite ends of the space. On each of the other two walls was a door. One might have gone to a bathroom and the other maybe to a bedroom. Except the one on the farthest wall from where they now stood had a keypad and looked more like a panic room door. That was the direction in which they headed, and dread swelled like a rock inside her stomach.

"Where is Vito?" She jerked at the man's hold. "I need to speak with him."

"In due time," the thug said. The keypad had the usual numbers for entering a code, but it also had a biometric pad. The man pressed his thumb there and the door swung inward.

He pushed Marissa inside. Digging in her heels, she didn't make it easy.

Lacon was shoved in right behind her.

"Make yourselves at home," the thug who'd dragged her here said. "For now." He laughed until the door closed, blocking the awful sound and any possibility of escape.

"You okay?" Lacon touched her arm.

She stared at the angry red marks the man's grip had created. "He didn't hurt me. Just made me mad as hell."

He pulled her into his arms and hugged her. "Don't try to be a hero, Issy. Just do what they ask until help comes."

She drew back and stared up at him, searching his pale brown eyes. With every fiber of her being, she had feared this moment would come. "How do you know they'll be able to find us?"

He smiled. "It's the Colby Agency. They always do."

She couldn't do this. She should never have involved anyone else. Somehow she had to rectify that mistake.

"Lacon, I appreciate how well you've taken care of me the past few days." She drew out of his embrace and squared her shoulders, hanging on to the last threads of her courage. "But I don't want you to do anything else. I want you to just stop. Right now."

"What?" The word came out on a choked laugh. "Are you firing me again?"

"Yes. I'm firing you as my bodyguard." She folded her arms over her chest in hopes he wouldn't notice the way her body had started to tremble. "You…" She cleared the emotion from her throat. "You are not to take any additional measures to defend me in any way. From this moment, your only concern is staying alive."

For ten or so seconds he stared at her as if he were too stunned to speak. To escape his daunting stare, she allowed herself to look around the room and fully assess the situation for the first time. It was far larger than the room outside that door. No warm paneling or soft carpet. Just cold concrete walls and floors. There were only two chairs, and each had straps to secure a person's arms and legs. Her body trembled harder when she considered the steel table, much like the one found in an operating room, complete with straps for securing whoever might end up stretched out on it.

Nearby, a glass-front cabinet displayed drug vials, very similar to those found in the dispensary at the Edge, along its top shelf. The other shelves were filled with what could only be called the tools of torture. Scalpels, knives, a hammer, small forceps, a hacksaw and a multitude of others she couldn't fully see.

She had to look away. It didn't help. Her gaze next landed on a heavy chain that hung from the ceiling. The hook on the end suggested it was for hanging something or...*someone*. Another small table, this one with wheels, sat close by. A control box of some sort with various attached cables sat atop it. She could only imagine what it was.

"Did you have anything else you wanted to say?" Lacon stared at her, his hands resting on his lean hips.

Emotion tangled in her throat. "No." She cleared her throat. "I guess that's all I have to say."

He laughed as he, too, took stock of their situation. "Well, you picked a hell of a time to decide to fire me."

A tear escaped her fierce hold, and she swiped at the nuisance. "Sorry. I don't have a lot of experience with this sort of thing."

He grabbed her and pulled her against him. "You can't fire me, Issy," he said, his tone as desperate as the look in his eyes. "This stopped being about work the first time I kissed you."

Those damned tears spilled past her lashes in spite

of all she did to attempt to staunch them. "I do not want you to risk your life for me. Just do whatever they tell you until…until we get out of here. All I need is your word that you'll do as I say."

He smiled and her heart reacted. "I can't promise you that, Issy. We're in this together, and I'm not backing down. I'll do whatever I have to do to keep you safe. That's what people who care about each other do, so don't ask me to do otherwise."

She exhaled a frustrated breath. "Fine. Just don't take any unnecessary risks."

He grunted a sound that couldn't be called an agreement. Before she could argue her point further, he took her by the hand and ushered her along to the cabinet near the steel table. He checked the doors. Locked. She doubted he had expected otherwise.

"Stand back," he ordered.

She moved a few feet away as he turned his back to the cabinet and then elbowed one of the glass doors. The glass shattered. He reached inside and grabbed a knife and the hammer. What in the world would he be able to do with those?

The glass crackled under his boots as he walked back to where she waited. He offered her the hammer. "You have a pretty mean swing, so here you go. A weapon."

Her trembling lips slid into a smile despite the fear and worry spiraling madly inside her. "My brother liked to play cops and robbers when we were kids. Conking him over the head was my favorite part. No matter how many times we played that game, he never resisted, even when he knew that bop on the head was coming."

Grinning, Lacon slid the knife into his waistband. "I think I like your brother." He hugged her again. This time he pressed his lips close to her ear and whispered, "There are cameras. They'll take these weapons away from us when they come back." He drew back a little and kissed her hard on the mouth, his right hand sliding down her back, fingers slipping into her hip pockets. He pulled his mouth from hers and hugged her again and murmured, "I'm hoping they won't find the scalpel I just slid into your back pocket on the right."

The door opened and they drew apart. Lacon grabbed her hand and ushered her behind him. Marissa wished she could think of something to say or do that would somehow change what she feared would happen next.

"Put the weapons down!" the thug she'd whacked with the poker shouted, his weapon trained on Lacon.

The thug's friend waltzed in next, his weapon leveled on Marissa. "Come with me," he ordered.

She shook her head. "Only if he goes, too."

"No can do." He motioned with his weapon for her to come with him. "The boss only wants you."

Fear blasted through her veins. "If you want me, you'll have to come and get me." She gripped the hammer a little tighter.

The one with his weapon aimed at Lacon was taller and older, and he walked closer. "Do as he says or I'll shoot your boyfriend."

Fear exploded in her chest. What the hell did she do now? She divided her attention between the two men coming closer.

"Put the hammer down," Lacon said, "and do like he said."

She swung her gaze to him. "No."

He sent her a desperate but determined look. "You go with him. Don't worry, I'll catch up."

The younger thug grabbed her. She swung the hammer at his head, missed. Tried again to hit him before her pathetic weapon flew from her grasp. His arm went around her waist, and the barrel of his weapon nudged into her temple.

"You behave yourself, Doc, and I won't have to hurt you. Mr. Anastasia wouldn't be too happy about that."

Her eyes stayed on Lacon until the bastard dragged her out the door. She wanted to kill him. She wanted to scream. To cry.

Mostly she wanted to kill Vito Anastasia.

The man hauled her up the stairs and into the long hall that led back into the main living area of the house. She relaxed a little and didn't fight him as much. So far he hadn't checked for any other weapons. *Please don't let him look.*

He stopped at a door before they reached the grand entry hall. She wondered where the fancy butler and the kitchen staff were this evening. Did they all blindly go about their business while their boss did horrific things to their guests? The urge to scream burgeoned in her throat. The need surged with such intensity, it was all she could do to hold back the sound. But she didn't want to do anything that would make this thug angry. The one thing she had on her side was that scalpel.

Maybe that narrow piece of steel would be the miracle she needed.

The thug pushed the door open. The room was empty save a couple of wooden chairs and a video monitor mounted to the white walls. The floor, ceiling and walls were so white they were blinding.

"Sit," the thug ordered.

He pushed her toward one of the chairs, and she hit the floor in front of it on her hands and knees. She ignored the pain in her wrists and knees and climbed into the chair.

"Are you going to behave yourself or do I need to tie you to the damned chair?"

She glared up at him but didn't say a word. "What could I possibly do?"

"Good." He laughed. "I'll be back." He hesitated at the door and pointed to a place in the ceiling where the flow of white ballooned out like a basketball. "That's a camera. We'll be watching every move you make."

There had to be something she could do to stop this. "I want to see Vito. He will not be happy that you're treating me this way."

The man sneered at her. "He knows you're here. You'll see him soon enough. Just relax and enjoy the show."

She frowned. Show? What show?

The monitor on the wall flickered and then the image cleared. The scene on the screen was from the basement. Lacon and the older thug were still facing off—the thug's gun aimed at Lacon… Lacon still holding the knife.

"Oh my God." She stood, moved closer to the monitor.

There was no sound, so she couldn't hear what they were saying. The man with the gun gestured to the steel table. Lacon placed the knife there and backed away. The thug picked it up and pitched it aside. Then he gestured to the table again. This time Lacon hopped onto the table's edge and then lay down.

"No." Her hand went to her mouth.

The man made another motion with the gun and said something else she couldn't hear.

Lacon fastened the first of the straps, securing himself to the table.

Marissa touched the screen and began to scream.

Chapter Thirteen

The door opened and Marissa's personal thug charged into the room. "What the hell is wrong with you?" he demanded.

She pointed at the monitor. "If your friend hurts my friend, then I'm done here. My answer to Anastasia's proposal will be no."

The bastard laughed. "Don't you get it yet, Doc? No isn't an option."

The door behind him was open. If she could only get past him and to a phone. She turned back to the monitor and started to scream again.

He stormed across the expanse of tile that lay between them and reached up to turn off the monitor. That's when she bolted.

She ran for the entry hall. The front door was right there. With the house so close to the street, all she had to do was get outside and scream at the top of her lungs. Someone would surely hear her. All she needed was one person to call the police and report the disturbance. The Colby Agency would be looking for them already.

Afraid to slow down as she reached the entry hall,

she slammed against the door and twisted the lock. Her fingers curled around the door handle. Her heart swelled. Get out the door and—

"Open that door and your friend dies."

Her fingers stilled on the handle. Her heart thundered; her blood roared in her ears. But he was right... if she did this, they would kill Lacon. He probably had a gun pointed at her head even as he spoke. She had banked on the idea that he wouldn't shoot her for fear of Anastasia's wrath.

She dropped her hands to her sides and turned to face him. "I want to see Vito."

As if he'd been waiting just around the corner listening, Anastasia stepped into view. "Do we have a problem, Issy?"

"We need to talk." She steadied herself, met his gaze with defiance in her own. "Privately."

He smiled. "At last."

With a wave of his hand he dismissed the thug, then he gestured for her to come to him. Forcing one foot in front of the other, she moved closer and closer to the monster who would forevermore play the lead in all her nightmares—assuming she lived through this night.

With a hand at the small of her back, he ushered her toward the grand staircase.

"We'll have more privacy upstairs."

Doing all within her power to prevent her body from shaking with the new fear spreading through her, she ascended the stairs at his side. She needed him to believe she wanted to cooperate. If she could somehow barter Lacon's release, she might have to bide her time

until he and the Colby Agency figured out the best way
to rescue her.

As much as the idea sickened her, she would do whatever was necessary until then.

"Did the situation on South Calumet work itself out?"
she asked. Her voice was a little thinner than she would
have liked, but at least it wasn't shaking.

He smiled at her. Her stomach cramped with disgust.
"It did. Thank you for asking."

Upstairs, the house was as elegantly decorated as
downstairs. How was it such a vicious man could have
such opulent taste?

The spacious corridor went left and right. He di-
rected her to the right. At the end of the corridor stood
double doors. Renewed terror licked a path up her spine.
His private rooms, which probably included a bedroom.

Stay cool. You can do this. All she needed was one
minute with a phone to call for help. Then maybe both
she and Lacon would be rescued.

He opened the doors to a sitting room. More double
doors that stood beyond the sofa likely led to his more
private rooms. The windows on either side of the generous space offered magnificent views, as well as another opportunity for her. A small occasional chair sat
next to the sofa. She could probably pick it up and hurl
it toward the window. If she succeeded in breaking the
glass, the alarm would likely go off.

Pay attention, Issy. Find the right opportunity.

"Please." He gestured to the sofa. "Make yourself
comfortable and I'll open the champagne. This is reason to celebrate."

She sat down, felt the slim steel in her pocket that didn't give with the move. The scalpel's presence gave her comfort. *Thank you, Lacon.* "I'd like to discuss the terms of our arrangement, but first I have one condition."

The cork popped. "You're a brilliant woman, Issy. I expected you would have certain conditions."

Hearing the sizzle of the bubbly drink overflowing was when she realized that he'd had a bottle of champagne chilling in a silver bucket of ice. Two stemmed glasses sat on the table next to the bucket. He'd prepared for this moment. Asking her to give him an answer had only been another of his games. He had always planned to have his wish, one way or another. The possibility that nothing she said or did would impact how this turned out made her start to shake deep inside.

No. This was the twenty-first century. People didn't get to enslave other people in this country...unless they didn't get caught. Panic burgeoned inside her. She thought of the high-profile victims she'd read about in the news who had been held for years—decades— by men with far fewer resources than Vito Anastasia.

Focus, Issy. No losing hope.

While he poured the bubbly liquid, she collected herself. By the time he joined her at the sofa, she had decided to go with the strategy she'd already begun in her head. She accepted the glass he offered and announced, "This first condition is nonnegotiable."

He savored the drink. "I'm quite curious as to what that condition is."

"Let him go. You let him go and my answer is yes— assuming we agree on a couple of other terms."

He smiled. "By him, you mean your friend—your bodyguard who held you and kissed you like a lover."

She shrugged. "Being a physician is a demanding job. You get lonely. Sometimes a woman as busy as I am needs someone, even if I am paying him for other services. Handy is sometimes the only option." She prayed he didn't see the lie in her words.

He nodded. "I understand. My position is much the same. Loneliness goes with the territory." He draped his arm over the back of the sofa and touched her hair. "But neither of us has to be alone again."

As difficult as it proved, she forced a smile, resisting the need to shudder. "Then you agree to my first condition."

"I will consider it." He finished his glass and set it on the cocktail table. "But I fear there may be a glitch in doing so."

She frowned. "What glitch?"

"I pride myself in my ability to measure a man. This man will not willingly ride off into the sunset, leaving you behind."

"He will do exactly what I tell him to do." If her heart pounded any harder, she was sure he would see it threatening to burst from her chest.

"He'll only bring the authorities and others from his agency, and I fear if that happens you might not stand by our agreement."

"You have my word." She sipped her drink. "Now, if that's settled, let's move on. I'll need to give the Edge a two-week notice. Otherwise my reputation will be damaged, and I've worked too hard to allow that to happen."

Another sip for her dry throat. "I'm going to want four times my current salary. I'm sure that's far more than you paid William but I'm a far better physician than he was, and smarter."

One side of his mouth lifted in a smile. "Your excitement sounds quite convincing, Issy. What changed your mind?"

Keep him talking. Keep him off guard. Lacon's backup would be calling his boss and the police by now. Help would come.

"Oh I'm not finished yet." She placed her glass on the table. "I will not live in that carriage house. Too cramped, too confining. I noticed a very nice town house across the street. It's not for sale, but I'm certain you can take care of that."

He studied her, appeared to be amused. "Either you've considered the situation at length, or you're playing me to buy time." The amusement vanished. "Which is it, Issy?"

"You're right. I've spent a great deal of time pondering my dilemma. Since I don't want to end up like William, and the police don't seem capable of stopping you, why fight the inevitable? I've always considered myself quite pragmatic in matters related to my career and my financial future."

His narrowed gaze relaxed. "Assuming I meet your first condition and your other terms."

"Assuming so, yes."

He stood. Her heart stumbled. She pushed to her feet and followed him to the windows that overlooked the back of his property. *Think!* Whatever was happening to Lacon, she had to stop it now.

"If your people harm him, I'm afraid our negotiations will be over."

Anastasia shifted his attention to her once more. "You present quite the quandary, Issy."

"It's really quite simple. You let him go—I stay."

He reached out, touched the pulse at the base of her throat. "You want me to believe you're calm and confident, that your decision is made. But I can feel your terror, Issy. How am I supposed to trust your words when your body tells me a completely different story?"

"You want me here with you, isn't that right?" She moved nearer to him. "Not just my ability as a physician, but *me*." She held her breath, touched his face, traced the line of his jaw. He stood stone still, but his eyes gave her the answer she sought. She was right. "I'm here and I'm willing to stay."

He smiled, the expression tight, angry. "Do you believe me a fool?"

She fought to keep the trembling at bay. "Why would I think that?"

"I saw the way he kissed you. The way you responded. You will sacrifice yourself for him, and then you will run the first opportunity that presents itself."

She set her hands on her hips. "You had me brought here like a prisoner. I've offered you a deal and you don't seem interested. Why don't you take me back home, and when you make up *your* mind, you can call me."

Every ounce of courage she possessed was required

to turn her back on him and to start walking toward the door.

If he had a weapon, he could draw it right now and shoot her. It was a risk she had to take. Lacon could be dying at this very moment. She had to help him.

A ruthless grip curled around her left arm. "No one walks away from me." He yanked her around to face him. "You will do exactly as I say, or everyone you care about will die, starting with your friend downstairs."

Stay strong. Don't let him see more than he already has.

"I offered to do exactly as you say. I gave you my terms."

"This is not a negotiation, as you appear to believe." His grip tightened on her arm. "You are now my property. There are no other terms or conditions. I've warned you of the consequences if you refuse to cooperate."

"You're right. I don't know what I was thinking." She hooked the thumb of her free hand in her right pocket. "I will do whatever you say. Just let my friend go and I'm good."

His evil smile was back. "I'm afraid it's too late for your friend. You see, Raeford fancies himself a coroner. He often practices on those we find in our way."

"You asshole," she snarled.

He threw his head back and laughed. "You should see your face."

While he continued to laugh, her fingers dipped into her back pocket, wrapped around the handle of the scalpel.

"I hope you're wrong, Vito," she warned.

He shook his head and laughed some more. "Oh, I'm not wrong, Issy. I'm never wrong."

"Too bad."

She stepped toward him and stabbed the scalpel into his throat.

He twisted. The cold steel sank into him.

He howled and reached for the scalpel. Blood seeped between his fingers.

She ran.

He had moved, so she missed the artery she had been aiming for. If she was really, really lucky, maybe she'd landed a fatal wound anyway. There were several veins and arteries in the neck.

A gunshot exploded in the air. The bullet hit the doorframe as she rushed from the room.

She ran faster, hoping the pain and any bleeding would slow him down.

Stairs.

She hit the stairs running. Two at a time. She almost fell. Grabbed the railing to catch herself and kept going.

Another shot.

The bullet pinged on the metal railing right behind her.

He was still coming.

Oh God.

TOP THUG TIGHTENED the strap on Lacon's right wrist. "I apologize for the delay, Mr. Traynor. Sometimes my associate feels he doesn't ever get to be in on the real fun stuff." He moved on to the end of the table and reached for the first of the two straps there. "These younger guys, they think they're owed something for doing nothing more than breathing." He laughed. "But he'll learn, or who knows, maybe I'll lose my patience and blow his head off."

The two men had almost come to punches arguing about who would have the pleasure of torturing Lacon and who would coordinate the security team outside. Both men were fully aware that the Colby Agency would send backup when it became apparent their client and investigator were missing in action.

The good news was that the argument had given Lacon the opportunity to unfasten the strap on his left hand since the disagreement had broken out before his right was restrained. He'd quickly arranged the strap so that it still looked fastened.

Top Thug returned to Lacon's side. "Now we're ready to begin."

"Where's Dr. Frasier?" He had asked that question three times already, mostly just to make the man hesitate.

"She's conferring with Mr. Anastasia." He grinned. "I imagine he's learning all her secrets by now."

Fury stormed through Lacon. He gritted his teeth and stayed perfectly still while the older man opened the cabinet. More broken glass scattered on the floor.

"This should do nicely." He turned back to the table, the other scalpel Lacon had noticed among the tools in his hand. "I'm so intrigued by the inner workings of the human body. I should have become a surgeon."

"I'll bet Dr. Frasier could give you a few pointers." He laughed again. "I doubt she'll be very happy with me when she learns what I've done to you. You won't care one way or another because you'll be dead." He placed the scalpel on the table between Lacon's legs. "Let's start with the chest. So much to work with there. I almost always start with the torso."

One by one he released the buttons of Lacon's shirt. He pushed back the sides to expose his chest. "Here we go." He reached for the scalpel.

Lacon made his move. He socked the older man in the face, sending him tumbling backward and falling into the cabinet. Lacon shook his hand, ignoring the pain from the impact that had no doubt broken the old bastard's nose. He unfastened the strap on his right hand and the one around his waist. He had his right foot free before the man staggered back to the table, blood pouring down his face.

"You son of a bitch." Top Thug drew his weapon.

Lacon kicked his wrist, sending the weapon flying. A second kick hit him in the chest. Top Thug slammed to the floor this time.

Lacon released his left foot and jumped off the table. He snagged the gun before the bastard could reach it. "On the table! Now!"

Top Thug started to argue, but Lacon shoved the gun in his face. "On the table."

The older man scooted onto the table. Lacon quickly strapped him in and felt in his pockets for his cell phone. "What's the code for the door?"

The man laughed. "Don't you wish you knew?"

The keypad also had a biometric thumb print scanner. "No problem." Lacon rounded the table and snagged the hacksaw from the cabinet. "Which hand do you want to keep?"

He shouted the code.

"Where did Anastasia take her?"

"To his suite. Upstairs."

Lacon rushed from the room and raced up the stairs to the first floor. He cracked the door open and listened before stepping out into the deserted hall.

The sound of a gunshot in the main living area had him bursting into the corridor.

He eased in that direction, listening for more trouble.

A scream.

Issy.

He charged forward, ran headlong into the younger thug who'd brought them here. He whipped the barrel of his weapon toward Lacon, but he didn't fire quickly enough—the bullet from Lacon's weapon nailed him center chest. The thug dropped like a rock. Lacon grabbed the downed man's weapon and shoved it into the waistband of his jeans.

He made it as far as the entry hall without encountering anyone else. There, the front door abruptly opened. A man dressed all in black, including a face mask, stepped inside. Perimeter security. Lacon fired in his direction. He scrambled back out the door.

Another scream.

Lacon shifted toward the staircase.

Anastasia was dragging Issy up the steps.

Lacon rushed for the stairs. The front door opened again. This time he didn't fire wide of his target. He popped the guy in the shoulder. He disappeared outside the door again.

Lacon took the stairs three at a time. He was at the top before the man in black made another attempt to come inside.

Shouting sounded somewhere in the vicinity of the back of the downstairs area. Kitchen or den. More of Anastasia's men were coming. Damn it. They were running out of time.

The double doors at the end of the hall closed as Lacon headed down that corridor. Lacon sent Michaels an SOS text and the address in case he hadn't already narrowed down where they might be.

He shoved the phone into his pocket and moved slowly toward the double doors, listening for the slightest sound from the room.

Voices. Heated words. They were arguing.

Lacon stood to one side and turned the knob. He opened the door a narrow crack and peeked beyond it.

Anastasia had Issy by the hair, the muzzle of his weapon shoved against her throat. Blood oozed from a wound in his neck. The scalpel, Lacon decided. *Good girl, Issy.*

"Join us, won't you, Mr. Traynor."

Lacon cleared his mind and focused on one thing: stopping this bastard. He stepped in the room, then to his right, putting his back to the wall so none of Anastasia's men could sneak up on him. There was blood on her T-shirt. Fear ignited in his veins. "You okay, Issy?"

"Yes."

She didn't sound okay.

"Let her go," he offered, "and you and I will finish this. The winner takes all."

Anastasia laughed. "This," he glared at Lacon, "is my world. You don't get to set the rules, Mr. Traynor. You're both going to die."

"If that's your final decision," Lacon said, "I can live with that."

Anastasia swung his weapon, aiming it toward Lacon. "I just told you that you're going to die."

Lacon didn't bother responding. He put a bullet in the guy's head.

The weapon fell from his hand and he crumpled to the floor.

Issy rushed to him. "Are you hurt?" She looked him up and down.

"You're the one with blood all over you."

She threw her arms around him and hugged him hard. "They were going to kill you."

"We're not in the clear yet," he warned.

He'd no more said the words than the sound of running footfalls echoed from the corridor.

He jerked his head toward the nearest door. Issy didn't look happy, but she disappeared behind it.

Lacon moved into a firing stance facing the double doors and held his breath to calm the blood roaring in his ears. A man in black rushed into the room, his weapon drawn. He spotted his boss and as if he'd sensed Lacon's presence he whirled toward him.

"You could leave now," Lacon offered, "and live."

"But then I'd miss the fun of watching your brains splatter on the wall."

The door behind which Issy had disappeared suddenly opened. The other man glanced in that direction. Lacon took the shot.

The man dropped.

But there was at least one more in the corridor.

Lacon braced for his arrival.

The sound of footsteps disappearing in the opposite direction made him smile. The other guy was retreating.

"Chicago PD! Drop your weapon!"

The proclamation echoed from somewhere downstairs.

The cavalry was here.

Issy stepped from her hiding place and looked from him to the man on the floor. "Did I hear the police?"

Lacon nodded. "Thanks." When her gaze met his in question, he went on. "You probably saved my life when you opened that door."

She shrugged. "I could hear what was happening and I didn't know what else to do to distract him."

More footfalls thundered up the stairs. Lacon placed his weapon in his waistband and held his hands up.

SWAT poured into the room. By the time they had determined that Lacon and Issy were the good guys, Michaels, Nader and Watts were walking through the door.

It was over. He glanced at Issy as she answered Nader's questions.

And they were both still alive.

Chapter Fourteen

Hampden Court, Saturday, July 14, 6:55 p.m.

The doorbell chimed its tune through the house.

Marissa's nerves jangled. She checked her reflection in the full-length mirror once more. She had pinned her wild curls up in a makeshift French twist with a few spiral wisps clinging to her temple and her neck. Good as it gets, she decided. Now for a little mascara, a touch of peppermint-flavored, shiny lip gloss and she was ready.

She drew in a deep breath for courage. The black dress hit four inches above her knees, not too modest yet not overly brazen. Sleeveless, scooped neck but not too revealing. The fit of the soft fabric made her feel sexy. The dress hugged her curves, adding a distinct sense of femininity without going overboard.

Then there were the shoes. Decent three-inch heels in a classic open-toed pump.

The chime came again, making her pulse flutter.

No more dawdling.

Taking her time, mostly to ensure she didn't break her neck in the heels, she descended the stairs. She spent so much time in comfortable work shoes, strutting around in heels was not one of her better skills.

When she reached the door, she paused. Had she forgotten a dab of perfume? She thought for a moment before distinctly recalling picking up the cut-glass bottle.

"No need to be nervous, Issy," she murmured as she wrapped her fingers around the knob and gave it a twist. She smiled. "Hi."

There were a host of other things she'd intended to say, like "come in" and "nice to see you" and "oh what lovely flowers." The rest of the words deserted her as her hungry gaze drank in the gorgeous man standing at her door.

Lacon Traynor wore jeans, as usual, plus a cotton button-up in a soft blue that emphasized his tanned skin. And those well-loved cowboy boots. She noted the white daisies, purple roses and bright yellow sunflowers in his hand on her tour back up to his handsome face. His sandy blond hair was combed as if it was Sunday morning and he was ready to go to church. His golden eyes were watching her admire him, and she didn't mind at all. She did admire him, in so many ways.

"Hey." He smiled and her heart melted.

"Come in." She drew the door open wider, held on for fear her knees would give out on her. She'd never met a man who could so easily make her swoon. In fact, she was fairly certain she'd never swooned before meeting Lacon Traynor.

He stepped inside and she closed the door. He offered her the flowers. "There's a flower stand in my neighborhood that swears all their flowers come fresh from a farm outside the city. I hope you like them."

She accepted the bouquet. "They're beautiful. Have a seat while I put these in water."

She took a couple of steps backward. "I'll only be a minute."

In the kitchen she rummaged under the sink for a pitcher, then placed it in the sink and filled it with water. Her hands shook as she loosened the ribbon around the arrangement. There was no need to be nervous. She knew this man. They had shared their bodies, laughed and cried and narrowly escaped death during a four-day period. Even in that short time, they had made memories that would forever be inscribed on the surface of her heart.

Wherever their fledgling relationship went from here, she couldn't be certain, but she had never in her life wanted to explore the possibilities with anyone more than she did with Lacon.

He walked up beside her, picked up a rose from the bundle and tucked it into the vase with the rest. "I made dinner reservations at your favorite restaurant."

Marissa picked up the vase. "You did?"

"Eva said Boka is your favorite."

She smiled. "Wow. I'm impressed you went to so much trouble."

He took the vase from her. Lifted his eyebrows in question.

"The table." She gestured to the dining room.

"No trouble." He placed the vase with its gorgeous

arrangement on the table. "I wanted to take you some-place special."

They had talked about this. Or she had, rather. She'd spent her adult life immersed in school and then in her career. Eighty-hour weeks at work, the rest of her time spent at home sleeping or blindly walking through life with a man she never really knew. She had no idea if William had had a hobby, much less what restaurant was his favorite. They were always too busy. Their marriage had been nothing more than a mutually advantageous living arrangement with the occasional fringe benefit of handy sex. The latter had become as rare as a blue moon the final months they were together.

She never wanted that sort of relationship again. This go-around, she wanted complete intimacy. She wanted to share her entire life with her partner. She wanted to know him inside and out, and she wanted him to know her the same way. No secrets. No lies. Utter honesty and the sharing of all things, good, bad and otherwise.

No one was perfect, not her, not Lacon, and she wanted their relationship to embrace those imperfections.

If he wanted the same.

After all, four days was not even a week, which was why they had agreed to stay apart for two weeks. They had needed distance and time to know if this was real. Except they only made it just shy of twelve days.

The longest eleven plus days of her life.

He reached out, traced the line of her jaw. "I've missed you."

She smiled, his words sending desire singing through her veins. "I missed you, too."

His fingers slid down her arm, tugged her closer. "Is this where we start?"

"Do you still want to move forward?"

His arms went around her waist, pulled her snug against his body. "I have spent the past eleven days, ten hours and forty—" he checked his phone "—forty-four minutes thinking about nothing but you. I've relived every moment we spent together at least a hundred times. I go to sleep needing you and wake up still wanting you. My life before walking into this house and seeing you for the first time feels like someone else's. This is my life now...*you* are my life now."

When she stared, speechless, at him, he smiled. "Does that answer your question?"

He dipped his head, placed a tender kiss on her lips. "I want to take you all the places you dream of going. I want to make pretty babies with you." He nuzzled the sensitive skin under her ear. "I love you, Issy. I want to be the one who grows old with you."

She cupped his face in her hands and looked into his eyes. "I think maybe you should cancel that dinner reservation."

He followed her up the stairs as he made the call. She kicked her shoes off at the door to her room and waited, trembling with anticipation, while he unzipped her dress. He kissed each vertebra as he revealed it. By the time the dress slid down her body, she was burning up for him. He turned her around and surveyed the lacy black bra and skimpy panties in the same racy black lace.

"Oh man, I don't know how much of this I can take without losing it."

She laughed, the happiness filling her chest and erupting from her, making her heart glad. Together they released the buttons of his shirt, peeled it from his muscular body. She smoothed her palms over those gorgeous ridges and planes. He walked backward, his lips locked with hers until they reached the bed. She pushed him into a sitting position and reached for a boot.

The boots and socks landed near her shoes. He lay back and allowed her to dispense with his jeans, as well. She slid the well-fitting denim over his hips and down his muscular legs. Then she reached for the briefs, tugging them away from his thick, fully aroused penis.

Twelve days she had waited to have him inside her again. She straddled his body. He used his magic fingers to push aside the flimsy strap of silk between her thighs and to guide himself into her.

Her eyes closed as she slid fully down onto him. He growled with need. His hands slipped beneath the lacy cups and squeezed her breasts. She wanted to tell him how very much she had missed him…how desperately she had wanted to call him each and every damned night.

He watched her coming undone, and for a moment she paused and leaned down close enough to taste his lips. "I love you, Lacon Traynor. I can't imagine spending my life with anyone else. We will make pretty babies."

Feeling his body tremble beneath her, she sat up and

ground herself into him, the urgency forcing her to start that frantic rhythm once more. She rode him faster and faster as the sweet throb of orgasm started deep inside, claiming her all too soon. Before she could catch her breath, he had rolled her onto her back and started the whole mind-blowing journey over again.

She didn't care if they ever left the house again. She had everything she wanted right here.

Chapter Fifteen

The Colby Agency, Monday, July 16, 9:30 a.m.

Victoria Colby-Camp sat behind her desk and smiled at Lucas as they waited for Jamie, their beloved grand-daughter, to arrive.

"I worry that she's only nineteen," Victoria confessed. "Are we getting ahead of ourselves here?"

Lucas, her cherished husband, propped his hands on his cane and considered the question for a moment. "We both know that Jamie is not like the average nineteen-year-old."

Victoria couldn't argue that observation. "I've spoken with Jim and Tasha, and they believe it's an excellent step."

Lucas shrugged. "Well, they are her parents. If they're comfortable, we should be as well, I suppose."

Lucas leaned back in his chair, setting his cane to the side. "Perhaps we should begin with a trial period. Three to six months, whichever you believe is best. We can revisit our concerns at that time. If all is well, then we'll continue. If not, we can always put someone else in charge of the program."

Victoria took a breath. "All right. When she arrives, we'll brief her and see how she feels about our suggestions."

Lucas nodded. "Agreed." He stroked his chin a moment. "Did I hear Ian say Eva and Todd Christian were getting married the end of this month?"

"They are," Victoria confirmed. "Bella and Devon are making plans for early next year. They're planning a beautiful wedding in Aspen. Eva and Todd prefer a small wedding and a long honeymoon."

Lucas frowned. "Why am I always the last one to know?"

Victoria laughed. "You are certainly not the last one to know, Lucas. You've just been preoccupied with other things."

He grunted. "I suppose Traynor and Dr. Frasier will be next."

Victoria nodded. "I have no doubt. Love, as you know, comes in its own time."

"That I do." His gray eyes twinkled with mischief. "Ours certainly took quite the journey."

"It did indeed."

A soft rap on the door preceded Jamie's entrance. Victoria's heart leaped as her granddaughter entered the room. Like her father, she had the blond hair and blue eyes of a Colby. She was tall and thin, but strong and incredibly intelligent. Victoria could not be more proud of her.

"Good morning, little girl," Lucas teased. He'd always called Jamie *little girl*.

Jamie leaned down and gave him a peck on the

cheek. "Morning, Grandfather." She rounded Victoria's desk and gave her a kiss on the cheek, as well. "You look beautiful as always, Grandmother."

"Thank you, sweetheart. Shall we begin?"

"I can't wait." Jamie settled into the chair next to Lucas. The blue suit she wore set off her beautiful eyes.

"As you're aware," Victoria began, "we've been working with Missing, the international network focused solely on finding missing persons."

"Yes."

It was impossible not to see the excitement in her eyes.

"The Colby Agency is very excited to be a part of the plan to broaden and deepen the search for those who've gone missing, especially the most vulnerable. Since many of the most vulnerable are children and young adults, we have decided it's imperative that someone who can better fit into that world should oversee this new outreach program."

Jamie nodded. "A reasonable conclusion."

"The program will be small in the beginning. Since the work will be completely pro bono, we need to be quite selective in the cases we choose."

"If our program is successful," Jamie offered, "I'm certain we'll be able to extend the scope of it with funds from generous donors."

There was another of Jamie's uncanny skills. Fundraising. The girl had a flair for the work. By the time she was in high school, she was already working for half a dozen local charities.

"For now, we'll take it one step at a time," Lucas cautioned. "This is hard, emotionally charged work. Your grandmother and I want to be absolutely certain that you comprehend the challenge before you."

"This is what I want to do," Jamie assured him. "I can think of no more fulfilling work than to reunite the lost with their loved ones."

"There isn't always a happy ending," Victoria cautioned. "Oftentimes, finding those who are lost means finding remains or merely finding the truth and nothing else."

Jamie squared her shoulders and lifted her chin in defiance of their warnings. "I understand and I'm ready to face those challenges."

"It's a fine cause, Jamie," Victoria said, finding it difficult to keep her voice steady. This was a very emotional subject for her. "You've made it clear that you feel deeply about this program. Does what happened to your father have anything to do with those feelings?"

Though Jamie had only heard the stories, she understood what a nightmare that time had been. Her father, Jim, had been stolen from Victoria when he was only seven years old and he remained missing, presumed dead, for more than two decades. Victoria felt certain she would never know all the horrors he had suffered. His journey back to Victoria had not been easy for either of them, but they had survived. Now he had a wonderful wife and two beautiful children, Jamie and her younger brother, Luke. Jim worked alongside Victoria at this agency—the agency she and his father, James Colby, had built. Even now, thinking of those awful years had tears burning her eyes.

"Of course, my decision is rooted in my father's history," Jamie said. "I want to do all within my power to ensure no other child has to go through that nightmare. I know I can't save them all. But I will save everyone that I can. This is how I choose to spend my life, Grandmother. Please help me do that."

"Done." Victoria smiled. "You may begin organizing your team right away."

Jamie hugged them both.

It was a good decision. Victoria's heart was full with the realization that her son and her granddaughter would carry on the work that meant so very much to her.

A new generation of Colbys. Time to celebrate.

* * * * *

SAVED BY THE SHERIFF

CINDI MYERS

For Lucy

Chapter One

Lacy Milligan flinched as the heavy steel door clanged shut behind her. After almost three years, that sound still sent a chill through her. She reminded herself she wouldn't ever have to hear that sound again after today. Today she was a free woman.

She followed the guard down the gleaming tiled hallway, the smell of disinfectant stinging her nose. At the door to a reception room at the front of the building she stopped and waited while a second guard unlocked and opened the door. Her lawyer, Anisha Cook, stood on the other side, beaming. She pulled Lacy to her in a hug and Lacy stiffened. That was something else she would have to get used to—being touched. Touching wasn't allowed in prison—even something as simple as a hug could lead to extra searches, even punishment. But those rules didn't apply to her anymore, she reminded herself, and awkwardly returned the other woman's embrace. Anisha, still smiling, released her, and Lacy noticed there were other people in the room— the warden, reporters, her parents.

"Lacy, what are your feelings, now that your conviction has been overturned?" A sandy-haired man shoved a microphone at her.

"I'm happy, of course," she said. "Ready to go home."

"Do you have anything to say to Rayford County Sheriff Travis Walker?" another reporter asked.

So Travis was the sheriff now. Putting a murderer behind bars had probably earned him points with the right people in town. Except he had arrested the wrong person. "I don't have anything to say to him," she said.

"Even though he's the one who came forward with the evidence that cleared your name?" the reporter asked.

Travis had done that? She shot a look at Anisha, who nodded. Lacy would have to get the whole story from her later. "That doesn't make up for the three years I spent behind bars for a crime I didn't commit," Lacy said. Three years of her life she would never get back.

"What are your plans now that you're free?" the sandy-haired reporter asked.

Plans? Plans were something a person with a future made—something Lacy hadn't had until yesterday, when word came down that she was to be released. She had been afraid to believe it was really going to happen until now. "I'm going to go home with my parents and consider my options," she said.

She caught her mother's eye across the room. Jeanette Milligan was openly weeping, tears running down her cheeks, while Lacy's dad held her tightly.

"We need to be going now," Anisha said. "We ask that you respect Lacy's privacy as she settles in." She put her arm around Lacy's shoulders and guided her toward the door.

Outside, her mother's green Subaru Outback waited—the same car she had had when Lacy had entered the Denver Women's Correctional Facility three years before. Lacy's dad embraced her and kissed her cheek, then it was her mother's turn. "I have your old room all ready for you," her mom said. "And we're having steak for dinner, and chocolate cake."

"Great, Mom." Lacy forced a smile. Moving back home had seemed the best choice right now, since she had almost no money and no job. It would only be temporary, until she figured out what she was going to do with the rest of her life and got back on her feet. But it still felt like going back in time while the rest of the world moved forward.

"We'll get together next week for coffee or something," Anisha said. "If you need anything before then, just call." She waved and headed for her own car, then Lacy slid into the back seat of her parents' car and they were off.

They tried to make small talk for a while, but soon fell silent. Lacy rested her head against the window and stared out at the summer-browned city landscape, which quickly gave way to the green foothills, and then the Rocky Mountains. Only five more hours until she was home in Eagle Mountain, the little resort town where her family had settled when Lacy was fourteen. Once upon a time, she had thought she would stay in Eagle Mountain forever, but now she wasn't so sure. Maybe there were too many bad memories there for her to ever be comfortable again.

Lacy slept, and woke only when her dad pulled the car into the driveway of the Victorian cottage just off Eagle Mountain's main street that had been their home for the past ten years. A lump rose in Lacy's throat as she studied the stone walkway that led up to the front porch that spanned the width of the house, with its white-painted posts and railings and lacelike gin-

gerbread trim. The peonies under the railings were in
full bloom, like big pink pom-poms filling the flower
beds. A banner over the front steps declared Welcome
Home Lacy!

She took her time getting out of the car, fighting the
instinct to run up the steps and straight into her room.
She was going to have to get used to facing people
again, to dealing with their questions about what she
had been through and what she planned to do next. She
had never been good at that kind of thing, but she was
going to have to find a way to cope.

She started up the walkway, but at the top of the
steps, she noticed the uniformed man seated in the
porch swing and froze. Travis Walker, all six feet of
him, made even taller by the cowboy boots and Stetson he wore, stood and moved toward her. "What are
you doing here?" Lacy asked, heart pounding madly.
Had there been some mistake? Had he come to arrest
her again?

Travis removed his hat, revealing thick brown hair
that fell boyishly over his forehead. When Lacy had
first met him in high school, she had thought he was
the handsomest boy she had ever seen. Too much had
passed between them for her to think that now. "I came
to apologize," he said. "I know it doesn't make up for all
I put you through, but I wanted to say I'm truly sorry.
I've done what I can to make up for my mistakes."

"Your mistakes cost me three years of my life!" Lacy
hated the way her voice broke on the words. "You hu-
miliated me in front of everyone I knew. In front of
people I've never even met. You accused me of the most
horrible crime anyone could commit."

His face showed the strain he was feeling, his brown

eyes pained. "I would give anything to take all of it back," he said. "But I can't. All I can do is say again that I'm sorry, and I hope you'll find it in your heart one day to forgive me."

"You don't deserve my forgiveness," she said, and rushed past him, tears stinging her eyes. She refused to break down in front of him.

She paused in the darkened living room, fighting for composure. Her father's quiet voice drifted to her through the opened screen door. "Give it a few days. This is hard for her—for all of us."

"I didn't mean to intrude on your first day back together," Travis said. "I just wanted her to know how I felt. It didn't seem right to wait any longer to apologize. It doesn't make up for anything, but it had to be said."

"And we appreciate it," her dad said. "We appreciate all you've done for her. It says a lot about a man when he's willing to admit he was wrong."

"I'll leave you alone now," Travis said. "You deserve your privacy and I have a lot of work to do."

"Thank goodness there's not a lot of crime in Rayford County, but I imagine the job has its challenges," her dad said.

"It does," Travis said. "But right now my priority is finding out who really killed Andy Stenson. I know now that Lacy didn't kill him, but I have to bring to justice the person who did."

TRAVIS WALKED AWAY from the Milligan home, down the street shaded by tall evergreens and cottonwoods, up a block to Main. He liked that the town of Eagle Mountain—the only incorporated town in Rayford County—was small enough, and the sheriff's department centrally located enough, that he could walk almost anywhere. A big part of policing in a rural area like this was simply being a presence. Seeing uniforms on the street made people feel safer, and it made troublemakers think twice about acting up.

He passed under the large banner advertising Eagle Mountain Pioneer Days Festival, the biggest tourist attraction of the summer for the little town, with a parade and fireworks, outdoor concerts, crafts booths and anything else the town council could think of that would entertain people and induce them to stay a few days and spend money.

"Sheriff!"

He turned to see Mayor Larry Rowe striding toward him. Solidly built and energetic, Rowe was a relative newcomer to town who, after a year on the county planning committee, had spent a significant amount of money on his campaign for mayor two years ago—unusual in a town where most public officials ran unopposed. "Mayor." Travis stopped and waited for the older man to catch up.

"Sheriff, I wanted to talk to you about security for the festival," Rowe said.

"We'll have plenty of officers patrolling," Travis said. "I'm putting all of the reserves on duty, and as many of the full-time staff as possible."

Rowe nodded. "We don't want any trouble to detract from the festivities." He stared down the street, in the direction Travis had come. "I understand Lacy Milligan is back in town."

"Yes, I stopped by to see her."

"Oh?" The lines on either side of Rowe's mouth deepened. "How is she?"

"She's still processing everything that's happened, I think."

"I hope she doesn't have any plans to sue the city," Rowe said. "I'll have to consult our attorney, prepare for that possibility."

"I don't think she has any plans to sue," Travis said.

"Do whatever you can to see that she doesn't. I have to go now. You'll keep me posted if any problems arise with the Milligans."

"Yes, sir."

The mayor moved on, and Travis resumed the walk to his office. Though he didn't consider Rowe a friend, he appreciated that the mayor rarely involved himself in the operation of the sheriff's department. Travis was free to do his job as he saw fit.

A ten-minute stroll took Travis back to the office. His office manager, sixty-eight-year-old Adelaide Kinkaid, who refused to even consider retiring—and was sharper than most thirty-year-olds—looked up from her computer screen. "How did it go?" she asked.

"About like I expected." Travis hung his Stetson on the rack by the door. "She told me I'd ruined her life and tried not to let me see she was crying." He shrugged. "In her place, I'd probably feel the same way. I guess I'm lucky she didn't punch me."

"You're already beating yourself up enough," Adelaide said.

"Why are you beating yourself up?" Deputy Gage Walker, Travis's younger brother, emerged from his office. Taller than Travis by two inches and lighter than him by twenty pounds, Gage looked like the basketball forward he had been in high school, lean and quick.

"I went over to see Lacy Milligan," Travis said.

Gage's face sobered. "Ouch! That took guts."

"It was the least she deserved. Not that she thinks so."

"You did what you could," Gage said. "Now the ball is in her court."

"Not exactly."

"What do you mean?" Gage asked.

"I mean, I still have to find Andy Stenson's killer. And doing that will be easier with her help."

"Wait a minute—you proved she was innocent—but you think she knows something?" Gage asked.

"She can at least walk me through Andy's records, tell me about his clients. She was his only employee. She may have encountered his murderer, without knowing it."

"What about Andy's widow?" Adelaide asked.

"Brenda knows nothing about the business," Travis said. "She's told me everything she knows, but it's not enough. I need Lacy to help me."

"And I need a million dollars," Gage said. "But I'm not going to get it."

Travis moved into his office and dropped into his chair behind his desk, staring at the stack of papers in his inbox, thinking about Lacy. She was the first murderer he had ever arrested—the only one, actually. He was a deputy with only a few years on the force at the time, and murder was a rare crime in Rayford County. Sheriff's department calls ran more toward theft, vandalism, domestic violence and what he thought of as tourist calls—lost hikers, lost wallets, lost dogs and people who had locked themselves out of their cars.

The murder of young attorney Andy Stenson had been a shock to everyone, but the chief suspect had been pretty clear. Lacy Milligan's prints had been found on the murder weapon, she had been overheard arguing with Andy that afternoon and someone had seen a woman who matched Lacy's description—from her build to her dark hair—outside the office shortly before the time of Andy's death.

Travis hadn't wanted to believe Lacy was a killer. She had always been the pretty, quiet girl in high school. After she had graduated high school and had gone to work for Andy, Travis had occasionally seen her downtown and they would say hello. He had even thought about asking her out, but had never gotten around to it.

But then Andy had died and the only evidence Travis could find pointed to Lacy. She hadn't been able to produce anyone who could confirm her alibi—that she had been almost two hours away at her cousin's basketball game. The cousin hadn't seen her there, and no one else could remember her being there. And then the prosecutor had discovered funds missing from the law firm's account, and a deposit in almost the same amount in Lacy's account.

The jury had deliberated only a few hours before handing down a conviction. Travis had felt sick as he watched the bailiff lead Lacy from court, but he had been convinced he had done his job. He had found a murderer.

And then, only two months ago, he had been whiling away the time online and had come across a video someone had posted of a college basketball game—a game in which a promising young player—now a major NBA star—had made a series of free throws that hinted at his future greatness. Watching the video, Travis had recognized a familiar face on the sidelines. Lacy Milligan—a smiling, carefree Lacy—had stared out at him from the screen. A time stamp on the video corroborated her story of being at her cousin's game. Further research backed this up. Here was her alibi. When Andy Stenson was stabbed in the heart, Lacy Milligan was two hours away.

From there, the rest of the evidence began to fall apart. Travis hired a former detective to review the case and the detective—who had retired to Eagle Mountain after a storied career with the Los Angeles Police Department—determined that what had looked like missing funds was merely a bookkeeping error, and the deposit in Lacy's account was, as she had said, the proceeds from the sale of some jewelry she had inherited.

Travis had felt sick over the error. He hadn't been able to eat or sleep as he worked feverishly to see that the decision in the case was vacated. He also did what he could to publicize his efforts to clear the name of the woman he had wronged. He wanted everyone to know that Lacy was innocent.

Now she was home. He didn't blame her for hating him, though it hurt to see the scorn in her eyes. All he knew to do now was to work even harder to find the real killer.

The phone rang and he heard Adelaide answer. A moment later, his extension buzzed. "Sheriff, it's for you," Adelaide said. "It's George Milligan."

Lacy's dad. Travis snatched up the receiver. "Mr. Milligan, how can I help you?"

"I think you need to come over here, Sheriff." George Milligan's voice held the strain of someone who had taken almost more than he could bear. "We've had a, well, I'm not sure how to describe it. An incident."

Travis sat up straighter, his stomach knotting. "What's happened? Is someone hurt? Is Lacy hurt?"

"Someone threw a rock through our front window." George's voice broke. "It had a...a note tied to it. Just one word on the note—*murderer*."

"I'll be right over," Travis said. Hadn't these people suffered enough? Hadn't they all suffered enough?

Chapter Two

Lacy stared at the grapefruit-sized chunk of red granite that sat in the middle of the library table beneath the front window of her family home, shards of glass like fractured ice scattered about it. Strands of thin wire held the note in place, a single word scrawled crookedly in red marker, like an accusation made in blood.

Murderer! She had worn the label for three years, but she would never get used to it. Seeing it here, in the place she had thought of as a refuge, when she had believed her ordeal over, hurt more than she had imagined. Worse, the word hurt her parents, who had put their own lives on hold, and even mortgaged their home, to save her.

A black-and-white SUV pulled into the driveway and Lacy watched out the window as Travis Walker slid out of the vehicle and strode up the walkway to the door. Everything about him radiated competence and authority, from his muscular frame filling out the crisp lines of his brown sheriff's uniform to the determined expression on his handsome face. When he said something was right, it must be right. So when he had said she had murdered Andy Stenson, everyone had believed him. Men like Travis didn't make mistakes.

Except he had.

The doorbell rang and her father opened it and ushered Travis inside. Lacy steeled herself to face him. Travis hadn't thrown the rock through her parents' window, but as far as she was concerned, he was to blame.

"Hello, Lacy." Ever the gentleman, Travis touched the brim of his hat and nodded to her.

She nodded and took a step back, away from the rock—and away from him. He walked over and looked down at the projectile, his gaze taking in the broken window, the shattered glass and the note. He leaned closer to study the note. "Has anything like this happened before?" he asked.

It took her a moment to realize he had addressed the question to her. She shrugged. "Not really. There were a few letters to the editor in the paper during my trial, and a few times when I would walk into a place and everyone would stop talking and stare at me."

"But no direct threats or name calling?" he asked.

She shook her head. "No."

"I can't understand why anyone would do this now." Her father joined them. Her mother was upstairs, lying down with a headache. "Lacy has been cleared. Everyone knows that."

"Maybe not everyone." Travis straightened. "I'll get an evidence kit from my car. Maybe we'll get some fingerprints off the note."

Lacy doubted whoever threw that rock would be stupid enough to leave fingerprints, but she didn't bother arguing. Travis went outside and stopped on the sidewalk to survey the flower bed. Maybe he was looking for footprints? Or maybe he liked flowers.

He returned a few moments later, wearing latex

gloves and carrying a cardboard box. He lifted the rock and settled it in the box. "In order to hurl the rock through the window like this, whoever threw it would have to be close—either standing on the porch or in the flower beds," he said, as he taped up the box and labeled it. "I didn't see any footprints in the flower beds, or disturbed plants, so I'm guessing porch. Did you see or hear anyone?"

"We were all in the back of the house, preparing dinner in the kitchen," her father said.

"I'll talk to the neighbors, see if any of them saw anything," Travis said. "After the window shattered, did you hear anything—anyone running away, or a car driving away?"

"No," her father said.

Both men looked at Lacy. "No," she said. "I didn't hear anything."

"Who would do something like this?" her father asked. His face sagged with weariness, and he looked years older. Guilt made a knot in Lacy's stomach. Even though she hadn't thrown the rock, she was the target. She had brought this intrusion into her parents' peaceful life. Maybe moving back home had been a bad idea.

"I don't know," Travis said. "There are mean people in the world. Obviously, someone doesn't believe Lacy is innocent."

"The paper has run articles," her father said. "It's been on all the television stations—I don't know what else we can do."

"You can help me find the real murderer."

He was addressing Lacy, not her dad, his gaze pinning her. She remembered him looking at her that way the day he arrested her, the intensity of his stare making it clear she wasn't going to get away with not answering his questions.

"Why should I help you?" she asked.

"You worked closely with Andy," he said. "You knew his clients. You can walk me through his records. I'm convinced he knew his murderer."

"What if you try to pin this on the wrong person again?"

He didn't even flinch. "I won't make that mistake again."

"Honey, I think maybe Travis is right," her father said. "You probably know more about Andy's job than anyone."

"What about Brenda?" Lacy asked. "She was his wife. He would have told her if someone was threatening him before he told me."

"He never said anything like that to her," Travis said. "And she doesn't know anything about his law practice."

"I'm pretty sure all the files from the business are still in storage," she said. "You don't need my help going through them."

"I do if I'm going to figure out what any of it means. You can help me avoid wasting time on irrelevant files and focus on anything that might be important."

His intense gaze pinned her, making her feel trapped. She wanted to say no, to avoid having anything to do with him. But what if he was right and he needed her help to solve the case? What if, by doing nothing, she was letting the real killer get away with murder? "All right," she said. "I'll help you."

"Thank you. I'll call you tomorrow or the next day and set up a time to get together." He picked up the box with the rock, touched the brim of his hat again and left.

Lacy sank into a nearby arm chair. This wasn't how she had envisioned her homecoming. She had hoped to be able to put the past behind her once and for all. Now she was volunteering to dive right back into it.

TRAVIS CRUISED EAGLE MOUNTAIN'S main street, surveying the groups of tourists waiting for tables at Kate's Kitchen or Moe's Pub, the men filling the park benches outside the row of boutiques, chatting while they waited for their wives. He waved to Paige Riddell as he passed her bed-and-breakfast, drove past the library and post office, then turned past the Episcopal Church, the fire station and the elementary school before he turned toward his office. The rock someone had hurled through Lacy's front window sat in the box on the passenger seat, a very ordinary chunk of iron-ore-infused granite that could have come from almost any roadside or backyard in the area.

Who would hurl such a weapon—and its hateful message—through the window of a woman who had already endured too much because of mistakes made by Travis and others? Eagle Mountain wasn't a perfect place, but it wasn't known for violent dissension. Disagreements tended to play themselves out in the form of letters to the editor of the local paper or the occasional shouting match after a few too many beers at one of the local taverns.

When Travis had arrested Lacy for the murder of Andy Stenson, he had received more than one angry phone call, and a few people had refused to speak to him ever since. When he had issued a public statement declaring Lacy's innocence, most people had responded positively, if not jubilantly, to the news. He couldn't recall hearing even a whisper from anyone that a single person believed Lacy was still a murderer.

On impulse, he drove past the police station and two blocks north, to the former Eagle Mountain Hospital, now home to the county Historical Society and Museum. As he had hoped, Brenda Stenson was just locking up for the day when Travis parked and climbed out of his SUV. "Hello, Travis," she said as she tucked the key into her purse. A slender blonde with delicate features and a smattering of freckles across her upturned nose, Brenda seemed to be regaining some of the vivacity that had all but vanished when her husband of only three years had been murdered. "What's up?"

"Lacy came home today," he said. "I was just over at her folks' place."

"How is she? I saw her mom yesterday and told her to tell Lacy I would stop by tomorrow—I thought maybe the family would like a little time alone before the crowds of well-wishers descend."

"So you don't have any problem with her being out?" Travis asked, watching her carefully.

She pushed a fall of long blond hair out of her eyes. "Lacy didn't kill Andy," she said. "I should have spoken on her behalf at the trial, but I was so torn up about Andy—it was all I could do to get out of bed in the morning. Later on..." She shrugged. "I didn't know what to think. I'm glad she's out."

"Except that now we don't know who is responsible for Andy's death," Travis said.

"No, we don't. It makes it hard to move on, but sometimes these things never get solved, do they? I hate to think that, but I'm trying to be realistic."

"I want to find the real murderer," Travis said. "I feel like I owe it to you and Andy—and to Lacy."

"You didn't try and convict her all by yourself,"

Brenda said. "And you fought harder than anyone to free her once you figured out the truth."

"But I started the ball rolling," he said. "And this isn't really going to be over for any of us until we find out what really happened that day."

She sighed. "So what's the next move?"

"I know we've been over this before, but humor me. Do you know of anyone who was angry or upset with Andy—about anything? An angry husband whose wife Andy represented in a divorce? A drunk driving case he lost?"

"Andy hadn't been practicing law long enough to make enemies," Brenda said. "And Eagle Mountain is a small town—I know pretty much everyone who was ever a client of his. None of them seem like a murderer to me."

"I think the odds that the killer was a random stranger are pretty low," Travis said. "So one of those nice local people is likely the murderer."

Brenda rubbed her hands up and down her arms, as if trying to warm herself. "It makes me sick to think about it," she said.

"If I can convince Lacy to help me, would you mind if we go through Andy's case files?" Travis asked. "I figure she would have known his clients almost as well as he did."

"Of course I don't mind. Everything is in storage. I haven't had the heart to go through anything myself."

"I don't know if it will help, but it seems like a good place to start," he said.

"Stop by whenever you're ready and I'll give you the key to my storage unit," she said.

They said good-night and Travis returned to his

SUV. He had just started the vehicle when his cell phone buzzed. "Hello?"

"Sheriff, Wade Tomlinson called to report a shoplifter at their store," Adelaide said. "He said he saw you drive past a few minutes ago and wondered if you could swing by."

"Tell him I'll be there in a couple of minutes." Travis ended the call and turned the SUV back toward Main, where Wade Tomlinson and Brock Ryan operated Eagle Mountain Outfitters, a hunting, fishing and climbing store that catered to locals and tourists alike. Technically, a call like this should have been routed through the countywide dispatch center. The dispatcher would then contact the appropriate department and the officer who was closest to the scene would respond. But locals were just as likely to call the sheriff department's direct line and ask for Travis or Gage or one of the other officers by name.

Wade Tomlinson met Travis on the sidewalk in front of their store. "Thanks for stopping by, Sheriff," he said. He crossed his arms over his beefy chest, the eagle tattoo on his biceps flexing. A vein pulsed in his shaved head. "Though I guess we wasted your time."

"Adelaide said you had a shoplifter?"

"Yeah, but he got away, right after I called." He led the way inside the shop, which smelled of canvas, leather and rope. Climbing rope in every color of the rainbow hung from hooks along the back wall, while everything from stainless-steel coffee mugs to ice axes and crampons filled the shelves.

Wade's business partner, Brock Ryan, looked up from rearranging a display of T-shirts. The one in his hand, Travis noted, bore the legend *Do It In the Out-*

doors. "Hey, Travis," he said. "You didn't pass a skinny teenager in a red beanie on your way over here, did you?"

"No," Travis said. "Was that your shoplifter?"

"Yeah. I caught him red-handed shoving a hundred-dollar water filter down his pants. I sat him down up front by the register and told him we would wait until you got here before we decided whether or not to file charges."

Unlike Wade, who was short and stocky, Brock was tall and lean, with the squinting gaze of a man who had spent long hours in the sun and wind.

"What happened after that?" Travis asked.

"I turned my back to get a tray of fishing flies out of the case for a customer and the kid took off," Brock said, his face reddening.

"Did the kid give you a name?" Travis asked. "Did you recognize him?"

Both men shook their heads. "He wasn't from around here," Wade said. "He wouldn't say anything to us, so we figured we'd let you see if you could get anything out of him."

"Maybe you two scared him enough he won't come back," Travis said.

"Burns me up when somebody comes in here and tries to take what we've worked hard for," Brock said. He punched his hand in his fist. "If that kid ever shows his face here again, I'll make sure he never tries to steal from me again."

Travis put a hand on the tall man's shoulder. "Don't let your temper get the best of you," he said. "If the kid comes back, call the office and one of us will take care of it."

Brock hesitated, then nodded. "Right."

A third man emerged from a door at the back of the shop—a lean, broad-shouldered guy in a black knit beanie. He looked as if he had been carved from iron—all sharp angles and hard muscle. He scanned Travis from head to toe, lingering a moment on the badge on his chest, and Travis wouldn't have called his expression friendly. "Do you have a new employee?" Travis asked, nodding toward the man.

Brock glanced over his shoulder. "That's Ian," he said. "A friend of mine."

Ian nodded, but didn't offer to shake hands. "I'll wait in back," he said to Brock, and exited the way he had come.

"Your friend got a problem with cops?" Travis asked.

"He's not comfortable with new people," Wade said. "He did four tours in Iraq and Afghanistan. He has trouble sometimes with PTSD."

Travis nodded. Maybe that explained the hostility he had felt from the guy. Or maybe Travis was more suspicious than most people. A hazard of the job, he supposed. "I doubt you'll have any more trouble from your shoplifter," he said to Wade and Brock. "You probably scared him off. But I'll keep my eyes open."

"Thanks."

Travis returned to his SUV and climbed in. He started the vehicle and was about to pull out of his parking spot when he glanced over at the passenger seat and slammed on the brakes. The box and the rock that had been thrown through Lacy's window were gone.

Chapter Three

"Why would someone steal the rock?" Lacy folded her arms over her chest and took a step back from Travis. He had shown up at her house this morning—supposedly to "check on" her and her family. But then he had come out with this crazy story about someone taking the rock that had been thrown through her window. "Do you think I took it or something?"

"No!" He put up his hands, as if he wanted to reach for her, then put them down. "I wanted you to know because you're the victim in this case, and you have a right to know what's going on."

She unfolded her arms, relaxing a little. She had insisted on talking with him on the front porch—mainly so her parents wouldn't overhear. Her mom and dad meant well, but they tended to hover now that she was back home. "So someone just opened the door of your sheriff's department vehicle and took the evidence box?" she asked. "How does that happen? Wasn't your door locked?"

"No one locks their car doors around here." He looked sheepish—an endearing expression, really—and she didn't want to feel anything like that for him. "Besides, it's a cop car. Who breaks into a cop car? And to steal a rock?"

"Maybe they didn't know what was in the box?" she said. "Or maybe somebody is pranking you—wants to give you a hard time."

"Maybe." He put one booted foot up on a metal foot-locker her mom used as a side table on the porch, and she tried not to notice the way the khaki fabric stretched over his muscular thigh. She didn't like being around Travis, but apparently her body couldn't ignore the fact that he was the sexiest guy she'd been near in three years. "Or maybe whoever threw the rock took it because they thought I could use it somehow to link them to the crime," he added.

She forced her mind away from ogling the sheriff's hot body to what was surely a more important matter. "Can you do that?" she asked. "Would a rock have fingerprints on it or something?"

"The surface was too rough to give good latent prints, and it looked like a common enough rock."

"What about DNA?" she asked.

He laughed. "No offense, but no one does DNA testing for an act of vandalism. It's expensive, and the results take a while to come back."

She lowered herself to the cushioned rattan love seat. Her mother had made the cushions out of flowered chintz, faded now by the summer sun, but all the more comfortable and homey for it. "If the person who threw the rock stole it out of your SUV, that means they knew you had it. They must have been watching and seen you come to the house to get it."

Travis sat beside her, the cushion dipping under his weight. She caught the scent of soap and starch and clean man, and fought to keep from leaning toward him. "Maybe," he said. "Or maybe they knew your family would call my office to report the threat, they saw my SUV and decided to take a look inside."

"Either way, I'm completely creeped out." She gripped the edge of the love seat. She had thought when she walked out of prison that she would feel free again, but she still felt trapped. Watched.

"I talked to Brenda Stenson yesterday," Travis said. "She's okay with us going through Andy's files."

Lacy nodded. "I'm not looking forward to that, you know."

"I understand. But I'm hoping coming at the files cold after a few years away, you'll spot something or remember something that didn't seem relevant before."

"What about the other evidence from the crime scene?" she asked. "Wasn't there anything that pointed to someone besides me as the murderer? Or did you conveniently overlook that?" She didn't even try to keep the sharp edge from her voice.

"I guess I deserved that," Travis said. "But no—there wasn't anything. Wade Tomlinson reported seeing a woman who looked like you near the office shortly before Andy would have died. Obviously, that wasn't you. It might help if we could find this woman, but we don't have much to go on—Wade admitted he only saw her from the back, and only for a few seconds, before she entered the office. I'll question him again, but I doubt he'll have anything useful to add."

"Right. Who remembers anything very clearly that happened three years ago?" Lacy sighed.

"I think Andy's files are the best place for us to start," Travis said.

"Andy hadn't been in practice very long," Lacy said. "Still, he had a couple of big cabinets full of files. Everything was backed up on the computer, too, but he had been trained by a man who liked to keep paper copies of everything, and Andy was the same way. It will take a while to go through everything."

"We can do a couple of boxes at a time. You could even bring them back here to look through."

"Do you trust me to look through them by myself?" she asked.

"It would look better in court if we went through them together," Travis said. "Otherwise, a good defense attorney would point out that you had a strong motive to make people believe someone else murdered Andy. They could suggest you planted evidence in the files."

She fought against her inclination to bristle at what sounded to her ears like an accusation. After all, she knew all too well how attorneys could twist the most mundane events to make someone look guilty to a jury. "I guess you're right," she admitted. She stretched her legs out in front of her. "So how do you want to do this?"

"I'll get together with Brenda this afternoon and go over to the storage unit with her. I'll select a couple of boxes to go through first, seal them in her presence, get her to sign off on them, then bring them here. We'll open them together and start going through the contents. Maybe I'll even video everything, just in case there's any question."

"You're very thorough."

"I'm determined not to make any mistakes this time."

And I'm determined not to let you, she thought.

ANDY STENSON'S STORAGE unit was located in a long metal shed at the end of Fireline Road on the edge of town. Weedy fields extended beyond the chain-link fence that surrounded the shed on all sides, the land sloping upward from there toward Dakota Ridge and the mountains beyond. With no traffic and no neighbors, the location was peaceful, even beautiful, with the first summer wildflowers blooming in the fields and a china blue sky arching overhead. But there wasn't anything beautiful about Travis's errand here today.

Brenda agreed to meet him, and when he pulled into the rutted drive, he found her waiting at the far end, key in hand. "You open it," she said, pushing the key at him. "I haven't been in here since before Andy died. I paid a cleaning company to move all his stuff out here."

"Are you okay being here now?" Travis asked, studying her face. Tension lines fanned out from her mouth, but she didn't look on the verge of a breakdown.

"I'm okay," she said. "I just want to get this over with."

He unfastened the padlock and rolled up the metal door of the unit. Sunlight illuminated jumbled stacks of file boxes. Furniture filled one corner of the unit—several filing cabinets and some chairs and Andy's desk, scarred and dusty. The chair he had been sitting in when he died, stained with his blood, was in a police storage unit, logged as evidence.

Brenda traced a finger across the dust on the desktop. Was she thinking about her young husband, who had been taken from her when they were still practically newlyweds? She squared her shoulders and turned to study the file boxes. "There's a lot of stuff here," she said. "Do you know what you want?"

"I want to look at his case files." Travis studied the labels on the boxes, then removed the lid from one with the notation Clients, A through C. "I know you said you didn't know much about his work, but who would you say was his biggest client at the time he died?"

"That one's easy enough. Hake Development." She pointed to a box on the bottom of the pile, with the single word *HAKE* scrawled on the end. "Andy couldn't believe his luck when Henry Hake hired him instead of one of the big-city firms. Mr. Hake said he wanted to support local business." She chuckled. "He did that, all right. Hake Development accounted for a big percentage of Andy's income that year." Her voice trailed away at these last words, as if she was remembering once more the reason the good fortune had ended.

"All right, I'll start with this one." Travis moved aside the stack of boxes to retrieve the Hake files, and found a second box, also marked Hake, behind it.

He set the boxes on the desk, then went to his car and retrieved the evidence tape and seals. "You're verifying that I haven't opened the boxes or tampered with them in any way," he said.

"I am." He ran a strip of wide tape horizontally and vertically across each box, sealing the tops in place, then asked Brenda to write her name across each piece of tape.

"I'll video opening the boxes," he said. "With Lacy's parents as witnesses. That ought to satisfy any court that we aren't up to anything underhanded."

Brenda watched him, arms folded across her chest. "I hope you find something useful in there," she said. "Though I can't imagine what."

"What was Andy doing for Hake, do you know?" Travis asked.

"Just the legal paperwork for the mining claims Henry Hake had bought and planned to develop as a vacation resort. It wouldn't have been a big deal, except that environmental group got an injunction against the development and Andy was fighting that."

"I remember a little about that," Travis said. "They had a Ute Indian chief speak at a council meeting or something like that?"

"He wasn't a chief, just a tribal representative—a friend of Paige Riddell's. She was president of the group, I believe."

"Maybe someone who didn't want the development thought taking out Hake's lawyer would stop the threat of the injunction being overturned," Travis said.

"If they thought that, they were wrong. Hake hired another firm to represent him—someone out of Denver this time. I don't know what happened after that, though I guess he hasn't done anything with the property yet."

"Wouldn't hurt to check it out," Travis said.

He picked up the first box as his phone beeped. Setting it down, he answered the call. "A car just crashed through the front window of the Cake Walk Café." Adelaide sounded out of breath with excitement. "Gage is headed there. Dwight and Roberta are in training today. I can call someone from another shift in if you want me to. The ambulance is en route from Junction."

"I'll handle it. I'm on my way." Travis hung up the phone and studied the boxes. He could take them with him, but after what happened yesterday, he didn't want to risk someone trying to get hold of them. He returned the keys to Brenda. "Lock up after I've left. I'll have to send someone to retrieve these later."

"Is everything okay?" she asked.

"Apparently, someone crashed into the café."

Brenda covered her mouth with her hand. "I hope no one was hurt."

"Me, too."

In the car, he called Lacy. "I picked out two boxes of files from Andy's storage and got them sealed, but now I have to go on a call. It will be a while before I can get back to them."

"I can pick them up," she said. "If they're already sealed, it shouldn't make any difference, should it?"

He debated as he guided his SUV down the rutted dirt road leading away from the storage facility. "Ride out here with Brenda and have her deliver you and the boxes back to your house." Before she could protest, he added, "It's not that I don't trust you, but I don't want to give any lawyers the opportunity to object."

"All right. I'd like to visit with Brenda, anyway."

"I'll get back with you to set a time for the two of us to get together," he said, and ended the call. As much as he wanted to find the person who had killed Andy Stenson, his job wouldn't allow him to focus all his attention on one case. Right now he had a mess to clean up at the café.

LACY ENDED THE call from Travis and looked out the front window. The glass company had been out this morning to replace the broken pane and she had a clear view of the street. The car she had noticed earlier was still there—a faded blue sedan that had been parked in front of a vacation cottage three doors down and across the street from her parents' house. The cottage had a For Sale sign in front, but Lacy was pretty sure no potential buyer had been inside the cottage all this time.

She retrieved her mother's bird-watching binoculars

from the bookcase by the door and returned to the window, training the glasses on the car. A man sat behind the wheel, head bent, attention on the phone in his hand. He was middle-aged, with light brown hair and narrow shoulders. He didn't look particularly threatening, but then again, looks could be deceiving. And it wasn't as if it would have taken that much brawn to throw that rock through the window yesterday afternoon.

She shifted the binoculars to the license plate on the car. BRH575. She'd remember the number and think about asking Travis to check it out. He owed her more than a few favors, didn't he? She had almost mentioned the car to him while they were talking just now, but she didn't want to give him the idea that she needed him for anything. She didn't like to think of herself as hardened, but three years in prison had taught her to look out for herself.

She brought the glasses up to the man in the car and gasped as it registered that he had raised his own pair of binoculars and was focused on her. She took two steps back, fairly certain that he couldn't see her inside the house, but unwilling to take chances. What was he doing out there, watching the house? Watching *her*? She replaced the binoculars on the shelf and headed toward the back of the house. As she passed her mother's home office, Jeanette looked up from her computer. A former teacher, she now worked as an online tutor. "Who was that on the phone?" she asked.

Lacy started to lie, but couldn't think of one that sounded convincing enough. "Travis canceled our meeting to go over Andy's files," she said. "He had to go on a call."

"I hope everything's all right." Jeanette swiveled her

chair around to face her daughter. "You're okay, working with Travis?" she asked. "I know you don't have the warmest feelings toward him, and I'll admit, I had my doubts, too. But when I saw how hard he worked to clear your name..." She compressed her lips, struggling for control. "I really don't think you'd be standing here right now if it wasn't for him."

"I wouldn't have been in prison in the first place if it wasn't for him, either," Lacy said.

Jeanette said nothing, merely gave Lacy a pleading look.

"I'm okay working with him," Lacy said. "I don't know how much good going through those old files will do, but I'm willing to help." She turned away again.

"Where are you going?" her mother asked.

"I thought I'd take a walk."

"That's nice."

Lacy didn't wait for more, but hurried toward the back door. All the houses on this street backed up to the river, and a public trail ran along the bank. She let herself out the back gate and followed this trail up past four houses, then slipped alongside the fourth house, crossed the street behind the blue sedan, and walked up to the passenger side of the vehicle. The driver had lowered the front windows a few inches, so Lacy leaned in and said, loudly, "What do you think you're doing, spying on me?"

The man juggled his phone, then dropped it. "You— you startled me!" he gasped.

"I saw you watching me," Lacy said. "I want to know why."

"I didn't want to intrude. I was merely trying to get a feel for the neighborhood, and see how you were doing."

"Who are you, and why do you care how I'm doing?" She was getting more annoyed with this guy by the second.

"I'm sorry. I should have introduced myself. Alvin Exeter. I'm a writer. I specialize in true-crime stories." He leaned across the seat and extended his hand toward her.

She ignored the outstretched hand. "I didn't commit a crime," she said. "Or don't you read the papers?"

"No, of course. And that's what I want to write about," he said. "I'm planning a book on your wrongful conviction and its aftermath."

"And you were planning to write about me without telling me?"

"No, no, of course not. I would love to interview you for the book, get your side of the story. I was merely looking for the right opportunity to approach you."

"Get lost, Mr. Exeter," she said. "And if you try to write about me, I'll sue."

"You could try," he said. "But you're a public figure now. I have every right to tell your story, based on court documents, news articles and interviews with anyone associated with you. Though, of course, the story will be more complete if you agree to cooperate with me."

"No one I know will talk to you," she said. Though how could she be sure of that, really?

"That's not true. Sheriff Travis Walker has already agreed to speak with me."

"Travis is going to talk to you about my case?"

"We have an appointment in a couple days." Alvin leaned back in his seat, relaxed. "What do you think the public will make of the man who sent you to prison speaking, while you remain silent?"

"I think you can both go to hell," she said, and turned

and walked away. She could feel his eyes on her all the way back to the house, but she wouldn't give him the satisfaction of seeing her turn around. She marched onto the porch and yanked at the door—but of course it was locked, and she didn't have her key. She had to ring the doorbell and wait for her mother to answer.

"Lacy, where is your key?" Jeanette asked as she followed Lacy into the house.

"I forgot and left it in my room." Lacy stalked into the kitchen and filled a glass of water.

"What's wrong?" Jeanette asked. "You look all flushed. Did something happen to upset you?"

"I'll be fine, Mother." She would be fine as soon as she talked to Travis, and told him what he could do with Andy's client files. Travis Walker was the last person she would ever help with anything.

Chapter Four

Travis waited while Tammy Patterson snapped another photo of the red Camry with its nose buried in the pile of crumbling brick that had once been the front wall of the Cake Walk Café. She stepped back and gave him a grateful smile. "Thanks, Sheriff. This is going to look great on the front page of the next issue."

"I'll want a copy of those pictures for my insurance company." Iris Desmet, owner of the Cake Walk, joined Tammy and Travis on the sidewalk.

"Sure thing, Ms. Desmet," Tammy said. "And I'm really sorry about the café. I didn't mean to sound like this accident was good news or anything."

"I know you didn't, dear." Iris patted Tammy's shoulder. "I'm just relieved no one was hurt. It was our slow time of day and I didn't have anyone sitting up front."

Tammy pulled out her notebook and began scribbling away. Twenty-three but looking about fifteen, Tammy was working her very first job out of college for the tiny *Eagle Mountain Examiner*. What she lacked in experience, she made up for in enthusiasm. "The paramedic told me they think the driver of the car is going to be okay, too. They think he had some kind of episode with his blood sugar."

"Better confirm that with the hospital before you go printing it," Travis said.

"Oh, yes, sir. I sure will." She flashed another smile and hurried away, no doubt thrilled to have something more exciting to write about than the town council's budget meeting or the school board's decision to remove soda machines from the lunchroom.

Iris moved closer to Travis. "Do you think the guy will lose his license over this?" she asked, nodding toward the pile of rubble.

"I don't know," Travis said. "Maybe. Either way, he's probably going to have trouble finding someone to insure him."

"I hope he's got good insurance," Iris said.

"I guess you'll have to close the café for a while, to remodel," Travis said.

"I imagine so. Then again, I've been thinking how nice it would be to visit my sister for a few days. She and her husband live up on Lake Coeur d'Alene, in Idaho. Pretty country up there. Still, it'll be hard on my employees."

"I'll keep my ears open, let you know if I hear of anyone looking for short-term help, until you can get open again."

"Thanks, Sheriff." She looked him up and down. "And how are you doing?"

"I'm fine."

"I guess it's a load off your mind, with Lacy Milligan being home again, out of prison."

"I'm glad she's home," he said, cautious.

"But now you're back to the question you started with—who killed Andy Stenson?"

"I'm working on that," he said. "Do you have any ideas?"

"No. But I've been thinking, the way you do when you live alone and wake up in the middle of the night and can't sleep. I've always wondered about that woman."

"What woman?" Travis asked.

"The dark-haired one Wade testified he saw going into Andy's office shortly before Andy was killed," Iris said. "If it wasn't Lacy—and I guess it wasn't, since she was at that basketball game—but if it wasn't her, who was it?"

"Maybe it was Andy's killer," Travis said. "Or someone who saw the killer. But again—we don't know who it was. Do you have any ideas?"

"Maybe look for a client of Andy's who fits that description?" Iris shook her head. "I know I'm not helping, I just like to think about these things."

"Well, if you think of anything else, let me know," Travis said.

He walked back to his SUV and drove to the office. Adelaide rose to meet him. "Sheriff—"

"Not now, Adelaide," he said. "I'm not in the mood to talk."

"But, Sheriff—"

He walked past her, into his office, and collided with Lacy Milligan.

As collisions went, this one was more pleasurable than most, he thought, as he wrapped his arms around Lacy to steady them both. She squirmed against him, giving him plenty of opportunity to enjoy the sensation of her soft curves sliding against him. But he wasn't the kind to take advantage of the situation. As soon as he was certain neither of them was going to fall, he released his hold on her. "What can I do for you, Lacy?" he asked.

"Do for me? You've done enough for me," she said, voice rising along with the flush of pink to her cheeks. "I want you to stop. I want you to leave me alone."

Aware of Adelaide's sharp ears attuned to every word, Travis reached back and shut the door to his office. "Let's sit down and you can tell me what this is about. Is there something specific I've done that has you so upset?"

He lowered himself into the chair behind his desk, but she remained mobile, prowling the small office like a caged animal. "Alvin Exeter," she said. "How could you even think of talking to that man about me?"

Travis squinted, thinking. "Who is Alvin Exeter?"

"He's a horrible man who says he's writing a book about me—about what happened to me. He said he has an appointment to talk with you."

Travis picked up his phone and pressed the button to ring Adelaide. She picked up right away and he put her on speaker. "Do you want me to bring in coffee for you and your guest?" she asked.

"No. Do I have an appointment with someone named Alvin Exeter tomorrow?"

"Two days from now, 9:30 a.m."

"So you asked me if I wanted to talk to this Exeter guy and I said yes?"

He could picture her scowl as she assumed her chilliest schoolmarm tone. "I didn't have to ask you. You have a stated open-door policy for citizens who want to speak to you."

So he did. "What does he want to talk to me about?" Travis asked.

"He said he's writing a human interest story on rural law enforcement."

"Thanks." Travis hung up the phone and looked at Lacy. "Did you get all that?"

"You really didn't know you had an appointment with him?"

"No." Which perhaps made him look like a poor manager in her eyes, but better than looking like a traitor. "And, apparently, Adelaide didn't know the real reason behind the appointment. He lied about his purpose in wanting to see me."

"Are you still going to talk to him?"

"Only to tell him to leave you alone. That's really all I can do. I can't keep him from approaching other people and asking them questions. Though if he bothers you again, I can arrest him for harassment."

She dropped into a chair and glared at him. The memory of her warmth still clung to him, making him conscious of the short distance between them, of how beautiful and prickly and vulnerable she was—and how mixed up and charged his feelings for her were.

"You really are making this difficult, you know?" she said.

"Making what difficult?"

"For me to hate you. I spent the last three years building you up in my mind as this horrible monster and now that you're here, in front of me, you insist on being so... so decent!"

He told himself he wouldn't laugh. He wouldn't even smile. "If anyone bothers you—Exeter or anyone else— let me know," he said. "I've got your back."

"I don't need you to be my bodyguard," she said.

"My job is to protect the citizens of this county, and you're one of them."

"So that's what I am to you, then? Your job?"

"No." She was his biggest regret. His responsibility, even. He'd helped ruin her life and now he felt obligated to help her put it back together. If she had asked he would have found her a job or given her money, but she wouldn't ask for those things—she wouldn't take them if he offered. But he could do everything in his power to protect her—to shield her from the aftereffects of the damage he'd done to her. He couldn't tell her any of that, so instead, he tapped the badge on his chest. "You're someone I hurt and I want to make that up to you, but mostly, I want to make sure you aren't hurt again."

She looked away, cheeks still flushed, then shoved out of the chair. "I'd better go. I... I'll look at those files whenever you're ready."

"Iris Desmet over at the Cake Walk said something interesting to me this afternoon," Travis said. "She said we should look for any client of Andy's who matched the description Wade Tomlinson gave of the woman whom he saw at Andy's office about the time Andy would have been killed."

"I don't remember any clients who looked like me," she said.

"Think about it. Maybe a name will come to you."

"So that's your new theory about who killed Andy—this mysterious woman?"

"Not necessarily. But if she was around near the time when Andy was killed, maybe she saw something or remembers something." He frowned. "I should have followed up on that when Wade first mentioned her."

"But you didn't, because you thought he was talking about me," she said.

"That was a mistake. A big one on my part." One he wouldn't make again.

She turned to leave. "Let me know how it goes with Alvin Exeter," she said. "I'm curious to know what he has to say."

He walked her to the door. Even with her bad prison haircut and too-pale skin she was beautiful. The kind of woman a lot of men might underestimate, but not him. He would never underestimate Lacy Milligan again.

"IT'S SO GOOD to see you." Brenda greeted Lacy on the front porch of the Milligans' house the next morning with these words and a hug that surprised her with its fierceness. When Brenda pulled away, her eyes glinted with unshed tears. "I'm sorrier than you can know that I didn't contact you while you were in prison," she said. "I started to write more than once, but I just couldn't think what to say."

"I wouldn't have known what to say, either," Lacy said. After all, she had been convicted of murdering Brenda's husband. That went far beyond merely awkward. "I'm just really glad you don't have any hard feelings now."

"I'm thrilled you're home," Brenda said. "I could never accept that you had anything to do with Andy's death. When Travis told me he had found evidence that proved you were innocent, I was so relieved."

"Even though it means the real killer is still out there?" Lacy asked.

"I didn't think of that until later."

"So Travis told you he was going to try to free me?" Lacy asked.

"He told me before he told the press. He wanted to make sure I was prepared." Brenda touched Lacy's arm. "He told me you still have bad feelings toward him, and I don't blame you. But he really is a good man—one of the best men I know."

Lacy nodded. She might not be ready to forgive Travis Walker for stealing three years of her life, but she was woman enough to see the good in him, in spite of his mistakes. "I guess he told you why we're looking through Andy's files," she said.

"Yes. I don't think you'll find anything useful, but I guess we can hope." She pulled her keys from her purse. "Are you ready to go get the boxes? I would have swung by the storage unit and picked them up myself, but Travis said it was better to do things this way."

"After the mistakes he made at my trial, I guess he's being extra cautious," Lacy said.

"I can't help but hope that this time he finds the real murderer," Brenda said. "I think it would help all of us put this behind us." She climbed into the driver's seat of her car, while Lacy slid into the passenger seat.

"I do want to put this behind me," Lacy said. "I'm still adjusting to the idea that I'm really free."

"Do you think you'll stay in Eagle Mountain?" Brenda asked.

"I don't know," Lacy said. "This is my home, but even in three years, things have changed."

"Not that much, surely," Brenda said. She turned the car onto Main.

"There are new houses, new businesses, new people I don't know. We even have a new mayor." Lacy gestured toward the banner that hung over the street. "And what's this Pioneer Days Festival?" she asked. "That wasn't around when I left."

"It's a whole weekend of events celebrating local history," Brenda said. "Jan came up with the idea when she was mayor and it's really been a boon for the town coffers." Jan Selkirk had been mayor when Lacy had left town, and, after leaving office, had taken over management of the history museum where Brenda worked.

"I guess I remember some talk about a local celebration to commemorate the town's founding," Lacy said. "I didn't think it would be such a big deal."

"I guess it morphed over time into a really big deal," Brenda said. "Tourists come and stay all weekend. All the local motels and inns are sold out, and we have all kinds of special events at the museum."

"Sounds like fun." Lacy swiveled in her seat as they passed a pile of wreckage. "What happened to the Cake Walk?" she asked.

"You didn't hear?" Brenda slowed as they passed the rubble, which was cordoned off with orange tape. "That was why Travis had to leave without picking up the file boxes. A guy ran his car right into it yesterday afternoon. Jan told me she heard the poor man had a stroke. They ended up taking him to the hospital. Fortunately, no one inside was hurt."

"I was at the sheriff's office yesterday afternoon and Travis never said a word about it," Lacy said.

"Oh? Why were you at the sheriff's office?" Brenda didn't try to hide her curiosity.

Lacy leaned back in the seat and sighed. "There's a man in town who says he's writing a book about me. I complained to Travis about him." No point in going into her accusations that Travis was selling her out to this writer.

"Oh, dear. I suppose that was bound to happen," Brenda said.

"I'm surprised he hasn't gotten in touch with you yet."

"When he does, I'll tell him what he can do with his book project," Brenda said.

"He said he was going to write about me, whether I cooperate or not. I guess I'll have to get used to that kind of thing. He said I was a public figure now."

"Oh, Lacy." Brenda reached over and rubbed her arm. "I'm sorry."

Lacy straightened and forced a smile onto her lips. "It'll be okay. What's one lousy book in the scheme of things?"

For the next twenty minutes, the two friends discussed the Pioneer Days Festival, new businesses that had moved to town in Lacy's absence and a new television series they were both watching. By the time they reached the storage facility, they had relaxed into the easy banter of old friends.

"I remember this place," Lacy said as she climbed out of the car at the storage unit. "I used to give Andy a hard time about it being so far out here on the edge of town."

"I guess nobody really wants a place like this in their backyard," Brenda said. "Plus, the land is cheaper out here." She undid the lock and pulled up the door.

The first thing Lacy spotted was a Victorian lamp that had sat on her desk in the front office of Andy Stenson's law practice. Seeing it now, shade crooked and grayed with dust, gave her a jolt. Her gaze shifted to the big walnut desk where Andy had sat. It had usually been covered in papers, but she recognized the lovely dark finish. So odd to see these familiar things out of context.

"After Andy died, I was such a wreck," Brenda said, as if reading Lacy's mind. "I hired a couple of guys to clean out the office and put everything here. I hadn't even looked at any of it until I was out here with Travis yesterday."

"There was no reason you should have had to look at it," Lacy said. "I hope Travis is right, and we find something useful in all these papers."

"These are the two boxes he wants to start with." Brenda pointed to two white file boxes, their tops crisscrossed with red and white tape. "All the files for Hake Development."

"I was surprised when my mom told me Mr. Hake still hasn't done anything with that property," Lacy said. "I remember he had big plans for a bunch of luxury homes—even a golf course."

"An environmental group successfully got an injunction to delay construction," Brenda said. "I'm not sure what's going on with it now. Maybe Henry Hake changed his mind."

"Maybe." Lacy picked up one box, while Brenda carried the other to the car. Boxes safely in the back seat, Brenda locked up again and the two friends set out once more.

"They haven't done much to fix this road," Lacy said as they bumped over a series of ruts on the gravel track that led away from the storage units.

"I guess with no one living out this way, it's not a priority," Brenda said.

"Right." Lacy looked over her shoulder to make sure the file boxes hadn't slid off the seat, and was surprised to see a pickup truck following them. "If no one lives out here, I wonder who that is?" she asked.

Brenda glanced in the rearview mirror. "I don't recognize the truck," she said.

"Maybe it's a tourist," Lacy said. "He could be looking for somewhere to hike. Or maybe it's someone else with a storage unit."

"It looks like a ranch truck, with that brush guard on the front." The heavy pipe, gate-like structure attached to the front bumper would protect the headlights and grill from being damaged by brush when a rancher drove through the fields.

"I didn't see any other vehicles there," Lacy said. "And we didn't pass anyone on our way out here."

"Whoever he is, he's driving way too fast for this road," Brenda said.

Lacy glanced over her shoulder again. The truck was gaining on them, a great plume of dust rising up in its wake. "He's going to have to slow down," she said. "Or run us off the road."

Even as she spoke, the truck zoomed up, its front bumper almost touching the rear bumper of Brenda's car. The lone occupant wore a ball cap pulled low on his forehead, a black bandanna tied over his mouth and nose.

"What does he think he's doing?" Brenda's voice rose in alarm. The car lurched as she tapped the brakes and Lacy grabbed on to the door for support. The screech of metal on metal filled the vehicle, which jolted again as the bumpers connected.

Brenda cursed, and struggled to hold on to the wheel.

Lacy wrenched around to stare at the driver once more, but she could make out nothing of his face. He backed off and she sagged back into her seat once more.

"He's crazy," Brenda said. The car sped up, bumping along the rough road. "As soon as I can, I'm going to pull over and let him pa—"

She never finished the sentence, as the truck slammed into them once again, sending them skidding off the road and rolling down the embankment.

Chapter Five

"All units report to Fireline Road for a vehicular accident with possible injuries." The dispatcher's voice sounded clear on the otherwise quiet radio. Travis, on his way to lunch, hit the button to respond. "Unit one headed to Fireline Road," he said. He switched on his siren and headed out, falling in behind Gage, an ambulance bringing up the rear of their little parade.

As he drove, he checked the GPS location the dispatcher had sent over. The accident looked to have occurred about two miles this side of the storage units, an area with a sharp curve and a steep drop-off. He slowed as the screen on his dash indicated they were nearing the site. Gage pulled to the side of the road and Travis parked behind him. He joined his brother on the rough shoulder, and stared down at a white Subaru Outback, resting on its side on the steep slope, wedged against a solitary lodgepole pine tree.

Gage raised binoculars to his eyes. "Looks like there's at least one person in there—maybe two," he said.

Two EMTs joined them—a freckle-faced young guy Travis didn't know, and Emmet Baxter, a rescue service veteran. "OnStar called it in," Baxter said, nodding to the wrecked Subaru. "They tried to contact the driver but no one responded. Since the airbags had deployed, it triggered an automatic call."

"I'll call in the plate," Gage said. "See if we can get a possible ID on the driver."

"Go ahead, but I know who it is," Travis said, the tightness in his chest making it difficult to take a full breath. "That's Brenda Stenson's car. And the passenger is probably Lacy Milligan. The two of them were supposed to drive out here to pick up some of Andy Stenson's files from storage." He pulled out his phone and punched in Brenda's number. It rang five times before going to voice mail. He got the same results with Lacy's number. He swore and stuffed the phone back in the case on his hip, then stepped down off the edge of the road.

Gage grabbed his arm and pulled him back. "Where do you think you're going?"

"I'm going down to them. They could be hurt."

"Yeah, and one wrong move could send the vehicle the rest of the way down the slope and you with it," Gage said.

Travis studied the car and realized Gage was right. "Get Search and Rescue out here. And a wrecker. We'll have to stabilize the car, then get the women out."

Gage made the call and then there was nothing to do but wait. Travis walked the roadside, studying the surface for clues to what had happened. Soon, Gage joined him. "You can see the skid marks where they went off here," Travis said, pointing to the long tracks in the gravel.

"Doesn't really look like an overcorrection, or like she was going too fast and missed the curve," Gage said.

Travis shook his head. "Brenda's not that kind of

driver. Anyway, look at this." He pointed to another set of skid marks behind the first, these veering away from the edge of the road.

"Another vehicle?" Gage asked.

"Yeah." Travis walked a little farther and squatted down at a place where broken glass glittered amid the gravel in the road. "This is probably where it struck her car—broke the rear headlights." He glanced back as the first of the Search and Rescue team arrived.

"Accident or deliberate?" Gage asked.

"They left the scene. That's a crime, even if the collision itself was an accident. But this feels deliberate to me. The weather's good, light's good. No way a person traveling behind Brenda's car wouldn't have seen her."

"Maybe the other driver's brakes failed?"

Travis straightened. "How often does that really happen?"

He and Gage walked back to meet the SAR volunteers. Travis was relieved to see an orthopedic doctor who worked weekends at the emergency clinic in Gunnison, as well as a local mountain guide, Jacob Zander. "You remember Dr. Pete, right?" Jacob said.

The men shook hands, then turned their attention to the wrecked car. "We've got two women in the vehicle," Travis said. "We don't know how badly they're hurt, but they didn't respond to OnStar."

"We need to secure the vehicle before we can do anything," Dr. Pete said.

Another carload of SAR volunteers pulled onto the shoulder, followed by a flatbed wrecker with a driver and passenger. The wrecker driver climbed out and shambled over to join them.

"Got a challenge for you," Gage said, nodding to the wedged car.

The driver, whose jacket identified him as Bud, considered the scene below, then shrugged. "I've seen worse."

"Can you secure the vehicle so that the EMTs can get down to take care of the driver and passenger?" Travis asked.

"I'll take care of it." He returned to the wrecker and his passenger—who turned out to be a woman with curly brown hair—climbed out. They conferred for a moment, then both started climbing down the slope, draped in ropes and chains. Dr. Pete and Jacob followed.

"What should we do now?" Gage asked.

Travis leaned back against his SUV, arms crossed, eyes fixed on the scene below. "We wait," he said. And pray that his search for whoever had run Brenda and Lacy off the road didn't turn into a hunt for a killer.

LACY WOKE TO pain in her head, and the taste of blood in her mouth. She moaned and forced herself to open her eyes against the searing pain. "What's happening?" she asked.

The words came out garbled, and her mouth hurt.

"Don't try to talk, ma'am. You were in an accident."

"An accident?" She blinked, and the face of the man who was speaking came into focus. He was blond, with freckles and glasses.

"It looks like you hit your head," he said. "Can you tell me if it hurts anywhere else?"

"No… I don't know."

The man leaned in through the passenger-side window, which was broken. He shined a light into her eyes and she moaned again and turned her head away. When she opened her eyes, she stared at Brenda, who lay in the driver's seat, mouth slack, white powder covering her face and shoulders. "Brenda!" Lacy tried to lean toward her.

"We're taking care of your friend. We need you to stay calm." Her rescuer reached around behind her. "I'm going to put this brace on your neck," he said. "It's just a precaution. What's your name?"

"Lacy. Lacy Milligan." The brace felt stiff and awkward, and smelled of disinfectant. Her head felt clearer now—she was remembering what had happened. But with memory came fear. "Where is the truck that ran us off the road?" she asked.

"I don't know about any truck." She heard the ripping sound of a hook and loop tape being pulled apart and repositioned. "My name is Pete. I'm a doctor."

Then a second man was leaning in beside Pete. "Lacy, it's Travis. How are you doing?"

"My head hurts." She closed her eyes again.

"Stay with us, Lacy," Dr. Pete said. "Open your eyes for me."

"Tell me about the truck, Lacy," Travis said.

She struggled to do as they asked, fighting against a wave of nausea and extreme fatigue. "The truck was black," she said. "With one of those big things on the front—iron pipe welded to the front bumper."

"A brush guard?" Travis asked.

"Yes. One of those. And it came up behind us really fast. It just—shoved us and we went over." Her heart raced, and she fought to draw a deep breath as panic squeezed her chest. "Is Brenda going to be all right?"

"We're looking after Brenda," Dr. Pete said. "Try not to get upset."

"Do you remember anything else about this truck?" Travis asked. "Did you see the driver? Was there a passenger?"

"No. I mean, I don't know. The windows were so dark I couldn't see much of anything. I think he was wearing a ball cap. And a bandanna tied over his face—like a bank robber in a B movie. It all happened so fast." She tried to shake her head and pain exploded through her with a burst of light behind her eyes. She groaned.

"Do you remember anything about the license plate?" Travis's voice cut through the fog that was trying to overwhelm her. "Or what kind of truck it was?"

"I'm sorry, no."

"Okay, everybody get back, we're going to open this door." The voice came from beyond Lacy's field of vision. Travis and the doctor moved away. A deafening screech rent the air and the car rocked and slipped to the side. Lacy let out a cry and grabbed at nothing. Then the door was wrenched off the driver's side and two men rushed forward. One worked to cut away the steering wheel while two others slashed the seat belt and carefully moved Brenda onto a stretcher. Moments later, someone leaned in the passenger-side window and began sawing at Lacy's seat belt with a blade.

After that, things happened very quickly. A man helped Lacy move into the driver's seat, then she, too, was lifted onto a stretcher. As they strapped her in, Travis leaned over her, his eyes boring into hers. "I'm going to find who did this," he said.

Tears blurred her eyes. "My parents…"

"I'm going there now, to tell them in person and take them to the hospital," he said. "We'll meet you there."

And then he was gone, and all she could see was blue sky, as a group of people she didn't even know worked to carry her to help.

She told herself she was safe now. She was surrounded by people who would help her. But fear still made a cold fist in the middle of her stomach, and she couldn't shake the memory of the impact of that truck on Brenda's car, and the feeling of falling down the mountainside, knowing it was because someone wanted her dead.

TRAVIS PACED THE hallway outside Lacy's room, phone pressed tightly to his ear, shutting out the intercom summons for doctors to report to the emergency room and the rattle of carts as nurses traveled between rooms. "Tell me you've found something," he said when Gage answered the phone.

"I put out the APB like you asked," Gage said. "But we don't have much to go on. There are probably a hundred black trucks in this county alone, and a lot of them are beat-up old ranch trucks. You wouldn't be able to tell at a glance if any of the dents were new or had been there for ten years."

"There was only one black truck that was out on Fireline Road this afternoon," Travis said.

"Face it, Trav, that truck could be in New Mexico by now," Gage said. "Without more to go on, it's going to take a massive stroke of luck to find it."

"Yeah, and nothing about this whole investigation has been lucky. Did you at least get the files out of Brenda's car?" he asked.

"I picked them up myself," Gage said. "They'd been thrown around a bunch in the crash, but that tape you put on the lids actually held pretty well. One of them is kind of split on one side, but everything is in there. I put them on your desk."

"Lock the door to my office and leave it locked until I get there," Travis said.

"You think the guy who ran Brenda and Lacy off the road was after something in those files?" Gage asked.

"I don't know," Travis said. "But we can't afford to overlook anything."

"How are Brenda and Lacy?" Gage asked.

"Lacy has a concussion and a bunch of bruises," Travis said. "They're keeping her overnight for observation, but she should be able to go home with her parents tomorrow. Brenda regained consciousness briefly on the ambulance ride over, but has been drifting in and out ever since. Her head injury is worse, and she had three broken ribs and a punctured lung. They're keeping her in ICU."

"Are Lacy's folks there with her?" Gage asked.

"Yes." They had followed him to the hospital in their car. He had run lights and sirens the whole way, clearing the route, but when they arrived it was clear Jeanette Milligan had been crying, and George was as pale as paper. "They're understandably upset and afraid."

A woman in light blue scrubs came around the corner. "Are you Travis?" she asked.

Travis looked up. "Yes?"

"Ms. Milligan is asking for you."

"Got to go," Travis said, and ended the call.

Mr. and Mrs. Milligan stood on the far side of Lacy's hospital bed when Travis entered the room. Lacy wore a dark pink hospital gown, the black thread from a row of stitches just to the left of her right temple standing out against her pale skin. Both her eyes had begun to blacken, and her upper lip was swollen. Travis must not have done a good job of hiding his shock at her appearance, because she gave him a crooked smile. "They won't let me look in the mirror, but Dad says I look like I lost a boxing match," she said.

"Maybe if anyone asks, that's what you should tell them," Travis said. He moved closer and wrapped both hands around the bed rail, wishing instead that he could hold her hand. But she probably wouldn't welcome the gesture and it wouldn't be the most professional behavior for the county sheriff. Someone had placed a vase of flowers on the bedside table and the peppery-sweet scent of carnations cut through the antiseptic smell.

"Have you found out anything more about the person or people who did this?" Lacy's father asked.

"George." Jeanette gripped her husband's arm.

"It's all right, Mom," Lacy said. "I want to know, too."

All three looked at Travis. "We don't have anything yet," he said. "If you think of anything else that could help us, let me know."

"I'm sorry, no." She shook her head. "Brenda and I went to the storage units and picked up the two boxes you had marked. There wasn't anyone else around while we were there. I mean, there weren't any other vehicles, and it's not that big a place."

"Maybe they parked behind the storage sheds in the back. A truck could probably hide back there."

"Maybe," Lacy said. "It's not like we were looking around for anyone. But they would have had to have been there before we arrived. You can see the gate from the storage unit. That's the only way in, and you have to stop and enter a code to open it."

"It's bad luck no one else was out there who might have seen the guy who hit you," Travis said. "There aren't any houses out that direction, either. We're putting a plea out on the local radio station, and it will be in tomorrow's paper, asking anyone with any information to come forward. Maybe we'll get lucky and someone will know something useful."

"Why would someone do this?" Jeanette asked. "Why would anyone want to hurt Brenda or Lacy? Or was it just a madman, wanting to cause a wreck for kicks?"

"We don't know," Travis said.

"Do you think this is related to the rock that was thrown through our window?" George asked. "Maybe the same person? One of Andy's friends or relatives who still blames Lacy for his murder."

"I'll look into that angle," Travis said. "Though Brenda is the only relative of Andy's I've ever met. I don't remember any parents or siblings attending the trial."

"He was an only child," Lacy said. "His father was dead and his mother had remarried and lives in Hawaii. He didn't see her much. I don't think they were close."

"Still, I'll check and see what I can find," Travis said. "Maybe it was random, or maybe it was related to something else."

"The files!" Lacy put a hand to her mouth. "I just remembered. What happened to the files?"

"Gage got them out of Brenda's car and they're safe for now. Don't worry about them."

"Have you seen Brenda?" Lacy asked. "They told me she's in ICU?"

"I saw her for a few minutes," Travis said. "She's going to be okay, it's just going to take her a little longer. Her head injury was more severe, and she broke some ribs."

"I hope they're giving her good pain meds," Lacy said. "I feel as if, well, as if I was run over by a truck." She gave a small, hysterical laugh.

Her mother squeezed her arm. "You're getting tired," she said. "You need to rest."

"I'll go now," Travis said.

"Please let us know what you find out," Jeanette said. "We're anxious to put this all behind us."

"I will."

He was walking down the hall and was surprised to see Wade Tomlinson walking toward him. "I heard about the accident," Wade said. "I came to see if I could give blood or do anything else to help." He extended his arm to show the bandage wrapped around the crook of his elbow. "They said they didn't need it for Brenda or Lacy, but they could always use donations, and as long as I was here..." He shrugged.

"That was good of you," Travis said. "I was just in to see Lacy. She's pretty banged up, but she'll be okay. Her parents are with her now."

Wade nodded. "That's good. I hear Brenda is in ICU. Do you know what happened? I mean, the weather was good today, and Brenda doesn't strike me as the type to drive too fast on these mountain roads. Or maybe a deer ran out in front of her and she swerved or something."

Travis debated how much he should say about the accident. Then again, by the time the wrecker driver and the EMTs and the SAR volunteers got finished telling their stories, everyone in town would know what had happened. "Someone deliberately ran them off the road," he said.

Wade's eyes narrowed. "You're kidding me."

"I'm not. Do you know anybody who drives a black truck with a brush guard who might want to do something like that?"

"Half of our customers probably drive black trucks, and a lot of them have brush guards," he said. "Why would someone do something like that?"

"I don't know. But I'm going to find out."

The two men stopped at the elevators. "I'm glad I ran into you," Travis said. "I was going to stop by the store today or tomorrow to talk to you."

"What about?"

"The day Andy was killed—you said you saw a woman going into his office, about the time he would have died."

Wade nodded. "I thought it was Lacy—but I didn't really get a good look at her. I just saw her from the back. She had hair the color of Lacy's and she was the same height and build."

"Is there anything at all about her that you remember—anything that stood out?"

Wade shook his head. "That was more than three years ago," he said. "I couldn't tell you what I had for breakfast last week, so details about something that happened that long ago—they're just not there."

"I know it's a long shot, but if you think of anything, let me know."

"Sure thing. And I hope you find whoever did this to Brenda and Lacy." The elevator doors opened and they stepped in. "I guess the car is pretty wrecked, huh?" Wade asked.

"I imagine the insurance company will total it," Travis said.

"Brock said he saw Bud O'Brien's wrecker hauling it through town. He said looking at it you wouldn't guess anybody could walk away from the crash."

Lacy and Brenda hadn't exactly walked away, but Travis knew what he meant. "They were lucky," he said. "Whoever did this to them won't be when I find him."

"Bud can add the car to the collection at his yard," Wade said.

"We'll go over it for evidence first," Travis said. "I'm hoping the forensics team can get some paint samples from the vehicle that hit them."

"Yeah. I guess they can do all kinds of things like that these days." The door opened on the ground floor. "Good seeing you again, Sheriff."

Travis checked in with the office on his way to his SUV. "Gage put Eddie Carstairs on traffic patrol out on Fireline Road," Adelaide reported. "We had so many rubberneckers driving out there to see the crash site that he was afraid there would be another accident. And Eddie needs the training hours, anyway."

"Good idea," Travis said. "I'm leaving the hospital now. And before you ask, Lacy is banged up but awake and should be going home in the morning. Brenda is in ICU with a head injury and broken ribs, but she should recover fine."

"That poor woman." Adelaide clucked her tongue. "As if she hasn't been through enough already."

"I'm headed back out to the crash site," Travis said. "I know Gage and the crime scene techs already took pictures and measurements, but I want another look on my own. Call if anything urgent comes up."

"Will do, Sheriff."

As he was leaving the parking lot, Travis recognized Wade's truck in front of him. It was red, with the Eagle Mountain Outfitters logo on the tailgate. But Wade wasn't alone. A man sat in the passenger seat. As Wade turned right, Travis got a look at the passenger's profile and recognized Ian. Odd that Wade hadn't mentioned that Ian was with him. Then again, maybe they had been headed somewhere else when Wade decided to swing by the hospital. Wade had said that Ian was uncomfortable around new people, so maybe it wasn't surprising he had decided to wait in the truck.

Travis was halfway back to Eagle Mountain when his phone showed a call from Gage. "We may have found the truck," Gage said when Travis answered. "Though I don't know what good it's going to do us."

Chapter Six

"What do you mean, you don't know how much good the truck will do us?" Travis asked.

"Somebody set it on fire," Gage said. "A hiker saw the smoke and called it in. By the time the volunteer firefighters got there, it was toast. No license plates, and I'm betting when we examine the wreckage we'll find the VIN had been tampered with or removed."

"Where is it?" Travis asked.

Gage gave a location on the edge of a state wilderness area—but still in the sheriff department's jurisdiction. "I'll be there in about forty-five minutes," Travis said.

"I'm going off shift in fifteen minutes," Gage said. "Dwight is coming on to relieve me, but I can stick around if you need me to."

"Don't you have a class tonight?" Travis asked. His brother was studying for the sergeant's exam.

"I do, but I could miss it one time."

"No. Go to your class. Dwight can handle things."

Travis checked the clock on his dash—almost three, and he hadn't eaten since breakfast. He swung through a drive-through for a chicken burrito to go, then headed out to view this burned-out truck.

A fire truck and crew stood watching the smoldering

remains of the blaze when Travis pulled up, along with Sheriff's Deputy Dwight Prentice. Dwight walked out to meet the sheriff. A rangy young officer who walked with the shambling, slightly bowlegged gait of a man who had spent most of his life on horseback, Dwight had surprised everyone when he had decided to seek a career in law enforcement after his return from active duty in Afghanistan, rather than take over the family ranch. "Good afternoon, Sheriff," he said when Travis climbed out of his SUV.

Travis nodded and looked toward the blackened remains of what had once been a pickup truck, the metal frame and parts of the seats and engine still visible amid the ashes. "That was about all that was left of it when I arrived," Dwight said.

The two men walked closer. Tendrils of smoke curled up from the wreckage and heat still radiated from it. "And why do we think this is the truck we've been looking for?" Travis asked.

"The hikers who called in the fire said it was a late-model black Chevy," Dwight said. "With a brush guard. You can still see the guard up front there."

The brush guard lay in the ashes near the front of the truck, blackened but intact. "Something like that would make it easy to ram another vehicle without tearing up your own ride," Dwight said.

"But we still don't know that this is the truck," Travis said.

"True," Dwight said. "But it looks like the fire was deliberate."

"Oh, it was deliberate, all right." Assistant Fire Chief Tom Reynolds joined them. "You can see they loaded up the bed with gas cans before they lit it." He pointed to the twisted remains of the cans in front of the rear axle. "The hikers said they heard a big explosion, and a couple of other people called it in, too."

"Adelaide said one woman called the station and wanted to know if they were blasting up at the Lazy Susan Mine again," Dwight said. "And it's been shut down for thirty years."

"I reckon whoever did this stood way back and set the fire by firing a flare gun into the gas cans," Tom said. "As soon as everything cools down enough to search, we'll get our arson investigator in here. He might be able to find the remains of the flare."

Travis nodded and looked around them. The country up here was pretty desolate—rocky and covered with knots of Gambel oak scrub, prickly pear cactus and stunted juniper trees. In the fall, hunters swarmed the area hoping to bag a mule deer or elk, but this time of year the only people who came to the area were more adventurous hikers, looking for a challenging route over Dakota Ridge, which rose on the horizon to the north. "If somebody drove the truck up here to dump it, then set it on fire, how did they leave? Did the hikers report seeing another vehicle?"

"Gage asked them that and they said no," Dwight said. "But it's possible they weren't in a position to see the road, so whoever did this could have had a second vehicle waiting to drive away. Or they could have walked out cross-county." He gestured past the burned-out vehicle. "There are a couple of trails you can access from here that will take you back to the highway. It would only be a hike of three or four miles."

"We'll ask around, but I'm not holding out a lot of

hope." He turned to Tom. "When is the arson investigator coming out?"

"Tomorrow morning. It would be a good idea if you posted someone here to guard the scene until we can give it a good look."

"I'll stay here until my shift ends at midnight," Dwight said. "Then Eddie will relieve me."

"I thought Eddie was on traffic duty on Fireline Road," Travis said.

"Gage sent him home, since the lookie-loos had apparently had enough. He told him to come back out here at midnight to relieve me."

"All right." Travis studied the still-smoldering wreckage. "What do you think a late-model Chevy is worth these days?"

"Depends on how old, but thirty or forty thousand at least."

"That's a lot of money to burn up," Travis said. "If this is the truck we were looking for, somebody was willing to get rid of it rather than risk getting caught."

"Some people will do anything to avoid going to jail," Dwight said.

"A good lawyer would try to plead down to reckless driving. Someone without a record might get off with probation and community service, maybe lose their license for a while."

"Or somebody who already had a criminal record might be looking at serious time," Dwight said.

"Or whoever did this is involved in something else they don't want us to find out about." Travis shook his head.

"Do you think this is connected to Andy Stenson's murder?" Dwight asked.

"Do you?" Travis asked.

Dwight nudged his Stetson farther back on his head. "Brenda is Andy's widow. Lacy was the woman everyone thought killed him. Targeting them seems like more than a coincidence. Maybe the real killer thinks they know something—or could learn something—that would point back to him or her."

"Maybe," Travis said. "Which makes me think the sooner I can see what's in Andy's files, the better."

"Every inch of me hurts, but I don't even care, I'm just so glad to be alive." Lacy sat on the wicker settee on her parents' front porch, a bowl of popcorn on one side of her, a glass of lemonade on the other, talking to her attorney, Anisha Cook, on the phone. The sweet scent of peonies drifted to her on the breeze and in spite of everything, she felt happier than she had since she had walked out of the door of the Denver Women's Correctional Facility. Although, who was to say some of that wasn't due to the painkillers the hospital had sent her home with?

"Do the police know who did this?" Anisha asked. "Are the drivers that bad over on your side of the Divide?"

Some of Lacy's euphoria evaporated. "Whoever did this deliberately hit us," she said. "I don't think the chances are very good that the police will find them, though Travis is apparently out questioning anyone and everyone."

"Travis? Do you mean Sheriff Travis Walker?"

"Yes. He seems to be taking this attack on me personally."

"Well, that is in-ter-est-ing." Anisha drew out the last word, a hint of laughter in her voice. "Looks like he's appointed himself your personal knight in shining armor."

"Don't be ridiculous." The settee creaked as Lacy shifted position.

"It's no secret he feels guilty about what happened to you," Anisha said. "I had my doubts when he first came to me with the evidence he had found to clear you, but I think he might be the genuine article."

"What do you mean?" Lacy asked.

"A nice guy. And he's definitely easy on the eyes."

Lacy's cheeks felt hot, and she was glad Anisha wasn't here to see her. "You didn't call me to talk about Travis Walker," she said.

"No. I have some good news for you."

"What is it?"

"The state is cutting you a check for $210,000."

Lacy almost dropped the phone. "What?"

"It's the money they owe you for your wrongful incarceration—seventy thousand dollars a year for three years. All duly authorized by state law."

Lacy collapsed against the back of the settee. "I don't know what to say," she said. "I'm stunned."

"It's no less than you deserve," Anisha said. "It's money for you to use to start over. Maybe you want to use it for your education, to start a new career."

"I don't know what I want to do," Lacy said. "I haven't had time to think."

"There's always law," Anisha said. "I can recommend some good schools."

Lacy laughed. "I'm so grateful for everything you've done for me, but I'm not sure I'm cut out to be a lawyer. I'll have to think."

"You do that. And let me know if the check doesn't

show up in a couple of days. They're supposed to be sending it directly to you."

Lacy ended the call and sat back, trying to let the news sink in. The money didn't feel real yet, but then, nothing about her situation did.

The door into the house opened and her mother stepped out onto the porch. "How are you doing out here?" she asked. "Do you need anything?"

"I'm doing well," Lacy said. "Great, even. I just heard from Anisha. The state is paying me a bunch of money. I guess there's a state law that says they have to."

Jeanette hugged her daughter. "That's wonderful. I'm so happy for you." She sat next to Lacy.

"I should use the money to pay you and Dad back for all you've done for me," Lacy said. "I know you took out a second mortgage on this house to pay my legal bills, and you used your savings..."

"Don't say another word." Jeanette put a hand over Lacy's. "We want you to use the money for your education, and for things you need—a car, maybe, or a place to live, though you are welcome to stay here as long as you like."

Lacy nodded. She would need all those things, wouldn't she? After so many months with no hope, she was going to have to get used to planning for the future again.

A familiar black-and-white SUV moved slowly down the street toward them. Lacy's heart sped up, though not, she had to admit, from fear. She no longer feared Travis Walker. And she had stopped hating him. But she wasn't indifferent to him, either. She couldn't decide where he fit in her categorization of people. He wasn't her enemy anymore, but was she ready to accept him as a friend?

Travis parked at the curb and strode up the walkway, confident and oh-so-masculine. He was one of those men who never looked rumpled or out of shape. "Good afternoon, ladies." He touched the brim of his Stetson. "I heard they let you out of the hospital, Lacy. How are you feeling?"

"Sore, but I'll live. Too bad it isn't Halloween, though. My face could be my costume."

He leaned closer to examine her face. "The bruises are turning Technicolor," he said. "Better start embellishing your story. Who did you say beat you in that boxing match?"

Lacy laughed in spite of herself. So much for keeping her emotions in check around this man. "What brings you here?" she asked. "Or did you just stop by to see how I'm doing?"

"I thought I should let you know the latest on the case, before the news got back to you through the Eagle Mountain grapevine."

"Eagle Mountain has a grapevine?" she asked.

"You know it. And half the time it starts in my office, with Adelaide Kinkaid."

"Sit down, Travis." Jeanette pulled up a chair. "Tell us what you've found out."

He sat. "We think we found the truck that ran you off the road," he said. "Someone drove it to an isolated area and set it on fire. We can't be 100 percent sure that it's the right one, but we think so. The Vehicle Identification Number was removed and there were no license plates. I don't know if we'll ever identify the owner."

"I wish you could find him," Jeanette said. "I hate thinking someone like that is out there, running free."

"We're doing the best we can," Travis said.

"I know that. And we appreciate it." She stood. "I have to get back to work. You stay and talk to Lacy."

They waited until her mother had shut the door behind her before either of them said anything. "I talked to—" she began.

"How are you—" he said.

"You first," he said, and motioned for her to continue.

"I talked to Brenda today," Lacy said. "She was pretty groggy, but awake. She thinks the doctors will let her go home tomorrow or the next day."

"That's great news."

"I got some more good news," she said. "The state is paying me a settlement. Apparently they have to, according to state law."

"I guess I had heard something about that," he said. "I'm glad. You can use the money to make a fresh start."

"I'm still trying to decide what to do with the money, but it does feel good to know it's there."

"I spoke to a friend of yours this morning," he said, a teasing glint in his eye.

"Oh? Who was that?"

"Alvin Exeter. We had an appointment, remember?"

"And what did he have to say?"

"I told him I knew he wasn't writing a piece on rural law enforcement and that I wouldn't talk to him about anything else. He said I must have spoken to you, but that refusing to do an interview with him wouldn't stop the book. He told me if I cooperated and spoke to him, he would be sure to present my side of the story. Otherwise I could come off looking like a stupid hick cop who took the easy way out on a case and got it wrong."

"He threatened you!" she said. "What a miserable worm. If I see him again—"

Travis's hand on her arm silenced her. "He isn't that wrong, you know," he said. "I did take the easy way out and I did get it wrong."

"You were inexperienced." She said the words without thinking. But she realized they were true. She had been twenty when she was sentenced for murder, but Travis had only been twenty-three. And he had never handled a murder case before.

"I should have done a better job," he said. "I will this time."

Lacy believed him, and she vowed to do what she could to help him. After all, she would only be helping herself. "I've been thinking about what happened," she said. "I have to wonder if whoever ran us off the road did so because he didn't want us to examine those files. It wouldn't be that difficult to figure out what we were doing out at Andy's storage unit. If he was watching us, he would have seen us put the files in Brenda's car."

Travis nodded. "I've thought of that, too."

"Where are the files now?" she asked.

"They're in my SUV." He nodded toward the vehicle parked at the curb. "I'm not trying to rush you, but when you're ready, I'd like to go through them."

"I'm ready now." She stood, fighting not to show how much it hurt.

"You just came home from the hospital," he protested.

"And I'm going nuts, sitting here doing nothing. Trust me, this is just what I need to distract me."

Chapter Seven

Lacy waited on the porch while Travis retrieved both boxes from the car and she held the door while he carried them inside. "Go through that archway on the right," she said. "We can use the dining table."

She flicked the light switch as she followed him into the room, illuminating the chandelier that cast a golden glow over the cherry dining set for eight that the family only used for holidays and formal occasions. Travis set the boxes on the table. "I'll be right back," he said, and went out again.

He returned moments later, carrying a video camera on a tripod. "This is probably overkill," he said as he positioned the camera. "But I didn't want to take any chances."

Camera in place and running, he broke the seal on the first box and removed the lid. The first file he opened on the table between them was the contract Henry Hake had signed, as president and CEO of Hake Development, with Andrew Stenson as his legal representative in the matter of Eagle Mountain Resort, a high-altitude luxury resort development.

"I remember the day Andy signed that contract," Lacy said. "He took me and Brenda to lunch and insisted on ordering champagne. We teased him that he was going to get a reputation as a lush, drinking at noon."

"It was a big contract for a fairly new lawyer," Travis said.

"The biggest. And totally out of the blue. We couldn't believe our luck when Mr. Hake contacted us. He said he wanted someone fresh, with new ideas, and that he believed in supporting local talent."

"Still, this development looks like a big deal," Travis said. "I'm surprised he didn't want someone who was more experienced in real estate law." He removed a folded paper from an envelope labeled Plat and spread it across the table. "Tell me about this," he said.

Lacy leaned over his shoulder, the soap and starch scent of him sending a tingle through her midsection. She forced herself to focus on the plat of the development, instead of on the way his shoulders stretched tight the crisp cotton of his uniform shirt, or the way his dark hair curled up at the collar, exposing a scant half inch of skin...

"These were all old mining claims, right?" Travis prompted.

"Right. Mining claims." She swallowed and shifted her gaze to the blue lines on the creamy paper. "Hake Development was able to buy up approximately fifty mining claims, all above nine thousand feet, an area that has traditionally been deemed unsuitable for development."

"Why is that?" Travis asked.

"Mostly because there's so much snow up there in the winter it makes it difficult to maintain roads," Lacy said. "Plus, there's a higher avalanche danger. Up at the higher elevations, above treeline, the ground is tundra, frozen year-round. That makes it unstable to build on. Hake had engineers who had devised plans for getting around those limitations—foundations anchored on rock deep in the ground, regular avalanche mitigation, roads on traditional mining trails, water piped up from far below in an elaborate network of aqueducts."

Travis whistled. "Sounds expensive."

"Oh, it was. But Hake swore he knew plenty of people who would pay a premium price to live with the kind of views and privacy you get at those elevations."

"Not everyone was thrilled about his plans, I'm sure."

"Oh, no. The Ute Indian tribe objected because some of that terrain overlaps areas they deem sacred. And the environmentalists were in an uproar over the potential damage to fragile tundra. They succeeded in getting an injunction to stop the development until environmental studies could be done."

"And were the studies done?" he asked.

"I don't know," she said. "But we could probably find out." The idea excited her. She had missed this—working on something constructive, researching and finding out things, instead of simply sitting back and letting each day stretch forward with no goal or purpose.

"You find out what you can about the injunction and any studies," Travis said. "Meanwhile, I'll talk to Henry Hake, and ask him to update us on the project."

"My mom said they haven't built anything up there," Lacy said. "Maybe he couldn't beat the injunction. Or he decided the project was too expensive to pursue. He supposedly had a lot of investors who wanted to put money into the resort, but maybe the injunction caused them to change their minds."

"I'll find out." He pulled another stack of files from

the box and handed her half. "Let's see if anything stands out in these."

As Lacy read through the contents, it was as if she was sitting back in the little office on Fourth Street, twenty years old and ready to take on the world, excited to have found interesting work right here in Eagle Mountain, the place she loved best in the world. From the window by her desk she could look up and see Dakota Ridge, and the road leading out of town, Mount Rayford peeking up over the ridge, snowcapped year-round.

As she flipped through the files, she remembered typing memos and motions, and discussing the work with Andy over sandwiches at their desks. Sometimes Brenda would stop by to say hello and share a story about her work at the history museum. Though the world hadn't been perfect back then, it had sure seemed so at times.

"Find anything interesting?" Travis asked after they had been reading silently for almost an hour.

"Not really," she said. "Most of it is just routine stuff—surveyor's reports and court motions, tax paperwork—nothing out of the ordinary. How about you?"

"I found this." He pushed a piece of paper across to her. "Any idea what it means?"

The note was written on the blank side of a "While You Were Out" message slip. *Ask Hake about notes.*

Lacy made a face. "This is Andy's handwriting, but I don't know what notes he's referring to."

Travis set the paper aside and they searched through the rest of the first box. Lacy could tell when her pain medication wore off, as her head began to throb, her vision blurring from the pain. She put a hand to her temple, grimacing. "We should stop now," Travis said. "We can do the other box later."

"I guess you're right." Fatigue dragged at her—she could have put her head down and gone to sleep right there beside him.

"I appreciate your help," Travis said. "But don't overdo it."

She nodded. "What will you do now?" she asked.

Travis picked up the slip of paper he had set aside earlier. "I think I'll start by asking Hake about this."

GETTING AN INTERVIEW with Henry Hake proved to be more difficult than Travis had expected. When he had telephoned the number for Hake Development yesterday, a brisk-sounding woman informed him that Mr. Hake was out of town. "I can ask him to call you when he returns," she said. "But it may be some time before you hear from him."

"This is a police matter. I need to hear from him sooner, rather than later."

"Oh. Well, I'll certainly let him know."

"So you're sure you don't know when he'll be back in town."

The silence on the other end of the line went on so long Travis wondered if they had lost their connection. "Are you still there?" he asked.

"Mr. Hake may be back tomorrow—but you didn't hear that from me."

"What's the status of the Eagle Mountain Resort development?" Travis asked.

"I don't have any information on that to give you," she said.

"Is that because you don't know or because the official policy is to keep silent?" he asked.

"I'm sure I don't know what you mean," she said. "Is there anything else I can help you with?"

"No, thank you." He ended the call, then called Adelaide. "I need you to track down Henry Hake's personal number and address."

"Will do, Sheriff."

Travis turned to his computer and found a report from the county's arson investigator in his inbox. He settled back to read, finding no surprises. The truck was a standard model, probably from the last two or three years, judging by what little remained of the frame and engine. No VIN, no plates. The only nonstandard feature was the brush guard, which had been welded of heavy pipe and wasn't the sort of thing that could be ordered from a catalog. Travis called Adelaide again. "Who's on shift right now?" he asked.

"Dwight just came on. He's probably still in the parking lot, if you need him for something."

"See if you can grab him and tell him I want to talk to him for a minute."

A few minutes later, Dwight entered Travis's office. "What can I do for you, Sheriff?"

"I need you to check with any metal fabricators or welders around here, see if any of them made a brush guard like this for a guy with a black Chevy pickup." He slid a note across the desk with the description and dimensions of the brush guard.

"Sure." Dwight pocketed the note. "This have anything to do with the guy that ran Lacy Milligan and Brenda Stenson off Fireline Road?" he asked.

"Yes. I'm hoping we'll get lucky and turn up a lead, but it's a long shot."

Dwight hesitated in the doorway. "Is there something else?" Travis asked.

"I was just wondering how Mrs. Stenson is doing?" Dwight said. "I heard she was hurt pretty bad in the accident."

"She's doing much better," Travis said. "She should get to come home in a few days."

Dwight nodded, his expression solemn. "I'm glad to hear it. She and I were in school together. She was always a real sweet girl."

Dwight left and Travis sat back in his chair, staring at the computer, wondering what he should do next. He was tempted to call Lacy and brainstorm with her about the case—or better yet, go by and see her. He discarded the idea immediately. Though she had seemed to enjoy the time they had spent together, he wasn't going to delude himself into thinking she was helping him out of anything other than self-interest. Maybe once upon a time the two of them could have hit it off and been a couple. But too much had come between them now.

"Why are you sitting there with that moony look on your face?"

Travis looked up to find his brother standing in the doorway of his office. He sat up straight and assumed his best all-business expression. "I just sent Dwight out to try to track down the welder who made the brush guard on that burned-out truck," he said. "And I've got a call in to Henry Hake, trying to find out about a note we found in Andy Stenson's files."

"I thought Hake was out of town," Gage said.

"When I pressed his assistant, she admitted that he's supposed to return today."

"So you've been busy." Gage crossed to the visitor's

chair across from the desk and sat. "When this is all over—when we've closed the case—are you going to ask her out?"

"Ask who out?" Travis stared at his computer screen, the words of the arson investigator's report blurring together.

"Lacy. And don't lie to me and say you aren't gone over her. You acted this same way about Didi Samuelson. I recognize the signs."

"Didi Samuelson was in eighth grade," Travis protested.

"Which only proves that love reduces all of us to immature shadows of ourselves," Gage said.

"And you know this because you've been in love so much."

Gage stretched his arms over his head. "I know this because I've studied how to successfully avoid falling victim to the dreaded love disease," he said. "And stop trying to change the subject. We're talking about you here, not me."

"I am not in love with Lacy Milligan." Travis kept his voice down, hoping Adelaide wasn't listening in, but doubting he would be so lucky. The woman had ears like a cat's. "I hardly know her."

"Right. So you only tied yourself in knots and practically killed yourself clearing her name because you wanted to do the right thing."

"Yes. Of course. I would have done that for anyone."

Gage laughed. "Pardon me if I have a hard time believing you would have gotten quite so worked up about some ugly guy with tattoos and a rap sheet as long as my arm."

"I made a mistake arresting her and I had to make up for it."

Gage leaned forward, his expression no longer mocking. "You did your job," he said. "You arrested her because the evidence pointed to her as the perpetrator of the crime."

"It was a sloppy investigation. The follow-up proved that. The money missing from the business account was a bookkeeping error. The money in Lacy's account really was from selling her grandmother's ring. She really wasn't in town at the time Andy was killed. If I had done my job and taken a closer look at the evidence, I would have found that out."

"You know what they say—hindsight is twenty-twenty. You could have looked at that evidence ten times back then and you might not have seen anything different."

"But I might have," Travis said. That knowledge would haunt him for the rest of his life. It had changed the way he looked at every case now.

"I know one thing," Gage said. "This whole situation has made you a better cop. And it's made all of us who work under you better cops."

"Yeah, it taught you not to make the mistakes I did," Travis said.

Gage sat back again. "And it taught us to man up and admit it when we do make a mistake, and to do what we can to right the wrong."

"Glad I could be such a shining example," Travis said sourly.

Gage stood and hitched up his utility belt. "Lacy is still speaking to you, in spite of everything," he said. "That has to be a good sign."

"She's a good person."

"And so are you. Don't sell yourself short. I'm not saying you have to rush things, but don't give up before you start." He pointed a finger at Travis. "You taught me that, too."

He left the office. Travis stared after him, an unsettled feeling in his chest he wasn't sure he wanted to examine too closely. It could be his brother had stirred up something inside him—something like hope.

BRENDA CAME HOME from the hospital the next day, and the day after that Lacy delivered a box of fancy chocolates and a chicken casserole to her friend's door. "The casserole is from my mom, but the chocolates are from me," Lacy said as she carried her gifts into Brenda's house. It was the same house she and Andy had purchased shortly after moving to Eagle Mountain—a former forest ranger's residence originally built by the Civilian Conservation Corps in the 1930s, constructed of native stone and cedar, with hand-carved shutters and door lintels. They had updated the house with new windows and roof and a new heating system, part of the improvements paid for with money from Henry Hake's retainer.

"Thank you for both," Brenda said, gingerly lowering herself to the sofa.

"It still hurts, doesn't it?" Lacy asked, as Brenda sucked in her breath and winced.

"The doctor taped the ribs, but all I can do is wait for them to heal," Brenda said. "I still get dizzy from the head injury, and I can't read for long without getting a headache. The neurologist said those symptoms could take months to disappear, though she reassured me there's no permanent damage."

"That's going to make it tough at work, isn't it?" Lacy asked.

"Jan already called and told me not to worry. I know not everyone gets along with her, but ever since Andy died, she's been an absolute peach." She leaned forward to study Lacy's face. "You look pretty beat up yourself," she said. "How are you feeling?"

"Much better, actually," Lacy said. "The headaches are almost gone. I'm still a little stiff and sore, but that will go away eventually." She made a face. "I was hoping makeup would cover the worst of the bruising, but no such luck."

"You're still beautiful and it makes you look... I don't know—tough."

"That would have come in handy when I was in prison." At Brenda's stricken look, Lacy laughed. "It's okay, really," she said. "I don't mind talking about it. I figure better to get it out in the open and own it than to worry everyone's talking about it behind my back—which you know they are."

"I guess people are curious," Brenda said weakly.

"Of course they are. I would be, too. So don't be afraid to ask me questions. I'll answer if I can."

Brenda shook her head. "I don't want to know anything. All I care about is that you're here now. Though if I could ask a question of someone, I would want to know who tried to kill us the other day. And why?"

"Travis is following every lead, but he hasn't come up with much yet," Lacy said. "He and I started going through some of Andy's files, hoping we could find some clue—in case the guy who hit us was trying to stop us from looking through the files."

"Did you find anything?" Brenda asked.

"Only a note on the back of a 'While You Were Out' slip. It was in Andy's handwriting, and it said, 'Ask Hake about the notes.' Do you have any idea what that might mean?"

Brenda frowned. "I have no idea what it means. You know Andy—he was always making notes to himself about things he wanted to do or find out. For weeks after he died I would find little scraps of paper around the house."

"I'm sorry," Lacy said. "I didn't mean to upset you."

"No, it's okay." She straightened her shoulders. "It's actually been a lot better since you came home. I think I had that burden of guilt hanging over me, keeping me from moving on."

"I'd think it would be easier to move on if you knew who actually killed Andy," Lacy said.

"It would. But I'm getting used to the idea that that might never happen. I still have to live my life, so that's what I'm trying to do."

"You're still young. Maybe one day you'll meet another man you can love."

"Maybe. Though dating in a small town can be problematic."

"You mean, you can't really keep a relationship secret," Lacy said. "But at least we're luckier than some places. Single men still outnumber single women in these mountain towns, so we have a better selection to choose from."

"I don't care about a selection," Brenda said. "I just want to find the one right guy. But enough about me. How many guys have asked you out since you came home?"

Lacy blinked. "None. Why would they?"

"Hello? Didn't we just say there are more single men

than women around here? And here you are, a beautiful young woman who hasn't had a date in at least three years. I'm surprised they aren't lined up at your door."

Once again, Lacy cursed her tendency to blush so easily. "I was single before I went to prison, too," she said. "And I never dated that much." In fact, she had never had a serious relationship. She had always put it down to men seeing her more as a best friend than as a lover.

"There's a new guy in town who looks pretty interesting," Brenda said. "I saw him with Brock Ryan at the climbing wall in Ute Park when I cut through there to deliver an ad to the *Examiner* office. He was about halfway up the wall and, well, I'm not ashamed to admit I stopped and stared. And I wasn't the only one. The two of them had drawn quite an audience of female admirers. Adelaide Kinkaid was there, too."

"Adelaide is old enough to be Brock's grandmother," Lacy said.

"You'd have to be dead not to notice those two," Brenda said. "I mean, Brock is good-looking, but this new guy..." She fanned herself. "He was like a statue of some Greek god. Amazing."

"Then I hope I get a chance to check him out," Lacy said. "What's his name?"

"Tammy Patterson at the paper told me his name is Ian Barnes. He's a veteran and she thinks he's in town visiting Brock and staying at his place. She tried to get him to do an interview with her for the paper, but he wasn't interested."

"I don't guess I know Tammy," Lacy said.

"She moved here last year from Minnesota. Sweet kid, fresh out of college. She works weekends at Moe's Pub."

"That sounds like a good place to run into good-looking men," Lacy said.

"Except Tammy is apparently engaged to her high school sweetheart back in Duluth and staying true to him," Brenda said. "Which doesn't keep the men in town from pursuing her. I guess playing hard to get really is an effective strategy."

"You really do know all the gossip," Lacy said. "Is that because you've been studying, preparing to dive back into the dating game?"

"It's really because Jan keeps tabs on everything and everyone in town, and passes the information on to me," Brenda said. "She may not be mayor of Eagle Mountain anymore, but she still wants to know what's going on."

"I was surprised to find out she didn't run for reelection when her term ended," Lacy said. "She seemed to enjoy the job so much, and she was good at it."

"She said it was time to move on to something else. And Larry had already declared his intention to run, and he seemed really serious about wanting the job, so I guess she figured it was a good time to bow out."

"Maybe we should talk to her about Andy," Lacy said. "Maybe she knows something about the mysterious woman Brock saw near his office the day he died, or someone with a black truck who might have had it in for us."

"She holds court at a back table at Kate's Kitchen every Thursday morning," Brenda said. "We could go there tomorrow if you like."

"I would like, if you're up to it."

"It's a date, then." Brenda picked up the box of chocolates. "Now, let's try out your gift. I get dibs on the caramels."

Chapter Eight

Henry Hake lived in a stone-and-cedar mansion near the base of Mount Rayford. A black iron gate blocked the winding paved drive, so Travis parked and called Hake's private number on his cell phone. "Hello?" The voice that answered was hesitant and higher-pitched than Travis had expected.

"This is Rayford County Sheriff Travis Walker. I need you to open the gate so I can come up and see you."

"What is this about?"

"We'll discuss that when I get there. Open the gate, please."

"I really don't have time for this. I'm on my way out."

"Then you shouldn't waste any more time discussing this. Open the gate and I'll be out of your way as quickly as possible." Silence stretched between them, but Travis could hear the other man breathing and knew he hadn't disconnected. He resisted the temptation to speak, letting the tension build. Finally, the gate groaned and began to swing open.

"I'll be up in a minute," Travis said, and ended the call.

He returned to his car and drove the quarter mile up to the house. Hake met him at the door. "Hurry. I don't have time to waste," he said, ushering Travis inside. A portly man in a light gray suit with worn cuffs, Henry Hake looked more like a schoolteacher than a millionaire businessman. Travis followed him down a mahogany-paneled hallway to a small, dark office, where Hake took a seat behind a cluttered desk. Dust coated the side tables and floated in the shaft of sunlight from the single window, where a leggy geranium sprawled across the sill. "What do you want?" Hake asked.

"I want to talk to you about Andy Stenson," he said.

Hake blinked. He clearly hadn't been expecting this topic of conversation. "What about him? He's dead."

"I'm trying to find out who killed him."

"Got that wrong the first time, didn't you?" Hake pawed through the papers on the desk until he unearthed a cell phone. He stared at the screen, then back up at Travis. "You've got five minutes."

"Why did you hire Andy Stenson to represent you and Eagle Mountain Resort?" Travis asked. "Why not a more experienced lawyer?"

"I wanted to give the kid a chance."

"Did you know him previously? How did you decide on him?"

"Never heard of the kid. A business associate suggested it."

"Who is this business associate?"

"That doesn't really matter. You're wasting your time."

The five-minute deadline was a bluff, Travis decided. As far as he could tell, Hake was alone in the house. It wasn't likely he could throw Travis out by himself. "What's the status of Eagle Mountain Resort?" he asked.

"We're restructuring."

"Who is we?"

"I have business partners—some of whom prefer to remain silent."

"You went to a lot of trouble to buy up the mining claims and develop plans for the resort. Why didn't you go through with them?"

"I really can't talk about that."

"Why not?"

Hake snatched the phone from his desk and shoved it into the inside pocket of his jacket. "It ought to be obvious to you, if you've done any investigating, that someone doesn't want that project to go forward."

"Who?" Travis asked. "The environmentalists?"

"Maybe. There was some sabotage that might have been their doing. What do they call it—monkey-wrenching? We had equipment destroyed, some property stolen."

Travis hadn't heard any of this. "Did you report this to the police?"

"We didn't want the bad publicity. We handled it ourselves by posting private security. After that we didn't have any more troubles."

"Who is we?"

Hake waved a hand as if shooing a fly. "The organization. Who doesn't really matter."

Travis took Andy's note from his pocket and passed it to Hake. "What can you tell me about this?"

Hake studied it. "What is this? It doesn't make sense."

"I found it in Andy Stenson's files."

Hake tossed the paper back toward Travis. "I have no idea what it's about."

Travis had given a lot of thought to what the note might mean. He risked a guess. "Was someone writing you threatening letters? Is that what Andy wanted to know more about?"

Hake's face registered an internal struggle. "There were a couple of nasty notes," he said finally. "I never should have mentioned them to Andy, but I thought it would be a good idea if someone knew—for insurance."

"Do you think Andy decided to look into the threats on his own?" Travis said. "Is that what led to his death?"

Hake pushed out his lower lip. He had a cut on his chin, maybe from shaving. "I wondered at first, if maybe he had gotten too close to someone who didn't want to be found out."

"Why didn't you say something?" Travis tried to rein in his anger. "Your suspicions might have led us to look at other suspects in the murder."

"I thought if I opened my mouth whoever had killed Andy would come after me next."

"Who do you think killed him?" Travis leaned toward him. "If you have any ideas, tell me."

"I don't know who. And if I did, I'm smart enough to keep my mouth shut. I was so terrified at the time, I hired a bodyguard."

"Who did you hire?" Maybe the bodyguard knew more about these threats.

"A professional. He came highly recommended, but I don't remember his name. He didn't work for me for long."

"Why not?"

"After Andy died, the threats went away. The injunction stopped the development, so I guess our opponents got what they wanted."

"I'll need the names of your business partners so that I can talk to them, too. Maybe they know more about the source of the threats."

"They don't know anything, I promise. Some of them

aren't even alive anymore, and the others won't talk to you."

"Tell me their names, anyway."

"I'm sorry, I really can't help you. And I have another appointment." He rose.

Travis stood, also. "Did you keep any of the threatening notes you received?" he asked.

"No. I destroyed them a long time ago."

"And you have no idea who sent them?"

"None. As I said, it happened a long time ago." His eyes met Travis's. "I've put it behind me, and you should, too."

He walked Travis to the front door. As Travis drove away from the mansion, Hake's final words replayed in his head. Was the developer merely offering advice, or was he making a threat?

LACY AND BRENDA walked into Kate's Kitchen a few minutes after nine o'clock the next morning and found Jan Selkirk having coffee with Adelaide Kinkaid and two other women at a table near the back. The former mayor—a striking, fortysomething woman with big brown eyes and ash-blond hair in a tumble of curls around her shoulders—looked up and smiled at their approach. "Good morning, Brenda. I didn't expect to see you out and about so soon."

"I was going crazy, sitting around the house," Brenda said. She pulled out a chair and carefully lowered herself into it. "You know Lacy Milligan, don't you?"

Lacy leaned forward and offered her hand.

"I do. It's been a while," Jan said, with a firm handshake. "I hope you won't be offended, dear, but you look like you took a real beating. I'm so sorry. And the police have no idea who attacked you two?"

"If there's a clue to be found, Travis will find it," Adelaide said. "The poor man is working himself into the ground." She studied Lacy over her coffee cup. "I thought things would settle down once he got Lacy home, but I guess we're not going to be so lucky."

Lacy tried not to resent the implication that she was personally responsible for a new local crime wave. She took the chair next to Brenda and accepted the carafe of coffee one of the women passed her.

"We have a few questions since, as former mayor, you know pretty much everyone in town," Brenda said.

"What you mean is that she has the dirt on everyone," Adelaide said. She pushed out her chair and stood. "Come on, ladies. Let's leave these young women to it. I need to get to the station, anyway. If I don't, Gage will make the coffee and it will be so strong you could strip paint with it."

When Lacy and Brenda were alone with Jan, the older woman leaned back in her chair and studied them. "What do you want to know?" she asked.

"At my trial, Wade Tomlinson testified that he saw a woman outside Andy's office about the time Andy was killed—a woman who looked like me," Lacy said. "Obviously, that wasn't me, so do you know who it might have been?"

"I have no idea," Jan said. "I was too busy being mayor at the time to pay attention to anything that didn't pertain to the job."

"Yes, but can you think of anyone who was living in the area at the time—or visiting—who looked like Lacy?" Brenda asked. "A slim young woman with dark hair?"

Jan put a hand to her own blond locks. "No one comes to mind," she said. "It could have been anyone."

"Maybe she was a client of Andy's," Lacy said. "I've tried to think if any of his clients had dark hair, but it was too long ago. I'm hoping when Travis and I look at the rest of Andy's files, it will jog my memory."

"You and Travis are going through Andy's files?" Jan looked amused. "I'll bet that's interesting. As I remember, there was no love lost between you and our young sheriff."

"We've decided to keep the past in the past," Lacy said, eyes downcast. No sense letting the town gossips think anything differently. Lacy's feelings about Travis were so all over the map she didn't need other people weighing in with their opinions.

"What about a newish black truck with a welded brush guard?" Brenda asked. "Do you know anyone with a truck like that?"

"Only half the ranchers in the county," Jan said. "I heard they found the one they think hit you burned out over on the edge of the public land out toward Dakota Ridge."

"Yes, but they don't know who was driving it," Lacy said.

"Whoever it is, let's hope he doesn't try again," Jan said. "Frankly, if I were you two I wouldn't want to be seen out in public together."

"Why do you say that?" Brenda asked.

"Well, since there's no way of putting it delicately, I'll just say it—you don't know who this maniac was really after, do you—you or Lacy. If you're not the one he wants, why take chances hanging out with the one he does?"

Lacy was still trying to digest this take on the situation when the door to the restaurant opened and a man entered. He wore a black watch cap, along with a black T-shirt that fit like a second skin, showing off every chiseled muscle of his shoulders and torso. Every female head in the room—including the two waitresses and the woman at the cash register—swiveled to track his progress to a table by the window. Jan leaned forward. "That's Ian Barnes," she said softly. "Now that is one beautiful man."

"I don't know," Lacy said, turning her back to him. "He's almost too beautiful. And does he ever smile? He looks almost...dangerous."

"Mmmm," Jan purred. "Some women like men like that. And you may not be interested in him, but he's definitely interested in you. He's looking right at you."

Lacy shifted in her chair. "I wish he wouldn't," she said. "Maybe someone should point out that it's rude to stare. He makes me nervous."

"He doesn't drive a black truck," Jan said. "I saw him yesterday in a beat-up Jeep." She sat back and sipped her coffee. "But I swear I've seen him somewhere before. That's not a body—or a face—a woman forgets. But I can't put my finger on where." She shrugged. "I'm sure it will come to me."

The door opened and a second man entered. Lacy let out a groan and turned back around. "Do you know him?" Jan asked.

"His name is Alvin Exeter," Lacy said. "He's a writer who says he's working on a book about me."

"I don't just say it, I'm writing it." Alvin stopped behind Lacy's chair, and the thought passed through her mind that this was what it must feel like for a mouse when a hawk hovered over it. Except she wasn't a mouse.

She turned to look up at the man. "Go away," she said.

"No." He pulled out the chair on her other side and sat.

"I don't have anything to say to you," Lacy said.

"I didn't come to talk to you. I came to talk to Ms. Selkirk."

"Oh?" Jan looked interested. "What about?"

"I understand you were mayor of Eagle Mountain when Andy Stenson was murdered," Alvin said. "I thought you would be the perfect person to give me a picture of what life was like here during that time."

Jan glanced at Lacy, then smiled at Alvin, coral-lip-sticked mouth stretched over big teeth. "I'm sorry, Mr. Exeter, but you'll have to write your book without my help. In fact, I think Lacy should write her own book. After all, it's her story to tell."

"Maybe I will," Lacy said, taking her cue, though she had no intention of reliving the last three years on paper.

Alvin's expression turned stormy. "If you don't help me, you have no say in how you're portrayed," he said.

"You're assuming we care," Jan said.

He shoved back his chair and left the café. Jan picked up the carafe and refilled their coffee cups. "What an unpleasant little man," she said.

"I caught him watching my house through binoculars," Lacy said.

"I don't suppose he owns a black truck," Jan said.

Lacy shook her head. "When I saw him, he was in a blue sedan."

"A pity. He's just the type I would like for the villain."

"I met plenty of very ordinary-looking people in

prison who did horrible things," Lacy said. "For a while I celled with a white-haired grandmother who had poisoned three husbands."

The sudden silence that blanketed the café made her aware that everyone in the place was staring at her. Jan leaned forward and broke the tension. "Keep talking that way and they're all going to want to see your prison tattoos," she said.

"I don't have any prison tattoos," Lacy said, her cheeks burning.

"Everyone will be so disappointed," Jan said. "When people come through a horrible experience like that, we expect them to wear their scars on the outside." She leaned forward and grasped Lacy's hand. "Don't be afraid of shocking people. Sometimes that's exactly what we need to wake us up to the real world. It's very easy to get complacent, hidden away in this little town. We start to think we're special—protected from the bad things that plague other people. We don't like it when things—like murder—happen to remind us that's not true, but sometimes it's exactly what we need. You're exactly what we need."

Chapter Nine

Lacy was still trying to figure out what Jan Selkirk had meant at Kate's that morning when Travis called. "Do you have time today to get together with me?" he asked. "I have some more questions for you."

"I don't know," she said. "Let me check my calendar. After all, I'm so busy these days, what with being unemployed and losing that boxing match and all. Well, what do you know? I have an opening."

He chuckled. "Why don't I stop by around lunch time?"

"Are you offering to take me to lunch? Because I'm going crazy sitting around the house."

"All right."

When he pulled up in his SUV a little before noon, Lacy was waiting on the front porch and walked out to the street to meet him. "The bruises don't look so bad today," he said.

"You sure know how to lay on the compliments, Sheriff." She opened the passenger door and slid in. "Thanks for agreeing to go out. My mom has been through so much, I don't want to lose my temper with her, but her hovering is driving me nuts."

"She worries about you."

"Yes, but I need a little breathing space."

"Is it okay if lunch is a picnic?" he asked. "I picked up some sandwiches and stuff from Iris Desmet."

"The Cake Walk is open again?"

"No, but she's doing some catering and stuff out of her home. I guess being idle didn't suit her any more than it does you."

"A picnic is fine," Lacy said. "In fact, it would be nice to eat without everyone in the restaurant watching me. I'm beginning to feel a little bit like the local freak on display."

"People are curious, but it will pass," he said. "But it suits me if we skip the restaurant today. Your mother and my office manager aren't the only people in town who are interested in what we have to say to each other. And it's never a good idea to discuss a case in public. You never know who might overhear something they shouldn't."

"I don't think I was prepared for all the attention I'm attracting," she said. "I was in Kate's this morning and said something about being in prison and you would have thought I had confessed to kicking small children for fun."

"They'll get over it," he said.

"I guess that curiosity is what sells books like the one Alvin Exeter is writing," she said. "By the way, he came by Kate's this morning and tried to interview Jan Selkirk. She shut him down."

"Jan is quite a formidable woman. One of her last acts as mayor was to invite—or rather insist—that I present a report to the town council. She wanted to know what the youngest sheriff the county had ever had was planning for their community. It was like standing for inspection with an army drill sergeant. I thought she would send me away if I had a scuff on my boots or a spot on my tie."

"She told me I was what the town needed, to remind them they aren't as special and safe as people think they are here." She stared out the window, at the passing vista of mountains and wildflowers. "I was kind of hoping it *would* be special and safe here."

"I guess if that was really true, I wouldn't have a job," he said. "Though I would just as soon stick to helping lost tourists and chasing off the occasional shoplifter."

"You'd be bored silly if that was the case," she said. "Admit it—you like the adrenaline rush of going after the bad guys. You wouldn't be a cop if that wasn't true."

His hands tightened on the steering wheel. "All right. Maybe some of that is true."

"It's okay," she said. "I don't hold it against you." She could even say she admired that about him—his determination to right wrongs. Though that aspect of his character had helped put her in jail, it had also made him work tirelessly until she was free. Another man might not have been so willing to admit he had made a mistake.

He headed over the bridge out of town, to a picnic area on a small lake with a view of Mount Rayford. "I remember coming here for a cookout with the senior class of Eagle Mountain High," she said as she helped him carry their lunch to one of the concrete tables. They had the place to themselves and settled in the shade of the canopy over the table.

"A local tradition," he said. "The year of our picnic it rained. You'd be surprised how many teenagers you can fit under one of these canopies."

"That all seems so long ago," she said. She had been a different person then, one who had thought the bad things of the world would never touch her.

"They still do those senior picnics," Travis said as he laid out their own meal. "One of the advantages of a smaller school—you're able to keep up traditions like that."

"It's nice to know some things haven't changed," she said. "I was only away three years and there's so many things I don't recognize—new people and businesses. And this Pioneer Days Festival—that's new."

"Some people thought Jan was crazy to suggest it," he said. "But it's been a big success. It's a real boost for local business. Though I'll admit, it keeps our depart-ment busy. Nothing big, but you bring a lot of people in from other places and crowd them all together, and you're bound to see an uptick in petty crime—shoplift-ing, public drunkenness, minor things like that."

"At least you're not up to your ears in serious crimes," she said. She bit into a ham sandwich.

"I went out to see Henry Hake this morning," he said, reminding her of the one very serious crime he was in-vestigating. "He says he got some threatening letters from people who didn't want the resort project to go forward and Andy was looking into them."

Lacy set down the sandwich. A chill shuddered through her in spite of the warm day. "So whoever wrote the letters might have killed Andy to stop him?"

"Maybe. Did Andy mention anything like that to you?"

"No," she said. "What did the letters say?"

"I don't know. Hake said he destroyed them. But they frightened him enough that he hired a bodyguard for a while."

"The only people I know who were against the development were the Utes and Paige Riddell's environmental group. But they weren't subtle about their objections to the development—they went after Hake directly—in court. And they won."

"And Hake says after they won—well, after Andy died—the threats stopped. And the development never did go forward."

"That surprises me," Lacy said. "From what I remember, they had sunk a lot of money into the project."

"He says they're restructuring—'they' being him and some partners he insists want to remain silent." He took a bite of sandwich and chewed.

"I wonder if the partners know any more about the source of the threats?" Lacy asked.

"I'm going to see if the district attorney can subpoena him for the names," Travis said. "But that will take a while, and Hake says some of the original partners are dead."

"And that makes me wonder how they died." She plucked a grape from the bunch he had set in the middle of the table. "Then again, maybe I read too many murder mysteries. The prison library was full of them."

"I like that you don't mind talking about it," he said. "Especially around me."

"I can't pretend it never happened." She crunched down on the grape. "Later, I hope I don't think about it so much, but I'm still too close to it. I still wake up in the morning thinking I'm back there. I've missed head count and I'm going to lose my exercise privileges, or access to the commissary, or any one of a dozen punishments they can mete out for the slightest infraction."

He nodded, his mouth tight, the lines around his eyes deepening.

"I'm not telling you this to make you feel bad," she said.

"Why are you telling me, then?"

She considered the question, a warmth blossoming in her chest as the answer came to her. "Because I want you to know me," she said softly. "And that's part of me."

He slid his hand across the table and took hers, his fingers warm and slightly rough against hers. They sat that way for a long moment, holding on to something precious, neither wanting to break the spell.

A gray jay circled overhead, screeching at them in a bid for part of their lunch. Lacy pulled away and straightened, suddenly self-conscious. "I shouldn't keep you from your work," she said. "And my mother will be wondering where I've gotten to."

"I was hoping you'd have time to go through that second file box this afternoon," he said. "I want to see if we can find anything more about these threats of Hake's silent partners."

"As I said before, my afternoon just happens to be free."

TRAVIS FELT WARMED by more than the sun as he drove Lacy back to her house. There in the park, he had felt her truly softening toward him. When she talked about her time in prison, she didn't come across as someone who had been scarred by the experience. He would give her back those lost years, if there was any way possible, but at least he could let go of the feeling that he had ruined her life.

In the Milligans' dining room, they opened the second file box and each took half the papers. This box contained mostly legal documents—the deeds for the various mining claims that made up the proposed resort, copies of surveys, title searches, newspaper articles about the project and dense legal contracts relating to everything from water and mineral rights to public right of way on historic trails. After an hour, Travis tossed aside a sheaf of papers and rubbed his eyes. "I think I've found a cure for insomnia," he said.

Lacy laughed. "It does get a little dense at times," she said. "One reason I'd never want to be a lawyer."

"Have you found anything interesting?" he asked.

She shook her head. "Not a thing."

She stretched her arms over her head, a gesture that lifted her breasts and made his mouth go dry. He looked away and cleared his throat. "Maybe we'll find something in the other boxes."

"Let's go out there now," she said. "That is, if you have time."

"Let me check in with the office and see."

Adelaide reported that the office was "as dead as Methuselah's cat," and Travis wondered if she lay awake nights trying to come up with colorful expressions to add to her repertoire. "I'm going to make a run out to Andy Stenson's storage facility to look at some more files," he said. "Call me if anything pops up."

"Who else would I call?" Adelaide said breezily. "Say hello to Lacy for me."

"How did you know I'm with Lacy?"

"Your SUV is parked in front of her house. If you really want to sneak around, you're going to have to learn to be more subtle."

"I am not sneaking a—" But Adelaide had already hung up.

Lacy said goodbye to her parents and she and Travis headed out the door. They were almost to his vehicle when Alvin Exeter stepped out from his car, which was parked across the street, and held a cell phone to his eye.

Lacy froze. "Did you just take our picture?" she asked.

Alvin grinned. "You two make a handsome couple—or you will when those bruises heal." He studied the screen of his camera. "This makes a more touching image, I think. The victim and the lawman."

"You're on thin ice, Exeter," Travis said, barely controlling his anger. "I've warned you about harassing Ms. Milligan."

"I'm standing in a public street and so are you. I know my rights as a writer."

Lacy took Travis's arm. "Come on, let's go," she said.

Travis held the passenger door for her, then went around the driver's side. Exeter watched, smirking and taking picture after picture with his camera. "I'd like to rip that phone out of his hand and stomp on it," Travis said.

"He gets a charge out of being confrontational," she said. "The best way to deal with someone like him is to ignore them."

Travis glanced at her. "You're pretty smart for someone so young."

"I keep telling myself the old children's rhyme still holds true," she said. "Sticks and stones may break my bones but words can never harm me."

He pulled into the street and headed for Main. "Words can do plenty of harm and we both know it," he said when they had left Exeter behind.

"Only if I let them," she said. "Being in prison was hard, but it taught me that I need to be my own best friend. I can't really rely on anyone else."

"You can rely on me," he said.

He could feel her eyes on him, though he kept his gaze on the road. "Yes, I'm beginning to believe that," she said.

They were both silent until he turned onto Fireline Road. A dusty brown Jeep blew past them and sped onto the highway.

"I think that was Ian Barnes," Lacy said, looking over her shoulder at the dust that hung in the wake of the Jeep's passing. "Jan said he drove an old Jeep. What was he doing out here?"

"There are some rock cliffs out this way that are popular with climbers," Travis said. "Maybe he was checking them out."

Lacy faced forward once more. "What do you know about him?" she asked.

"Not much. I met him at Eagle Mountain Outfitters. I think he's a friend of the owners. Wade Tomlinson told me he's an Iraq and Afghanistan veteran and suffers from PTSD. Why?"

She shrugged. "I don't know. There's just something about him I find...unsettling. Maybe it's the way he watches me."

"Maybe he's trying to work up the nerve to ask you out." His throat felt tight as he said the words.

"Hah! Trust me, the way the women around here are always ogling him, he could get a date with any one of them. He doesn't need me."

"But maybe you're the one he's attracted to."

"Right." She brushed a lock of hair off her face. "Because I'm so attractive with two black eyes, a busted lip and a row of stitches across my head. Though maybe he's into zombie chic."

"So you don't go for the chiseled look?" he asked, keeping his voice light.

"Chiseled is right. He looked like someone carved him from granite."

"I wouldn't want to meet him in a dark alley. He looks like he could take me apart with his bare hands."

"You look like you could hold your own in a fight, Sheriff."

The air between them felt suddenly charged. "Are you saying you've been checking me out?" he asked.

"I've been locked up with nine hundred other women for three years," she said. "I check out every man I meet." But her smile seemed to say that she liked what she had seen when she looked at him. He had to fight the urge not to puff out his chest.

He stopped at the entrance to the storage facility and punched in the code Brenda had given him. The barrier rose and he drove to the first row of units on the right and parked. "I don't see anyone else out here," Lacy said as she and Travis climbed out of his SUV.

"I checked and only about half the units are rented," Travis said as he fitted the key into the padlock on the Stensons' unit. "Tom Reynolds owns the place and he told me most of the time people stash their stuff out here and don't look at it for years. The payment comes out of their bank account automatically every month and they probably never even think about the boxes of old clothes and papers or Grandma's furniture or whatever it is they're paying to store."

He shoved up the rolling metal door and it rose with a

groan. Everything looked exactly as he had left it when he was here with Brenda, boxes and furniture piled haphazardly, everything smelling of dust and old paper. "Let me get the video recorder set up before you go in," Travis said. "We might as well do all this by the book."

Lacy waited while he set up the recorder on its tripod, then she moved into the unit ahead of him. "Where do we start?" she asked.

"The boxes are labeled alphabetically," Travis said. "Why don't you glance through a couple and see if anything catches your eye." He lifted a box from a stack and set it on top of Andy's desk. "And look for any *H*'s. The boxes we looked at already were labeled Hake, but maybe some papers related to the development ended up mixed in with the general files."

"All right." Lacy accepted the box he slid toward her and began flipping through the papers. Every few seconds she would pull up a file folder and examine it more closely. The sun beat down on the metal building and even with the door open, it grew stifling.

Lacy stopped to wipe sweat from her forehead. "Maybe we should just grab a couple and take them back to the house," she said.

"Good idea," Travis said. "Let me get my tape from the SUV and we'll seal up a couple to go through later."

He turned and had taken two steps toward the door when an explosion ripped through the air and knocked him to the ground.

Chapter Ten

The concussion from the blast slammed Lacy to the concrete floor of the storage unit and sent a tower of boxes tumbling over her. She lay stunned, head spinning, trying to make sense of the roaring in her ears and the pain in her knees and hands.

"Lacy!" Travis's voice rose above the roar.

She lifted her head. "I'm here!" she cried, the sound weak and barely audible even to her own ears. She took a deep breath, inhaling smoke, and coughed violently, then tried again. "Here!" she shouted, hoarse.

"Can you move?" Travis shouted. "Head toward my voice."

She rose up on her knees and shoved boxes and papers away from her. Then she felt the heat of the fire licking at her back. Terror sent her lunging forward, fighting against a wall of boxes and scattered furniture. "Help!" she shouted. "Help me!"

"I'm coming!" The wall of debris shifted, and a hand reached in, groping wildly for her.

Lacy took the hand and was yanked forward, half carried toward a blast of fresh air. Then she and Travis were rolling in the gravel, his hands beating at her back, and the flames that licked there. Then he pulled her to her feet and they ran, away from the burning storage unit, into the field beyond, where they collapsed, arms still tightly wrapped around each other. Even there, the tower of flame that reached toward the sky radiated heat over them.

Lacy's eyes filled with tears as she looked into his soot-streaked face. His eyes met hers, and he rested the back of his hand to her cheek. "I thought I'd lost you," he whispered.

She took his face in both hands and pressed her lips to his, the kiss desperate in its intensity. He wrapped both arms around her and rolled onto his back, carrying her with him, their lips still locked together, her body stretched atop his. Tears ran down her face and mixed with the soot. She tasted the salt of them as she opened her mouth to deepen the kiss. Everything—the roar of the fire, the ache in her knees, the stench of the smoke—receded, burned away by passion. Some part of her, banked and given up for dead all these years, roared to life, fueled by the feel of his hard, male body beneath her, by his searching lips and caressing hands. She wanted. She needed. She took.

He was the first to pull away, breaking the kiss and rolling her aside, then sitting up and taking both her hands in his. "I need to call this in," he said.

She nodded, unable to speak, adrenaline still pumping through her body. He released her hands, only to caress her cheek again. "You're the most amazing woman," he said.

"You're making a habit of saving my life," she said.

His expression hardened and he dropped his hand. "You don't owe me anything."

"This isn't about debts and payments," she said.

"Then what is it about?"

"It's about you making me feel more alive than I have in years. It's about… I don't know." She looked away. She had almost said "love," but that was absurd.

"Maybe it doesn't matter why right now," he said. He pulled her close again, so that her head rested on his shoulder. "I'm just glad you're okay. That we're both okay."

She turned her head to watch the fire. Other storage units had caught now, their contents feeding the blaze into even more of an inferno. "I heard an explosion," she said.

He nodded and, with one arm still wrapped around her, shifted to take out his phone. "This is Rayford County Sheriff Travis Walker. The storage units at the end of Fireline Road are burning. There was an explosion. We need the fire crew, an ambulance and a crime scene team out here." He listened a moment. "Just some burns. No fatalities. Get an officer out here to block the road," he said. "I don't want anyone back here but emergency personnel."

He ended the call and replaced his phone on his belt. "Why do we need an ambulance?" she asked.

"You've got blood on your hands, and you might have some burns." He took her wrist and turned her palm up to reveal the drying blood there.

"I scraped my hands and knees on the concrete when the blast threw me down," she said. "What about you? Are you hurt?"

He shook his head. "I was closer to the door, so the blast threw me forward." He squinted toward the blaze, black smoke billowing to the sky. "My SUV is probably on fire by now. And all of Andy's files."

"Do you think that's why this happened?" she asked. "So that we couldn't get to those files?"

"That would be my guess. I know one thing—I want to talk to Ian Barnes and find out what he was doing out here."

"Do you think he booby-trapped the storage unit or something?"

"Or something," Travis said. "Maybe he was just checking out places to climb, but he might have seen someone else out here."

Sirens sounded in the distance. Travis shoved to his feet, then offered her his hand and pulled her up beside him. "Sounds like the cavalry is on the way," he said. "Let's see if we can circle around to the road and meet them."

Lacy kept her hand in his as they hiked over the rough ground, around the still-raging blaze and out to the road. She had kissed him in an adrenaline rush of fear and elation, but she didn't regret the impetuous gesture. Danger hadn't changed her feelings for Travis, but it had made her see the foolishness of playing hide-and-seek with her emotions. Crazy as it seemed on the surface, the man who had been her worst enemy was fast becoming her best friend.

THE FRONT PAGE of the *Eagle Mountain Examiner* had a three-column color photo of the fire at the storage units, with a smaller inset picture of Travis and Lacy, scorched and ragged, standing surrounded by half a dozen emergency personnel. "You look like two extras in a low-budget horror film," Adelaide said as she laid the paper on Travis's desk.

Travis scowled at the photo. "I didn't even know this was taken."

"Tammy was at Kate's this morning, crowing about getting the story in just under deadline," Adelaide said. "You bumped a piece about the Eighth Grade Science Fair. She had to move the pictures of Olivia Dexter's first-place exhibit on DNA testing to page four."

"My apologies to Olivia," he said. "Have we heard anything from the arson examiner?"

"He says you're keeping him busy," Adelaide said. "He sent over his preliminary findings this morning—it was definitely a bomb, with some kind of trip mechanism, probably set to go off on a delay once someone triggered it."

"Adelaide, you aren't supposed to read official reports addressed to me."

"He sent it to the general office email and I'm in charge of the general office." She waited while he logged on to his computer and opened the email from the county's arson investigator. "You know, I think I read terrorists use those kind of bombs over in Iraq and Afghanistan," she said. "That way they can make sure all our soldiers are inside a building before they blow them all up."

"Go back to work, Adelaide," Travis said. "And close the door behind you."

He read the investigator's report, though everything was as Adelaide had said. The bomb wasn't sophisticated, but it was effective, and the kind of thing anyone with a rudimentary knowledge of explosives could use. He closed the file and left his office.

"Where are you going?" Adelaide asked as he passed her desk.

"Out."

He drove instead of walked, wanting the security of

a vehicle around him. His SUV had been consumed in the blaze, so he was using the department's "spare" vehicle, an ancient 4Runner with a dented door, sagging seats and no air-conditioning. He would have to petition the county commissioners for funds for a new vehicle and probably wait for an insurance settlement to come through before he could get a new ride.

He parked in front of Eagle Mountain Outfitters and went inside. Wade looked up from the cash register, an outdoor magazine open on the counter in front of him. "Hey, Sheriff, what can we do for you?" he asked.

"I'm looking for your friend Ian," Travis said.

"He isn't here."

"Where is he?" Travis asked.

"Is something wrong, Sheriff?" Wade asked.

"I need to speak to Barnes. Where is he?"

"He's staying over at the Bear's Den," Wade said. "Paige Riddell's place. Why do you need to see Ian?"

"I just want to talk to him." Before Wade could question him further, Travis left the store, got back in his vehicle and drove three blocks to Paige Riddell's Bear's Den Inn. The faded brown Jeep he and Lacy had seen turning off Fireline Road yesterday sat in the driveway of the two-story Victorian home, next to Paige's red Prius. Paige answered when he rang the doorbell. She was a tall woman, with straight, shoulder-length, honey-blond hair and serious gray eyes. In addition to operating the bed-and-breakfast, she taught yoga at the local gym and headed up Eagle Mountain Conservationists, the environmental group that had succeeded in getting an injunction to stop Henry Hake's resort development. "Sheriff Walker," she said. "What can I do for you?"

"I need to talk to one of your guests—Ian Barnes."

Her eyes narrowed. "What about?"

"That's none of your business and you know it, Paige. Can I come in?"

She opened the door wider and let him walk past. "Ian is uncomfortable with strangers," she said. "He suffered horribly in the war."

Travis turned to study her. In her midthirties, and a little too serious for his tastes, but she might appeal to a man like Barnes. "You and he are friends?"

"No. But I respect his privacy."

"So do I. Which is why I won't tell you what this about. Is he here?"

"He's upstairs, in the sunroom off the back of the house." She nodded toward a set of carpeted stairs.

Travis took the stairs quickly, but Ian met him at the top. The muscular veteran in the black knit cap filled the doorway to the sunroom, his expression blank. "Sheriff," he said, no inflection to the word.

"Let's go into the sunroom where we can talk in private," Travis said.

Barnes backed into the room, keeping his gaze fixed on Travis. He sat in a square, heavy wood rocker in the back corner of the room. Travis pulled up a wrought-iron armchair. "I saw you out on Fireline Road yesterday afternoon," he said. "What were you doing out there?"

"I was looking for places to climb. I heard there were some good routes up Dakota Ridge back that way."

"Did you go by the storage units at the end of the road? Maybe turn around there, or stop and take a look around?"

"No." His expression and his voice never changed, both as cold as a robot's. In Travis's experience, being interviewed by the police made most people a little nervous, even if they were innocent of any wrongdoing. The first time he had interviewed Lacy after Andy's murder, she had fidgeted constantly, and practically vibrated with tension. At the time, he had mistaken her unease for a sign of guilt.

Ian Barnes might have been talking to a store clerk or a complete stranger, for all the emotion he displayed. Was he that unfeeling—or simply more experienced at dealing with law enforcement? "You know about the bomb that went off out at the storage units yesterday afternoon," Travis said.

"I saw the paper."

"But you don't know anything about it."

"No."

"Someone suggested to me that this might have been the type of bomb used by terrorists in Iraq and Afghanistan, with a delayed timer. You must have run into that sort of device while you were serving over there."

"Yes."

"So you would know how to put one together. How to deploy it."

"I know a lot of things. Yesterday I was looking for places to climb. I don't know anything about your bomb." He stood, an imposing figure looming over Travis. It was hard not to read the gesture as an intentional threat.

Travis rose also, and found that he and Barnes were almost the same height. He looked the other man in the eye. "Why are you in Eagle Mountain, Mr. Barnes?" he asked.

"I'm visiting friends. Doing some climbing."

"Have you been to the area before?"

Something flickered in those impassive brown eyes, a shadow of something—guilt? Fear? "No."

Travis knew he was lying. All his words thus far might

have been lies, but Travis was certain about this one. Ian could have said he had visited Wade and Brock before, or come here on vacation. Instead, he had lied. Why?

"If you had something to do with this, I'll find out," he said. He turned to leave, but at the door, Ian's words stopped him.

"If you want to know who has it in for you and your girlfriend, you should talk to that writer, Exeter," he said.

Travis turned to face Ian again. He could have protested that Lacy wasn't his girlfriend, but the memory of her in his arms after the fire cast doubt on the truth of that statement. "Why Exeter?" he asked instead.

"He was in Moe's Pub the other night, mouthing off about the power of the written word and making Lacy pay for being so rude to him."

"What did he say, exactly?" Travis asked.

Ian sat in the rocker again and picked up a book from the table beside it. "Ask him," he said, then opened the book, ignoring Travis.

Paige met Travis at the bottom of the stairs. "Did you upset him?" she asked.

"Do you really think anything upsets him?" Travis asked.

"Not everyone wears his feelings on his sleeve," she said. "Some are more stoic."

Travis headed for the door, then thought better of it and faced her again. "When that environmental group you head was opposing Henry Hake's resort development, did any of your members do more than protest?"

She wrinkled her forehead. "What do you mean? We filed an injunction against him in court and we won. We succeeded in stopping the development—which was a ridiculous idea, anyway. The environment at those el-

evations is far too delicate to support the kind of infra-
structure Hake wanted to build—all so a few ultrarich
people could enjoy looking down on the rest of us from
their ridiculously oversize homes."

"Did you write threatening letters to him? Destroy
equipment?"

Her eyes widened. "No! Our group doesn't just work
for the environment—we're committed to peace. It's
part of our core values and mission statement."

"But you don't control all your members," he said.
"Maybe one of them stepped out of line."

"Not that I'm aware of."

Travis glanced up the stairs, wondering if Barnes
was listening. "Someone threatened Henry Hake back
then. Someone destroyed machinery on his property.
Andy Stenson was looking into those threats. It may
have been what got him killed."

Paige looked pained. "I don't know anything about
that," she said. "It's horrible to even think about."

"Think about it," Travis said. "And maybe ask your
guest upstairs how many men he's killed."

He left, shutting the door a little harder than necessary behind him. Maybe his last words had been a low
blow. He hadn't meant to frighten Paige, only to warn
her about the kind of man she might be harboring. Travis couldn't see how Ian Barnes had had anything to
do with Andy Stenson, but his presence out on Fireline
Road yesterday had to be more than coincidence. And
when Travis looked into Barnes's eyes, he saw a man
with no conscience. A man like that might do anything.

Chapter Eleven

Lacy stared at the check in her hand, at the machine-printed numbers—210,000 dollars. More money than she had ever seen in her life. "I'll have to open a bank account to deposit it," she said. She hadn't had a bank account since before she went to prison.

"Have you thought about what classes you'd like to take?" her father asked. "What career you'd like to pursue?"

She shook her head. "I don't know. I think I'd like to get a car first." Her eyes met his over the top of the check. "Nothing flashy. It doesn't even have to be new, but I'd like to be able to go places without borrowing Mom's car."

"Of course." Jeanette rubbed her daughter's shoulder. "And you have until August to decide about school. You might even be able to take some courses online at first, until you decide for sure on a major."

"Yeah. That's a good idea."

"Do you want me to take you to the bank now?" her father asked.

"Sure, Dad. That's a great idea. I'll just go upstairs and get my purse."

When she came back down, both her parents were

waiting by the front door. "I think this calls for a celebration," her mother said. "Maybe a special dinner."

"Sure." Lacy forced a smile. "But maybe here at home? We could order takeout so you don't have to cook."

"I don't mind cooking," Jeanette said. "We'll stop at the grocery store after the bank. We'll keep it simple—steaks and a salad. Is there anyone you'd like to invite?"

No. Yes. "Maybe... Travis?" Was she ready for that? Dinner with her family?

Jeanette's smile widened. "That's a wonderful idea."

Lacy wanted to tell her mother not to read too much into this. Travis was a friend. A friend she had been ready to jump right there on the ground next to the burning storage units, but she could blame at least part of that reaction on the sheer euphoria of surviving the explosion, right? "He might have to work," she said.

"Why don't you call right now and ask him?" Jeanette said. "We'll wait."

She realized both her parents were prepared to stand right there while she made the call, so she turned around and retraced her steps to her room, where she pulled out her cell phone—the one her parents had had waiting for her when she first arrived home, a first real symbol of her freedom.

Travis answered on the second ring. "Lacy. Is everything okay?"

"Why wouldn't it be okay?"

"You've never called me before."

"I wanted to invite you to dinner. At my house. With my parents. We're kind of celebrating. I got my check from the state." She said everything quickly, wanting to get it all out before she lost courage.

"Tonight?"

"Yes. I told them you might have to work, but I thought I would call and—"

"I'll be there. Unless some emergency comes up."

"Great. Be here about six."

She ended the call, feeling a little giddy, and almost floated down the stairs.

"He must have said yes," her mother said as Lacy joined her parents by the door.

"What makes you say that?" Lacy did her best to act nonchalant.

"You have that look in your eye," her mother said.

"What look?"

"A very pleased-with-yourself look." She reached out and touched the ends of Lacy's hair, where it skimmed her shoulder blades. One of the women on her prison block had cut it with a pair of contraband nail scissors in exchange for cookies Lacy purchased in the prison commissary. "We could stop by Lou's Salon on the way home and see if she could work you in," she said. "Maybe shape it up a little."

Lacy started to protest that she didn't want that— then realized she did. She wasn't an inmate who didn't care about her appearance anymore. "All right," she said. "That would be nice."

She was surprised at how nervous she felt about opening a bank account, but the clerk was professional and didn't even blink when Lacy handed over the check. "Would you like to deposit a portion of this in an investment account?" she asked. "I could make an appointment for you to speak to one of our financial counselors."

"Not today," Lacy said. "But next week would be good." One step at a time.

With a pad of temporary checks tucked in her purse, Lacy left the bank and headed across the parking lot with her parents. Her mother nudged her and leaned close to whisper in her ear. "Who is that good-looking young man who is staring at you?" she asked.

Lacy looked over her shoulder, starting when she recognized Ian Barnes.

Her father, who had just unlocked the driver's door, looked over the top of the car. "I think he's friends with the two guys who run Eagle Mountain Outfitters," he said. "I went in there looking for a bite valve to replace the one on my hydration pack that's been leaking and he was there. I think he's ex Special Forces or something."

"Well, he's certainly impressive," Jeanette said. She slid into the front passenger seat and cast a sideways glance at her husband, her cheeks rosy. "Well, he is. In an overly muscular kind of way."

"I wonder how he knows the mayor?" her father asked.

Only then did Lacy realize Ian was standing with Mayor Larry Rowe. She looked back and Larry clapped the younger man on the shoulder, then walked away.

"You know Larry," her mother said. "He makes it his business to know everyone in town. A good quality in a mayor, I guess. Lacy, have you met him before?"

"The mayor?" Lacy asked, deliberately misunderstanding her mother's question.

"No—that good-looking young man."

Lacy decided it was time to change the subject. "What's this Pioneer Days Festival like?" she asked. "Have you been?"

"It's quite the production," her father said. "There's a parade and a special display at the museum. Last year

Brenda and Jan dressed in 1890s swimming costumes and sold lemonade and sugar cookies. There's a stage in the park with bands and crafts vendors, a baseball game and foot races and I forget what else."

"Fireworks," her mother said. "They shoot them off above town. They do a wonderful job."

"The whole thing was Jan Selkirk's idea," her father said. "She spent two years persuading the town fathers to adopt the idea, and then was able to gloat when it turned out to be such a big success. The new mayor, Larry Rowe, and his council have expanded on her original idea and attracted quite a bit of attention to our little town."

"They keep talking about creating a similar festival for winter, when business is slow," Jeanette said. "But the weather can be so iffy then."

"A big snow and avalanches could cut off Dakota Pass and everyone could be snowed in," George said. "The locals are used to it, but tourists might raise a fuss."

"I think it's enough having all those tourists in town for the summer," Jeanette said.

"Yes, but you're not a local businessperson," her husband countered.

Her parents continued the argument on the drive to the grocery store. Lacy sat in the back seat and let her mind drift to the place it always ended up these days— back with Travis and the kiss they had shared after the explosion. When she closed her eyes, she could still feel the scrape of the beard just beneath his skin as she pressed her cheek to his, the hard plane of his chest crushed against her breasts, the implements on his belt digging into her belly—the length of his desire confirming that he wanted her as much as she wanted him.

So what did she do? Instead of arranging to see him privately, where maybe they could see where that desire would take them, she had invited him to a family dinner, where she would be too uptight to even risk a kiss under her parents' watchful eyes. Not that her mother and father were prudes, but a new relationship—one she didn't even know how to define—required privacy.

Her father stopped and signaled for the turn into the parking lot of Eagle Grocery. A black-and-white sheriff's department vehicle, lights flashing and sirens blaring, sped by, followed closely by a second vehicle and an ambulance.

"My goodness, what's that all about?" her mother asked.

Lacy had already dug her phone from her purse and punched in the number for the sheriff's department. Adelaide answered immediately. "What's going on?" Lacy demanded.

"I'm not allowed to give out information about sheriff's department calls over the phone," Adelaide said. "You people ought to know that by now."

"This is Lacy Milligan. Just tell me—is Travis hurt?"

The silence that followed lasted so long Lacy thought Adelaide had hung up on her. "You can't tell anyone where you heard this," Adelaide said finally, her voice lowered.

"I won't. I promise."

"We had a report of an officer down, out at the storage units on Fireline Road. We don't know that it's Travis."

"Even I know the sheriff's department doesn't have that many officers," Lacy said. "We just saw two cars go by. If Travis wasn't in either one of those..."

"I have to go now, Lacy. I have a lot of other calls coming in. Try not to worry, but it wouldn't hurt to say a prayer."

Lacy ended the call to Adelaide and let the phone fall into her lap. "What is it, dear?" her mother asked.

Lacy swallowed, her mouth too dry to speak. *Keep it together*, she scolded herself. "There was an Officer in Distress call," she said.

"Travis?" her father asked.

"They don't know." The awfulness of those words settled over her like a smothering blanket, and it was all she could do to remain seated upright and breathing.

TRAVIS WAS AT the motel out on the highway, trying to track down Alvin Exeter, when the Officer in Distress call went out. As soon as he heard the address, he raced to his car, dialing his phone as he ran. He tried the office first, but the line was busy. No surprise there. Half the town had probably called in to see what was going on. The line was supposed to be for sheriff's department business only, but too many people knew about it and felt free to use it any time they wanted. He could have called Adelaide on the radio, but he didn't have time to waste.

He started the Toyota and hit the speed dial for Gage. "What's up?" he asked as he sped from the parking lot.

"Travis! Thank God!" Gage almost shouted the words. "We got the Officer in Distress call from Dispatch and they didn't know what unit. Since it was out at the storage units, I thought—"

"Where's Dwight?" Travis cut off his brother's relieved babbling.

"He's right behind me."

"No one else should be on duty," Travis said.

"They aren't."

"Then who put in the call?" He eased off the gas pedal, mind racing. "Is this some kind of trap?"

"Dispatch thought it was legit. Are we gonna risk not checking it out?"

"No, we aren't. But we need to be careful."

He was closer to Fireline Road than the other two units, but it wasn't long before they fell in behind him, a wailing, flashing parade of three sheriff's department vehicles, an ambulance and one state highway patrol car. Travis wouldn't have been surprised to see the fire department and Search and Rescue trailing them.

A red Jeep Wagoneer was parked in front of the gate at the entrance to the storage units. Travis swore when he recognized the vehicle. Gage's voice came on the radio. "Eddie," he said. "What's he doing out here?"

Eddie Carstairs was one of the reserve officers, called in when someone was out sick or on vacation, or when Travis needed extra manpower to work an accident or a festival. At twenty-two, Eddie looked about sixteen. His straight black hair flopped over a high forehead, and his face was long and droopy, which had led to the nickname Gage had saddled him with—"Hound Dog."

Travis pulled in beside Eddie's Jeep and shut off the Toyota, the engine sputtering twice in protest. From here he could make out a figure in jeans and a T-shirt, face down on the dirt a few yards from the blackened area that marked the reach of the fire. Travis pulled out his phone and called Eddie's number. "Officer Carstairs, this is Sheriff Walker. Can you hear me?"

The body on the ground didn't move.

Travis scanned the area around the body, then the hills beyond, searching for some clue as to what had happened. Gage and Dwight moved to his window, crouching down so that they were shielded between the Toyota and the Jeep. "What do you think?" Gage asked.

"What did Dispatch say about the call?" Travis asked.

"It came in on a private cell, not a police number," Gage said. "I called the dispatcher, Sally—you know her, the big blonde with the twins?" That was typical Gage. After five minutes with almost anyone, he would know their life history.

"What did she say about the call?" Travis prompted.

"She said the man on the other end sounded like he was having trouble breathing—or was in pain. All he said was 'Officer down'—and gave the address. Then he hung up or got disconnected."

Travis stared at the prone body, willing it to move. He took his binoculars from the field kit on the passenger-side floorboard and trained them on the figure.

"I think he's breathing," Dwight said.

"I think so, too," Travis said. Or was he imagining the faint rise and fall of the back? He laid aside the field glasses and looked at his two officers. "You two wearing your vests?"

They nodded in unison. "You think he was shot?" Dwight asked.

"That seems the most likely scenario."

"Could be a sniper," Gage said. "Up in the hills."

"If it is, I'm not risking him picking us off one by one," Travis said.

"If one of us could get behind one of the storage

buildings, we could shoot up into the hills, maybe draw his fire," Dwight said.

"A smart shooter wouldn't fall for that," Travis said. "He'd wait until we were out in the open, where he could get a clear shot." He considered the situation again. "Gage, do you have the sniper rifle with you?"

"Yes. And two ARs and a shotgun, some smoke grenades and a case of ammo." At Travis's raised eyebrows, he shrugged. "When the call came in, I unlocked the arsenal and took everything I could grab. You never know what you're going to need."

"You take the sniper rifle and one of the ARs," Travis said. "Dwight, you get one of the ARs. I want one of you set up behind each of the intact buildings on either side of Eddie."

"Where are you going to be?" Gage asked.

"I'm going out to get Eddie. You're going to cover me."

Chapter Twelve

All thoughts of celebration vanished as Lacy and her parents drove home. Lacy started to suggest her dad drive out to Fireline Road to see what had happened, but quickly dismissed the idea. The officers didn't need civilians in the way. And it wasn't as if she could do anything to help. She would just have to sit at the house and wait.

She was surprised to find Jan and Brenda seated on the settee on the front porch when her dad pulled the car into the driveway. "We heard what happened," Jan said. "It's all anybody in town is talking about."

"But it might not be Travis," Brenda said, giving Lacy's arm a squeeze. "I called the dispatcher, Sally Graham, and she said the man who called didn't identify himself, but it wasn't Travis's phone number."

"Why don't we all go inside," Jeanette said. "I'll make coffee."

They all trooped inside and into the Milligans' living room, which overlooked the street. Jeanette and George left the three younger women sitting on the sofa and love seat and went to make the coffee. "Alvin Exeter came by the history museum this morning," Jan said. "He wanted to talk to me and to Brenda."

"We both refused to speak with him," Brenda said. "But he didn't want to take no for an answer. He was really nasty about it, too."

"He said he's thinking of taking the approach that you really got away with murder," Jan said. "Since no one is coming forward to contest that theory, he figures it will be an even better story than the one of your wrongful conviction—the kind of thing that's sure to attract a lot of attention and boost sales."

"I don't care what he says," Lacy said. "He can say I murdered ten people and it won't make any difference to me. He's just trying to bait people into talking to him."

Brenda glanced toward the kitchen, then leaned toward Lacy, her voice low. "You might not care, but your parents will," she said. "It would hurt them so much."

Lacy nodded. "There's nothing I can do to stop him."

Jan and Brenda exchanged glances. "You could talk to him."

"No," Lacy said. "Just…no."

"Or," Brenda said. "You could find out who really murdered Andy."

"That's what Travis has been trying to do," Lacy said. And because of that, he might even now be dead. She shoved the thought away. No. He would be okay. He had to be okay.

"There must be something in those files," Brenda said. "Something we forgot or overlooked."

"It doesn't matter now," Lacy said. "The files are gone. Destroyed by the bomb."

"It's horrible to think it, but all this violence must mean you're getting close to finding the real killer," Brenda said. "Otherwise, why go to so much trouble to stop you?"

"We thought it must have something to do with Hake Development, because that was Andy's biggest client," Lacy said. "But what if that's not it at all? After all, he had lots of clients. Maybe it's something small that we aren't thinking of at all."

"I still have Andy's computer," Brenda said. "I haven't turned it on since he died—I don't even know if it still works."

Jan and Lacy stared at her. "Why didn't you say something before?" Lacy asked.

"I didn't think of it," Brenda said. "Andy kept hard copies of everything. I figured anything important would be in his files."

"He probably had copies of a lot of stuff on his computer," Lacy said, excitement growing. "And if you haven't even turned it on in years, it should be just fine."

"I promise I'll take it to Travis first thing tomorrow," Brenda said.

"Better let him come to you," Jan said. "I wouldn't take a chance going anywhere with anything the killer might want."

"If Travis is okay," Lacy said.

Lacy's parents returned to the living room with a tray of cups and a coffeepot. "I turned on the radio to see if we could get a news report and find out what's going on," her father said. "But I couldn't find anything."

"Lacy, you have Travis's phone number, don't you?" her mother asked.

"Yes," she said. "I called him on it earlier."

"Have you tried calling him since all this has happened?"

"Mom, he'll be too busy to talk—" She fell silent, heart leaping in her chest. She laughed at her own foolishness and pulled out her phone. She didn't care if Travis yelled at her for interrupting him while he worked, as long as he answered.

She punched in his number and waited while the call connected and the ringer buzzed—once, twice, three times. "This is Sheriff Travis Walker. Leave a message at the beep."

She had heard the expression "crushed" before, but had never fully comprehended what it meant. She felt as if someone had dumped a truckload of bricks in the middle of her chest. She ended the call without leaving a message. "No answer," she said.

Brenda leaned over and squeezed her hand. "Don't give up hope," she said.

"I won't." Lacy took a deep breath and straightened. Three years in prison had taught her how to survive when things looked bleak—the only difference now was that so much more was at stake.

TRAVIS WAITED UNTIL Gage and Dwight were in position, then exited the Toyota. He wore a pack that contained blankets, a first-aid kit and water, and had unholstered his duty weapon and held it in his right hand. Eddie still hadn't moved, though a second check through the binoculars had revealed no pooling blood or obvious injuries. Still, he could be bleeding out from a chest wound or a gut shot and they might not be able to tell.

Gage signaled that they were ready and Travis began moving around to the west. His plan was to move far to the side, then rush in low, with Gage and Dwight laying down a screen of fire aimed at the hills within firing distance of Eddie. It wasn't the best plan in the world, but it was the only one he had right now. He could have waited for a helicopter or an armored vehicle from a neighboring department, but arranging that kind of backup could take hours, and Eddie might not have that kind of time.

He was halfway to the cover of the first storage unit, where Dwight waited, when his phone rang. He ignored it and silenced the phone. Everyone he needed to talk to was here right now and had better ways of communicating with him.

He stopped when he reached Dwight, who had been scanning the hills above the site with a pair of binoculars. "See anything?" Travis asked.

"Nothing." He lowered the glasses. "Could be our shooter is gone."

"Maybe." If he was, that meant they had lost their chance to pin him down, but it also meant it would be easier to get help for Eddie. He put his hand on Dwight's shoulder, the hard edge of the tactical vest beneath his palm. "You ready?"

"Ready."

Travis looked across at Gage, who nodded in acknowledgment, then took a deep breath. "Okay. I'm going out there."

He ran bent over, on a zigzagging path that was supposed to make it harder for a shooter to target him. Behind him, bullets ripped from the magazines of the two ARs fired by his deputies in a deafening blast. Travis couldn't tell if anyone returned fire or not, though no rounds hit the dirt around him—and more important, none hit him.

The shooting stopped as he knelt beside Eddie. He put a hand on the younger man's back and relief left him shaking as he felt the steady rise and fall of his breath. "Eddie." He shook the body. "Eddie, wake up."

Eddie groaned. Travis knelt in front of him and shoved him over. The younger man landed heavily on his back with a groan.

The first thing he noticed was that Eddie's nose looked broken. It was definitely crooked, with blood crusting around the nostrils, purpling bruises under both eyes. More blood seeped from a gash in the middle of his forehead. That might explain why the young man was unconscious. So what had happened? Had they gone to all this trouble because Eddie was clumsy and had tripped and knocked himself out?

Then Travis saw the wound—a dark, round hole in his shoulder, rimmed with blackish blood. He pressed on the wound and more blood seeped out, and Eddie groaned and stirred. His eyelids fluttered and he stared up at Travis. "Sheriff?" he asked hoarsely, and tried to sit up.

Travis pushed him back down. "Lie still," he said. "I'm going to call in the paramedics."

Thirty seconds later, a pair of paramedics swarmed around the wounded young man. Gage and Dwight, weapons in hand, emerged from the cover of the storage units and joined the growing crowd of law enforcement personnel who were milling around the area. "Get these people out of here," Travis said to Gage. "They could be compromising a crime scene."

"So he *was* shot," Dwight said.

"At least once, in the shoulder," Travis said. "Hit his head pretty good and broke his nose, too. That may be what knocked him out."

"What was he doing out here?" Dwight asked.

"Oh, he's going to explain all that, I promise," Travis said.

"My guess is he came out to look at the bomb site," Gage said. "He was hoping to be a hero and find something the arson investigator or the rest of us missed."

"So whoever set the bomb was *guarding* the place?" Dwight asked. "Why? There can't be anything in those ashes worth finding."

"I don't know," Travis said. "Maybe extra insurance? They're so paranoid they don't want to leave anything to chance?"

"Nobody is that paranoid," Gage said.

"You never worked for a big corporation, did you?" Dwight asked. "Or the government—especially the military. Some of those people are majorly paranoid."

"Ian Barnes was in the military," Travis said. "Maybe he's that paranoid. We'd better find out where he was and what he was doing when Eddie was shot."

A second team of paramedics wheeled a gurney over the rough ground to Eddie and lifted him onto it. One of the original first responders joined Travis, Gage and Dwight. "The bullet is still in him, but he's stable," he said. "We'll know more when they get some X-rays but my guess is he'll be okay."

"What about the head injury and his nose?" Travis asked.

The paramedic grinned. "He said he was trying to run for cover when he tripped and hit a big rock. Broke his nose and knocked himself clean out."

"It's a miracle the shooter didn't take the opportunity to finish him off," Gage said.

"Maybe he thought he had killed him and didn't want to stick around and find out," Dwight said.

"Or maybe killing him wasn't the point," Travis said. "Maybe he was just sending a warning."

"Yeah," Gage said. "After all, Eddie wasn't in uniform. He wasn't driving a police vehicle. The shooter probably didn't know he's a cop."

Travis watched as the paramedics strapped Eddie onto the gurney and fitted an oxygen mask over his face. He waited until they had rolled him away toward the ambulance before he moved over to examine the place where he had fallen. By now most of the other law enforcement personnel had moved on, but he had no doubt that within a couple of hours everyone in the county would have heard about the reserve officer who had knocked himself out fleeing from a shooter. Hound Dog might never live that story down.

"Here's where he hit his head," Gage said, nudging a cantaloupe-sized chunk of granite with the toe of his boot.

"There's some scuff marks here, like this was where he was standing when he was hit," Dwight said, indicating an area on the edge of the scorch marks where the Stensons' storage unit had once stood.

Travis moved to stand beside him, and stared up into the hills. He pointed to clump of pinion trees about halfway up the slope. "What do you think? In there somewhere?"

Gage squinted up toward the area Travis indicated, then nodded. "Yeah, I think so. Good cover, shade, a good view of this area, a good angle to shoot, with the sun behind you or directly overhead most of the day, after it came up over that ridge there."

"About two hundred yards," Dwight said. "You'd have to have a high-powered rifle and be a good shot."

"I could make it," Gage said. "So could you. So could a lot of people."

"All right. Let's go up there and see what we can find," Travis said, and led the way up the slope.

ADELAIDE KINKAID TELEPHONED Lacy at four thirty. "Travis is fine," she said. "Though when I see him, I'm going to read him the riot act for not letting me know himself. I had to find out from Pamela Sue Windsor, over at the hospital in Junction, when she called to get Eddie Carstairs's insurance information. That fool Eddie was up there, poking around at the bomb site where he had no business being, and got himself shot."

Lacy didn't know or care who Pamela Sue Windsor or Eddie Carstairs were. "Travis is okay?" she asked, collapsing back against the sofa. Around her, her parents and Jan and Brenda broke into relieved smiles.

"He's fine," Adelaide said. "He and Gage and Dwight are still out there, investigating the scene. Eddie is fine, too. They're operating to remove the bullet and they have to set his broken nose because the fool tripped on a rock and knocked himself out while he was trying to run away. I swear, that rock is probably smarter than he is. I'll tell Travis you called when he comes in. Or maybe I'll leave him a note, since it's almost time for me to go home."

"Oh, no, don't tell him," Lacy said. "Please don't." She was embarrassed to have him know how panicked she had been at the idea of him hurt or dead. Whatever was between them felt too new—too fragile for that.

"Have it your way, dear. I have to go now. I have a few more calls to make. I think I remember that Eddie has a girlfriend over in Delta—I'll need to get in touch with her and hold her hand a little. These men have no consideration."

Lacy slipped the phone back into her pocket and realized everyone in the room was looking at her. "He's fine," she said. "It was another officer who was hurt, but he's going to be okay."

"You have to know more than that," Jan said. "We want the whole scoop. What happened?"

"I don't know." Lacy held out her hand to stave off the chorus of protests. "I really don't. Adelaide said this other officer—Eddie—was out at the storage units and someone shot him. And I guess he tripped and fell and broke his nose and knocked himself out, but I guess he was able to call for help before that." She shook her head. "That's all I know, really." And Travis was okay. She knew that—and that was really the most important fact. The only one she cared about.

"I'm glad I decided to have a yard sale instead of renting a storage unit," Jan said. "Who knew they could be so hazardous."

"I think the sooner I get Andy's computer out of my house, the better I'll feel," Brenda said. "Whatever was in those files of his, someone wanted to protect the information badly enough to try to kill me and Lacy and Travis and now this Eddie fellow."

"Maybe they did kill Andy," Lacy said.

Jan stood. "Come on. We'll go get the computer now and take it to the sheriff's office," she said.

"Maybe you should wait and have Travis or one of his deputies go with you," George said.

"I'll go with you," Lacy said.

"Lacy—" Her mother managed to freight the one word with a wealth of worry.

"It's better than sitting around here," Lacy said. "It will be fine. I promise." And if they timed their arrival at the sheriff's department right, she might even run into Travis, and be able to see for herself that he was all right.

Chapter Thirteen

"I still can't believe you're only just now mentioning that you had Andy's computer," Jan said as she followed Brenda and Lacy into Brenda's house. "You knew the sheriff was looking for any information Andy might have had."

"I simply forgot it existed," Brenda said. "I was in the basement the other day, looking for that box of fossils I told you my father had given me—you remember we talked about using them in that ancient history display at the museum. I pulled a big plastic storage container out from under the stairs and when I opened it, I realized it was full of stuff from Andy's office. I thought everything was out at the storage unit, but apparently not. The computer was sitting right on top of everything else. I suppose whoever packed the stuff up for me thought I would want it here, but I'm not sure I ever knew I had it."

"If it's been safely packed away all this time, I'm sure it still works," Lacy said. "And computer files should be easier to search than paper ones."

"That doesn't mean there's going to be anything useful on it," Jan said.

"No," Lacy agreed. "But maybe it will help."

"I'll just go down in the basement and get it out of the storage box," Brenda said, crossing the kitchen to a set of stairs that led down. "You two can wait up here."

"I'll go," Jan said. "I know it's upsetting for you to see Andy's things."

"It was a shock, seeing them yesterday," Brenda said. "But I'm over that now. After all, it's been over three years. I'm not going to break down because I see an old law book that used to belong to him."

"Still, I'm sure I can go right to it, you've described the location so well." Jan moved past Brenda and Lacy to the top of the stairs. "Why don't you open a bottle of wine for us?" she said as she started down the stairs.

Lacy and Brenda's eyes met. "Is Jan always this bossy?" Lacy whispered.

"Jan is the type of person who likes to be in charge of any project," Brenda said. She opened a kitchen cabinet and pulled out three tall glasses. "Understanding that has helped me get along with her at work. I think instead of wine, we should have iced tea. I don't think we all want to show up at the sheriff's office with alcohol on our breaths."

While Brenda filled glasses with ice, Lacy descended the stairs to the basement. "Did you find it?" she called. She rounded the corner and spotted Jan bent over a large blue plastic bin.

Jan jerked her head up and saw Lacy, then straightened. The contents of the bin in front of her were all in a jumble—as if they had been hurriedly pawed through. "Brenda said the computer was right on top," Lacy said. "You shouldn't have to dig through the boxes."

Jan snapped the lid back onto the bin, then pulled a laptop computer off the shelf next to her. "I've been

thinking," she said. "Maybe I should talk to that reporter—Alvin Exeter."

Just the mention of Alvin made Lacy's stomach
churn. "Why would you want to do that?"

"Maybe if someone appeared to cooperate with him,
he'd give up this crazy idea of portraying you as guilty."
She led the way up the stairs. "I wouldn't tell him anything much about you, personally. I'd focus on the town,
how much of a shock the crime was—and, of course,
how we all knew all along that you couldn't possibly
have murdered Andy."

Lacy couldn't help but wonder where "all" these people who knew she was innocent had been during her
trial, but she could see little point in bringing that up
now. "You're free to talk to whoever you like," she said,
"but I doubt if you'll change his mind about anything.
He strikes me as a generally nasty person."

Brenda met them at the top of the stairs. "I see you
found the laptop." She reached out and Jan handed it
over.

"There are actually several bins of things from Andy's office down there," Jan said. "I peeked in a couple
of them and there are some books that might be worth
some money if you want to sell them. And I saw a couple of photographs you might want to donate to the museum. I'll come over one day and we can go through
them, if you like."

"Sure," Brenda said. "That would be great." She set
the computer on the kitchen table and handed Lacy
and Jan glasses of tea. "I decided we could wait on the
wine until after we stop by the sheriff's department,"
she said.

"We don't have to all go see the sheriff," Jan said.

"When I leave here I'll take Lacy home, then drop this off on the way to my house." She opened the computer. "We ought to see if this turns on, don't you think?" Before Brenda could answer, she pressed the power button and the computer hummed to life.

"Looks like it's password protected," Lacy said, looking over Jan's shoulder at the screen that asked for the password. She and Jan looked at Brenda.

"I have no idea what the password is," she said. "We could guess, but I really don't care what's on there. I prefer to leave the snooping to the police."

"But snooping can be so fun," Jan teased. But she shut down the computer and closed the lid. "You'll feel better—and so will I—when you have this thing out of your house. Hopefully, whoever was out to destroy those files doesn't know yet that you have it."

Brenda froze, the glass of tea halfway to her lips. "How could they? I didn't even know myself until yesterday."

"One of the movers who helped clean out Andy's office might have remembered it," Jan said. She finished off her tea, then set down the glass and picked up the computer. "But probably not. Come on, Lacy. Let's take care of this. It's early enough, maybe you and Travis can have dinner together after all."

"How did you know about that?" Lacy asked.

"Your mother told me while you were in the bathroom," Jan said. She grinned. "I can't help it if I have a talent for finding out things about people. You'd be surprised how useful it can be."

She started toward the living room and the others followed. They were almost to the door when the bell rang. Brenda hurried forward to answer it.

Travis's uniform was streaked with soot and something dark that might have been blood. He had more soot smudged on one cheek and his nose, and he needed a shave, but Lacy had never seen a more welcome sight. She wanted to rush forward and throw her arms around him, but she held back, hovering behind Brenda as her friend ushered the sheriff inside.

He looked past the other two women and found Lacy, his eyes meeting hers. "Your mother told me I'd find you here," he said.

"I'm glad you're okay," she said.

"Sorry if I worried you," he said. "The dispatcher didn't know the name of the officer who called in, and people jumped to conclusions. By the time I got back to the station half the town thought I was the officer who had been wounded and the other half were ready to start planning my funeral."

"I'm sorry about the officer who was shot," Lacy said. "Is he going to be okay?"

"He will be."

"Do you know who shot him?" Jan asked.

"No." Travis was still watching Lacy. "I stopped by to see if you'd still like to have dinner with me."

"Um, sure." She was so aware of the other two women watching. She tried hard to appear casual and indifferent.

"Good." He looked down at the floor and for a long moment, no one said anything.

"Oh, really, go on, you two," Jan said. "It's at times like these that I'm reminded that the saying 'three's a crowd' is so true."

"But before you go." Brenda reached over and tugged

the computer from Jan's grasp. "We were going to bring this to your office, but you can take it with you."

"A laptop?" Travis examined the computer.

"It was Andy's," Brenda said. "I didn't even realize I had it until I was looking for something in the basement and found it in a box of books and other stuff from his office. It's password protected and I don't know the password, but I thought maybe the sheriff's department could get past that. So many things, like notes and letters and photographs, Andy kept in his files, but contracts and correspondence will probably be on there. Maybe you'll find something to help you."

"This is great," Travis said. "We'll find someone to get the information off it. Thank you, Brenda."

"I'm sorry I didn't think of it before," she said.

"Are you ready to go, Lacy?" he asked.

"I'm ready."

She followed him out the door and down the walkway, aware of the other two women watching them. "This is the oldest vehicle in our little fleet," he said as he opened the passenger door of the Toyota. "It's pretty rough."

"It doesn't matter," she said, sliding into the seat. She watched as he tucked the computer into a large plastic bag, filled out a label on the front of the bag, then sealed it. He laid the bag with the computer in it on the rear floorboard. "We'll put that in an evidence locker at the station." He looked up and his eye caught hers. "Later."

"Mom was thrilled you accepted her invitation to dinner," Lacy said, as he turned onto Main. "I was, too, of course. I thought maybe you would be too tired or too busy or…"

He put his hand over hers and she stopped talking. "It's okay," he said. "You don't have to be nervous."

"I'm not sure why I am," she said. She watched him through half-lowered lashes, not wanting him to look into her eyes and see the powerful desire and attraction that had her feeling a little out of control.

He laced his fingers with hers. "I told your mother I needed to take a rain check on the family dinner," he said. "I wanted some time for the two of us to be alone."

Lacy swallowed, her heart beating faster. "Oh."

"Is that okay with you?"

"Yes." She looked into his eyes. "More than okay."

He kissed the back of her hand, then turned it over and kissed her palm, and she suddenly felt hot and a little light-headed. "Where are we going for dinner?" she asked.

"How about my place?"

"Yes."

They held hands on the drive to the condo he rented in a development on the river. He retrieved the computer in its evidence bag from the Toyota and carried it inside, where he locked it inside a cabinet by the door. When he straightened, Lacy didn't hesitate, but moved into his arms.

The kiss was urgent, a little rough, his unshaven chin abrading her cheek, his lips crushing the still-healing cut on her mouth. But sheer pleasure overwhelmed the discomfort, and she angled her head to deepen the contact, reveling in the heat and strength of him. She wrapped her arms around him, pressing herself fully to him, and he slid his hands down to cup her bottom and draw her tight against him, leaving no doubt how much he wanted her.

When he finally lifted his head and looked into her eyes, she was shaky, her heart pounding. "Wow," she said.

"About dinner—" he began.

She wriggled against him. "I'm thinking maybe we should enjoy dessert first."

She whooped as he lifted her, his hands under her thighs, wrapping her legs around his waist. He kissed her again, bracing her back against the wall in the foyer. She squirmed, delighted at the way he groaned in response—then she was the one groaning as he brought one hand up to caress the side of her breast, and began tracing a series of warm, wet kisses along the line of her jaw.

She tugged at his shirt, frustrated by the equipment that jangled and poked from the belt at his waist. Even when she succeeded in undoing the top two buttons, she was blocked from further exploration by the hard black wall of his bulletproof vest. By this time he had her T-shirt pushed up under her arms and was trailing his tongue along the lace at the top of her bra.

"This isn't fair," she protested. "You're wearing too much stuff."

He raised his head and laughed, then wrapped his hands around her waist and gently lowered her to the floor. "Am I rushing things?" he asked, looking into her eyes.

"More like going too slow." She pulled his head down to kiss him again, then nipped his upper lip. "You're welcome to get naked right here and take me up against the wall, but don't you think a bed might be more comfortable?"

She whooped again as he picked her up once more,

this time scooping her up behind her knees and shoulders. He carried her down a short hallway to a large bedroom. She had a passing impression of dark furniture and a king-size bed before he dropped her onto the mattress.

She propped herself on her elbows and watched as he stripped off his utility belt and draped it on the arm of a chair next to the bed. He kicked off his boots, then finished unbuttoning the shirt and removed it. This was the kind of male body she could admire—masculine but not too hard, handsome but not too perfect.

There was nothing particularly sexy about the black protective vest he wore under the shirt—except that he was wearing it. He peeled it off, his skin damp in places beneath it. "I should take a shower," he said.

"Only if you take me with you," she said. His eyes met hers and she felt the force of the look deep inside, a tugging heat that settled between her legs. He finished undressing, then pulled her up from the bed. When she was standing beside him she pulled her T-shirt off over her head. Before she could remove her bra, he had unfastened it and was tracing his tongue around one nipple, and then the next, until she was swaying, her kneecaps having apparently melted in the onslaught.

Some time after that the rest of her clothes ended up somewhere on the bedroom floor, and the two of them tumbled into the shower, where warm water rushed over them, and she discovered how sensual the feel of soap-suds between two naked bodies could be.

She slid soapy fingers over the jut of his shoulders and the swell of his biceps, tracing the ridges of his ribs and smoothing across the flat plane of his stomach. When she wrapped her hand around his erection, he let out his breath and his eyes glazed.

He curled a hand around her wrist. "Better slow down," he said.

She smiled up at him. "I don't know," she said. "I kind of like having you at my mercy."

"Is that so?" His grin held a hint of wickedness that sent another thrill through her. The grin gave way to a slack-jawed sigh as he reached down and slid a finger into her, stroking gently. "Now...now who needs to go...slow," she stammered as he slid the finger in and out. "Remember...it's been a while for me."

With his free hand, he reached over and shut off the water, then kissed her again, their lips remaining locked together even as they moved out of the shower and wrapped themselves in towels.

They were still damp when they returned to the bed and tumbled onto the dark blue comforter. She scooted back onto the pillows and beckoned him to her. "I don't want to wait any longer," she said.

He leaned over and took a condom from the drawer of the bedside table. "Just so you don't get the wrong impression, these have been in there awhile," he said, holding up the foil packet. "But I think they're still good."

"Stop talking and put that baby on," she said.

"Yes, ma'am."

Watching him roll on that condom was enough to have her breathing hard again. When he finally moved over her she was more than ready for him, pulling her to him and sighing with happiness as he entered her.

She had expected a lot from this moment—physical satisfaction, a kind of completion, the thrill of being so close to him. But she hadn't counted on his gentleness, or how much he would *care* for her. He moved slowly at first, his eyes locked to hers, his focus entirely on her. He shifted slightly, and she felt the movement deep inside her. "Do you like that?" he asked.

"Yes."

"How about this?" He reached down to fondle her and her eyes lost focus. *Yeesss.* His hands and his hips worked a kind of magic over her, and she surrendered to it. "That's it," he whispered, his fingers caressing a sensitive place she hadn't even known existed. "Don't be afraid to let go."

So she let go, and rode the waves of pleasure each thrust of his body sent through her. She dug her fingers into his back and responded to his every movement, opening her eyes when she felt him still and tense, watching his release reflected on his face, then pulling him to her to hold him even closer, until they rolled to the side, still joined, to gaze into each other's eyes.

"To quote you—wow," he said, and he slid out of her. He disposed of the condom in the trash basket next to the bed, then lay back down beside her.

She laughed, feeling impossibly light, as if she might float off the bed. "Yeah—wow." She trailed one finger down his nose. "Now you're making me think I missed out in high school, not flirting with you."

"I like to think I've learned a few things since high school."

"Life has a way of doing that—teaching us things whether we want to learn them or not. You taught me that people can change—or at least, they can change their minds. You changed your mind about me. And I changed my mind about you."

He slid over to lay his head on her shoulder. "Let's

put that behind us," he said. "I want to focus on our future, not our past."

"Except we can't really put the past behind us," she said. "Not until we find Andy's killer—or whoever it is who keeps coming after us."

"You're right," he said. "We're going to stop them."

She eased him off her and sat up. "Why don't we start by taking a look at that laptop?" she said.

"What good will that do?" Travis asked. "Brenda said it's password protected."

"Yes, but I think I know the password. It's probably the same one Andy used for everything. That's what most people do, isn't it?"

The look he gave her held frank admiration. "I was right when I said you'd be the key to solving this case," he said.

"We haven't solved anything yet," she reminded him.

"No, but we will. And soon. I can feel it." He slid off the bed and took her hand. "Let's go check that laptop."

Chapter Fourteen

Travis couldn't stop looking at Lacy. He liked watching her when she was like this—completely relaxed and happy, her attention focused on the computer that was open on the coffee table between them. They sat on the sofa in his living room, thighs touching. She had put on one of his dress shirts, the cuffs folded back, the tails hanging down to midthigh. He had pulled on a pair of jeans. Just as well he didn't have the video camera here to film this, though he had made her sign off on the custody sheet, keeping to proper procedure.

"Andy's password for most things was brenda812," Lacy said as she typed. "They were married in August of 2012." She hit Enter and the screen shifted to reveal the desktop menu. "Eureka!" she cried, and clicked on a folder labeled Office.

A list of file names filled the screen. Travis leaned in closer. "Do you see anything?" he asked.

She highlighted the file named "Eagle_mtn_resort." The first thing that came up was a report from the county road commissioner. "It's about the roads in and around the resort," she said, scanning the page. "That doesn't look too pertinent."

She started to close the file, but Travis put out a hand

to stop her. "Wait a minute. Look at this." He dragged his finger across the touch pad to highlight a paragraph that began at the bottom of the page. "This mentions Fireline Road, see?"

She squinted at the screen. "It says they'll need to extend Fireline Road up over the ridge to provide a second access route to the resort." She looked at Travis. "Does that mean the resort is just over the ridge from the storage facility?"

He nodded. "Which would make it easy for anyone on the ridge to keep an eye on the storage facility, too. Maybe whoever shot Eddie was on Hake's land and saw Eddie from there."

"That still doesn't tell us why they would do something like that."

"No, but I think first thing tomorrow I'll drive to the resort property and see if it looks like anyone has been up there. Henry Hake said the group is restructuring, so I wouldn't think there would be any work going on."

"Don't go by yourself," she said.

"No. I'll take Gage or Dwight with me. And I'll be careful."

She turned back to the computer. "Let's see if there's anything else interesting on here." She scrolled through the list of file names and stopped when she came to a file named jan.

"Jan as in January?" Travis asked.

"Or Jan as in Jan Selkirk?" Lacy opened the file. The first page was a list of dates. 04/06/14, 07/29/14— seventeen different dates altogether.

"Those are all from the months prior to Andy's death," Travis said.

Lacy scrolled to the second page of the file. This

one was a photograph. She enlarged the photo on the screen. "That's Jan Selkirk," she said, staring at the wide-mouth brunette who was sitting on the lap of a burly blond man. "She's changed her hair color, but that has to be her. And is that—"

"Henry Hake," Travis said. "Keep scrolling."

The next four pages in the file were more pictures of Jan Selkirk and Henry Hake—the last two of them kissing passionately, his hand up her skirt.

Lacy scrolled until her cursor reached the end of the file. "That's all there is," she said.

"Jan Selkirk is married to Barry Selkirk," Travis said. "She has been for years."

"So Jan and Henry Hake were having an affair?" Lacy stared at the last picture, of the former mayor and the developer locked in a steamy kiss. "This explains why Jan was acting so strangely at Brenda's house this afternoon."

"Strange in what way?"

"She insisted on going into Brenda's basement to retrieve the computer herself, and when I went down to see what was taking her so long, I found her going through a box of things from Andy's office. Then she volunteered to take the computer to the sheriff's office herself. But then you showed up and foiled that plan."

"She must have suspected Andy had something on here that would damage her reputation," Travis said. "Not to mention her marriage."

Lacy looked ill. "Do you think Andy was blackmailing her?" she asked.

"If he was, that might have given her reason to want him dead." Travis tapped the screen. "Notice anything else about these pictures?"

"Her hair—it's dark brown, like mine."

"I don't remember when she changed it, but it may have been about the time Andy died," he said. "We might be able to find pictures in the newspaper archives."

"The woman Wade Tomlinson saw outside Andy's office the day he died—that could have been Jan."

"Maybe so." He tapped the keys to shut down the computer. "I need to take you home," he said. "I have to get this down to the station." He bent down and kissed her cheek. "Sorry we never got around to dinner."

"Oh, I don't know." Her smile sent heat curling through his stomach. "I thought dessert was pretty good."

"Only pretty good?"

"Awfully good." She kissed him on the mouth, then stood. "Let me know what happens with Jan," she said.

"I will. I'd like to put an end to this case as soon as possible."

"Yeah, I hate to think of Jan as a murderer."

"I'm going to make sure of her guilt before I ask the DA to file charges," Travis said. "I want to bring Andy's killer to justice, but I want to be sure we've got the right person this time."

"If you want to discuss security for Pioneer Days, I don't see why we couldn't have done so at my office at the museum." Jan Selkirk swept into the Rayford County Sheriff's Department on a wave of expensive perfume, a bright blue Questions? Ask Me! button affixed to her blouse.

"What's with the button?" Gage asked as he escorted her into an interview room.

She glanced down at the four-inch button. "It's for Pioneer Days. I'm an information helper. We'll have them stationed throughout town. Anyone who sees this button knows they can approach that person and find out the schedule of activities, or where the restrooms are located or anything else they need to know."

Travis came into the interview room and closed the door behind him. Jan's smile faltered. "Why are we in here?" she asked. "Couldn't we go in your office?"

"I didn't ask you here to talk about the festival," Travis said.

Her color paled beneath her makeup. "What is going on, Sheriff?" she asked. "I don't have time to waste on trivial matters."

"Oh, I don't think this is a trivial matter. Sit down." He motioned to a seat at the conference table, then took the chair across the table for himself.

Jan hesitated, then sat. She glanced up at Gage, who remained standing by the door. "Am I under arrest?" she asked.

"Not at this time. We just want to ask you a few questions. You're free to go anytime."

She looked toward the door, as if debating leaving. Travis was gambling that she wouldn't. "I'm going to record the conversation," he said, and switched on the recorder that sat at one end of the table. "That's for your protection, as well as ours."

"You're making me very nervous," she said. "What is this about?"

Travis opened a folder and slid out a stack of photos—three of the pictures taken from Andy Stenson's computer enlarged to eight-by-ten-inch glossies. He arranged the photos in front of Jan. "Recognize these?"

She stared at the pictures, all the color bleached from her face. "Where did you get these?" she whispered.

"They were on Andy Stenson's laptop," Travis said. "You knew they might be there. They're why you tried so hard to get the laptop away from Brenda. I think you planned to destroy the machine, or maybe just erase the files."

"I don't know what you're talking about." But she continued to stare at the photographs, pain reflected in her eyes.

"You were having an affair with Henry Hake," Travis said. "An affair you didn't want your husband and the town council to know about. I looked up some council minutes from that time period and you were one of the strongest supporters for Hake's resort development, urging the council to pass resolutions that would make it easier for him to build his high-altitude luxury homes."

"I supported the development because it was a good idea. Not because I was sleeping with Henry Hake." Her voice was stronger, though the fear hadn't left her eyes.

Travis waited until her eyes met his before he spoke. "Was Andy blackmailing you?" he asked.

"No. Of course not!" She sat back, hands clutching the edge of the table. "You're thinking if he was I would have a good reason to kill him but I didn't kill him, I promise."

"We're going to subpoena your financial records," Travis said. "As well as Andy's bank accounts. They'll show if you were paying him to keep this quiet."

She shifted in her chair, hands clenching and unclenching. "All right—yes. He was blackmailing me. He said he wouldn't tell Barry or anyone else about the affair as long as I paid. He said he needed the money to finish the remodeling on his house. He let Brenda think all the money came from Henry Hake." She laughed, a hysterical sound. "I suppose in a way that was true, since I had to borrow money from Henry to pay Andy. But I didn't kill him. I wouldn't do something like that."

"A slim woman with dark brown hair was seen outside Andy's office about the time he died," Gage said. "We know now that woman wasn't Lacy—was it you?"

"I didn't kill him," she said. "I went there to talk to him—to tell him I couldn't keep paying him. I told him if he didn't stop harassing me I would make Henry Hake cancel his contract with Andy."

"I'm surprised you hadn't thought of that before," Travis said.

She made a face. "Henry didn't really have a say in who represented the development corporation," she said. "He was the public face of the company, but his business partners—the people behind the scenes—made all the decisions. Henry didn't think Andy was experienced enough to represent the group, but his objection was overruled."

"What happened when you went to talk to Andy that day?" Travis asked.

Her mouth tightened. "He laughed at me. He laughed. I didn't say half of what I wanted to say before he started laughing. He said he wasn't about to give up his very lucrative 'side job' and I'd better focus on finding a way to pay. He said Henry wouldn't fire him because he knew things about Henry that his business partners wouldn't want to know."

"What happened then?" Gage leaned over the table toward her. "Did you attack him in a fit of rage? Stab him in the heart with the letter opener he kept on his desk?"

"No! I ran out of there. I left by the back door so no one would see me. I was crying and I didn't want to have to make up some excuse if I ran into anyone."

"So you didn't see anyone when you were leaving?" Travis asked.

"No. The next day I heard Andy had been murdered and I was terrified. You can't imagine my relief when I heard Lacy had been arrested."

Travis tamped down his anger. "You really thought she killed Andy?" he asked.

"I just assumed he had been blackmailing her, too." Jan sniffed. "I wouldn't be surprised if Andy was getting money from other people in town. Everybody thought he was such a nice young man, but he had a sly streak."

"Who else do you think he was blackmailing?" Gage asked. "Besides you and possibly Henry Hake?"

"I don't know." She straightened, some steel back in her spine. "And I've said enough. Too much. I want a lawyer."

Travis slid back his chair and stood. "Call him. You can wait for him in here." He and Gage left the room, locking the door behind them.

Outside, at the end of the hallway, the brothers conferred. "What do you think?" Travis asked.

"She admits she was in Andy's office that day," Gage said. "It had to have been only minutes before he died. She's got a motive, since he was threatening to tell her husband about the affair."

"I don't think it's enough to hold her," Travis said.

"If we don't arrest her, she's liable to leave town and try to disappear," Gage said. "She's got money and I bet she's got a passport."

"I wish we had more evidence against her."

"You're afraid of making the same mistake with her you made with Lacy," Gage said. "That isn't going to happen a second time."

"Let me call the DA, see what he says," Travis said.

The DA agreed with Travis that they probably didn't have enough evidence to arrest Jan at this time, but that she was a strong suspect. By this time both Barry Selkirk and the lawyer Jan had hired to represent her had arrived at the police station.

"My client—"

"My wife—"

Travis waved away the attorney and the husband's protests. "You're free to go, Jan," he said. "But I'll need you to stay close, in case I have more questions."

"I get it. Don't leave town." She stood, gathering her dignity. "Obviously, I've done some things I'm not proud of." She slanted a look at her husband. "But I did not kill Andy Stenson."

They watched her walk out of the door, flanked by her lawyer and her husband. "Do you believe her?" Gage asked.

"Yeah." Travis shoved his hands in his pockets, shoulders hunched. "Right now, anyway, I do."

"So what now?"

"I'm going to talk to Henry Hake and I'm going to check out the site of Eagle Mountain Resort. Why don't you search through Andy's computer and see if you can find anyone else he was blackmailing?"

"We might end up with a whole town full of suspects," Gage said.

"The only one I care about is the person who really killed him," Travis said. "Find him or her and we'll tie up a whole lot of loose ends."

"BLACKMAIL! AND JAN SELKIRK? I just can't believe it." Brenda sat between Lacy and Jeanette Milligan on the Milligans' sofa, a cup of coffee steadied on one knee.

"I was shocked, too," Lacy said. "I never would have believed Andy would do something like that. I knew he was doing better financially, but he told me you had inherited a little money from a favorite aunt, and that was enough for you to finish the remodeling on your house."

"I thought the money came from Henry Hake and the other new clients he had." Brenda sipped her coffee. Her eyes were red and puffy, and Lacy knew she must have been mourning this new revelation about her husband. "I thought I knew him so well," she said. "And to think all this time he was lying." Her voice caught on the last word and she bowed her head.

Jeanette pulled her close and handed her several tissues. "Andy was misguided, but he loved you," she said. "That's what you have to remember."

"Mom is right." Lacy patted Brenda's hand. "Andy did love you. I never knew him to even look twice at another woman."

Brenda nodded and raised her head. "To think I've worked with Jan all this time and I never knew she cheated on her husband. But I can't believe she killed Andy over it."

"I'm shocked, too," Lacy said. "Of course, I don't know her well, but the way Andy died—it never struck me as something a woman would do. It was just so… brutal." She glanced at Brenda. "Sorry. I shouldn't have said that."

"No, it's okay," Brenda said. "It *was* brutal. The trial kind of numbed me to the whole thing, but I agree. It never set well with me when the prosecutor said Andy was killed by a woman. For one thing, he was a young, strong guy. You and Jan Selkirk just aren't big, physical women. I think Andy could have fought her off easily."

"I've been trying to think if there was anyone else Andy might have been trying to get money from," Lacy said. "Someone besides Jan who might have had a reason to kill him. There's Henry Hake, of course. He might not have wanted news of the affair getting out, and he certainly had a lot more money than Jan."

"I'm sure Travis has already thought of that," Jeanette said.

"Speaking of Travis." Brenda sat up straighter and dabbed at her eyes. "I don't think I was imagining the sparks flying between the two of you yesterday when he picked you up at my house."

"He canceled dinner with us in favor of a *private* dinner with Lacy," Jeanette said. "Though come to think of it, when she came in several hours later, she said she was starved because they had never gotten around to eating."

"Hmm. I wonder what two people could do for several hours that would make them forget all about food?" Brenda said.

Lacy's cheeks burned and she refused to look her mother or Brenda in the eye. "Travis and I have gotten close," she said.

Jeanette covered her ears. "I don't think I want to hear any more." She lowered her hands and smiled. "But your father and I think he's a very nice young man. And it's good to see you so happy."

"If anyone deserves it, you do," Brenda said.

"You deserve to be happy, too," Lacy said. "I'm so sorry about Andy. It feels as if he died all over again."

"There's something else about all this that's bothering me," Brenda said.

"What's that?" Lacy asked.

"Do the police think Jan is the person who ran us off the road in that truck, then burned the truck, and blew up the storage unit while you and Travis were inside?" Brenda asked. "And if she was, who shot Eddie Carstairs? Jan was with me when that happened—and then the two of us were with you."

Lacy stared at her. "I've been so focused on Jan as a suspect in Andy's murder that I didn't think of that," she said.

"If she could kill Andy, she might not hesitate to kill you or anyone else who threatened her," Jeanette said.

"Yes, but with a big truck?" Brenda asked. "Or a bomb? What does Jan know about trucks or bombs? And then she sets the truck on fire and hikes home cross-country?"

"I don't know her as well as you do, but I can't picture her doing any of that," Lacy said. She put a hand over her stomach, which felt as if she had eaten way too much pie. "I hope Travis isn't making another mistake."

"You should call and talk to him," Brenda said. "Not that you should tell him how to do his job, but maybe he'll put your mind at ease. He might have an explanation that we haven't thought of yet."

"Or maybe he thinks Jan had an accomplice or something," Lacy said. She slipped her phone from her pocket and tapped in Travis's cell number. After two rings the call went to voice mail. "Call me when you get a chance," she said, hesitant to say more—especially with Brenda and her mother listening in.

Brenda set aside her half-empty coffee cup and

stood. "Thanks for letting me vent," she said. "I have to get to work."

"The museum is open, even with Jan under suspicion?" Jeanette asked.

"Oh, yes. We're redoing all the displays and adding new ones for Pioneer Days." She picked up her purse and slung the strap over her shoulder. "It's coming up quickly, so I'd better get busy."

"I can help." Lacy stood, also. "I don't know the first thing about history, but I can put things where you tell me," she said. "Consider me your newest volunteer."

"That's the best offer I've had all day," Brenda said.

Jeanette rose and walked with them to the door. "If Travis stops by, I'll let him know you're at the museum," she said.

"Mom, you don't have to be my personal secretary."

"I know this is a little awkward," Jeanette said. "After all, you're not a teenager anymore. But just so we won't worry, if you're going to stay out overnight, text and let us know you're safe."

"Umm. Okay."

Lacy followed Brenda out to her car. "Did your mom just give you permission to spend the night with Travis?" Brenda asked.

"Yes. Talk about awkward!" Lacy rolled her eyes. She could joke about it with Brenda, but she added "look for own apartment" to the top of her to-do list.

THE BIG IRON gate across Henry Hake's drive stood wide-open when Travis visited the house later that day. The sheriff parked in the paved circular drive and walked up to the massive oak entry doors. He rang the bell three times, but received no answer. No one answered when he called Henry Hake's private number, either.

Travis walked around the house, peering in windows, his boots crunching on the heavy layer of bark mulch in the immaculately tended landscape. Hake didn't strike Travis as the type to want to get his hands dirty, so he imagined an army of gardeners tending the lilacs and creeping juniper. The garage had no windows, so Travis couldn't tell if a car was parked inside, but the house itself had a deserted look, with no lights showing from within.

He returned to his vehicle and called the office of Hake Development. "This is Rayford County Sheriff Travis Walker," he told the woman who answered. "I'm out at Henry Hake's house and he doesn't appear to be home. It's important that I reach him."

"I'll put you through to Mr. Hake's administrative assistant," the woman on the other end of the line said.

Seconds later, the brisk woman Travis had spoken with before answered. Travis introduced himself once more. "It's very important that I speak with Mr. Hake," he said.

"You're from the police, you say?"

"The sheriff's office, in Rayford County, where Mr. Hake lives. I believe we spoke the other day. I'm at Mr. Hake's house now and he isn't home."

"Yes, I remember speaking with you. I was thinking I should call you later today, if I hadn't heard from Mr. Hake," she said.

"What about?" Travis asked.

"I'm afraid I can't tell you where Mr. Hake is right now, because I don't know. I haven't heard from him in a couple of days, and I'm starting to get worried."

"Does he often disappear without telling you where he's going?" Travis asked.

"Oh, no. He always stays in touch. That's why this is so unusual. And why I was going to call you."

"I'm not sure I understand," Travis said. "Do you think something has happened to Mr. Hake?"

"I couldn't say. All I know is that Mr. Hake is missing."

Chapter Fifteen

Volunteering at the history museum was not the most exciting work Lacy had ever done, but she enjoyed spending time with Brenda, and the work gave her something to do. Now that she had adjusted to life at home once more, she was growing restless. She needed a job, but a small town like Eagle Mountain didn't offer many employment opportunities, so for now at least, volunteering seemed the best solution.

The museum occupied the building that had once been Eagle Mountain's hospital, back at the turn of the nineteenth century, when the town had boasted five grocery stores, a dairy, a lumberyard, a train depot and a population five times what it was these days. The various rooms of the hospital housed themed displays, with space in the back for a classroom, archives and a workroom. Everyone from schoolchildren to tourists regularly filed through the building, which had developed a reputation as one of the finest small-town museums in the state.

Lacy finished tacking red, white and blue bunting around the large front windows and turned to find Brenda frowning at a computer screen behind the front desk. "What are you looking at that put that sour look on your face?" she asked.

Brenda turned away from the computer. "A customer came in yesterday, asking about a book we usually keep in stock, but were out of. I was trying to see if I could find out where Jan orders our books so I could get this lady a copy, but I'm having a hard time figuring out her system for organizing things."

"What will happen if Jan is arrested?" Lacy asked, joining her friend at the museum's front counter, which served as both check-in desk and retail checkout.

"Even if she didn't kill Andy—and I still can't believe she did—her affair will be a scandal," Brenda said. "The town owns this museum and I doubt if they'll keep her on."

"Will you apply to be the director, then?"

"I'd like to." She studied Lacy's face. "What about you? Want to be my assistant?"

"I would love to work for you, but I'm not in love with history the way you are." Lacy picked up an antique paperweight from the counter and turned it over in her hand. "I think I should use the money I got from the state to go to school."

"Do you know what kind of career you want to pursue?" Brenda asked.

"I was thinking maybe…education. My mom is a teacher and I like kids." She set the paperweight back on the counter. "I think I'd be good at the job."

"We certainly need good teachers. You should go for it."

"I already did some research," Lacy said. "I can enroll in the university in Junction and commute to classes from here."

"So you'd stay in Eagle Mountain?"

"This is home." Even with everything that had happened here—the tragedy of Andy's death and those awful months before and during her trial—Lacy still felt more comfortable here than she had anywhere else. "I don't want to leave."

"And a certain handsome sheriff is here…" Brenda's eyes sparkled.

Lacy laughed. "There is that. But I think I'd like to find my own place to live. My parents are happy to have me stay with them as long as I like, but it feels too much like I'm in high school, with them watching my every move."

"I know a place you can rent," Brenda said.

That got Lacy's attention. Rentals, like jobs, were scarce in small towns like Eagle Mountain. "Where?"

"Andy and I fixed up an apartment over our garage, thinking we would use it when relatives visited. It's been sitting empty all this time, but I'd love to rent it to you. You'd have your own entrance and could come and go as you please."

"That sounds perfect." Lacy leaned over the counter to hug her friend. "Just tell me when I can move in."

Brenda returned the hug. "You should look at the place first, make sure it's what you want," she said.

"Does it have room for a bed and my own bathroom?"

"And a tiny kitchen and living room," Brenda said.

"Then I love it already."

The bell on the front door rang, announcing someone had entered the museum. "I'll take care of this," Brenda said. "Would you go into the workroom and look in the closet and take out the box marked Pioneer Days Costumes? We need to go through those before the festival."

Lacy found the box in question and looked around for a pair of scissors to cut the tape. But voices from the front of the museum caught her attention and she froze, listening. "I didn't know you were interested in local history, Mr. Barnes," Brenda said.

Lacy tiptoed to the door of the workroom and peered out at the front reception area. Ian Barnes, his black Eagle Mountain Outfitters T-shirt stretched like a second skin over his powerful chest and shoulders, stood across from Brenda at the front counter. "Somebody told me you have a display of old climbing gear and some pictures," he said.

Brenda handed him some change and an admission token. "We do. It's in the Local Sports room—second door on the left." She indicated the hallway to her right.

Ian replaced his wallet in his back pocket. "Hello, Lacy," he said.

Lacy jumped. She hadn't realized she was standing where Ian could see her. Reluctantly, she stepped into the front room. "Hello," she said.

"Do you work here, too?" Ian asked.

"No. I'm, uh, volunteering."

He put his hand lightly at her back—a touch that sent a shiver up her spine. "Why don't you show me where this Local Sports room is?"

"Go ahead and go with him, Lacy," Brenda said.

"It's down this way." Lacy hurried forward, away from his touch, and led him to the room, which, in addition to historic photos of rock climbers and skiers, included a feature on a 1930s boxing champion who had hailed from the area and jerseys from local sports teams.

Ian stepped inside the room and Lacy turned to leave, but he grabbed her by the wrist. "Stay a minute and tell me more about yourself," he said.

She pressed her back against the door frame, tamping down the urge to flee. Why did this man leave her feeling so unsettled? While every other woman in town seemed gone over the fact that he was so good-looking, what she felt in his presence wasn't attraction, but fear. "Why do you want to know about me?" she asked, keeping her voice light and focusing her gaze on the displays in the room.

"Oh, the usual reason." He smiled, and the effect was dazzling.

"What is the usual reason?"

"I'm a single guy, you're a pretty single woman." He leaned toward her, one hand on the doorjamb, over her head. "I'd like to get to know you better."

"I'm involved with someone, Mr. Barnes," she said, wincing inwardly at the primness of her words.

"The county sheriff. I've seen you two together. But you're not engaged or anything, right?"

"No."

He flashed the smile again. "Then you can't blame a guy for trying." To her great relief, he lowered his hand and turned to study the sepia-toned pictures of men in woolen knickers and heavy boots climbing up Dakota Ridge. "Somebody told me you used to work for that lawyer who was killed."

"Yes."

"I guess you knew all about all his clients then."

"Actually, no, I didn't." She edged toward the door. Why was he asking about Andy's clients?

"I think maybe you know more than you're saying," he said. "That's good. It's always good to know when to keep a secret."

The skin along Lacy's arms stood up in gooseflesh. Did Ian Barnes know about the blackmail? Had Andy blackmailed *him*? She backed out of the room. "I don't have anything to say to you or anyone else," she said.

"That's good." He turned and his eyes met hers, and the look in them froze her blood. His earlier flirtatiousness had been replaced by pure menace. "If I were you, I wouldn't tell my boyfriend, the sheriff, about our little conversation," he said. "After all, your parents have suffered enough, haven't they?"

Lacy all but ran back to the front room, past Brenda and into the workroom. Brenda hurried after her. "Lacy, what is it?" she asked. "You're white as a ghost. Did Ian do something to upset you? Should I call Travis?"

Lacy shook her head. "No. No, I'm fine. I just…" She put a hand to her head. "I just had a dizzy spell. I didn't eat breakfast this morning." She struggled to pull herself together, not to let her friend see how terrified she was. She felt confident enough to stand up to someone like Ian Barnes on her own. But when he threatened her family, he left her defenseless.

"Have some water." Brenda took a bottle from a small refrigerator under the counter and handed it to Lacy. "Are you sure this doesn't have something to do with Ian?"

Lacy drank some water and began to feel a little steadier. "He just makes me uncomfortable, that's all," she said.

"Yeah, he may be gorgeous, but have you noticed he never smiles?"

Lacy shuddered as she remembered the smile he had fixed on her like a weapon. "I don't like him," she said, keeping her voice low.

"I'm sorry," Brenda said. "If he comes around again, I'll offer to give him a tour myself." She moved back up front and Lacy sagged against the counter and drank more water. Should she tell Travis about her encounter with Ian? Maybe he could find something on Andy's computer that would point to Ian as the victim of blackmail.

But what if word got back to Ian that she had told, and he made good on his threat to hurt her parents? Travis would offer to protect her family, but what if he couldn't?

"That's funny." Brenda came back into the workroom. "Ian left already."

"Did he say anything?" Lacy asked.

"No. When I walked back into the front room just now he was headed out. I called after him, but he must not have heard me. He got in that Jeep of his and drove away." She shrugged. "I guess all he wanted to see was the climbing gear and pictures. Some people are like that—they're only interested in items related to their hobby or history or family or whatever."

"Right." Lacy finished her water and tossed the bottle in the recycling bin. "I guess we'd better get back to work," she said. "What's next on the list?"

"Costumes." Brenda walked to the box Lacy had taken from the closet, opened it and pulled out a blue-and-white striped dress. Or, Lacy thought it was a dress—until she saw the attached bloomers.

"What is that?" she asked.

"It's an 1890s bathing costume." Brenda held the garment up to her body. "It's wool, and comes complete with a lace-trimmed cap and lace-up slippers. Jan and I wore them last year for Pioneer Days and they were a hit."

"You'll look adorable," Lacy said, trying hard not to laugh at the image she had of Brenda in the old-fashioned garment.

"Oh, I won't be alone." Brenda reached into the box and pulled out a second costume—this one red, with white ruffles at the neck and hem. "You and Jan are about the same size." She tossed the suit to Lacy. "And don't you dare say no. You promised to help, remember?"

"So I did." Lacy held the bathing costume at arm's length and made a face. It reminded her of a flannel nightgown. Not exactly the thing to turn the head of a certain sheriff.

"Please, Lacy," Brenda pleaded. "Don't make me look ridiculous all by myself. And I could really use the help."

"I'll wear it," Lacy said. "After all, you're going to be renting me my sweet new apartment." And at least volunteering at the festival would help take her mind off Ian Barnes. When she had a little more distance from her encounter with him, she would decide what to do.

TRAVIS SUMMONED HIS DEPUTIES, both regular and reserve, to the sheriff's department for a strategy session. "Eddie is out of the hospital but on medical leave," he said to begin the meeting. "Which may be permanent leave, when I've had more time to review his conduct that day. I don't need reserve officers who decide to interfere with investigations—on their days off or any other time." The pointed look he gave the two other reserve officers in attendance was enough to make them squirm.

"On to the next item of business," he continued. "Pioneer Days is this weekend. The sheriff's office has agreed to supply a couple of officers to help with crowd and traffic control, but four of us will be on duty throughout the weekend, and available to head off trouble if we see it developing."

"Check your schedules," Gage said to the reserves. "With Eddie out, I had to juggle things a bit."

"Moving on." Travis consulted his notes. "Henry Hake's administrative assistant, Marsha Caldwell, filed a missing person's report on him this morning. No one has seen or heard from him in the last forty-eight hours. There's no activity on his phone or credit cards, and his car is missing. But there's no sign of a struggle or violence at his home or office, so it's still possible he took a trip somewhere without telling anyone. He wouldn't be the first company executive to decide to take a break and shut off his phone for a long weekend."

"But you don't really think that's what happened," Gage said.

"No. Everything we've been dealing with lately—the reopening of the investigation into Andy Stenson's murder, the attack on Brenda and Lacy, the bombing of the storage unit, even Eddie's shooting—all have connections to Eagle Mountain Resort. We need to keep digging and see how they all link up."

"What's the next step?" Dwight asked.

"I want to check out the site Hake had planned for his resort. And I want you and Gage to go with me."

The meeting ended a few minutes later. The reserve officers left. Adelaide met Travis, Gage and Dwight in the front office. "It's a wonder your ears aren't burning, considering how the revelation that Andy Stenson was blackmailing Jan Selkirk, and Henry Hake's disappearance are all anybody can talk about."

"Anybody else confess to having been blackmailed by Andy Stenson?" Gage asked.

"Nah. Though Josh Lindberg at the hardware store is supposedly taking bets on whether Henry Hake left town because of the scandal with Jan, or whether Barry Selkirk ran him out of the county."

"That doesn't sound like Barry's style to me," Dwight said. "My guess is he'd be more likely to run Jan out of town."

"Word is he's sticking by her," Adelaide said. "Paid for a top lawyer from Denver and everything."

"I hope they work it out," Travis said. "We're headed up to the resort site to check things out. You know how to reach us if anything happens."

"I'd say we've had more than enough happen lately," Adelaide said. "I'm ready for the crime wave to be over. People are going to get the wrong idea about Eagle Mountain if this keeps up."

They set out, Gage and Dwight together in one SUV, Travis leading the way in the Toyota. The town was abuzz with preparations for the festival the following day. Wade Tomlinson and Brock Ryan were setting up a climbing wall for kids in front of Eagle Mountain Outfitters, and the Elks Club members were transforming the park into a mini-carnival, complete with a test-your-strength game, designed to look like a pioneer chopping wood, and a series of water troughs set up so that kids could pan for gold.

Travis had heard that Lacy was helping Brenda at the museum, but he hadn't had a chance to talk to her, what with the craziness of Jan's confession that she was blackmailed and Henry Hake's disappearance. But they had made a date to meet up the day of the festival to watch the fireworks together. And maybe, he thought, go back to his place afterward and make a few fireworks of their own.

The proposed site for Eagle Mountain Resort was eight miles out of the town proper, near the top of Dakota Ridge, but Eagle Mountain had annexed the land three years previously, largely at the urging of then-mayor Jan Selkirk, on the theory that the luxury development would be a tax boon to the community. So far, that prediction hadn't come true. The sheriff's department vehicles drove through the twin stone pillars that marked the entrance to the resort, into a landscape of crumbling asphalt and abandoned building foundations. Grass and even small shrubs broke through the neglected streets, and the stakes marking lot lines had fallen over or were barely visible through the underbrush that had taken over. Staked trees and other landscaping that had died from neglect dotted the landscape.

They parked in front of a five-foot-by-four-foot sign that touted the amenities of the resort, with an artist's rendering of the development, the homes all soaring redwood beams and glass walls, luxury four-wheel-drive vehicles parked on cobblestone drives while elegantly dressed men and women smiled and laughed.

"Yeah, it sure doesn't look anything like that now," Gage observed.

"I never could understand how Hake thought he was going to sell a bunch of people on living way up here," Dwight said. "It's eight miles down the mountain to town, and in winter you could end up stuck up here for days. Not to mention the avalanche potential." He looked behind them, up the slope of Dakota Ridge.

"These aren't the kinds of homes people live in fulltime," Gage said. He indicated the illustration on the sign. "People who build these kinds of places spend a few weeks in them at a time. When the weather gets bad they move to their villa in Tuscany or something."

"Let's take a look around," Travis said. He began walking, heading for a trio of curved metal air vents jutting up from a concrete pad.

"Looks like air vents," Dwight said. "Maybe venting an old mine, or an underground utility plant for the development."

"Maybe," Travis agreed. "They don't look that old, but maybe putting them in was one of the environmental requirements for building up here. Some of these old mines contain trapped gasses they might have had to vent."

"What exactly are we looking for?" Gage asked.

"Any signs of recent activity," Travis said. "I have a feeling whoever shot Eddie may have been coming from here."

"So you're thinking the shooting didn't have anything to do with the storage units?" Gage said.

"There wasn't any reason to shoot a man for digging through the ashes of a burned-out storage room," Travis said. "The fire destroyed everything, which even a casual observer could see. But if someone was coming over the ridge from this area—with something they didn't want anyone else to see—then they might be willing to kill for it."

The two brothers walked together along the development's main street, while Dwight explored among the foundations of buildings. "What does Eddie say about the shooter?" Gage asked.

"He doesn't remember anything," Travis said. "The knock on the head and the resultant concussion wiped out his short-term memory. He can't help us."

Mixed in among the modern foundations and survey markers were the signs of older occupation—weathered timbers with square iron nails and bent rusted spikes marked the path of tram lines that had carried raw ore from the mines. A new iron gate blocked the opening of a mine adit that had probably been constructed a hundred and fifty years before, and a rusting ore car positioned alongside the already-crumbling concrete foundation hinted at a future purpose as a flower planter.

"I may have something over here," Dwight called, about fifteen minutes into their search.

Gage and Travis joined him at the end of one of the streets, where the crumbling blacktop gave way to drying mud. Dwight pointed to a pair of impressions in the ground.

"Boots," Gage observed and squatted down for a closer look. "Some kind of work boots, or heavy-duty hiking boots."

"Army boots," Dwight said. "About a size thirteen from the looks of them. I've got the stuff in my unit to make casts of them if you want."

"Go ahead," Travis said. He walked from the mud in the direction of the storage units. Five feet farther on, he found a heel print that matched the boot print. Ten yards from there, he stood on a ledge that overlooked the storage facility and the end of Fireline Road.

"Sometimes you do know what you're doing," Gage said. He studied the ground at their feet. "I don't suppose we'd get lucky enough to find some shell casings."

"I think we're dealing with a pro," Travis said. "Someone who doesn't leave clues behind."

"The footprints were a mistake," Gage said.

"A mistake, or he knows they're not going to give us anything useful."

"It wasn't Jan Selkirk," Gage said.

"She was with Brenda when Eddie was shot," Travis said. "I'm not ruling her out for the murder, but not this. This was someone else."

"Come look at this." Dwight called them over.

On the back of a low rock wall that marked the boundary of the proposed resort, he had located tire imprints. "It's a good-sized truck," he said. "Not a tractor-trailer rig, but maybe a box truck. The tread pattern is still really sharp—they haven't had time to erode in the weather."

"So we know someone was up here," Travis said. He scanned the desolate surroundings. No trees grew taller than four feet, and the wind blew constantly. In summer, the sun burned through the thin air, fading paint, weathering wood and carrying an increased risk of skin cancer to anyone who stayed out in it very long. In winter, nighttime temperatures plunged to thirty below zero and snow piled up in drifts as tall as two-story buildings. Yes, the views were breathtaking, the air clear and the nighttime vista of stars unparalleled, but it seemed to Travis there were some places where it was better for people to visit and not try to dominate entirely.

They spent another half hour exploring the place, taking pictures and impressions of what they found. The few buildings that were intact were locked with heavy padlocks. "I'd love to see what's inside there," Travis said after he shook the door of a metal building half sunk in the side of a hill. "But I'd say our chances of getting a warrant to search this place are pretty much nil."

"Then why are we bothering with the impressions?" Gage asked.

"We had cause to come up here, tracking the shooter," Travis said. "If those impressions turn up anything, I'll make my case to a judge. But I'm not holding my breath we'll find anything."

They piled into their vehicles and headed back toward town. Halfway there, Travis got a call from Adelaide. "That writer, Alvin Exeter, is here in the office, demanding to speak with you," she said.

"Tell Mr. Exeter I have nothing to say to him."

"He says you'll want to talk to him," Adelaide said. "He says he has information about Eddie's shooting."

"Is he telling the truth, or only bluffing?" Travis asked.

"Well..." Adelaide paused, then said. "I don't know what kind of poker player he is, but I'm thinking you might want to talk to him."

Chapter Sixteen

Chapter Sixteen

Lacy had a restless night, replaying her interaction with Ian Barnes over and over again. By morning, she had decided she would tell Travis about Barnes and trust him to protect her and her family while dealing with Barnes's threats.

But when she came down to breakfast, she froze at the sight of a hunk of rusting metal resting in the middle of the kitchen table. She stared at it, a sinking feeling in her stomach that she had seen this artifact somewhere before—and recently. "What is that?" she asked.

"Your father thinks it's a piton," her mother said. "You know, the anchor things they drive into rock for climbers to attach safety lines to."

"Right." Lacy had a clear vision of a display of similar pitons on the wall in the Local Sports room at the history museum. "Where did you get it?" she asked.

Her father picked it up and turned it over in his hand. "The craziest thing—it was on the front porch this morning, right in front of the door. I can't imagine where it came from."

"Some climber probably dropped it in the street or it bounced out of a truck and the person who found it left it at the closest house," her mother said. "Though it looks old, antique, even."

"I thought if you were going to the museum again today you could take it down there," her father said. "Maybe they can use something like that—I sure can't."

Lacy had little doubt that she would find a missing space in the museum's display where, until yesterday afternoon, this exact piton had sat. Ian Barnes had brought it here and left it as a message to her. *I know where you live and I can practically come into your house without you ever knowing,* he was saying. *I can hurt you and the people you love and nothing you can do will stop me.*

"Lacy? Are you all right?" Jeanette put a hand on her daughter's shoulder. "You've gone all pale."

Lacy swallowed the bile that had risen in her throat. "I'm fine." She dropped into her chair at the table and forced a smile. "Nothing a cup of coffee won't fix."

"I'll wrap this up for you to take to the museum," her father said. "Tell Brenda hello from me."

Lacy had thought she would tell her parents that she had agreed to rent the apartment over Brenda's garage, but she needed to deal with Ian before she took that step. Living alone didn't seem like a good idea with him threatening her—and she needed to be near her parents to keep an eye on them.

"It's wonderful of you to help Brenda out at the museum." Lacy's mother placed a mug of coffee in front of her, then sat across from her. "That was so awful about Jan Selkirk. I couldn't believe it—her and Henry Hake. And Andy Stenson was blackmailing her?" She shook her head. "I couldn't say anything while Brenda was here yesterday, but it just goes to show you never can tell about people. I mean, I never would have thought Andy was a blackmailer, and I certainly wouldn't have picked Jan for a murderer."

"Mom, we don't know that Jan killed Andy," Lacy said. "We, of all people, should know better than to jump to conclusions about something so serious."

"Of course, dear." Jeanette stirred her coffee. "Still, someone killed Andy. I know it wasn't you, but knowing who really did it would finally put an end to all the speculation, and you wouldn't have any doubt hanging over your head. People think I haven't overheard their whispering. To some people you'll never be innocent until someone else is proven guilty."

"I don't care about those people," Lacy said. The only people she cared about were here in this room. And, well, Travis. She was beginning to care a great deal about him. Her gaze shifted once more to the rusted piton lying in the center of the table. She couldn't risk telling Travis about Ian. Not when there was so much at stake. She would never forgive herself if anything happened to her parents. And what if Ian hurt Travis?

She finished her breakfast, collected the piton her father had wrapped up for her and walked to the museum. She tried to slip through the door quietly, though the bell announced her arrival. The front room was empty, so she took the opportunity to tiptoe back to the Local Sports room and replace the piton in the display. By the time she made it back up front, Brenda had emerged from the workroom.

"I thought I heard you come in," Brenda said. "And just in time, too. The printer just delivered a bunch of brochures we have to fold and box up to hand out tomorrow. I'd forgotten Jan ordered them."

"I can definitely help with that," Lacy said, feigning cheerfulness. Though Brenda was as perfectly groomed and put together as ever, she had dark half-moons under her eyes, as if she, too, hadn't slept well last night. Between her hurt over the news about Andy and worry about her friend, Jan, she had a lot to deal with right now.

The two of them were well into the brochures when the bell over the door rang and Jan sashayed in. "Don't look so shocked to see me," she said. "There's lots of work to be done before tomorrow and until the town council relieves me of my duties, I'm still director of this museum."

She stashed her purse in the filing cabinet and locked the drawer, then turned to face them. "I'm only going to say this once, so pay attention. Brenda, I did not kill your husband. I was furious with him for extorting money from me and threatening to tell Barry about the affair, but really, I was furious with myself for getting into such a mess in the first place. I argued with Andy, but I never, never would have killed him. When I left his office that afternoon he was very much alive."

Brenda's eyes shone with tears. "I believe you," she said.

Jan turned to Lacy. "One of my biggest regrets is that I didn't speak out at your trial, when Wade Tomlinson told everyone he had seen you outside Andy's office that day. But I was too much of a coward. I told myself it didn't matter but I know I could have made a difference to you and I didn't. I don't blame you if you hate me for that."

Lacy told herself she should be angry with Jan, but the once-proud woman looked so pathetic. She seemed to have aged ten years overnight, her usually perfect manicured nails chipped and bitten, her lipstick crooked, her hair hanging limp. Jan would never be one of her favorite people, but she wasn't going to waste time hating her. "I'm through holding grudges," she said. Travis had taught her that lesson, hadn't he?

"What does Barry say?" Brenda asked.

Jan's expression grew more strained. "He's understandably upset, and he's moved into our guesthouse. But he's agreed we should see a counselor, so I'm hoping we can get past this."

"Did you know Henry Hake is missing?" Lacy asked. "I heard it on the news last night."

"I heard it, too," Jan said. "Travis contacted me to see if I knew anything about it. But I haven't seen the man in over a year, and we broke off our relationship before Andy died. That was one of the things I told Andy that day when I went to plead with him. I told Henry I couldn't take the stress and I wanted to try to make things better with Barry." She dropped into the chair behind the front counter. "Henry took the news much better than I expected. To tell you the truth, I was a little insulted that he took it so well. But I think I knew deep down inside that Henry was never really invested in a serious relationship. He's one of those perpetually distracted people—so many irons in the fire, so many deals and meetings. I was a bit of casual entertainment."

An awkward silence stretched between them, until Jan stood and picked up one of the brochures. "I'm not going to let my personal problems get in the way of making Pioneer Days as fabulous as possible. We have a lot of people counting on us."

"Right." Brenda picked up a stack of brochures. "Let's get to work, ladies."

ALVIN EXETER LOOKED as cocky as ever when Adelaide ushered him into Travis's office Friday afternoon, after Travis finally decided to talk to him. The writer offered a firm handshake, then dropped into the chair across from Travis's desk. "You're going to be glad you talked to me, Sheriff," he said. "All I ask in return is an interview for my book to get your side of the story. This is going to be great for both of us."

"I'm not interested in making any deals," Travis said. "If you know something that pertains to my case, you have an obligation to tell me."

"I don't know about that." Exeter pursed his lips. "After all, maybe I'm only speculating. And even if I did see something that might pertain to an investigation you're conducting, it's not a crime to keep it a secret, is it?"

"Then I have to ask myself—why would you say you know something about a shooting involving one of my officers unless you're an accessory to the crime?"

Exeter's mouth tightened. "There's no need to make threats."

Travis glared at the man. The guy really rubbed him the wrong way. "Either tell me what you know or quit wasting my time," he said.

Exeter sat back and crossed one leg over the other. "You suspect Jan Selkirk had something to do with the murder of Andrew Stenson," he said. "Don't deny it. The news is all over town. Her motive was that Stenson was blackmailing her over her affair with Henry Hake."

It was true what people said, Travis thought. You couldn't keep anything secret in a small town.

"So it stands to reason she's your chief suspect in the attack on Brenda Stenson and Lacy Milligan," Exeter continued. "As well as the explosion at the storage units."

"We haven't found any evidence linking her to those crimes," Travis said.

"But what if I could give you evidence?" Exeter uncrossed his legs and scooted to the edge of his chair. "That would be worth something to you, wouldn't it?"

"Get on with it, Exeter. I'm losing patience."

"What if I told you Jan Selkirk had an accomplice?" Exeter said. "A man who has the skills and the background to make him perfectly capable of running two women off the road or blowing up a building. And one who I don't think would hesitate to shoot a cop."

"Who are you talking about?" Travis asked.

Exeter grinned. "Ian Barnes."

Travis's heart beat a little faster at mention of the name. Barnes's military background certainly made him familiar with firearms, and explosives, too. And he had a certain menace about him. But looking tough didn't mean a man had broken the law. "What makes you think Jan and Barnes are working together?" he asked.

"Because I *saw* them. In the bar of the motel where I'm staying. Jan Selkirk was wearing sunglasses and a black wig, but I know it was her. She and Barnes had their heads together in a back booth, and then she handed over a stack of bills to him. He counted the money, slipped it into his wallet and told her she didn't have anything to worry about—he'd take care of things."

"What things?" Travis asked.

"He didn't elaborate, but I'm thinking it might be running those two women off the road, blowing up the storage unit—and maybe even shooting a cop."

Travis didn't know whether to be annoyed or intrigued by these revelations. "So you saw two people talking and one of them gave the other some money," he said. "That doesn't make either one of them guilty of a crime."

Exeter's expression hardened. "It does when one of them is a suspect in a murder case."

"Go back to your motel room and dream up a few more conspiracies, Exeter. Don't waste any more of my time."

The writer shoved to his feet. "You're not going to look into this?"

"I know how to do my job," Travis said. "You can leave now."

Exeter glared at Travis, then stormed out of the office. Adelaide swept in after him. "He didn't look too happy," she said.

"What's the local gossip about Ian Barnes?" Travis asked.

"Other than that it should be illegal for a man to look so good?" She grinned. "I heard he has PTSD, and that's what makes him so standoffish. He spends a lot of time in the mountains, climbing. I guess that's his big thing. He's friends with Wade and Brock, over at Eagle Mountain Outfitters. What else do you want to know?"

"Any links between him and Jan Selkirk?"

Adelaide hooted. "In her dreams. I think Jan's a little long in the tooth for Ian."

"Exeter said he saw them together and they were pretty cozy."

"If that's true, then she's more of a cougar than I ever expected," Adelaide said.

Travis rose and moved past Adelaide. "Where are you off to?" she asked.

"I'm going to have a chat with Mr. Barnes."

DWIGHT WAS ON DUTY, so Travis asked him to ride along to the Bear's Den B and B. Paige was clearly surprised to find two cops at her door. "Is there a problem?" she asked.

"We're looking for Ian Barnes," Travis said. "Is he around?"

"He checked out yesterday," she said.

"He wasn't going to stay around for the festival?" Dwight asked.

"He had a reservation through next week," Paige said. "But he said something had come up and he needed to leave." She shrugged. "I had a waiting list of people who wanted to stay here during the festival, so the early checkout didn't hurt me."

"Did he say why, exactly, he had to leave?" Travis asked.

"No, and I didn't ask. I believe in respecting people's privacy."

"So it didn't strike you as suspicious that he would leave so suddenly?" Travis asked.

"Work with the public long enough and nothing people do will surprise you," Paige said. "I thought maybe the idea of the crowds that are coming to town for the festival was stressing him out, so he decided to leave."

From the B and B, Travis and Dwight headed to Eagle Mountain Outfitters. Wade was manning the register and greeted the officers when they walked in. "No more sign of that shoplifter," he said.

"We're looking for Ian Barnes," Travis said.

"Haven't seen him for a couple of days," Wade said. "I think he was planning on doing some climbs out in Shakes Canyon. I'd have liked to go with him, but we've been too busy at the store."

"We were just over at the Bear's Den and Paige says he checked out yesterday afternoon," Travis said.

Wade frowned. "He didn't say anything to us. But then again, Ian's a different kind of guy."

"What do you mean by that?" Dwight asked.

"Oh, you know—standoffish. Not much for social niceties. He was probably just ready to leave and decided to go. It's a bummer, though, because he was supposed to help with the fireworks show tomorrow night."

"Why was Barnes helping with the fireworks?" Travis asked.

"Because he had experience with explosives in the military," Wade said. "We thought he'd be a natural to help set up the big fireworks display above town. The fire department and the Elks Club do most of the work, but they were happy to get an experienced volunteer."

"Where do they set up the display?" Dwight asked.

"Up the hills overlooking town. There's a big flat ledge there looking out over the town, with a backdrop of cliffs. The Elks cleared all the brush from the ledge years ago, so it makes the perfect spot to set up the explosives."

"Did Barnes say where he planned to head from here?" Travis asked.

"Nah. Ian doesn't like it when people ask too many questions. He's the kind of guy you have to accept at face value, on his own terms. He's an amazing climber, though. Being around him always ups my game."

They left the store. Out on the sidewalk, Travis studied the row of storefronts decorated for the festival. Tourists were swelling the population of the town and the festival promised to be bigger and better than ever. Not the time he wanted a possible shooter and arsonist on the loose. "Let's go talk to Jan," he said. "See what she knows."

"Where do we find her?" Dwight asked.

"Good question." Travis had assumed she would be at home, but what if her husband had kicked her out? He called the office. "Adelaide, where is Jan Selkirk staying right now?" he asked.

"She's still in her home. Barry moved into the guesthouse," Adelaide said. "But if you're looking for Jan, check the history museum. Amy Welch said she saw her over there this morning."

"Thanks."

They headed to the museum. Sure enough, Jan was there, along with Brenda and Lacy. "Hi, Travis," Lacy said, offering a wan smile. She was pale, with dark circles under her eyes, though the bruises from the accident had begun to fade. The stress of the whole situation with Jan must be getting to her.

He returned the smile, then turned to Jan. "We need to speak with you for a minute," he said.

He could tell she wanted to argue, but appeared to think better of doing so in front of Brenda and Lacy. "Come back here," she said, motioning them to follow her into a room at the back of the building. She shut the door behind them. "I've answered all the questions I'm going to without my lawyer, Sheriff," she said.

"Just tell me where Ian Barnes is headed," Travis said. "He checked out of the B and B yesterday. I want to know where he went."

"How should I know where's he going?"

"Because the two of you are friends, aren't you?"

She looked away.

"I have a witness who saw you with him," Travis pressed. "You were at a motel bar, and you gave Barnes money."

Her face crumpled and she let out a strangled sob. The sudden breakdown of a woman who had always struck Travis as having ice water in her veins was shocking. "What do you have to tell us, Jan?" he asked.

"It wasn't supposed to turn out that way," she said through her tears. "That wasn't what I wanted at all."

"What wasn't what you wanted?" Travis asked. He led her to a chair and gently urged her down in it, then pulled up another chair opposite her, while Dwight stationed himself by the door. "Tell me about Ian Barnes."

She sniffed, and dabbed at her eyes with the tissue Travis handed her. "He was Henry Hake's bodyguard," she said. "I hadn't seen him for years and I didn't recognize him when he first came to town—when I knew him before, he had longer hair and a moustache. And he didn't call himself Ian Barnes then—he was Jim Badger. But he remembered me. He showed up at here at the museum late one evening, when I was working by myself. He said if I knew what was good for me, I wouldn't tell anyone I had known him before."

"Did he say why he was back in the area?"

She shook her head. "No, and I didn't ask."

"What about the money you gave him?"

"I think I'd better call my lawyer," she said.

"Call him," Travis said. "But I'm warning you now that when I find Barnes, I'm arresting him. If I find out you gave him money and he's involved in any of the other crimes I'm trying to solve—including the attack on Lacy and Brenda and the shooting of my deputy, I'll charge you as an accessory to attempted murder—and possibly murder." The threat was a bluff. While his suspicions were growing that Barnes was involved in the recent spate of local crimes—and maybe even Andy Stenson's murder—Travis didn't yet have enough proof to actually arrest him.

"I didn't have anything to do with any of those things," Jan said. She bit her lower lip so hard it bled.

Travis softened his voice. "If you need to tell me something, you should do it now," he said.

She glanced toward Dwight, then shifted her gaze back to Travis. "All right, I did give him money. I paid him to burn down the storage unit. I wanted to be sure Andy's files were destroyed, so that you wouldn't find out about my affair with Henry. He said he could set a fire and no one would ever figure out who did it. I didn't know he was going to put a bomb out there—or that you and Lacy would end up hurt." She grew more agitated. "I swear I didn't know."

Travis stood. "Call your lawyer," he said. "Then I want you both to report to the sheriff's department. Turn yourself in and we'll talk to the DA about the charges."

He left her sobbing, with Dwight standing guard. Lacy met him outside the door. "What is going on?" she asked. "Is that Jan crying in there?"

"She's going to be all right," Travis said. "Are you okay?"

"A little stressed," she said, still watching the door to the workroom.

"It will all be over soon," Travis said. He touched her arm. "I can't say more, but trust me."

Her gaze met his and she nodded. More than anything just then, he wanted to kiss her, but the timing felt off. "I do trust you," she said.

"We're still on for the fireworks tomorrow night, right?" he said.

"Yes. I'm looking forward to it." Then she stood on tiptoe and gave him a quick kiss on the lips—a firm, warm pressure that sent a jolt of electricity through him. But before he could reach out and pull her closer, she had moved away. "I'd better let you get back to work," she said, and left the room.

But she had given him a good reminder of how much she was coming to mean to him. And of how much he wanted to clear this case, so that there would be nothing holding them back in the future.

Chapter Seventeen

Pioneer Days Festival in Eagle Mountain featured the kind of weather Coloradans love to brag about—balmy air, gentle breezes and a sky the color of blue china glaze, a few cottony clouds hanging around as if for the sole purpose of adding interest to photographs of the scenery. As it was, Lacy found herself part of that scenery. In her 1890s bathing costume, she handed out sugar cookies and lemonade and posed for photographs with families, children and a few grinning young men who flirted shamelessly but were otherwise harmless.

Crowds of people showed up to tour the museum, keeping Brenda and Lacy busy. Neither of them had seen or heard anything from Jan, who had left the museum the day before without saying a word. For once the town rumor mill wasn't churning with any information about the former mayor. Nobody had heard anything about her.

Mayor Larry Rowe made an appearance at the museum midafternoon to shake hands and congratulate everyone on helping to put together such a great festival. "Lacy, you're looking wonderful," he said, accepting a cup of lemonade. "I'm glad to see you're doing so well, making a fresh start."

What else was she supposed to do? she wondered, but she didn't voice the question out loud. She merely smiled and moved on to ladling more lemonade into cups.

Travis stopped by for a few minutes after the mayor left, but Lacy only managed to smile at him from behind the counter where she was pouring lemonade. He waved and moved on, but Lacy felt giddy from the brief encounter.

"You certainly look happy about something." Tammy, the reporter from the *Eagle Mountain Examiner*, focused her camera on Lacy. "Keep smiling like that." She clicked off half a dozen pictures, then studied the preview window of her camera. "Oh, those came out nice," she said. "You look great, and the museum and the crowds in the background might as well be an advertisement for Pioneer Days."

"I had no idea so many people would come to town for this," Lacy said.

"It's a draw," Tammy said. "Though we can thank the weather for the bigger-than-ever turnout, I think. And it's supposed to be perfect for the fireworks show tonight and, of course, the dance afterward." She snagged a sugar cookie from the tray to Lacy's left. "Only bad thing is that handsome Ian Barnes left town. I was hoping to wrangle at least one dance with that hunk. I probably wouldn't have worked up the nerve to ask him, but a girl can dream, right?" She took a bite of cookie.

"Ian left town?" Relief surged through Lacy.

"Yeah. Paige said he had reservations through the end of next week, but he came to her and said something had come up and he had to leave." She brushed cookie crumbs from the front of her shirt. "I'm thinking somebody told him about the crowds this festival attracts and he figured he didn't want to deal, you know?"

Lacy nodded absently. She leaned toward Tammy, her voice lowered. "Do you know what's up with Jan Selkirk?" she asked. "We haven't heard a word from her all day. It's like she's disappeared."

"Maybe she and her husband went away for a few days," Tammy said. "I heard they were trying to patch things up."

"Could she do that?" Lacy asked. "Would the sheriff let her leave town while the investigation is still ongoing?"

"I have no idea," Tammy said. "But I'll ask around. If I hear anything, I'll try to swing back by here and let you know."

"Thanks."

By six o'clock, when the museum closed, Lacy's feet ached and her head throbbed. But Travis had agreed to meet her at seven thirty. They planned to walk to the park and stake out a good spot from which to view the fireworks. They could do a little catching up while they waited for the show to begin, and maybe enjoy a glass of wine and a slice of pizza from one of the vendors in the park.

She walked back to the house without having to stop even once. The crowds had thinned and she guessed most of the tourists were eating supper or had headed to their hotels to change or put their feet up before the fireworks show and dance tonight. She let herself into the house and found a note on the hall table from her mom. "Having dinner with Dick and Patsy Shaw. Will probably get home after you leave. Love, Mom."

Lacy smiled. It was a rare occasion when she had the

house to herself. Too bad she didn't have time to enjoy it. She went upstairs and changed into capris and a knit tank with a matching cardigan for after dark, when the air would cool and she'd welcome another layer.

She still had half an hour before Travis would be here, so she poured a glass of iced tea and went out into the backyard. Here, where a wooden fence protected the space from hungry deer, her mother had created a sanctuary of flowers and fruit. Apple trees full of green apples gave way to paths lined with colorful hollyhocks. A copper birdbath and feeders attracted juncos, goldfinches, orioles and other birds, and wind chimes in the trees added their melody to the scene.

Lacy decided to pick a hollyhock for her hair, and headed toward a stand of dark pink blossoms near the back fence. As she leaned over to pluck the flower, something rustled in the bushes. Out of the corner of her eyes, she saw a flash of movement, then someone grabbed her from behind. She struggled as something was pulled over her head, blinding her, and she was thrown to the ground. "Make a sound and I swear I'll kill you now." The man's voice was low, his breath hot against her cheek. Something sharp pricked at the side of her breast and she sucked in a breath.

"That's right," the voice said. "Keep quiet or Mommy and Daddy will come home to find you butchered in their backyard."

AT SHORTLY AFTER SEVEN, Travis met Lacy's parents as they came up the walkway toward their house. "Are you coming to get Lacy?" Jeanette asked as George unlocked the front door.

"I stopped by the museum on my way over and

Brenda said she left about an hour ago to come home and change," he said, following them into the house.

"That old-fashioned swimsuit was so cute on her," Jeanette said. "Though she said the wool was a little itchy. Can you imagine wool for a swimsuit?" She stopped at the bottom of the stairs and called up. "Lacy! Travis is here!"

He waited, but heard no response. "Go on up," George said. "She's probably drying her hair or something and didn't hear you."

Travis climbed the stairs, though he heard no hair dryer or other noise as he neared the door to Lacy's room, which stood open. He paused in the doorway and knocked. "Lacy? Are you in here?" The antique swimsuit lay across the end of the neatly made bed. A laptop sat on her desk near the window, the top open but the machine shut off. Lacy's purse lay next to it, her phone tucked in a side pocket.

He checked the upstairs bathroom, and even peeked into a second bedroom he assumed belonged to her parents, but found no sign of Lacy.

"Did you find her?" Jeanette asked when he joined her and George in the kitchen.

"No. Her purse is on her desk in her room, but she's not upstairs."

George frowned. "That's odd. She's not down here." He looked at his wife.

"Maybe she decided to walk over to the park and meet you," Jeanette said.

"She would have taken her purse. Or at least her phone. It's upstairs in her purse." The bad feeling that had started when he had seen Lacy's empty bedroom was growing.

"Oh, this is just silly." Jeanette moved to the back

door. "She's probably sitting out here in the backyard and we're in here worrying."

But the Milligans' backyard was empty and silent, save for the faint sounds of celebration that drifted from the center of town and the gurgle of the creek just past their fence line. "Lacy!" Travis shouted.

But no answer came.

"What could have happened to her?" Jeanette clutched her husband's arm.

"She probably did walk downtown to meet me," Travis said, keeping his voice steady and his expression calm. "She's probably still not used to carrying a phone around with her and she forgot it. I'll go look for her."

"Let us know when you find her," George said.

"Of course."

He forced himself not to hurry out of the house, to assume the calm, easygoing saunter of a man who wasn't worried. But as soon as he was out of sight of the Milligans' home, he pulled out his phone and called Gage. "Lacy is missing," he said. "Spread the word to the others to keep an eye out for her."

"What do you mean, 'missing'?" Gage asked.

"She left the museum an hour ago and came home to change," Travis said. "Looks like she did that, but her purse and phone and keys are still here at her parents' house, only she's not."

"She probably just went downtown and forgot her phone," Gage said.

"I hope that's what happened," Travis said. "But I can't shake the feeling she's in trouble."

IAN BARNES HAD bundled Lacy into his Jeep and driven out of town, away from the crowds of people who might see her with him and act to help her. Once they had reached the vehicle, he had exchanged the knife for a gun and kept it pointed at her while he drove, one-handed, up a dirt road that led up Dakota Ridge.

"Where are you taking me?" she asked, hating the way her voice shook.

"I've been helping the Elks Club set up for the big fireworks show tonight," he said. "They were thrilled to get a guy with my experience with explosives to volunteer. They've cleared off a big ledge for the staging area for the show, but there's another ledge above that. Great view of the town, and when all the fireworks start going on, no one will be able to hear you when I kill you."

"Why are you going to kill me?" she asked, struggling to keep the tremor from her voice.

"Because you know too much."

"I don't know anything," she said. "Not anything to do with you."

"Some things you don't realize the significance of, but we can't risk you figuring them out later."

"Who is we?"

He gunned the Jeep up a steep slope, gravel pinging against the undercarriage, tires spinning until he gained traction. "That doesn't matter."

She stared at him, a cold, sick feeling washing over her. "You killed Andy, didn't you?" she asked.

Ian grinned. "I broke into the office while he was at lunch. I knew it was your day off and that he'd be alone. I hadn't counted on Jan coming by to see him, but it was easy enough to hide in the bathroom while she pleaded with him. She left out the back door and before he had time to even move, I stabbed him. He didn't suffer. I left by the back door and drove out of town."

"But why kill him?" she asked. "What did Andy ever do to you?"

"It was a job." He voice was matter-of-fact, as if he was talking about moving furniture or clearing brush. "He was poking his nose where it didn't belong. The people who hired me wanted him shut up."

"What was he poking his nose in?" She couldn't recall anything he had talked about, but that had been so long ago.

"I don't know and I don't care," Ian said.

"Did Henry Hake hire you?"

He laughed. "That loser? No. Hake had people above him who ran the show. They hired me."

"Why did you bother coming back to town? Why now?"

"I had a job to do."

"For the same people who hired you to kill Andy?"

"Maybe."

"Who are they?"

He glanced at her, his expression cold. "I don't see that that has anything to do with you."

"Were you the one who tried to run Brenda and me off the road that day?"

"Yes. I sacrificed a new truck to that one. It was hard, watching it go up in flames. But I had the old Jeep as backup."

"And the explosion?"

"Yeah, that was me. I miscalculated the delay on the timer, though. I should have set it for just a little longer."

"Did you shoot Travis's officer?"

"I can't tell you all my secrets, can I?" He parked the Jeep against a sheer rock face, shut off the engine, then leaned over and grabbed her by the arm. "Come on. The show starts in less than an hour. I want to be in place before everyone gets here."

TRAVIS PUSHED THROUGH the crowds of tourists and locals in the park, searching for Lacy. Once he thought he caught a glimpse of her dark hair in a group of women, but it turned out to be someone he had never seen before. As he circled the edge of the park, he came upon a group of firemen, climbing into the chief's truck. "Want to come help with the fireworks, Sheriff?" Assistant Fire Chief Tom Reynolds called.

"You don't need me in your way," Travis said.

"Come on," Tom urged. "We're a man short since Ian Barnes left town early."

"He left town?" a short, balding man next to Tom said. "That's funny, I could have sworn I saw his Jeep go by just a little while ago. I waved, but I guess he didn't see me."

"You saw Ian Barnes?" Travis asked.

"Yeah. I'm sure it was him. He had a woman with him."

Travis's heart pounded. "What did she look like?"

"I didn't see her face, but she had dark brown hair." He grinned. "Odds are, though, that she's a looker. A guy like that can have any woman he wants. My wife got this dazed look on her face every time she saw him."

"Which way was he headed?" Travis asked.

"The way we're going," the man said. "Hey, maybe he decided to stick around and help us and he went on ahead."

"Hey, Travis, where are you going?" Tom called as Travis took off across the park at a run.

Travis already had his phone out, calling Gage. "I

think Ian Barnes has Lacy," he said. "They're headed to that hill above town, where the Elks are getting ready to shoot off fireworks. Get Dwight and meet me up there. And alert Highway Patrol in case we need backup." He hung up as soon as his brother acknowledged the information. He had to get to Lacy. He only hoped he wasn't too late.

A LACEWORK PATTERN of glittering lights marked the town of Eagle Mountain, nestled in the valley below an uplift of mountains and cliffs. Lacy looked down at the town from the narrow ledge Ian had brought her to. Travis was down there somewhere, and her parents. They were probably wondering where she was, but she had no way of signaling to them, no way of letting them know what had happened to her.

Closer even than town, fifty feet below on a much larger ledge, a dozen men swarmed around the metal stands and boxes that contained the explosives set up for the fireworks display. If Lacy yelled, would they look up and see her here? Maybe—but if they did look up in response to her shout, likely all they would see was her death as Ian shot her. And then he would escape, driving away in his Jeep before anyone below had time to react.

"Come away from the edge," Ian said, and pulled her back against the cliff face. The gun dug hard into her side. "You don't want to fall, do you? A drop like that could kill you." He chuckled at his own joke, sending an icy tremor through her.

"Why are you doing this?" she asked again. "I haven't done anything to hurt you."

"It's nothing personal," he said. "It's a job. It pays well and it makes use of my talents." He leaned back against the cliff, his gaze still steady on her. "It's kind of a shame, though. I mean, you just got out of prison and you don't even get to enjoy a month of freedom before it's over. I'm sorry about that."

She looked away. How could she even comment on such an absurd statement?

"I was inside once," he said. "You did three years, right?"

"Yes."

"That's what I did, too. Course, I hear the women's prisons have it better than the men. But it wasn't too bad for me. I had friends inside and I knew how to work the system. You get respect, even inside, being a military veteran, and I never had to worry about anyone messing with me."

"I wouldn't know about that," she said.

"I remember you from before, you know," he said.

"From before what?"

"Before you went inside. When you worked for that lawyer."

"I don't remember you," she said. Surely she would remember if she had met him before.

"You never saw me. That's part of my job, too, not being seen. They won't see me when I kill you, and they won't see me when I leave."

She closed her eyes, not wanting him to read the fear there. Would those be the last words she ever heard?

THE BACK WHEELS of Travis's SUV skidded around a sharp curve as he trailed the fire department truck up the dirt road to the fireworks launch site. A number of men and vehicles were already at the site, their vehicles parked well away from the explosives, behind a protective wall of boulders. Travis drove right into the midst of the men working. "Something wrong, Sheriff?" one man asked, as Travis lowered his SUV's window.

"I'm looking for Ian Barnes," Travis said. "Have you seen him?"

"I haven't." The man looked around. "Anybody seen Ian Barnes?" he called.

"I thought he left town," someone said.

Tom walked up to Travis. "I don't see him or his Jeep," he said. "Maybe Walt was wrong about seeing him."

"I saw him." Walt walked up behind Tom. "But you're right that he's not here."

"Where else could he have gone?" Travis asked.

Both Tom and Walt registered confusion. "I don't know," Tom said. "There's nothing else up here."

Travis scanned the area. The road he had driven up continued past this ledge. "Where does that road go?" he asked.

"It just climbs up a little ways then peters out," Tom said. "There's an old mine site. I've been up there looking for artifacts, but it's pretty picked over. There's an adit, but the tunnel's full of water and the timbers are falling down, so it's not safe to go inside. There are warning signs posted, but no gate."

A flooded mine shaft. The perfect place to dispose of a body. Travis shut off the SUV and got out. "What are you doing?" Tom asked. "You can't just leave your vehicle here—not with the fireworks so close."

"Then you move it." Travis tossed him the keys. "I'm going up there to look around. When Gage and Dwight get here, tell them where I'm at."

"Okay, Sheriff," Tom said.

The noise and activity of the preparations for the

fireworks show faded as Travis climbed. He kept to the shadows at the side of the road, moving stealthily, ears tuned to any sounds from above. The trail was steeper up here, and narrower, and Travis breathed hard on the climb. He doubted many people had the nerve to take a vehicle up something this steep, but Barnes apparently hadn't hesitated.

He crested the last rise and spotted Ian's Jeep first, the battered vehicle tucked in next to a cliff face. Freezing, he waited, listening. After a few seconds he heard the low murmur of voices—a man's, and then a woman's. A band tightened around his chest as he recognized Lacy's voice. He couldn't make out her words, but he felt the fear in her tone as a tightness in his own chest.

Travis drew his gun and began moving toward the voices, stealthily, placing one careful step at a time. By the time he reached the front bumper of the Jeep, he could make out the two shadowed figures against the cliff face and stopped.

He apparently hadn't been stealthy enough. "Step out where I can see you and toss your gun on the ground." Ian's voice was calm, the words chilling. "One wrong move and I'll blast her away right now."

Travis tossed the gun to the ground and raised his hands over his head. *Come on, Gage,* he thought. *Bring in the cavalry anytime now.*

"Come over here and stand next to your ladylove," Ian said. "When the fireworks start, I can shoot you both. And hurry up. They're almost ready."

At that moment, the first explosions from below shook the air. Lacy gave a cry of alarm and Ian turned to watch the first rockets soar overhead. "Now," he shouted, but before he could turn back to them and fire, Travis rushed him.

"Lacy, run!" Travis shouted.

LACY RAN, BUT not far. She made it only a few feet before she tripped and went sprawling. Gravel dug into her palms and her knees. Shaking with fear, she crawled to the cliff face and sat with her back against the rock wall, watching as Travis and Ian struggled on the ground. The two men rolled, grappling for the gun, while deafening explosions sounded overhead. Flashes of red and blue and gold illuminated the struggle, and bits of paper and ash rained down. Smoke and the smell of gunpowder stung her nose and eyes, but she blinked furiously and tried to keep track of what was happening.

Travis's discarded gun lay a few feet away. She crawled toward it and had almost reached it when a man stepped out of the shadows and scooped it up. "No offense, Lacy, but I'm probably a better shot with this than you are," Gage Walker said, joining her in the shadows.

"Are you alone?" she asked, looking over his shoulder.

"No. I've got Dwight and a couple of Highway Patrol deputies surrounding this place," he said. "But I'm not sure there's anything any of us can do right now but wait and hope one of us can get off a good shot."

Explosions continued to echo off the rocks. Lacy covered her ringing ears, but kept her eyes fixed on Travis and Ian, who continued to wrestle, gouging and kicking. In the flashes of light she thought Travis might be bleeding from a cut on his cheek, and Ian's shirt was torn. They rolled to the edge of the ledge, until Travis's feet hung over the edge. Lacy moaned. How could he win? He was in good shape, but Ian was phenomenal. She remembered Travis saying he wouldn't want to meet Ian in a dark alley. What about a dark mountain ledge?

The two men rolled away from the ledge, and Lacy let out her breath in a rush. Beside her, Gage did the same. She glanced over and saw that he was kneeling, steadying his gun with both hands, keeping it fixed on the two men as they moved. "All I need is one clear shot," he said in a lull between explosions.

The next round of volleys began, and then Travis was on top of Ian. He slammed the other man's head into the rocky ground, then lunged to his feet and staggered back.

"Freeze!" Gage yelled. "One move and I'll shoot."

"All right." Ian sat up, his hands over his head. "I give up." He struggled to his feet.

"I said freeze!" Gage shouted again, but already Ian had made his move, lunging toward Travis with a roar.

Gage fired, the explosion deafening, and Travis dodged to the side. With a scream that rose above the sound of fireworks and gunfire, Ian dove over the edge, the echo of his cry hanging in the air as he vanished.

Epilogue

"Goodbye, Jan. And good luck." Lacy faced the older woman, who had aged even more in the past few weeks. She had accepted a plea bargain in the charges against her involving her hiring of Ian Barnes to blow up the storage unit, and would serve a minimum of eighteen months in the Denver Women's Correctional Facility.

"It will be tough at first, but obey the rules and you'll get along fine," Lacy said. "Focus on doing your time and coming home."

"It helps a little, knowing you came out all right," Jan said. "I'm sorry again for all the trouble I caused you."

"I'm not worrying about the past anymore," Lacy said. "I'm focusing on the future, and so should you."

"You've got a lot to look forward to." Jan's gaze shifted to the man who stood behind Lacy.

Travis put a hand on Lacy's shoulder and nodded to Jan. "Good luck," he said. "I'll see you when you come home."

Jan turned away, and climbed into the sheriff's department van that would transport her to Denver. Lacy and Travis watched the van drive away. "I probably shouldn't, but I feel sorry for her," Lacy said.

"She brought it all on herself," Travis said. "And she got off lightly, considering."

She turned to face him and he pulled her close. She sighed—a sound of relief and contentment. "I'm just glad it's all over and you're all right."

"I'm all right. As for it being over—Henry Hake is still missing, you know."

In the whirl of activity in the days following the death of Ian Barnes, Lacy had forgotten all about the real estate developer. "No one has heard anything from him?" she asked.

"Not a word. According to the latest from Adelaide, public opinion is divided on whether he skipped town to avoid paying debts Eagle Mountain Resort had run up, or whether something has happened to him."

"Ian said people who were over Hake hired him to kill Andy," Lacy said. "Who was he talking about? I thought Henry Hake owned his own company."

"That's one thing I'm trying to find out," Travis said. "Ian may have been talking about investors—or maybe Hake had silent partners. And I'd like to know what Andy was looking into that got him killed. Knowing that might help me figure out who hired Barnes. Now that Exeter knows Barnes killed Andy, he has turned his focus to Barnes and Hake, as well."

"So there's still a lot of unanswered questions," Lacy said.

"I'm going to find the answers," Travis said. "It may take time, but I have plenty of that."

"Lacy! Travis!" Lacy looked up to see Brenda hurrying toward them. "Was that Jan leaving just now?" Brenda asked, a little out of breath as she joined them on the sidewalk in front of the sheriff's department.

"Yes," Travis said. "You just missed her."

"We said our goodbyes yesterday," Brenda said. "Though I meant to be here this morning. I got delayed at the museum." Brenda was the new director of the Eagle Mountain Historical Museum, a job that came with more responsibilities, but also a raise. Already, Lacy could see her friend blossoming in her new role.

"Have you seen Lacy's new apartment?" Brenda asked Travis. "She's fixed it up so cute."

"I have an invitation to dinner there tonight," Travis said.

Lacy hoped the blush that warmed her cheeks wasn't too evident. Now that she was settled into the apartment over Brenda's garage, she had invited Travis over for a little celebration, which she figured—hoped—would lead to him staying the night.

"I'd better get back to work," Travis said. "It was good seeing you, Brenda." He leaned over and kissed Lacy's cheek. "And I'll see you tonight."

"How are your parents taking the move?" Brenda asked, when Travis had disappeared inside the station.

"My mom cried, but then she cries at any change," Lacy said. "Truly, I think they're both happy for me." She and Brenda began walking back toward the museum.

"You may not need the apartment for long, if our county sheriff has a say in the matter," Brenda said.

"We've agreed to take it slowly," Lacy said. "I have a lot of adjustments to make. I start classes in just a few weeks. I'm pretty nervous about that."

"You'll do great." Brenda took her hand and squeezed it. "It's good to see you so happy. You deserve it."

"I'm happier than I ever thought I could be," Lacy

said. "While I was in prison, I told myself the key to surviving was to never give up. Now I know it can be just as important to have someone on the outside who will never give up on you."

"Travis was your someone," Brenda said.

"Yes." Travis Walker was her someone—her only one. The man who had saved her, and the one who had brought her back to herself. A man she thought she could love for a long time—for a lifetime.

*****

COMING SOON!

We really hope you enjoyed reading this book. If you're looking for more romance, be sure to head to the shops when new books are available on

Thursday
12th July